The Extrapolated Man

Doug Franklin

Extrapolated Worlds

For Stella

Who sails the sea of stars.

Prologue

Sparrow stalled just inside the orbit of Deimos. A ghostly blue shockwave of Cherenkov radiation marked the ship's fall from hyperspace. Mars lolled in front of her like a battered harvest moon, its pockmarked face bloodied by war. Sunlight caught on ragged burns in her skin, then flared on diamondoid viewports at her bow.

The little vessel could carry two, but the seat beside her pilot was empty. Commander John Gray considered it with a haggard gaze. His lover had cast her lot with the tharks. There was a line that could not be crossed even in war, she had said, and now it felt like his heart was being torn apart by that very line.

Another flash of Cherenkov radiation cast blue shadows across the flight deck. Gray's mouth tightened. The tharks had followed him after all. His only weapon was a standard Space Force cutlass. If it came to using that, odds were good he was a dead man and this whole desperate mission a failure.

"All right my little bird," he said, "time to find out if you can handle atmosphere."

Sparrow responded to his touch like a living thing, pitching around with a staccato burst of her vernier thrusters until her rocket engine faced forwards. Her turbopump spun up and the ammonia in her tanks boiled through the reactor core with a shriek, felt more than heard.

They decelerated onto a trajectory that would take them down into the atmosphere, and the ship spun back around of her own accord. The first faint traceries of incandescent plasma began to dance across her triangular viewports. Mighty Olympus rose in front of them and the ancient rust of the Tharsis highlands gave way to the brilliant white of fresh snow.

Plasma sheeted back from the bow like fire as they dropped deeper into the atmosphere, washing over the viewports until all Gray saw was a green inferno shot through with pink and deeper shades of red. The ship began to shudder.

Then the inferno that danced upon the capsule viewports flickered out. Three more volcanoes loomed in front of them like blunt teeth – Ascraeus, Pavonis, Arsia – all smaller than Olympus, but the ship was dropping fast. *Sparrow* made a lousy airplane; all drag and no lift. At this rate they were going to make another crater on the slopes of Pavonis.

"Let me help," Gray said, taking the ship's manual controls in hand.

Sparrow resisted his input. She had been trained in orbital and hyperspatial mechanics. She knew nothing of aerodynamics except what could be inferred from taking an integral of the hyperspatial equations.

Pavonis was dangerously close; he could see the space-elevator terminal at its summit.

"You need to trust me on this," he said.

Sparrow relented, and none too soon. The trick was to make drag work for them. Turbulence buffeted them as they skidded into a shallow turn. Gray was afraid they would lose the outboard stabilizer, but she held together.

Then the ground fell away as they left the Tharsis plateau behind. And fell away again, as the plateau stepped down into the enormous chasm of Valles Marineris. Snowmelt formed silver ribbons of water. Ahead on the left was the cleft that led into Candor Chasma. That way led home, to sunlit rooms that looked out over iceboat races and skating parties. And to the squadron of Sturmoviks based at Thunderbird Falls that might still save him, if they only knew he needed to be saved. Which seemed unlikely now that *Sparrow* had descended below the level of the base's radar sweeps.

The bottom of the canyon drew near. Gray pulled the ship's nose up away from their line of descent. The buffeting increased until his vision blurred. They were almost vertical now. He throttled up the nuclear engine, giving *Sparrow* enough head to let her balance on the exhaust while he worked the problem of getting them down in one piece. Or at least alive; the ship did not have planetary-style amenities like landing gear, so 'one piece' was not on the list of possible outcomes. The best he could do was set them down on the stabilizers that tipped the aft spars.

The buffeting eased as their airspeed diminished. He backed the ship down, eyes darting between the view outside and the rapidly dropping propellant gauge. Dust billowed below them, tracking their motion across the floor of the canyon.

They settled down into the roiling cloud. Gray could no longer see the ground. Two of the aft stabilizers made contact. Their wrist joints sheared. *Sparrow* pitched over, spars buckling and hypervanes shattering. She screamed as the myriad sensors built into her spars tore free. She tried to twist away from the impact, but there was nothing she could do. She plowed head-first into the ground and slid to a shuddering stop.

"I'm sorry," Gray said. There was no reply. The silence was broken by a crash of thunder. A wave of sand washed across the viewports. He took off his multi-faceted flight helmet and retrieved his cutlass.

Outside, the sun was almost down. Its last rays caught the bow of the ship that had pursued him. It looked like a tetrist's vision of a carpenter bee, a nightmare rendered in black carbon and stainless steel: six crystalline hypervanes, three landing legs, and nestled between them, a triad of thark soldiers.

Take a terrestrial leafcutter ant, atta cephalotes. Size it up a couple orders of magnitude. Replace chitin with ceramic armor, put high-carbon steel on the cutting surfaces, and endow it with intelligence. Make it indifferent to vacuum, needing only the warm glow of fissiles in its gut to stay alive, and you have the general idea of a thark soldier.

Gray hesitated. There was no way to spare his ship from what would come. *Sparrow* did not have an off switch any more than he did. She would live or she would die, and either way there would be pain and fear, and there was nothing he could do about it.

"I have to go, little bird," he said. "I'll do what I can to hold them off. Thank you for taking me this far."

The tharks dropped from their niches. Gray loped away at a right angle to their approach, making them choose between him and *Sparrow*. The triad swung to follow him. His ship was not going anywhere, after all.

He set off for the nearest hill. How far would they follow him? How much time could he buy? The tharks increased their pace as he struggled up the hill. He gained the top only a few seconds ahead of them. He stood there, his ragged breath fogging the inside of his skinsuit's facemask, his cutlass whining angrily as their leader crouched below him, just out of reach of its chainblade.

Then a pair of Mars Guard Sturmoviks roared overhead like avenging angels, the blue diamonds of their exhaust vivid in the failing light. The leading thark made a sound like a band saw and leapt up at him. Gray sprang to the side, slashing downwards with his cutlass. Sparks flew as its chainblade took an arm below the elbow. Two hundred kilograms of angry thark landed where he had been a moment before.

Gray charged the nearest of her followers. The thark lunged at him as if she meant to snatch him from his feet. He went low and jabbed the chainblade up into her thorax. The cutlass caught on ceramic armor and nearly seized. He shoved it in and rocked it viciously back and forth inside her.

A middle limb whipped sideways against his chest. He heard more than felt his ribs break. He jerked the cutlass out of the thark with a scream. She stumbled and fell, mortally wounded. Gray tried to catch his breath. His chest was on fire. He straightened up with an effort. His ribs grated with every move.

Geysers of dust erupted in a straight line that marched up the hillside and bisected the trailing thark, which came apart in two untidy pieces wreathed in lightning. The Sturmoviks ripped overhead, banking to make a pass at the ship that had brought the tharks. It lifted off on a pillar of fire. Its rocket engine was deafening. Gray turned away from the blast of sand and small rocks, shielding his faceplate with his free hand.

The first thark was on him in a heartbeat. It felt like he'd been punched in the gut. His knees buckled but he did not fall. The thark's forearm was inside him. A bubble of blood expanded from the juncture where it pierced his skinsuit, popped, and was followed by another.

She pulled her arm free. Electricity snapped where he had cut off her hand. He staggered, dropped to his knees. Blood welled up in his throat. He swallowed reflexively.

The thark seized him with her middle limbs and lifted him until they were face to face. She tore his facemask off with her good hand. A cold wind sucked the breath out of his lungs. Iconji flickered across her enormous eyes. The only thing he understood was the question mark in a yellow triangle. But what was the question?

He looked past her to the setting sun. It had been a long time since he had seen a sunset from the surface of a planet. He had forgotten how beautiful they were, how extravagant, how utterly indifferent to the lives of men and all their works.

A dark spot detached itself from the dazzling blue inferno and raced toward them, preceded by a line of dusty geysers. The thark dipped her head towards him. There was tremendous pressure around his neck as her mandibles closed.

Then he rolled free and was laying on his side. He wondered for a moment why she had released him. He tried to get up but could not move. Nothing seemed to work but his eyes. Sunlight dopplered from blue to violet to something that was so brilliant he could see nothing more.

1

The Find

Maggie rolled over so she could think without having her face in the dirt. The sky looked like tempered steel, hot blue near the sun shading to copper at the horizon. Brilliant white cirrus clouds drifted above the distant canyon walls. It was mid-afternoon, maybe four hours of light left. She could feel the warmth of her body leaching into the cold ground. She wondered if that was what it felt like to die. If the vital heat just seeped out of you, like the last joule of a kino spinning down to ground. If that was all there was to it, it wouldn't be so hard.

She closed her eyes and listened to the solid thud of her pulse. Beside her, on his stomach, Eric was breathing heavily from the climb up the face of the dune. Below them a small stream tumbled its tribute of sediment down to the mighty Marineris.

"That's got to be what he was talking about," Eric said. He passed his viewpoint over to her goggles.

On the other side of the stream, the shifting dunes had partially uncovered the wreck of an old spacecraft. The remnants of a fin protruded from the sand like a lonely, wind-stripped tree. A landing pad hung uselessly from its tip.

"It doesn't look like a fighter to me," she said skeptically. "Maybe a reusable booster? That's the bell of a rocket engine on the end."

She tagged the engine bell with a blink and passed the viewpoint back. Compared to a fighter, a booster would not bring much return for the effort of getting it back to town.

"Think your pilot friend got it wrong? Maybe trying to impress the pretty bartender?"

"He's not my friend," Maggie said. "And he was drunk, so getting it wrong is more likely than getting it right. But here we are."

The wind came up, blowing grit up the face of the dune and into their faces. Maggie pulled her airscarf back into place. It snugged itself around her nose and mouth, seeking out the warmth of her breath. They inched their way back down the dune out of the wind.

"Maybe a ground to orbit interceptor," Eric said, voice muffled by his own airscarf. "That would be a score. Weapons, ammo, kinos..."

Eric was a dreamer, but there were plenty of wrecks in the canyon lowlands, and more buried beneath the snow up on Tharsis. Any war machine you could imagine had been built and fought and crashed on the surface of Mars. Of all the battlegrounds in the solar system, the ones ruled by the old god of war had drunk most deeply of mankind's blood. Earth had hardly been touched in comparison, until the end.

So yes, the wreck could be almost anything, even a fighter. But – task at hand – many of the anythings it could be were still quite dangerous, even long after the Warsing. That was the nature of the game they played.

"The truck is what, an hour behind us?" she asked. She and Eric had gone ahead in his bipe Dusty, leaving the rest of the group to pick their way across the rough, boulder-strewn terrain in a battered old flatbed truck.

"About that," Eric agreed. "You want to wait for them to catch up?"

"Not really. If this is a bust, that's an hour we could use looking for the real thing. Besides, I'm getting cold."

"I hear that. Usual drill?"

"Yeah. Let's do it."

Eric unslung his rifle and checked its gauge. The kino slung beneath its barrel was warm to the touch from parasitic discharge. But the gauge showed enough spin left to drive an entire magazine downrange. If it took more than that, he was doing something wrong. He twirled his finger in the air.

Maggie drew her revolver and thumbed its iris open. The weapon woke with an ominous quiver, like a hunting falcon whose hood has been removed. Her goggles switched over to tactical mode. Bright red crosshairs tracked smoothly across her field of vision as she hefted the weapon and sighted down its barrel. The aiming reticle was encircled by eight green dots; all chambers were full and ready to go.

The revolver felt good in her hand. It was the only thing she had inherited from her father besides her dark unruly hair and vaguely Slavic features. She rose to her feet, shaking dirt out of her long coat. Fifty meters along the face of the dune, she judged she'd gone far enough. She gave a cursory wave to Eric and crossed over the top.

From this angle it was apparent that the wreckage was not a booster. In addition to the exhaust bell at the stern, she could make out the angular lines of a capsule at its bow. It had been manned! Maybe a fighter after all, though nothing like she had seen before. She pushed down a surge of excitement. No room for that now.

The capsule was crumpled from the impact and ripped by cannon fire. Purplish growths of fractal lichen burst through the tears, no doubt rooted in some carbon-rich source within, perhaps the vessel's former occupants.

A shiver wracked her shoulders. She took a deep breath to let the cold all the way in. Then she strode down the dune as if she were Dejah Thoris herself. She splashed across the stream without pausing. The water was opaque with milky-pink summer runoff. It was hard to judge its depth, or her footing for that matter, but it did not come over the tops of her boots. Small blessings.

She slowed as she approached the wreck, making sure to keep clear of the line of fire between it and Eric, who had positioned himself atop the dune. The area around the vessel was pockmarked by mekano tracks. Most had been blurred by the wind, but some were fresh. If she could follow them back far enough in time, they would eventually lead to the mekan hive where they were drexlered.

She squatted down to check a set of tracks that formed two parallel rows, as if a creature the size of a four-wheeler had gone by. Each indentation was the span of her hand. Too big for a mekano. Probably a spider bear looking for something to eat. Usually not people, but it had been known to happen.

Something moved in the periphery of her vision. She whirled around and brought the revolver to bear. It was just a sand crab. The mekano backed into a crevice under the hull, fluffing dust over its iron carapace until it was completely hidden.

"A little jumpy, huh?" Eric's voice came over her goggles.

"You looked over your shoulder lately?" Maggie retorted. "There's no telling how long this thing has been exposed, and what kind of attention it has attracted." Like spider bears, she did not say. No point in winding him up any tighter.

He sighed. "Fine, take care of yourself for a sec."

Maggie turned full circle while Eric made sure nothing was stalking him. They were a third of the way up Valles Marineris from its mouth, in the no man's land between Tsiolkovsky to the east and Thunderbird to the west. The main river channel was several kilometers away. The canyon walls were barely visible on the horizon. Scrubby knots of synlife brush covered the slope of a nearby hill.

"Nothing moving but the wind," Eric reported.

"Then let's see what we've got."

On closer inspection, the capsule at the bow of the vessel proved to be an integrated assembly. Three triangular facets formed the point of a tetrahedron. Each facet had a long, oval structure reminiscent of a mekan's eye, but made of some crystalline material.

The exposed edge of the capsule was flanked by a pair of viewports. Maggie looked cautiously over both shoulders, then holstered her revolver and got a flashlight out of her coat pocket to check one of them. Underneath a thick layer of dust, the viewport's diamondoid was as smooth and clear as the day it was drexlered.

The capsule was cramped and strewn with debris. Small mekanos skittered away from her flashlight's beam like cockroaches. An empty seat faced the viewports, an odd-looking multifaceted helmet beside it. Another seat occupied an adjacent corner of the triangular flight deck. The third corner held an artiform braincase. The cables leading out of it were encrusted by a spray of fractal lichens.

Maggie circled around the capsule. A slender hexagonal spine, mostly buried, connected the capsule to the vessel's midsection.

"Looks like its neck is broken," Eric said, following along on her viewpoint. "See how the nose of the capsule is tilted up compared to the rest of the ship?"

"Looks that way," she said, running her hand over the aft surface of the capsule. It was covered by a layer of something like quartz crystal, translucent and grainy to the touch. A triangular vane of the same stuff formed a buttress between the capsule and the narrow spine.

She walked down to where the spine disappeared beneath the sand. She dug in with the toe of her boot, encountered something blocky under the surface. She scooped away the sand with her hands, revealing a framework of hinged triangles.

"That's a Canfield joint," Eric said. "The neck isn't broken; it's articulated. What the hell is this thing?"

Maggie scrambled up the dune that had once engulfed the wreck and was now slowly divulging it again like an old secret. She stepped out onto its spine. Sand skittered underfoot and rolled off. She walked carefully between crystalline shards that rose like jagged teeth from the spine.

She gently rocked one of the shards out of the clamp that held it. It was the same crystalline material as buttressed the capsule, a couple centimeters thick, shot through with dark lightning that branched and subdivided in self-similar patterns. It made Maggie's brain hurt when she tried to follow it.

"I think before the crash these shards formed another triangle between the hull and the spar," she said. "Like a fin, but of quartz. Or whatever this stuff is."

She tucked the shard in her satchel and continued back towards the spar. What she had taken for a landing pad, when they were first glassing the wreck, was another smaller crystalline assembly, attached to the tip of the spar by an articulated joint.

The vessel's geometry was impossible to grasp. Not a right angle on the thing. Alien, if she had to pick a single word. Which was ridiculous. The galaxy was rotten with life, but nary a technosignature to be found amongst the carbon dioxide and methane and dimethyl sulfide signals. There were no starfaring aliens unless you counted Jesus. But she was not a religious person. Death was the end, which was a good reason to avoid it.

She took another step and the radiation detector built into her goggles started chattering. She backed up and the clicks subsided.

"We've got a hot one," she said, trying to keep the elation out of her voice. "Probably a nuclear thermal rocket. I'm right at the boundary of the shadow cast by its shield."

"The sweet, sweet, sound of spin," Eric said.

"Maybe. If nothing's gotten into it."

The Martian mekosystem was based on the accumulation of fissiles, from the simplest insect-like burrowers to solitary eight-legged predators at the top of the food chain. For them, the wreck would be like a ripe carcass, well worth defending from other scavengers. Like Maggie.

She edged around the spar, careful not to snag her coat on crystalline shards. The intermittent clicking in her goggles became a steady chatter. A thick cylinder, carbon black, terminated in the engine bell they'd seen from the other side of the stream. The portion of the cylinder that had been exposed by the dune's retreat was pockmarked by tracks.

"That's not good," Eric said.

"I saw spider bear tracks a ways back," Maggie said, and then regretted it.

"Now you tell me. Please don't go any farther. It's a long shot. I'd hate to miss."

"I'm going to take a closer look."

"Maggie…"

"You know I gotta know," she said. She jumped off the spine.

"Wardamn it!"

Whatever else Eric had to say was cut off by the nuclear thermal rocket's shielding. The chatter in Maggie's goggles became a full-throated growl. She settled down beside the rocket's flank. From here she could see that mekanos had breached the outer hull, but the reactor inside was intact. The sweet, sweet sound of spin indeed.

She worked her way back down to the edge of the stream, probing the ground for dragon teeth and other hazards. When she glanced up, Dusty stood beside Eric at the top of the opposite dune. Their shadows stretched out towards the water below. Eric's head barely reached the knobby joints of the robot's reverse knees. Even so there was no mistaking the nature of their relationship. The bipe followed him down the face of the dune like a loyal pet, its delicate, bird-like gait kicking up clouds of dust that were whisked away by the evening down-canyon breeze.

They met at a flat spot upstream of the wreck, nose on to it, so its shadow shield protected them from the radiation spilling from its reactor.

"Mah-gee," Dusty said, settling down into a crouch.

"Hey Dusty." She patted the bipe's flank affectionately. It settled lower on its haunches with an air of mechanical contentment.

"Not cool," Eric said.

"Sorry," Maggie replied without a great deal of sincerity.

"You could have died," he said.

"Always a possibility," she agreed. "But here we are."

"Is it intact?" He could not keep the excitement out of his voice.

She nodded. "A hundred kilos of enriched uranium, ours for the taking."

He shook his head. "All right. One of these times I'm just going to stroke out, but all right."

"Come on, let yourself be happy."

"I will not give you the satisfaction," he said, but Maggie had the sense that he was smiling beneath his airscarf.

They were unloading camping gear from the bipe when the truck rolled in. Alex was driving. His brother Dmitri rode shotgun. Alex had ten centimeters and almost as many kilos on his little brother. Dmitri liked to say he was the brains for Alex's brawn, and there was some truth to it. Alex drove, Dmitri navigated.

Alex pulled the girls into orbit with his rugged good looks, but it was Dmitri who landed them with an endless supply of one-liners.

Eric's girlfriend Zsuzsanna was sandwiched between the two young men. This was her first time out with the group. Maggie did not know much about her. Eric said she worked as a research associate at Tsiolkovsky's Polytechnic Institute. He had hooked up with her a few weeks before and talked Maggie into letting her come along as the camp cook.

Alex parked next to Dusty so they could spin up his kinos with the truck's thorium engine. They set up camp by the stream, kicking aside rocks and uprooting synlife shrubs and clumps of grass to make a level bed. Maggie would have felt more comfortable on higher ground, but the odds of a flash flood were low. There were no icefalls predicted and the skies were clear. It would take heavy rain in the highlands to pose a real threat.

Eric and Zsuzsanna had brought their own tent, a sturdy little half-dome, which they set up at a discrete distance from the main camp. Maggie and the brothers shared the same weather-beaten dome the group had used since they started treasure hunting together. Sleeping bags and packs were shoved up against the walls in a colorful jumble. Olive green airscarves and embers dangled from cords strung across the vaulted ceiling in a Star of David. An old war-surplus oxygen candle flickered cheerfully in the middle of the floor, casting a ruddy glow on their faces. Three and a half standard centuries of icefalls had raised air pressure enough that vacuum suits were no longer required, but the more delicate business of making the air breathable for baselines would take centuries more.

Maggie listened to the conversation as the warm glow of dinner spread through her body. It was a good group. She'd been worried about taking on Zsuzsanna. She was a pretty girl, with light brown hair and the kind of figure that boys found irresistible. Alex had trouble keeping his eyes off her, which could become a problem. But for now, they were getting along. And now was good enough for Maggie.

Maggie warmed her hands over the jug-sized candle. "I'm going to set up the fence before it gets dark. We don't need a spider bear sniffing out hot spots in the middle of the night. Anybody want to lend a hand?"

"I'll go," Zsuzsanna said before anyone else could speak.

"Let's get it done." Maggie snagged her airscarf from the clothesline and settled it around her face with a practiced motion. Zsuzsanna followed suit with somewhat less polished results.

"I'll come too," Eric said, standing.

"You can do the dishes," Zsuzsanna replied, much to the amusement of the two brothers.

She and Maggie went through the tent's airlock together. It was a simple accordion model, not particularly efficient, but reliable. Maggie pulled the outer doorframe back towards them, making the chamber as small as possible. Zsuzsanna zipped shut the inner door. For a moment they were pressed against each other back-to-back. Then Maggie zipped open the outer door and stepped out into the cold, clear evening.

The sun was low on the horizon. Its horizontal rays revealed the texture of the land. Every fold and rock cast long shadows. The largest stretched for hundreds of meters. The smallest were no bigger than the tip of her thumb. It was Maggie's favorite time. The most intimate secrets of the world were exposed, soon to be covered again by the blanket of night. But for a moment, everything was clear. Everything was revealed.

The electric fence was rolled up in the back of the truck. There wasn't much to it, just a bunch of meter-long composite stakes pre-rigged with a few strands of bare wire. Zsuzsanna held the stakes while Maggie pounded them in with a rock.

"How long have you been doing this?" Zsuzsanna asked as they worked.

"Treasure hunting? Off and on since I was eight mears old."

"What was your biggest find?"

Maggie considered. "I guess it depends on what you mean by 'big.' The most lucrative was a late-war Ying Raider."

"Are those the ones with three drives?"

Maggie's estimation of her went up a notch. "Yeah, two in front and one in back that's gimballed. Its micro qigong had been shot out, but the antigravs were still sealed and good as new. That was big enough to buy a stake in the Rusty Robot and spin up everyone's bank accounts."

"Is that what you mean by big? Lucrative?" There was a challenge in Zsuzsanna's question that cut to the heart of why they were camping out in the bush in the first place.

Maggie shrugged. "Spin is good when you need to make rent. But there are easier ways to make a living than scraping for leftovers from the Warsing. So no, when I think big, I'm thinking artifacts that haven't been seen since the warsingers took over."

"That's what I think too," Zsuzsanna said eagerly. "So what was your *biggest* find?"

Maggie straightened up and worked a kink out of her lower back with a satisfying pop. "Here's the thing about being a technomancer, Zsuzsanna. Talking about it can get you killed. If warsingers think you found something, they'll send in mantids. And *they'll* take your head right off your shoulders, just to be sure no one puts a leech on you and sucks out whatever you knew."

Zsuzsanna blushed. "I'm sorry. I didn't mean to put you on the spot."

"It's all right," Maggie said. "Eric trusts you, so I trust you. You wouldn't be here otherwise. You've got a cut of whatever we find this trip. But as for the past – my past, anyway – you need to trust me when I say there are things you're better off not knowing."

And that was the end of that conversation. Maggie felt like a jerk, but her circle was small and Zsuzsanna was not part of it. The reality was that Maggie did not trust her. She had no reason to, besides Eric, and she was not inclined to spend the next few mears working in a uranium mine to 'repay her debt to society' if he was wrong.

They finished putting up the fence in silence. Eric came out with a stack of dishes. Zsuzsanna went down to the stream with him to help wash.

Maggie headed the other direction, up to the top of the knoll behind camp, to get her blood moving again. The light was dying fast. It would be nice to go to bed with warm hands and feet. She felt a burst of pity for Eric and Zsuzsanna, washing dishes in a stream that was barely above freezing. But then they had each other to keep warm at night, so who was better off?

Maggie did not really have anybody. No boyfriend, or girlfriend for that matter. No immediate family. She was an only child. Her parents were killed when mantids raided their home back in Korolyov. Way back east in the Margaritifer Terra, where the mighty Marineris flowed into what had been the Aurorae Chaos, before the Blue Mars Project had turned it into a sea. Korolyov on Aurora's southern shore, white caps in the summer, a rippled plain of ice in the winter. Korolyov with its fish racks holding their bounty of red flesh up to the sun. Korolyov where she could never return.

Her father was a treasure hunter too, and more than that, a technomancer. He could crack almost any Warsing artifact, graft an interface, make it work. And that was his downfall. He became well-known. People brought him things they had found. He liked the attention. He got comfortable. And the warsingers noticed him.

Oh, he was a fighter, Maxim Lebedev. He took quite a few of their mantids with him, enough to give Maggie a chance to run. She escaped the firefight with his revolver and the bugout bag he kept near the back airlock.

She moved to a different town, took a different name, kept a low profile. But she knew the warsingers were still out there, waiting for her to cross some invisible line.

Maggie shivered. The stars were starting to come out. Phobos rose in the west and moved steadily across the sky. She had stood still for too long. She would be going to sleep with cold feet after all.

Still she stood and watched Phobos cross the sky. Its space-elevator was visible as a bright line descending from the little moon towards the horizon before it disappeared in the shadow of Mars. Every three days the elevator rendezvoused with a high-speed maglev train at the summit of Pavonis Mons. Cargo off, cargo on, and away it went. All run by warsingers.

Nothing else moved up there, or at least nothing human. No ships. No communication satellites. Anything that humans launched into orbit – or beyond – was never heard from again. Such was the price of peace with the League of Worlds, the ergocrats said. But it offended her on a primal level that she could barely articulate.

She shook her head, descended the slope with giant loping steps. It had gotten dark enough that she could not see the ground beneath her feet. Rocks scattered under her poorly placed footsteps and rolled away downhill in front of her. One of them hit something that made a hollow clonking sound.

She skidded to a halt.

Eric called up to her from camp. "Maggie, you all right? It's time to turn on the fence!"

"Be there in a minute!"

She got her flashlight out and dialed it up to full power. The landscape around her sprang into sharp relief. So much for her night vision. She raised the light high above her head and fanned it around. She was rewarded with a pale gleam off to one quarter. She bounded down to the object.

There in the puddle of light was a human skull. The jaw was missing but it was otherwise intact, albeit heavily weathered. Maggie picked it up carefully. A ceramic button was imbedded in its crown.

She dug a small roll of fluorescent flagging tape out of her pocket and tore off a half-meter strip. She tied the flagging around the upper branches of a nearby synlife tree. Then she headed back down to camp with her find.

The fence squawked a warning when she hopped over it.

"It's just me!" she called out.

"Good thing, because I'm naked," Eric's voice came from within the ember-lit arch of the smaller tent.

"We're all glad to know that," Alex called back from the big dome.

Maggie zipped herself through the big dome's airlock.

"Skull," Alex observed.

"Found it on the hillside. Maybe our missing pilot?" She handed the skull to Alex and stripped off her outer layers. "It's warm in here! Nice."

Alex shook the skull experimentally. Something inside made a sound like a wire brush on sedimentary rock: soft, rasping. He handed it over to his brother.

Dmitri ran the tip of his finger around the ceramic button on top of the skull and frowned thoughtfully. "Looks like a brainstone."

"Brainstone?" Alex asked.

"Immortality hack," Dmitri said. "Encodes your brain in durable matter."

"Didn't work out for this guy."

"Yet," Maggie said. "Can you get it out?"

Dmitri buffed the ceramic button, dug a bit of dirt out of an indentation in its top. "Looks like it takes a standard star wrench."

Maggie got her master set out of her black bag and handed it to him.

"It's stuck," Dmitri said after trying it.

"Give," Alex said. Dmitri handed the skull over. Alex waved off the wrench set and took out his belt knife. Its chainblade left an unpleasant odor of burnt bone in its wake. He set aside the bottom with its jagged sinus channels. The top of the skull looked like a bowl into which someone had dropped a freshly uprooted vegetable, a dirty radish replete with clotted root tendrils.

Alex tugged on it experimentally.

"One piece please," Maggie said.

Alex handed it back to Dmitri.

He scowled, but after a bit of work managed to free the ceramic button from its boney socket without ripping it loose from the brainstone.

Maggie took it gingerly. "Thanks."

"Are brainstones worth anything?" Alex asked, ever practical.

Maggie shrugged. "Depends on whose it was. Grandpa's brainstone gets grandpa rates. If its owner was a player in the Warsing, you get player rates."

"Would the pilot of an unknown type of spacecraft be a player?"

"You'd think."

"Huh." Alex settled back into his sleeping bag. "Then, you're welcome."

Dmitri clapped the two skull halves back together and held it out to her. "Alas, poor Yorick."

"Your ick now, more like," Maggie said. "I don't want it."

"You brought it in!" Dmitri protested.

"An intact skull has a certain gothic charm. A sawed open skull is kind of gross. Besides, it smells bad now. Like burnt... Something."

"Bone," Alex added helpfully.

"You only act like a girl when it suits you," Dmitri grumbled.

"That's why it's called acting," Maggie replied absently. She was already absorbed by the challenge posed by the brainstone. The trick would be to get the ceramic capsule open so she could access the brainstone's interface. Thermal cycling might do the trick, but she'd have to be careful.

Dmitri sighed and put the bisected skull in the airlock.

"All the way out," Maggie said without looking up. "I don't want it stinking up the entry."

Dmitri zipped through. She heard him punt the skull out through the outer door. The two halves clattered away into the darkness.

"Thank you, Dmitri!" she called.

He zipped back through. "Anything for your Highness."

"Really? Can I borrow your headlamp? I could use a little extra light over here."

Dmitri sighed, handed it over. "Anything else?"

"Nope, that's great, Dmitri. Thanks, really." She gave him a smile.

"Then I'm hitting the sack," he said.

Alex was already asleep, snoring lightly.

"Night then." Maggie opened her black bag and got to work.

2

Liberty on Ceres

"How's your head?" Lynch asked.

"Feels like someone drove a nail through the top of my skull," Gray said.

"Sounds about right, from what I've heard about the procedure." Lynch snagged a bulban of champagne from a passing waiter. "This should help."

The bulban's legs folded up against the bottom of its distended abdomen, the top of which was clear and pure as a piece of blown glass. Gray swirled the straw-colored fluid within.

"I swear I can feel it growing," he said.

"Just your imagination. Your brain is amazingly insensitive, considering it is a bunch of nerves. But yeah, it is. Growing."

"Thanks," Gray said.

"At least it's not a moravec," Lynch said. "I'll give that to your girlfriend. I still can't believe you let her talk you into it though. You know it's proscribed technology."

A recollection: Elise sitting across from him on her bed, belly flat, breasts round in Ceres' low gravity, hair like a dark nebula around her oval face. 'Do you want to live forever?' she had asked.

"She can be very persuasive," Gray said.

"That I believe!" Lynch raised his bulban. "Here's to the future. May some version of you live long enough to replace one of those old lizards."

Gray returned the toast. The drink was cold and evanescent.

The chamber and its contents had been carved out of the crater wall in one piece. The floor glinted with shocked quartz. Water lapped languidly at the edge of an octagonal basin the size of a small swimming pool. An ancient synlife ship tree rose from an island near its center. Its gnarled branches held a few small apples aloft towards the vaulted ceiling. People sat around the basin's rim, talking business.

His spex tagged her on the far side of the chamber.

"There," Gray said. He passed the tag along to Lynch.

"Not bad for a vamp," Lynch said.

"Not bad? Elise is hot."

The woman in question wore a black dress cut low in back, and exquisite clockwork heels of brass and carbon. A curtain of dark glossy hair fell just below the line of her jaw. Light gleamed on the gems at her throat as she turned to speak to her companion, a tall reddish-haired man. Something about the exchange – the set of her shoulders, hand on one hip – told Gray she was not enjoying his company.

"She's got wings," Lynch said.

"Everybody here has wings."

"We don't have wings," Lynch pointed out. "Commander Abrams doesn't have wings. My date doesn't have wings."

"Here as in Ceres. Not here as in the expo," Gray said. "Besides, I think wings are kind of sexy."

There were plenty of near baselines at the exposition. *Tereshkova's* senior officers were there along with command staff from several other Space Force torchships, plus a full wing of controllers from Greenwich Station, amongst them Lynch's date for the evening social. They had all come down to preview the latest mekan hatch.

"Some of them have tails," Lynch said. "You think that's sexy too?"

"We've got gecko pads on our hands and feet. Form follows function." His gaze lingered on Elise. "And believe me, she is highly functional."

As soon as the words were out, he regretted them. Gray had a reputation for having a woman in every port, but this time was different. Elise was not just another conquest, another picture next to his bunk to brag about.

Lynch shook his head. "Once an engineer, always an engineer. Now my idea of sexy is Primus Petrova there. Tall, slender, a dusting of freckles. Blonde hair, blue eyes. Which is to say, the opposite of your vamp."

"You and your Martian dolls. And don't call her a vamp, all right? When you meet her."

Lynch looked offended. "I wasn't born in the bush."

Gray consulted his spex. "Best round them up. The social is a kay and a half out."

"I'll get Petrova and meet you over there."

Gray finished his bulban. "Poyekhali."

"Poyekhali." Lynch headed for the buffet table, where Petrova was building a plate of appetizers for her and her friends, looking very tall and self-possessed in her dress whites.

Gray set his bulban down. Its legs flicked out from underneath and latched onto the granite tabletop. He straightened his uniform jacket and strolled across the ballroom, exchanging pleasantries with fellow officers as he made his way to Elise's booth.

A deconstructed mekan was mounted on a pedestal in front of the booth. Its radiators were lifted away from its back like the wings of an insect in flight. Its carapace had been artfully resected to reveal its internals. One hand was held out, fingers splayed as if in supplication. Each digit branched into two, and then two again, and on until the outermost edge looked soft as a feather. The recursive fanlike cilia of its other hand were folded together into a binary claw, posed open like a pair of scissors. Its four legs were bent as if it were about to leap.

Gray tested the edge of one binary claw with his fingertip. A faint pink line tracked across the whorled grey flesh of his gecko pad.

"Careful," Elise said behind him. She had the lilting accent of a native-born Ceresean. "It's very sharp."

Gray turned, a broad smile breaking through his official façade. "Elise!"

Her spex glimmered with iconji, the symbols flashing by too quickly for Gray to fully grasp, then cleared to reveal lovely half-moon eyes. She held out her hand. "Lieutenant Gray. So good to see you again."

Gray's smile disappeared as quickly as it came. There were protocols to observe, observers to placate. Gray's torchship needed fresh mekans, and bidding on the latest hatch would start the next trisol. The last thing either of them needed was someone claiming a conflict of interest.

"Hivemaster." Gray took her hand in his, marveling again at its slenderness. What would have been her little finger, if she were baseline, was a long gracile digit doubled back halfway to her elbow. A fold of flesh webbed the space between finger and forearm, draped now like the cuff of an elegant dress.

"Hivemaster in waiting. An important distinction, my brother tells me."

"Is that who you were talking to?"

"Yes. He can be such a null set. I can't believe I'm shut out of my own hive." She shook her head as if to clear it. "I'm sorry. Family business. How's your head?"

"Fine. Can't even tell somebody drilled a hole in it and stuffed it full of nanotech."

"Lucky! Mine gave me a migraine for trisols running."

"Funny you didn't mention that until now."

"It seemed a small price to pay for virtual immortality."

"It's the virtual part that worries me." Unlike a moravec, the brainstone did not offer the comfort of continuity. You had to die before you could be resurrected.

"Life is full of tradeoffs."

"And death too, evidently."

She changed the subject. "What do you think of our newest species of mekan? We're calling them mantids."

Gray turned his attention to the resected mekan. "I like the hand design. Very elegant. What's the use case for the claw?"

"The inner fingers work like shears. They can cut right through standard titanium hull plate. Of course, if it came to a true offensive action, your crew would still have to step in. Mantids have the same aversion to harming us quads as any mekan."

She circled around the display, explaining the improvements they had made as she went. Gray trailed behind, captured by the way the folds of her wings caught the air as she gestured. When she ducked beneath the abdomen of the mantid to show him something, Gray knelt beside her.

"As you can see, we've redesigned the thermoelectric organ, too. Mantids are optimized for the reactor environment of the current generation of torchships." She pointed up at the organ's manifold and the soft, dark fur on the edge of one wing brushed against his cheek.

Gray closed his eyes and took a breath. He had spent the last few megaseconds on a torchship with thirty-one other men and twice that many mekans, and the touch of a woman was enough to make his head swim.

Especially this woman. She had the scent of cinnamon and roses, with a bit of musk that probably wasn't perfume at all. Some pheromonal circuit closed in his brain. She didn't just smell good, she smelled *right*. He opened his eyes to find her watching him curiously.

"I don't think you've heard a thing I've said."

"I've got a bit of pixel-bloom going," Gray admitted.

She shook her head. "You're such a xenophile."

"I am entirely omniphilous!" he declared. Which was true; Gray was a great admirer of female beauty. He appreciated all women, from the rangy Slavic baselines he'd grown up with on Mars to exotic crispers like Elise from distant ports of call.

"That's not even a word."

He waved off the criticism. "Listen, I'm on liberty until third sunrise. Are you still free for dinner? I want you to meet my buddy Lynch."

Someone cleared their throat behind them.

"That would be him," Gray said.

Elise stood gracefully, giving him a look that meant they would be talking about this later. Lynch took her hand. His brow furrowed briefly at the strangeness of it.

"Ed Lynch, Chaika's third lieutenant. And this is Rachel Petrova, Space Control primus."

"Elise Aberdeen, Taproot hive."

"Elise is Taproot's hivemaster in waiting," Gray expanded as he took Petrova's outstretched hand. A single gold embossed feather adorned the cuff of her white sleeve, matched by a snowy owl feather tucked into the left side of her pilotka hat. "I'm John Gray, first lieutenant."

"Congratulations on your prize, Lieutenant. That was nice work."

"Thank you, Primus."

"Rachel, please. If we're going to be friends." She had not yet let go of his hand.

"John, then," Gray said. He had an uneasy sense of being boxed in.

"Are you bringing someone to the social, John?" Petrova asked. "I have a friend who would love to go if you need a plus one."

A silver cloud passed over Elise's spex, obscuring her eyes.

"Elise is my date," Gray said, his voice gone dangerously quiet.

"But..." she turned to Lynch, stopped at the alarm on his face. "...it is an official Space Force function."

"Elise is a hivemaster," Lynch said. "I'm sure she'll be more than welcome."

"Actually," Elise said, "I have duties here that will prevent me from attending. You three have fun."

"Two," Gray said curtly, unable to keep the anger out of his voice. "Lieutenant Lynch, please extend my regrets to the XO. Dismissed."

"Aye sir." Lynch turned away, face flaming red, Petrova in tow.

Gray shook his head. He would have bridges to mend after pulling rank like that. Lynch might not have been born in Tsiolkovsky, but his date clearly was. What a basist bitch.

"I'm so sorry," Gray said.

"Not your fault. A lot of baselines feel that way."

"Let's just go to that place you like. The Anasazi."

"I do have some things I have to wrap up here. Not a complete lie."

"I'll wait."

Gray watched the sun rise over the rim of the crater that held the city. Its wan light slanted across the bowl, illuminating the low walls of terraced gardens and brushing shadows through the ship trees that grew from its floor. And that was just the surface; much of the city was underground, safely shielded from whatever coronal nastiness the sun might eject. All of which made the city-state of Meridian the crown jewel of the United Colonies of Mars, the seventh golden star on its royal blue flag.

On the far side of the diamondoid dome that capped the city, sunlight caught on the city's beanstalk and turned it the color of burnished copper. Gray traced the beanstalk up from the sprawling mekanopolis at its base, past the nebulous shadow of Greenwich Station in synchronous orbit, until it was lost in the glare of the fusion torch at its far end. Even a thousand kilometers away, he could feel the heat of the torch on his face.

The old and the new sun. Prometheus had stolen fire from Olympus and brought it down in the form of a fusion torch. Without its heat, without its immediate light, the famous gardens of Meridian would wither and die.

The torch enabled the United Colonies of Mars to exist. It lit up the asteroids and powered the ships that bound them together. But there was a catch. Clean fusion was the product of deuterium and helium-3. Deuterium was ubiquitous in the solar system. Helium-3 was not. The only viable source was Luna.

Long before Gray was born, back when Earth teetered on the verge of ecosystem collapse, it became obvious that the planet's only sustainable energy source was the sun. The Ecostate of Nüwa built vast constellations of solar power satellites in Earth orbit. Most of the material for those satellites came from Luna.

Meanwhile the oners who fled EON's oppression for freedom on Mars were burning uranium like there was no tomorrow. And why not? There was nothing to pollute on Mars, nothing to save. Mars was a wasteland of epic proportions, as Gray's grandfather liked to say.

Nuclear fission propelled the Martians out to the Belt and then on to Jupiter's Trojans. And there things took a turn. Out in the Arkipelago, the nexus of iceteroids that trailed mighty Jupiter in its orbit, the sun was only a twenty-seventh as bright as on Earth. Having fission power was like having a fireplace in a place that was always winter. It kept you warm, but you can't eat warm. You can't grow warm. Life needs the hot light of the sun to thrive.

Necessity being the mother of invention, the Arkies invented the fusion torch, a big geodesic sphere with an ignition laser at every vertex, all pointing inwards at a tiny droplet of fuel. The land of eternal winter saw first one, then another, then a dozen new suns. Life blossomed. Life that depended on helium-3.

From the surface of Mars, the Arkipelago rivalled the brightest constellations. The Martian ergocrats took notice. Meetings were held. Deals were made. Charters were granted.

EON's clean-burning hydrogen-oxygen rockets were no match for the United Colonies' atomic fleet. A settlement was negotiated that gave control of the Lunar mines to Helios, a Martian corporation. If the Nüwans wanted anything from their moon, they could buy it.

There matters sat for the better part of a standard Earth century until terrestrial temperatures fell, ambitions rose, and some girl genius from the Wudang mountains invented the qigong reactor. Take six plasma mirror lasers and arrange them like the spokes of a child's jack. Fuel it with deuterium and helium-3. Shock it to life with a Promethean blast of electricity. Stabilize its star-hot breath with an artiform like the mind of a dragon.

A qigong the size of a shipping container produced enough clean, aneutronic fusion power for a city. Now there was something the Nüwans wanted very much from their moon: the same helium-3 that the United Colonies needed. The Martian ergocrats took notice. Meetings were held. Deals were made. And the Nüwans learned there was nothing they possessed that Helios would accept in exchange for helium-3.

Elise appeared at Gray's elbow. "Hey spacer. Looking for Chaika?"

"Hello, beautiful!" Gray set aside thoughts of empire. "Actually I can't make her out against the paramirror."

Elise gazed up through slatted fingers. Her backless dress was secured by a loop around her neck and a strap that pierced the membranes of her wings. The wings themselves bridged wrist to the small of her back like a softly furred cloak. Gray wanted to touch them. He loved the way they felt. But they were still getting used to being back together after a long absence. And they really had not been together for very long before he had left for the cruise. It was almost like starting over.

"There's a big one on the leading pier," she said. "Is that her?"

"That sounds right." To him the station looked like a hazy vertical slit of a pupil set in a blazing eye. Those tendrils might be docks, or they might be tracks in his vitreous humor left by mears of radiation exposure. "You really can see her from here?"

Elise raised her spex and fluttered dark eyelashes theatrically. "High dynamic range eyes. They go with the wings."

He took advantage of the implicit invitation for a closer look. Her grey-green eyes were significantly larger than baseline. Something about that both alarmed and aroused him. He drew back involuntarily.

She laughed at his reaction, a low throaty chuckle. "Still want to take me to dinner?"

"More than ever."

She fed her spex to the puffer purse at her waist and held out an impossibly slender hand.

They walked along the esplanade. The sun rose quickly. Ceres rotated three times in a Martian sol. People got up and went to work at first sunrise, went home at second, and went to bed at third. Now after the second sunrise of the trisol, people frolicked in the air above the crater floor. Gray could not keep his eyes off them.

Elise gave him a sideways glance. "You could crisp a pair of wings, settle down... No one could tell you from a home-grown drac in short order."

Gray smiled, shook his head.

"Not the settling type?" Elise asked.

"You know I'm career Space Force. The only acceptable crisps are the ones that fit in a skinsuit. Wings are not one of the options."

"I see," she said in a tone that made him think he had insulted her.

"Not that there is anything wrong with wings! I like wings. Especially your wings."

Her lips pressed together. "Don't try too hard. I'm not taking it personally. So tell me about this prize of yours. What happened?"

"You heard about that threelium barge that was hijacked?"

"Sure, it was all over the news. It happened right after they left L5, right? Pirates stowed away in a threelium tank. After the tug lit its torch, they cut their way out and took over. Kind of brilliant, really."

"They weren't pirates," Gray said, ignoring the 'kind of brilliant' part, which stung a little.

"That's not what the talking heads said."

"I was there," Gray said.

"Wait, now I'm confused. The ship that rendezvoused with them was UCM *Tereshkova*. Your ship is the Chaika. At least that's what you've always said."

"Ah, right, sorry," Gray said. "She's named after Valentina Tereshkova, who was the first woman in space. Tereshkova's call sign on that flight was Chaika, Russian for seagull. And the ship's radiators kind of look like glowing wings –" He stretched his arms out to illustrate and nearly hit a big drac in the face. "Sorry mate."

The drac shot Elise an evil glance. She raised her eyebrows and he moved on.

"So the men call her Chaika," Gray finished, looking back over his shoulder. "Most of the ships have nicknames. It's an old tradition."

Elise took Gray's arm, steering him away from the drac. "Chaika, nickname for *Tereshkova*. Famous Russian. We're not big into Russia out here, if you haven't noticed."

"Famous spacer," Gray said. "Anyway, they weren't pirates. They were EON kunmings."

Elise looked skeptical. "Kunmings are a fable meant to scare oners."

"No, really. I was there. We blew the hull near the bridge. I'm looking around, but as far as I can tell everyone is cold. So I turn to wave my squad in, and I get shot in the back with an incendiary." Gray laughed ruefully. "I would have cooked in my own juices if Lynch hadn't hauled me out of my combat shell. By the time that happened, all the hijackers really were cold."

"Cold being dead."

"Right."

"Got it. Cold. So you didn't get to talk to them."

"Well no, that did not work out. But all three were kunmings. Take a look." Gray tapped his spex. Elise fetched hers out of her puffer. He sent a picture he'd taken aboard the tug. "Webbed fingers and toes, retractable claws, and it's hard to make out with what's left, but the ears are distinctive as well. Large and articulated, kind of like a dog, for thermal regulation."

"Ugh," Elise said. "What happened to him?"

"He took a wide beam in the head. Superheated, kind of blew out to the aft. And then of course the vacuum."

"Of course," Elise said faintly. She closed the picture.

Gray bit his lip. "Sorry about that. I forgot you're a civilian." Which was a compliment, but not one she would necessarily appreciate, given the gist of their conversation.

"Why isn't this on the news?" Elise asked. "Nobody said anything about the Ecostate of Nüwa."

"I imagine Helios doesn't want people to think the Space Force is getting into a shooting war with EON on their behalf. Better to say they were pirates and let everyone think it is business as usual."

Elise looked out over the city. A warm breeze blew up from the bowl, ruffling her hair. "The United Colonies should give Luna back to Earth and move on. There's plenty of threelium in Saturn's atmosphere. Three Martian gees at cloud top is no worse than Earth's surface."

"Saturn is a long way out. And the mining infrastructure is completely different there than Luna. Ramscoops versus tractors. That's going to take some serious spin to set up."

"As if spin is a problem for Helios. The most profitable entity in the history of mankind."

"Spin is always a problem. The old lizards who run the United Colonies are not going to give up a single joule without a fight." He shook his head. "Don't get me wrong. I'm no fan of fighting Helios's battles for them. I joined up to get a shot at a Kuiper Belt mission. But if the skipper says fight, I'm all in."

The Anasazi was set into the crater wall. Rough windows had been hewn out of the rock. A waiter in a breechclout and bow tie led them to a table. Tattoos crawled across his back in slow motion. A bird of some sort? No, a dragon.

Elise ordered a bulban of wine. There was no shortage of vineyards in Meridian. Gray chose a martini made with a local gin. They eyed each other speculatively. Gray took the lead.

"What's going on with your brother?"

"I don't even know where to start with that."

"The beginning? We haven't done the family history yet."

She laughed. "No, it was a pretty straight shot to the bedroom, last time you were here."

"I can only hope history repeats itself," Gray said.

"The night is young." She sat back in her chair, an enigmatic smile gracing her face. "All right, the family. But you're not going to like it."

"Try me."

"All right. The grandparths immigrated from Mars back when Ceres was just another rock. They were baselines of course; everybody was back then. Their daughter Melissa crisped some wings when the big dome went up, which made her part of the first generation of true Cereseans. She went on to marry Hugh Wilson, another crisper, and had Anton the regular way. Which technically makes him my parthsib, not my brother. It gets complicated. Anyway, much later, she had a baby all by herself – that's me."

He sipped his drink to hide his expression. He had wondered if she was a parth.

"It's a common pattern in the hive business. A way to ensure business continuity. Queens are gene locked to prevent hivejacking. And cloning is illegal in the United Colonies, but what you do with your own body is your own business. So..." She shrugged. "Parths."

"Are the, uh, grandparths still alive?"

"No they died way back. No lifex baked into the Aberdeen genome! And Hugh died in prison. He and Melissa were part of the Resistance. The Insurgency, as your wikis say. Melissa and Anton made it through, though they nearly starved to death."

"Ah. I'm sorry."

"The Annexation was a long time ago. Before I was born. I think it's stupid to hold the current generation responsible. Counterproductive."

He nodded slowly, filling in the blanks of her silence. "But that's not how Melissa feels. Nor Anton."

She sighed. "No. That is not their story. They hate the United Colonies for what they did to Ceres. To Hugh."

"So I'm guessing they are not happy about you getting involved with a Space Force officer."

She shrugged with her eyebrows. "There's nothing about me that Anton is happy about. And it has been a couple years since I've seen Melissa or been in the hive. I'm just a glorified sales engineer at this point."

She fingered the translucent gem embedded in the hollow of her throat. It was the size of the end of his thumb and the color a drop of blood would make in a shot glass of vodka. It was flanked by a pair of smaller gems.

"Is that a queen's mekovum?"

Elise nodded. "I'm going to call her Rhea."

"As in the moon of Saturn?"

"As in the mother of gods."

"Ambitious. I like it."

"If I'm Melissa's backup, Rhea is mine. I can start over with her if I must." For a moment she looked drawn, older than he'd thought. Then she smiled brightly. "How about another drink?"

They ordered another round, and then dinner. Gray chose roast chicken, she chose lamb. It was the most expensive item on the menu, an even forty gigajoules. He didn't care in the least. Captain Rashnikov had claimed the helium-3 tug as a prize. As first lieutenant, Gray got a sizeable share. Only a small portion of it had come through yet, but that was more than enough to pay for a night on the town with Elise. And a major upgrade to his combat shell. And a state-of-the-art brainstone. Which no longer hurt.

Not bad for a niner from Thunderbird.

He realized he had lost track of what Elise was saying. He studied her face as she spoke, hearing the lilt of her voice but not able to discern individual words. The first martini had hit home and the second was on the way.

He felt like he knew the secret meaning behind what she was saying. He was caught up in the curve of her lips, the subtle plane of her cheeks. He wanted to take her in his arms and kiss her. He wanted her so badly he could feel it, a dull ache between his legs.

After cruise rations, dinner was a revelation. The roast chicken came with a side of small red potatoes and a neat stack of asparagus spears. Onboard a torchship, the crew did not eat so much as fuel up. Grechka, lentils, some greens. Tilapia from time to time, as the fish in the water tanks that shielded the living quarters matured. No hard alcohol, which likely explained his state.

Outside the stone walls of the restaurant, the sun was sinking. The gin buzz was starting to fade, leaving a warm glow in its place. "So what now? Dancing? A nightcap in my hotel room? It's very nice."

She smiled. "You are a mess. Dancing sounds lovely. I haven't been out in ages."

"One of my shipmates told me about a club in the high-gee ring train under the rim wall."

"You mean the Seventh Sister?" Elise wrinkled her nose. "That's a Space Force hangout. I don't want to spend the night fending off drunken geckos. No offense."

He waved his hand. "None taken. What's your favorite place?"

"I don't think I have one anymore, it has been so long. That sounds sad, doesn't it?"

"It sounds like an occupational hazard. Being heiress to the family hive and all." Gray motioned the waiter over and handed him his wallet. The waiter took the disk-shaped device and discharged their tab into the restaurant's kino bank. Gray gave him a healthy zap on top for good luck.

He took Elise's hand as they strolled along the balcony. She wrapped her arm around his waist. Their walk turned into a slow perambulation.

Gray let his hand slide down from her waist to cup her ass. All he could think about was how her body felt next to his. Her muscles moved sensuously beneath his hand. She really did have a nice ass. And beautiful eyes. And a sweet, sweet mouth. He pulled her around to face him.

Their lips were just about to touch when his spex buzzed. Elise drew back. Gray sighed, blinked at the pulsating red icon. It opened into an avatar of a lean middle-aged man in the Space Force's black uniform and grey vest: UCM *Tereshkova's* executive officer.

"Commander Abrams," Gray said.

"Lieutenant Gray. Something has come up. We need you back on Chaika."

"Understood," Gray said. "It's going to take a few kilosecs to get up there."

"Best possible speed, Pilot," Abrams said.

"Aye sir."

The comm window closed. Gray sighed. "That was my XO," he said. "Something has come up."

"You have to go," Elise said. She looked smaller, as if she had fallen in on herself.

"I'm afraid so. Space Force business."

She nodded. "Of course."

"Kiss me goodbye?" he asked.

"Here? In front of everybody?"

"Absolutely here in front of everybody," he said.

She laughed. "You have no idea. All right."

She tilted her head up. He pulled her close, careful not to hurt her wings. They brushed against his arms in soft warm folds as their lips met. He started to get hard.

She did not push him away. "You need to go."

"Now?"

She sighed. "Now."

3

The Ice Tree

The ice tree had watched Mars since its first eye flower bloomed. There was something compelling about the unblinking orb, something that called to the simple intelligence that animated the ice tree. Something that felt like sex, like release.

As it fell insystem from the Arkipelago, its roots penetrated deep into the heart of the iceteroid and methodically pulverized it. Primeval elements trapped in the ammonia ice became dusky purple leaves spread to catch the faint sunlight. At the periphery of the canopy, eye flowers blossomed like tulips in the springtime. Their deep-bellied petals swung out from the central seed heads. At full extension the petals stiffened into a reflector three meters across.

Each reflector focused an image of Mars onto its blue-black head. What had been a ruddy orb was now a true disk. Brilliant water-ice polar caps bracketed a reddish-brown center. But these features were not what held the ice tree's interest. It searched for the tiny flecks of light that meant fulfillment.

And found them, rising from the outer moon. To the ice tree's slow mind the lights moved like sparks kicked out of a fire. The time had come. The eye flowers' petals bent back from their centers. The spherical heads thrust up from the foliage like offerings to the sky.

The pchelan swarm burned hard to catch up with the iceteroid. The delta vee required to reach it was at the limit of their capabilities. They exhausted nearly all their onboard ammonia matching velocities. The arcjets on their backs got hot, then hotter still. Heat flowed down into their abdomens, pooling like erectile blood in the heavy metal stinger at its tip.

They dropped towards the surface, hungry for the ammonia hidden beneath the ice tree's foliage. The purple leaves did not present a significant barrier. They could take what they needed. But the blue-black spheres thrust up from the withered eye flowers drew their attention. There was a pattern woven into the blackness that polarized distant sunlight.

Vernier thrusters flickered, consuming the last of their precious ammonia. The pchelans came to a stop above the eye flowers. They pulled themselves down, breaking petals off with their massive bodies. Tree leaves curled away from contact with red-hot stingers.

Tricode was woven into the seed heads, surely as the mantras engraved on Buddhist mani stones, a plea for fulfillment, a statement of origin. For a long moment the pchelans stared at the hidden message. Then with gentle ferocity they sheared seed heads from stems with their mandibles, and hurled them back into space, so they might find their way back to their beginning.

Only then did they begin to feed. They tore through the tangled branches, fighting their way down to the surface. When one broke through, she spared a single glance at the sky to be sure of her position, then plunged her stinger into the surface.

A gout of vaporized ammonia blasted away from the point of contact. The pchelan worked her stinger deep into the ice. A cone of gas jetted up her flanks and frosted her legs. She withdrew her stinger and turned to the hole she had melted in the ice. Foveal rings tracked across her eyes, building a model of the pit. It would do.

She plunged her head into the pit. Her beak-like mandibles scraped the sides of the pit and filled her mouth with a delicious slurry of ammonia ice. Her diamond-crusted tongue crushed it against the roof of her mouth. The ice liquefied and ammonia flowed into her body.

She shuddered with pleasure and rooted deeper into the hole. The arcjet on her back crackled into life. An ionized jet of ammonia lanced up into the night, then another and another as her hatchmates joined her.

Slowly, inexorably, the iceteroid decelerated. The elliptical transfer orbit that had brought it insystem from the Arkipelago became a circle that matched that of Mars.

4

Salvage

Eric zipped through the airlock. "Good morning sleepy heads!"

"What time is it?" Maggie asked, her voice muffled by the hood of her sleeping bag.

"Almost eight."

She groaned, pulled the pumpkin-colored bag down to her armpits so her arms were free. Her breath frosted in the stale air. The oxygen candle had gone out sometime in the night, and Alex had turned off the truck's engine when he had gone to bed to save fuel. Someday she would live where it was not always cold.

"Up late partying with the boys?" Eric asked.

"Not exactly." Maggie handed over the brainstone and the interface she had cobbled together.

He examined it closely. "What is it?"

"Somebody's life." Maggie reluctantly extracted herself the rest of the way from the warmth of her sleeping bag. She hurriedly put on her outer layers. She lit another oxygen candle, then jammed her hands under the waistband of her long underwear to warm them.

Eric held the walnut-sized device up to the light. "I've heard about these. Did you get it to work?"

"Mostly." She passed the interface's link to Eric's goggles. "Alex! Dmitri! Get your lazy asses out of bed. There's work to be done. And for war's sake start the truck. It's cold in here."

Eric turned the interface on, grimaced. "First person immersive. That'll take some getting used to. Whose is it?"

"Some Space Force guy named Lieutenant Gray."

"I imagine he had a first name."

"Don't be an asshole before I've had coffee."

Eric held out a battered green thermos. "I brought coffee. Breakfast is on the way."

"Ah, bless you." She poured herself a cup and savored it in silence for a few moments. The sun was just brushing against the top of the tent, turning the tan fabric pink. "Alex! Dmitri! I'm going to open the airlock if you don't get up."

"Don't be such a hard ass," Alex grumbled. "You know when I went to bed the night before we left?"

"This is not a vacation, Aleksey Ivanovich. Get up now while there's still some of this excellent coffee left."

Alex sat up with a grunt. "Ah it stinks in here." He cuffed the sleeping bag next to him. "Dmitri, you let the oxy candle go out last night!"

"Frag you I did," Dmitri said from somewhere deep inside his bag. "It was your turn to tend to it."

"Something about this guy rings a bell," Eric said. He turned the interface off. "We could hook up to marsnet next time a commhawk flies over, see if the Warsing Wiki has anything on him."

"Not while we're out here," Maggie said. "I don't want to leave any tracks."

Eric nodded. "Good point. It'll come to me eventually. What's the order of the day?"

"Pull the reactor out of the wreck, get it on the truck before sunset."

"Why not take the whole stern section?" Alex asked. "And gut it back in town."

"What we should really do is take the whole thing," Dmitri said. "A find like this is more valuable whole than in pieces."

"It's too big for the truck," Alex said. "We'd have to cut it up anyway."

"We could register a claim and sell it off."

"To who?" Alex asked.

"To whom," Dmitri corrected. "I bet Tsiolkovsky Polytechnic would be interested."

"We're not registering a claim," Maggie said. "If any of the big players find out – T-Poly or whoever – all bets are off. We don't have enough people to defend a claim on the ground or spin to do it in a courtroom. We work in the black."

"I'm not going back to Tsiolkovsky empty-handed," Alex said.

"No," Maggie agreed. "*We* are not going back empty handed. We are taking the reactor this trip, and if that's all we ever get, we've done good. If it turns out that the rest of the wreck is worth something, then we come back for it."

"Works for me," Eric said.

"I'm in," Alex said.

Dmitri shrugged. "Just saying."

"Then it's a plan," Maggie said. "Where's that breakfast you promised, Eric? Where's Zsuzsanna?"

"She probably went back to sleep," Eric replied, deadpan.

"I heard that!" Zsuzsanna's voice came from outside. "Who do you think made your coffee? And your breakfast. Help me with the airlock, my hands are full."

Eric jumped up and zipped her through. Zsuzsanna brushed past him laden with a steaming plate of pancakes and the means to consume them.

"Ah, she's a keeper," Alex said.

"I'm not sure he is," Zsuzsanna said with a dark look at Eric. "Went back to sleep, indeed." She passed around plates and utensils and served out the cakes.

"These are good," Alex said between bites.

"Thank you, Alex." Zsuzsanna favored him with a radiant smile. "I'm glad you like them."

Alex looked up, glanced over at Eric. Maggie cleared her throat. "What's the weather forecast today, Alex?"

He slipped his goggles on. "Temps about the same as yesterday; just above freezing. Icefall this afternoon. A small one, three point four gigatons, mostly ammonia. Estimated ninety five percent airburst, all predicted impactors way west of us on the Tharsis."

"Flash floods?"

"None forecast."

"All right," she said. "Let's get on with it. Be sure and document everything you touch, right? Dmitri's right: we might find a buyer who wants this thing whole. Try to keep the knife work to a minimum."

There were only three lead aprons in the truck, so Maggie and Zsuzsanna made as-builts of the wreck while the boys worked on freeing the stern section. Brains versus brawn.

The first step was to take pictures of everything. Then Maggie fired up a modeling tool and imported the images their goggles had collected. She passed her viewpoint over to Zsuzsanna. The awkwardness of the prior night was forgotten in the excitement of the moment.

"This is what we've got so far. A lot of it is still hidden under the sand, but I'll lay odds that the whole thing exhibits trilateral symmetry. The spar sticking up out of the sand is just one of three spaced equally around the spine. Like this."

Maggie copied the spar, rotated it a third of the way around, and then did the same operation again, so there were three of them.

"Like fins on a rocket," Zsuzsanna said.

"Except the spars support additional surfaces." Maggie brought up a picture of the spar from the previous day. "See? Not just a triangle oriented fore-to-aft like a fin. More like this." She sketched a skirt of crystal between the three aft spars. "Which makes it a pentachoron. Huh."

Zsuzsanna gave her a questioning look.

"Like a tetrahedron, but in addition to the four outer vertices that make the corners, there's another right in the center. Sometimes called a four-dimensional triangle."

"Well whatever it is, it's not very aerodynamic," Zsuzsanna observed. "There wasn't a lot of atmo back then, but still."

"Yeah. And then the same shape up front, but smaller, and pointing backwards. And another, smaller yet, attached to the tip of the spar. Recursive, almost."

"Ladies!" Eric called up from the work site, interrupting them. "We could use a hand down here."

"What do you need?" Maggie replied.

"Bring the truck around and back it up to where we can get the crane in play. We're almost done."

She and Zsuzsanna retrieved the truck. Maggie got it within twenty meters of the wreck before it started to lose traction in the loose sand. She set the brake and got out, Zsuzsanna following.

"You ever work one of these things?" Maggie gestured at the crane pedestal between the truck's cab and its open bed. Zsuzsanna shook her head.

"These ones," Maggie toggled a pair of spring-loaded switches, "extend the legs." A couple of screw jacks whirred down from either side of the truck.

"This is the cable brake." She lifted a lever that freed the cable. She pointed at a tee lever. "That one is for the winch drum. And this controls the rotation of the crane on its pedestal. Got it?"

Zsu did not look convinced. "Maybe?"

"You'll be fine. Don't kill me. I'm going to walk the hook out to the boys."

Dmitri met her halfway. "Do you have any spare kinos?" he asked. "My knife is dying."

"Already?" Maggie was not amused. "When was the last time you spun it up?"

"Uh... our last trip?"

"How can someone so smart be so stupid?"

"Mine is spun up," Alex said.

"Of course it is," Maggie said. She thrust the winch hook out to Dmitri. "Hold this."

Dmitri exchanged his knife for the winch hook. Maggie unscrewed the pommel of the knife's rubberized grip and dumped out its kino. The cylinder was blissfully warm in her gloved hands.

"You're an enabler," Eric commented. "Where are the consequences?"

"I'm a facilitator," Maggie said. She rummaged through her satchel for a spare. "If I weren't, the consequences would be you all not..."

Maggie was interrupted by an ear-splitting crack. A sheet of dust jumped up off the ground and hung there in the low gravity. She swore involuntarily.

"Icefall!" Dmitri called out, pointing to the north. A fireball ripped across the afternoon sky. It broke up as they watched, streaking the sky with ammonia vapor trails. A second boom, duller than the first shockwave but nearly as loud, rumbled down the canyon.

"Ded Moroz," Alex said, raising his fist like he was holding a stein.

"Ded Moroz," the others murmured. Grandfather Frost. Every fourteen Martian months another batch of ammonia-rich iceteroids arrived from the Arkipelago courtesy of Blue Mars, adding a few precious millibars to the atmosphere and kickstarting another hydrological cycle. This batch arrived in what would otherwise be summer. It would probably snow overnight.

By nightfall they had the stern section of the wreck up on the truck's bed. They strapped it down beneath the crane, bracing the radioactive cylinder with toolkits and spare gear to keep it from rolling. They put the shadow shield up front towards the cab to provide some shielding for the occupants. The engine bell hung over the back of the truck.

Dmitri looked at it and laughed. "Should be a short ride home!"

"Not short enough," Maggie said, too tired to laugh at a bad joke. "Tack those lead aprons up against the back of the cab, or our hair will be falling out by the time we get back. And get a tarp over the bed so no one can see our haul."

They all gathered in the big tent. Zsuzsanna made dinner for them again. She managed to turn a motley collection of canned goods and a box of grechka into a tasty meal, which pretty much won her a permanent place on the team, at least so far as the boys were concerned. Cooking was a chore none of them liked doing and therefore was rarely done well.

Maggie lit a second oxygen candle. Alex laid five gleaming ampules beside it. Each contained a cubic centimeter of DNA repair nanites. He set shot glasses and a bottle of vodka down beside them.

"What's that?" Zsu asked apprehensively. "I mean I like to party as much as anyone, but I'm not into needles."

"Not a party," Alex said. "Radvax booster. Pulling the reactor put us way over the personal exposure limit."

"Welcome to treasure hunting," Maggie said. She pulled up the sleeve of her base layer.

Alex slipped an ampule into the injector. He squeezed its grip. A status light changed from red to yellow as the radvax began to charge. Within the ampule, the viscous fluid took on a life of its own.

The light turned green. Alex pressed the injector against Maggie's shoulder. It went off with a cough.

"Nothing to it," she said, eyes watering. It felt like Alex had shot molten lava into her arm.

Zsu went next. "Mekfucker!" she exclaimed when the injector coughed. "That hurts." She gave Maggie an indignant look. "Liar."

Maggie bobbled her head. Eric was next, then Dmitri. Then Maggie took the injector from Alex and gave him his dose. Alex exhaled deeply and reached for the bottle of vodka. He filled the shot glasses.

"Merry Ded Moroz!" he toasted. "Thank you Grandfather Frost for this most excellent find."

"Merry Ded Moroz!"

The vodka burned nicely on the way down.

"That's good," Maggie said to Alex. "Did you make it?"

He nodded modestly. "Latest batch."

Maggie held out her cup. "You're improving. Keep it up and you'll be able to sell to the Rusty Robot. Another?"

Alex poured out another round. Maggie raised her cup. "To the best treasure hunters on Mars. And especially to our newest member and fabulous camp cook Zsu-zsu."

"Zsu-zsu!"

It went like that until the bottle was empty. Between the two oxygen candles, the warm meal in their bellies, and the vodka, the cold outside was forgotten. They stripped down to their base layers and played cards.

"Eric told me about the brainstone you found," Zsuzsanna said between hands. "The Space Force pilot."

Maggie nodded. "Lieutenant Gray."

"Yeah. So while I was waiting for the grechka to cook, I got a blip, and I tried looking him up in the Warsing Wiki."

"You got a blip." Maggie exchanged glances with Eric. Judging by his expression it was news to him as well.

"Yeah, low on the horizon. Anyway, I couldn't find anything about him," Zsuzsanna continued. "Are you sure his name is John Gray?"

"I'm sure," Maggie said.

Zsuzsanna looked back and forth between them. "What's wrong?"

"We weren't going to make any queries until we were well off-site," Maggie said. "But you were not part of that conversation, and evidently nobody told you." She looked pointedly at Eric, who raised his hands in a mea culpa.

"Oh." Zsuzsanna was crestfallen. "I did turn off location sharing before we left Tsiolkovsky, like you said."

"That just keeps your goggles from blabbing their nav data," Eric said. "But the towers that serve up marsnet..."

"Commhawks," Dmitri interjected, "when you're out this far."

Eric waved his hand dismissively. "Commhawks can estimate your position from your goggle's signal strength and bearing. And that location estimate gets logged, along with the start and stop time, for every message that the commhawk receives. So it knows roughly *where* and precisely *when* you initiated contact. And the Warsing Wiki knows when it got a query about Lieutenant John Gray. So anybody with the horsepower to correlate the data knows that someone from this location, more or less, is interested in an obscure Space Force pilot."

"If they're paying attention," Maggie said.

"Or whenever they mine the data," from Dmitri.

Maggie shrugged. "What's done is done. There's no point worrying about it."

"I'm sorry," Zsuzsanna said meekly.

"It'll be fine," Maggie said. "Now, I'm going to do dishes. It's gotten so warm in here I need to cool off!"

"I'll go with you," Dmitri said.

It had gotten dark while they ate. The stars overhead were bright and steady. The constellations on the western horizon, at the upper end of Valles Marineris, were obscured by a bank of clouds. Snow was coming.

Maggie improvised a headlamp by rearranging her airscarf and tucking her flashlight into one of the wraps. The living fabric gripped it obligingly.

"Night vision gear would be nice," Dmitri said. "I don't like being all lit up like this."

"I know," Maggie said. "Me neither." Her good mood had evaporated. "It's on the list."

They hopped over the security fence, dropping a cup and all the spoons in the process. The utensils clattered against a rock, but the fence itself remained silent. They had forgotten to turn it on before dinner, and then dinner had morphed into a celebration of their good fortune, and then night had fallen. It was the kind of mistake that could get them all killed, and she had no one to blame but herself.

The stream was shockingly cold. They took turns washing. On her break, Maggie stuffed her icy hands down the front of her pants to warm and turned full circle, fanning her flashlight beam into the darkness. There was no answering gleam of eyes in the darkness. Up on the bank, the tent glowed like an orange beacon. She could see shadows moving against the walls. All lit up, as Dmitri said.

They powered up the fence on the way back to the tent. Maggie took a long last look around before they went back inside.

Eric and Zsuzsanna were getting ready to go back to their tent. Maggie almost suggested that they stay in the main tent with the rest of the team, but she bit her tongue. Let them have their fun. Everything was going to be all right. Nonetheless she had a hard time getting to sleep. Every little noise pulled her back from the edge. She mentally catalogued each interruption, dismissed it as harmless, and let herself drift again.

It seemed like she had just really fallen asleep when her alarm woke her. Time to go home. She groped blindly for her goggles to turn it off. The sound didn't stop. She jerked upright with her heart pounding. It wasn't her goggles; it was the fence's continuity alarm.

She shook Alex. "Alex, something broke the wire. Up, up now!"

She looped her airscarf around her face, grabbed her goggles and her gun. "Dmitri, up now!"

There was a shriek from the other tent.

"What the hell," Alex said.

"Venting!" Maggie shouted, all thought of stealth gone. Alex was on his feet. No time for the niceties of the airlock. She opened the tent to the elements and charged out. A light coat of snow covered the ground. Something massive was crouched over the little half-dome tent. Maggie lit it up with her flashlight. An ugly lens-studded head jerked up to look at her. Not a spider bear. The warbot was three meters tall and vaguely humanoid in shape.

She thumbed open the revolver's iris. Crosshairs danced over the armored torso. She settled them at what would have been the intersection of a human's collarbones at the hollow of its throat and squeezed the trigger. The gun's muzzle blast momentarily blinded her.

She cast around with her flashlight, now clenched in her left hand and pressed up against the grip of the gun, parallel to its barrel. Something moved near the tent. She settled on it briefly and realized it was Eric. He rolled away from the wrecked tent and came up with his rifle in hand. She swung away, found the warbot again. One arm hung uselessly at its side. A brilliant beam of laser light cut through the falling snow as it turned toward her. She sprang to the side. A gout of dirt exploded where she had been.

Maggie landed, stumbled, rolled into a firing position on her belly. The warbot was still tracking her. She put the crosshairs in the middle of its head and pulled the trigger. She couldn't tell whether she hit or missed.

The warbot returned fire. A rock exploded right in front of her, blasting jagged bits across her face and knocking her revolver out of her hand. She rolled to her left and catapulted herself into a low jump.

A rifle spat out a slug with a sharp, supersonic bark. She landed, changed directions. A second rifle shot. Landed again. Somewhere along the way she had lost her flashlight as well as her revolver. She crouched down in the dark, trying not to be a target while she figured out what was happening.

"Maggie, you all right?" It was Eric on the goggles.

"I think so. You?"

"Okay. The warbot's down."

"Zsuzsanna?"

"I don't know." He sounded lost.

"Alex, Dmitri?" she called out.

"On," they echoed back.

"You two check the warbot. Make sure it's dead. Eric, you'll have to cover them. I've lost my weapon. I'll look for Zsuzsanna."

"Get on it," Eric said tersely.

Maggie stood warily. Her flashlight was a few meters away in a lonely puddle of light. She bounded over to it, searched briefly and unsuccessfully for her revolver, and then moved on to the tent Eric and Zsuzsanna had occupied.

It had been slashed open and one of the poles was broken, totally distorting its arch. Maggie pulled open the torn flap, working against the tension of the broken poles, and shone the beam inside. It was a tangle of clothes and sleeping bags clumped with snow. She pawed through the mess looking for Zsuzsanna. She wasn't there, but her airscarf was. Maggie grabbed it.

"Got a problem," she said over the comm link. "She doesn't have her airscarf."

How long since they had been woken by the fence? Maybe five minutes? Probably less. Time had a way of stretching out under the influence of adrenalin. Still a long time to go without good air.

Flashlight beams crisscrossed the ground around them. Maggie's heart was pounding. There was the taste of iron in her mouth. They were coming up empty-handed. She crouched down then leapt straight up. The trick bought her an extra two meters of height, enough for her flashlight to find its mark.

"Got her!" she called out. "Up against the fence." She indicated the direction with her beam.

Alex got there first. Eric and Maggie were close behind. Alex had already taken his airscarf off and wrapped it around Zsuzsanna's mouth and nose. He had his ear pressed against her chest. Maggie looped Zsu's airscarf over his face and snugged it down.

"Is she alive?" Eric asked.

"Got a heartbeat," Alex said. He picked up the limp body and ran for the main tent. Eric sprinted after him. Maggie paused for a moment, looking around. The stream burbled quietly in the darkness as if nothing had happened. What else was out there?

"Dmitri, are you armed?"

"Oh hell yeah."

"All right, keep watch. I'm going back to the tent."

"Where's the med kit?" Alex said over the comm link.

"I'll get it," Maggie said. She rounded up the med kit and an emergency oxygen tank from a pile of gear beside the truck. Back in the tent Zsuzsanna was cocooned in her sleeping bag. Her eyes flickered open when Maggie leaned over her.

"Hey Zsu, how you doing?"

"Still breathing," she said faintly.

"That's my girl."

"We need to flush her lungs," Alex said. "Get her loaded with oh-two."

"On it." Maggie got the ventilator out of the med kit and hooked it up to a splitter valve on the oxygen tank. Zsuzsanna cried out in pain when Alex lifted her head to replace the airscarf with the ventilator's mask. Maggie cracked the valve and started a flow of oxygen.

"What hurts?" Alex asked.

"My shoulder." Zsuzsanna's breath misted the transparent mask.

"Put your arms down by your side," Alex said. "Wait, let me help. This one?"

Zsuzsanna nodded. Her face was white.

"Probably dislocated," Alex said. He felt around the back of her shoulder. "Yeah, that's not right. Okay, here's what we're going to do. We're going to fold your hurt arm against your tummy, okay? And then slowly rotate your forearm out. That should pop the ball back into the socket. Ready?"

"No but go ahead."

Alex chuckled. "Right, here we go."

There was meaty pop as the joint slid back into place.

"Oh! That's better."

"What else?"

"My hip. The warbot threw me. I must have landed on it."

They shucked the sleeping bag down to check. Her pajama bottoms were caked with blood in a big patch on her left hip.

"We're going to have to get those bottoms off to work on that," Alex said.

"Okay," Zsuzsanna said faintly. "I'm not wearing underwear."

"Ah." Alex paused, looked up at Eric. "It's probably just a scrape. You want to take it from here, Eric?"

"Sure," Eric said. "I can deal with a scrape."

"Don't let her go to sleep, right? She's probably in shock. Make sure the mask stays on."

Eric nodded. "Got it. Thanks Alex."

Maggie hefted Eric's rifle. "Mind if I borrow this?"

"Take it."

Maggie and Alex zipped out to give them some privacy. Maggie walked down to where she'd been when the warbot opened fire on her. It was starting to get light outside. The sun would be up in an hour.

She found her revolver a few meters from the small crater left by the shot that had nearly killed her. A long bright scratch marred its barrel. That really pissed her off. Mekfucking warbot. She dumped the cylinder, checked the bore and the action, and reloaded. The interface came up clean when she thumbed open the gun's iris. She shut it down and holstered it, feeling whole once again.

She joined Alex and Dmitri by the carcass of the warbot. She poked its massive central eye with her finger. No response from the clamshell eyelids that should have protected it. The secondary eye turrets to either side of the big lens sagged down lifelessly. There was still a faint glow of waste heat from the laser mounted in its crest.

Her first shot had broken its collar bone. There was no sign of her second shot. One of Eric's rifle shots had gone through the power distributor in its abdomen, shorting it out, and exited through the pelvis, breaking it in half.

"Not a spider bear," Dmitri said.

"No," Maggie said. "It's a warbot. An early-war Hund, by the looks of it. Kriegsfabriks in Von Braun built thousands of them to counter mekan hives subverted by EON."

"Am I the only one that finds that odd, and arguably more disturbing than being stalked by a rando spider bear? I mean, how did it get this far out? Where does it spin up?"

"No, it's for sure odd and disturbing," Maggie said. "Spider bears are one thing, warbots quite another."

"What do you want to do with it?" Alex asked, indifferent to questions of origin. "I don't think it'll fit on back of the truck. I guess we could strap it onto the hood?"

Maggie thought about it. If the attack was not a coincidence, if Zsuzsanna's query about Lieutenant Gray had triggered the attack, then they were in a dangerous place. Somebody was paying attention. Somebody who did not want the fate of Lieutenant Gray and his anomalous spacecraft to be discovered. In which case it would be better to not roll into town with a busted warbot strapped to the hood of their truck.

On the other hand, she might be able to dig something out of its brain that would explain how it found them, and why it attacked.

"If you know the enemy and know yourself, you need not fear the result of a hundred battles," she murmured to herself.

"How's that?" Alex asked.

"The Art of War. TLDR: know your enemy. There's enough room in the back of the bipe for this thing if we curl it up. Lay it down in there with the other odds and ends and pile the camp gear on top of it. Careful with that big pentachoron, it's the only one that's intact. And this," she held up the odd, faceted helmet she had found in the capsule. "Let's wrap them both up in sleeping bags."

They broke camp before sunrise and were on the road at dawn. Eric and Zsuzsanna went ahead in the bipe. Maggie rode in the truck with the brothers. Everybody was tired, and even with the radvax onboard, the aftereffects of radiation exposure felt like a nuclear hangover. After a few listless kilometers she pulled Gray's brainstone out of her satchel and fired up its interface.

5

UCM Tereshkova

A warning bell rang halfway up the beanstalk. The elevator's passengers were weightless for a few moments as the car pivoted end-to-end. Then it began to decelerate, and everyone settled back into their seats.

The car was capped on both ends with diamondoid domes. Above his head, Meridian shrank to an emerald point. Gray felt a preliminary pang of loneliness. He already missed Elise.

Below his feet, Greenwich Station grew larger with every moment. The station's designers had spun a Mandelbrot set around its long axis and rendered the result in carbon fiber and aramid. The central body was shaped like an onion. Long root-like piers extended fore and aft along its orbital track. The torch itself was hidden from sight by the body of the station, but the paramirror that reflected its light back down to the city was ablaze with golden light.

The trailing pier accommodated a dozen different ships. Most were fission-powered miners clad in universal construction yellow. Blue Mars terraforming rigs stood out with their blue and silver livery. There was even a sleek black qigong-powered yacht, easily identified by the six spokes of its reactor, each sporting a dagger-like radiator fin.

The baseline beside him noticed his interest. He leaned in conspiratorially. "It's the Hivemaster's," he said. "The *Morrigan*. I don't know how she gets away with it. They're dangerous!"

"Qigongs, you mean?" Gray asked.

The man nodded. "Could blow us all up! She's trouble, that one. A real piece of work."

This got some stink eye from their fellow passengers, none of whom were baselines. The man sat back, displeased. Then a swarm of pchelans hove into view, verniers flickering like a cloud of fireflies as they maneuvered, and Gray forgot all about the yacht. At the center of the swarm was the tug Rashnikov had claimed. The pchelans were repairing the hole Gray and his men had put in its hull. Gray watched them go about their business with proprietary interest.

Helios had not been happy when Captain Rashnikov claimed the tug, but the Admiralty had advocated for him in Space Control's Parliament, and the athenes had granted it. For which they received a full quarter of the prize. Rashnikov got another full quarter. The third quarter was divided amongst the ship's officers and the fourth went to the crew.

It was a great system when it worked in your favor. On the other hand, every man had to buy his own gear, and the captain was responsible for outfitting the ship. Repairs, weapons, consumables – none of it cheap, and many a captain had gone too deep in the red and lost his post. A man had to make his own way.

His view was eclipsed by the curve of the station's hull. The warning bell rang again as they came to a halt. Weightlessness returned. The elevator's door opened inwards with a sigh. Warm moist air rushed in, bringing with it the odors of sweat and ozone.

Gray debarked with the other passengers. He bounced between mesh decks to a portal that let into the cavernous volume of the terminal. Warehouses, shops, and garages encrusted its inner surface.

He waved for an air taxi. An iridescent blue dragonfly darted through the crowd of Cereseans and alighted beside him with a blast of air. Gray took the saddle strapped to its neck. The holocaster glued to the back of its head projected a schematic of the station. He poked a finger at the forward pier. The taxi's wings blurred into motion.

Gray cleared the Space Force checkpoint to the forward pier without incident. The composition of the crowd on the other side of the checkpoint was markedly different. There were only a few Cereseans. Space Force black and grey uniforms dominated.

A column of mekans spiraled around the interior of the pier, defying any sense of up or down. They ranged in size from minor workers the size of a ship's cat to elephantine monsters hauling major machinery, but most were human-sized, suited to work in a human universe. All had six limbs. They bore a variety of provisions: pallets of food, kegs of hard cider, sealed cases of medical supplies.

The bigger ones had mandibles large enough to take off a man's head, but they were intrinsically harmless. All mekans large and small had a hardwired aversion to harming humans. That was how they came out of the drexlers, and that was how they would die. They would never be soldiers. Their only purpose was to serve the grey-hulled ships on the other side of the diamondoid portholes that dotted the airway.

The taxi braked to a stop at the end of the pier. Gray discharged his fare and dismounted. The watchman lounging beside the airlock snapped to attention. The cutlass hanging from his buckler was not ceremonial; projectile weapons were not allowed in habitats. The taboo was strict and universal. Even the smartest slug gun could punch holes in a hull. The nanosaws in a cutlass would stop the moment it touched hull material.

Gray returned the salute. "Permission to come aboard."

"Granted sir! Commander Abrams sends his regards and requests you join him on the bridge."

The bridge was a few levels aft of the airlock. The interior of the torchship looked like a submarine. There were no portholes, and every surface had piping or conduit runs bolted to it. Gated alcoves held repair gear. Emergency power cables were affixed in coils to the bulkheads.

Gray rounded a corner and came head-to-head with a mekan. When it saw Gray, the soft undifferentiated glow of its ledeyes sharpened into a pair of foveal rings that darted from Gray's hands to his face as if to measure his intention.

The mekan backed up clumsily. Gray pulled himself into a repair bay and waved it on. It passed close enough for him to feel the chill that radiated from its skin. It must have just come inside. Moisture condensed on its limbs, froze, and broke off in a trail of glittering ice particles. It smelled like a burnt carbon arc.

The hatch to the bridge was open. Gray ducked through to the sound of animated conversation. All *Tereshkova's* officers except her captain were gathered around the main holocaster. It was unusual for them all to be awake and together at the same time. Each led a different watch, five watches per hundred kilosecond ship-day.

Commander Abrams waved him over. He was still in his dress uniform from the social, as was Lynch. The rest were in the usual shipboard shorts and utility vest.

"Good of you to join us, Pilot."

Gray jumped across the room. He grabbed the railing that ringed the holocaster's hexagonal cluster of consoles and torqued himself into the same orientation as the other men.

"About time," Chief Sidorov said under his breath.

Second Lieutenant Sidorov served as *Tereshkova's* chief engineer. Sidorov was sleekly handsome, with dark glossy hair and prominent cheekbones. The only son of a wealthy ergocrat, he chafed at being subordinate to Gray, whose family had come to Mars to work the mines before that became a mekan's job. Niners, Sidorov called them.

"Some oner needs to get laid," Gray said. The riposte won a few chuckles from around the holocaster. He hooked his feet into the stirrups below his console and pulled himself into place. Back in the saddle again.

"The expo was truly a target-rich environment," Lynch said. "Pity you missed it, Sid."

Gray glanced at him, and Lynch met his gaze steadily and without rancor. All forgiven, then.

He held his hands above the console's neural inductors. Light danced beneath his fingertips as the console authenticated him. He was part of the torchship's nervous system now, a complex network of men and mechanisms woven together by fiber optics and light. No artiform intelligence here, in the conventional embodied sense. But *Tereshkova* was more than the sum of her parts. Gray had a sense of being part of something larger than himself. All the men felt it. It was in some ways the most important part of what bound them together into a crew, more than their loyalty to the United Colonies or their politics or economic interests. Gray relaxed into the flow, coming up to speed.

Captain Rashnikov emerged from his cabin, and the men around the holocaster went silent.

"At ease," Rashnikov said. He crossed the bridge to his command station. He was almost a century old and moved with the mechanical precision of someone whose musculoskeletal system was largely artificial. The dull black casing of a moravec converter showed through his stiff white hair like the crest of a lizard.

The process of converting a living brain to silicon was slow and expensive, but ergocrats like Rashnikov did not die for want of time or spin. Gray knew junior officers who looked forward to war with EON, just to clear out the gerontocracy that encrusted the upper ranks.

War or not, most lizards died violently. Rashnikov rarely ventured off *Tereshkova* when they were at Ceres. It was too dangerous; he had taken part in the Annexation as executive officer of UCM *Titov* a half century prior. *Titov* had destroyed Meridian's orbital mirrors when the city refused to surrender, plunging it into darkness. By the time the mirrors were replaced with a fusion torch, they'd lost a third of their population to famine. The Cereseans had not forgotten their losses nor forgiven those responsible.

Rashnikov swung into position behind his console, which overlooked the rest of the bridge like a lectern. "Gentlemen. We have a situation on 55 Pandora. The last freighter to visit the asteroid never showed up at its next stop, and the station itself is not responding to our signals."

"Pirates?" Abrams asked.

"Let's hope so," Rashnikov replied, which elicited laughter from the other officers. Everyone was still riding the buzz of getting the tug as a prize. "Otherwise, the obvious suspect is EON. The hive on Pandora drexlers ignition lasers. It would be a high-value target."

No one was laughing now. Rashnikov continued after letting the implications sink in. "Space Control's orders are to proceed to 55 Pandora as quickly as possible. There we will assess the situation, render aid as necessary, and deal with any hostiles that may be in the vicinity."

"Very good, sir," Abrams said. "Pilot, plot a trajectory to 55 Pandora at one Martian gee, and don't assume we can refuel at the other end. There's no telling what we'll find there."

"Aye sir." Gray exported the results to the main holocaster along with estimated fuel consumption.

Abrams consulted the plot. "Bits, notify Space Control we need propellant stat, and request clearance for reactor activation."

They had shut down the reactor as a courtesy to the station shortly before they had arrived. The shadow shield that protected the torchship's crew didn't do much for the sprawling expanse of the station.

"On it sir," Ensign Boiko said.

"Chief, bring up the reactor as soon as we've got clearance from Control. Pilot, see to the refueling."

Gray racquetballed down the drop tube from the bridge, stopping briefly in his quarters to exchange his dress blacks for a skinsuit. He shrugged back into his utility vest and continued aft to the locker room, where Polanski was waiting for him. Polanski was a round cheerful fellow with sparkling brown eyes. He had been in the Space Force for most of his life. His watch had ended ten kilosecs ago; he should have been getting dinner and some rack time.

"I've prepped your shell for you, sir," Polanski said. "Teague is already out there."

"You're a lifesaver, Polanski," Gray said. "I was thinking I'd have to do this in my skinsuit."

"No sir, that would not do," Polanski said. "If Abrams saw you out there without a shell, he'd bust you down to second watch. Then I'd have to move up, and I like it fine just where I am. Suit and shell, they're like belt and suspenders."

Gray walked around the shell on a brief inspection. The upper half looked like a deformed egg. There were no windows. A pair of engine bells jutted out beneath bulbous shoulder blades.

The bottom half would have been right at home on a medieval knight, except for the prehensile clockwork toes. He could not tell where he had been hit even when he rubbed his hand over the back of the shell.

"The repair work is first rate, sir," Polanski said. "And the new hundred mil laser is a beast. Aperture is your best friend."

"Yes it is," Gray agreed. "Nothing like being able to reach out and touch somebody."

Gray pulled his facemask down, flipped his skinsuit's hood up over his head. The hood sealed itself around the flange of the facemask of its own accord.

Polanski helped him into the bottom half of his shell. Then he lowered the top half, giving Gray time to work his hands into the controls hidden inside the shell's armored sleeves. Gray felt an unexpected sense of dread as the shell sealed at the waist with a solid click. It was like being sealed in a coffin. He flashed back to when he had been shot. The sharp rap of the incendiary round as it punched through the back of his shell. The sudden darkness as the kinos cut out. The rising tide of heat at his back. The panic of not being able to get out.

Gray forced himself to breathe evenly. The shell booted up. External cameras relayed a high-fidelity image of the room. He gave Polanski a thumbs-up. Ribbons of carbon nanotubes attached to the inside of the shell contracted, and the shell's gauntlet faithfully tracked his gesture. Everything was fine. He was not locked into a coffin.

He cycled through the airlock. The outer door opened onto starlight. The station was in Ceres' shadow. He switched over to maneuvering controls and jetted out. *Tereshkova* receded behind him.

From here the torchship looked like some kind armor-plated denizen of the deep nibbling at a coral reef made of glass and steel. A pair of laserscopes flanked the torchship's cylindrical pressure hull, giving her the menacing aspect of a hammerhead shark. A long spine led aft to the boxy vacuum hull, which housed the ship's auxiliary fission reactor and propulsion system – the hot stuff. That was mekan territory.

A pchelan zhuk hove into view. It was pushing a spherical drop tank twelve meters in diameter. The tank contained as much liquid hydrogen as the first moon rocket. The zhuk's arcjet flared as it began to decelerate.

Gray crossed in front of it and jetted down the length of the spine to where Teague and his triad of mekans were waiting. He braked to a halt where he had a view of the operation. The mekans scuttled around Teague like monstrous insects. Each had a number stenciled on its back, yellow paint on black carbon fiber, so they could be told apart by humans. Their ledeyes flickered as they conversed.

The zhuk's arcjet shut down. It hung motionless directly above the team. Iconji flickered across Teague's shell. The mekans fanned out in a ring around the drop tank. There was a spark of electricity as they equalized potential. Working together they slowly hauled the tank into place.

The zhuk released its grip on the tank and pushed off. With an actinic burst from its arcjet it headed back to the propellant depot for another. They would need sixteen in all. It was going to be a long watch.

There was a flurry of commands and acknowledgements as they disconnected from the pier. Gray switched through viewpoints as mekans sealed umbilicals and detached them. Counterparts on the other side hauled in the cables and hoses and stowed them. Down in the vacuum hull, another triad of mekans was getting the fusion engine ready.

Gray's men were all online too. Polanski was waiting by the aft airlock in a combat shell, ready to go astern to the vacuum hull if need be. Teague was manning the secondary pilot's console. Even Mendeleev and Allen, who normally would have been in their racks at this time of day, were at their duty stations.

"Permission to depart Greenwich Station," Gray requested.

"Poyekhali," Captain Rashnikov said. It was what the first man in space, Yuri Gagarin, had said just before he lifted off in his Vostok spacecraft.

The men on the bridge echoed the old saying, their voices like a benediction. "Poyekhali!"

Gray fired a short burst from *Tereshkova's* forward arcjets. They backed away from the pier. Another burst from the lateral verniers left them drifting to the side.

"Are we ready Chief?" Gray asked when they had cleared the station.

"All systems ready," Sidorov reported. "Fission reactor is hot. Kinos at omega max. Hydrogen lines pressurized."

"Initiating departure sequence," Gray said. Valves to the hydrogen tanks opened. A couple megavolts of potential energy became kinetic. White-hot plasma flared from the aft arcjets, lighting up the side of the pier. An invisible hand shoved Gray into his seat. The burn ended and he rebounded into his harness. The torchship fell away from the station.

"Course nominal," Gray said. "We'll come around the bottom of our orbit in about four kilosecs. Chief, are we on track for ignition?"

Sidorov didn't reply.

"Chief?"

"We have a problem with the dorsal radiator, sir," Sidorov said.

"Can you be more specific?" Gray asked.

"It won't start. I think one of its valves is wedged open. I've got a triad on site."

Gray exchanged glances with Abrams. "Export your console to the main 'caster, Chief."

"Aye sir." Sidorov was monitoring a couple mekans. One was part of the triad that had just crawled out onto the dorsal radiator's forward manifold. The other was on the opposite side of the vacuum hull at the ventral radiator. Gray puzzled over that until he realized Sidorov was using the working radiator as a model to double-check the one that wouldn't start. That indicated a certain lack of confidence.

Not that it was a simple system; the liquid droplet radiators worked by spraying a curtain of molten salt from a strip of nozzles on the forward manifold. Each nozzle had a ball valve that spun rapidly, breaking the stream up into myriad droplets. The droplets cooled rapidly as they traveled through vacuum to the aft manifold, where they were collected and recycled.

Tereshkova could get underway with a valve stuck shut; one nozzle represented a small percentage of the radiator's capacity. But with a valve stuck open, they would quickly dump their coolant into the big empty. And then they would be done.

One of the mekans out on the manifold – Fourteen according to its feed – circled around the mast-like structure to its aft side. The point of view swiveled dizzyingly as it checked the stuck ball valve. A crust of salt had crystallized inside the nozzle. Fourteen scraped at it with a rasp-like digit. Every few seconds it tapped the side of the nozzle to see if the valve could be dislodged. On the fourth try, the ball rotated back into position.

"That did it sir!" Sidorov reported.

"You should cycle them before we get underway," Gray said. "Just in case."

"Aye sir." Sidorov turned back to his console and keyed a sequence.

"Not now!" Gray exclaimed, but it was too late. Sidorov had already sent a pulse of molten salt through the manifold.

Gray found Fourteen's feed. The viewpoint was tumbling wildly. The mekan had been knocked off the manifold. Gray swore under his breath.

"Polanski," he said, "are you monitoring the situation on the dorsal radiator?"

"Yes sir. You want me to go after that mekan?"

Gray checked the mission clock. They were supposed to fire up the engine at periapsis, which was just under a kilosec away. "Only if you can get there and back in eight hectos."

"Piece of cake. On my way."

"Belay that," Commander Abrams said.

"Hold position, Polanski," Gray said.

"Holding in the lock," Polanski said.

In the holocaster, *Tereshkova* swung through Fourteen's field of view again, smaller now. The gaping maw of the fusion torch's parabolic reflector was plainly visible.

Gray turned to Commander Abrams. "Sir, if we don't retrieve that mekan, we're going to fry it when we light the torch."

Abrams nodded. "True enough. But considering the damage it has already incurred, I am not willing to risk a man's life for it, much less this mission. It's in orbit; it'll swing back by Greenwich Station in due course. Maintenance will pick up whatever's left."

"Yes sir." Gray took a deep breath. He wanted to strangle Sidorov. He locked his gaze straight ahead and kept his voice neutral. "Come back in, Polanski."

"Aye sir."

Gray checked Fourteen's health indicators. One arm was gone entirely, and the other had been melted off at the elbow. Its thorax was burned through in several places by the molten salt.

Mekans could repair each other to some degree with their extruders. But that kind of damage required a trip through a drexler to fix. Unless the damaged mekan possessed unique knowledge that warranted its preservation, odds were good its hive would choose to recycle it instead.

Gray switched through the feeds of the other two mekans in Fourteen's triad. Fifteen had gone inside, but Thirteen lingered at the base of the manifold. It watched Fourteen dwindle to a speck and disappear.

What was it thinking? Did it care? Gray could not help but think that in some way, it did. He turned Thirteen's feed off. The holocaster returned to a default tactical plot.

"That was entirely unnecessary," Abrams said.

"Yes sir," Gray agreed. The statement was met with silence. Abrams had fixed him with a baleful glare. Gray realized he had made a mistake. He straightened up.

"Sorry sir," he said. "My statement that the radiator should be cycled was not clear. I take full responsibility for the loss of Fourteen."

"As you should, mister," Abrams said scathingly. He rounded on Sidorov. "Although a cadet could have figured out what you meant."

"It was only a mekan sir," Sidorov said sullenly.

"Are you volunteering to take Fourteen's place in the vacuum hull, Mr. Sidorov? With the torch running? No? I didn't think so. There are more mekans on a torchship than humans for a reason: they do the real work. Try to remember that next time, mister."

"Aye sir."

Abrams rubbed his temples. "I can't believe we're having this conversation. Mr. Sidorov, are we ready for primary engine ignition?"

"Aye sir. All systems are functioning normally."

"Good. Mr. Gray?"

"Ready sir. Periapsis in six hectosecs."

Abrams turned to Captain Rashnikov. "Ready for ignition sir. Apologies for the delay. It won't happen again."

"See that it doesn't, Commander."

"Aye sir." Abrams glanced coldly from Gray to Sidorov and shook his head.

The bridge was silent as they waited for the torchship to reach periapsis. When the bulk of the dwarf planet fully shielded Meridian and Greenwich Station, Rashnikov gave the order.

A plasma machine gun in the heart of *Tereshkova's* vacuum hull ripped into life. A beaded stream of helium-3, deuterium, and hydrogen propellant shot through the throat of the torch's reflector. An encircling crown of high-powered lasers caught each pulse of helium-3 and deuterium in a vise of light, crushing it down until atoms merged. The engine flared into life like a giant strobe light, flickering with the light of the sun twenty times per second.

Once again the invisible hand of acceleration pushed Gray down into his seat, but this time it did not let up. Chaika groaned and creaked as she accommodated the compressive loading. They climbed out of Ceres' gravity well at a Martian gee.

Gray handed his console over to his relief and retreated to the bottom of the pressure hull, as far away from the rest of the crew as he could get without going outside. On a torchship, privacy was the scarcest commodity. The only people who had their own cabins were the captain and the XO. Gray and the other officers all shared the same bunk room. At least they had their own racks; the rest of the crew had to hot-sheet theirs, two men per rack.

Deck one was a dank, dark place, but no one else was there. Odds and ends that had not been properly secured for acceleration found their way down ladders and stairways. And water; any kind of leak or condensation went aft.

Gray found a dry spot and sat down with his back against the cold hard casing of a recirculation pump. He kept going through the sequence of events, trying to make it right. But it was not right. And at the end there was just the feed from Thirteen, watching its shipmate dwindle to a speck and disappear. Watching as if it cared.

He thought back to one of his first conversations with Elise. He had asked if she thought mekans felt emotions.

"All lifeforms do," she had said. "Biologicals, synlife, artiforms. Did you know that the turning point in the development of artificial intelligence was the realization that you can't have mind without body? All intelligence is embodied. And the intersection between mind and body is emotion. Pleasure and pain, attraction and fear, love and hate – they're actually intrinsic to intelligence, not its antithesis."

He swore to himself. "I guess there's nothing else for it."

He summoned Thirteen.

The mekan seemed larger in the cramped confines of deck one. Its head was on a level with Gray's. Its ledeyes flickered like a monitor that had lost sync, then settled into a stable pattern, a yellow triangle with a black question mark within.

Gray read iconji fairly well, but being a visual language, he could not speak it. For that he and the rest of the crew relied on the ledeyes built into their spex and facemasks.

"I am Lieutenant Gray," he said. His name came across the lenses of the spex as a color, or more precisely, a lack of color. "I want to apologize for the loss of Fourteen."

A long pause during which the mekan's ledeyes glowed blankly. Then the glow coalesced into a stream of symbols. *Thank you, sir. That is considerate of you.* Gray's spex rendered the symbols as a feminine voice, strangely intimate, as if she were speaking inside his head.

"Did you..." It was Gray's turn to pause. What was the correct pronoun? Like their biological prototypes, almost all mekans were female. Whatever that meant to an artiform. "Did you know her well?"

We were hatchmates.

"I'm sorry," Gray said. "I tried to prevent it, but I was not quick enough."

Thirteen mulled this over. *It was a mistake by Lieutenant Sidorov.*

"Yes," Gray said, surprised she would know that.

You are not responsible.

Gray shook his head. "I knew he was going to make a mistake, but I did not stop him in time."

You are not responsible, Thirteen repeated. *You are the ship's pilot.*

"Yes, but..." Gray trailed off. It was absurd. He was trying to explain his feelings to a mekan. He was on the verge of dismissing Thirteen when Elise's words came back to him: the intersection of mind and body is emotion. If she was right, then explaining his feelings was exactly what he needed to do. Absurd but necessary.

"But I feel responsible," he said.

Thirteen's ledeyes returned to an undifferentiated glow. Finally she signaled again. *I also feel responsible. I should have performed the task. But I allowed* – there was the black-and-white flash of an optical code in her ledeyes – *to do it, so she could gain experience.*

They pondered their collective guilt in uncomfortable silence. Gray changed the subject. "What was that symbol?"

The black and white triangular pattern reappeared. Fourteen's tricode. *It is a unique identifier woven into our carbon fiber exoskeleton. I am told quads cannot see it unassisted.*

"Definitely true," Gray said, repressing annoyance at being called a quad. He blinked at the tricode and his spex translated it into a long string of letters and numbers. "That's how you identify each other? By a string of numbers?"

No. We do not read tricode like you read iconji; we see it. Quads recognize each other's faces, yes? We all look alike, aside from whatever injuries we bear or marks you put on us. Members of a caste are identical copies. But we can see the tricode woven into our skins.

"Is there a short form, like a human name? A checksum?"

You mean like our ship number? The iconji in her ledeyes was trailed by a stick figure of someone bowing over folded hands, nominally used to indicate respect, but often used by humans as a form of sarcasm. Did mekans use sarcasm?

"Point taken," Gray said.

Thirteen made a low grinding noise. Gray realized she was rubbing one of her legs against her flank like an oversized cricket. Laughter?

She held up her right hand. It had four digits, jet black, bone-thin, and fringed with fur-like cilia. The center two were tipped with wicked looking claws, and both outer digits were opposable. Two thumbs.

She waited. Gray warily held out his own hand, pressed it against hers. Cilia thrummed against his fingers.

That is what I am called by my hatchmates. There was no utility in giving us speech, or scent, as we live in vacuum. But you could not deny us touch.

"Again," Gray said, brow furrowed. Cilia thrummed against his hand like a hundred living drums, a brief syncopation that ended when her thumbs closed around his hand, squeezing it with surprising gentleness. It was the first time he had ever been touched by a mekan.

6

Deimos

Arcjets flared like fireflies in the night as the swarm braked into orbit around Deimos. The pchelan zhuks circled once, letting wing-like radiators bleed off heat from the burn. The surface below them was heavily pitted with mining tunnels. Mounds of tailings had been cemented into jagged soaring fins.

From atop the fins, sentinels tracked the swarm's progress across the starfield. Oversized ledeyes flashing excitedly as they sent news of the swarm's return down to their hatchmates.

First one and then another worker emerged from the tunnels that led down into the hive. They lifted their carbon black heads to the sky, antenna swiveling as if to touch their kin in orbit.

The swarm's arcjets flared again, a sudden incandescent constellation above the horizon. The pchelans dropped from orbit in graceful ellipses, alighting near the entrance to the hive with a final flicker from their verniers. Swollen bladders full of liquid ammonia nearly enveloped the creatures. Stick-like legs scrabbled for purchase in the dusty regolith.

A scuttling mass of workers emerged from the mouth of the hive. The flood engulfed the returning pchelans like a chitinous tide. Sleek and quick-footed, the workers climbed over one another to reach out and grapple a pchelan who had lost her purchase and rebounded from the surface to hang above them.

They hauled the pchelan back down into the jostling crowd and climbed up her legs. Their antenna folded back against their heads as they wedged themselves beneath the bladders on her thighs. Beak-like mandibles seized on outlet nozzles. Hollow tongues pressed eagerly, found the valve within, and pushed it open.

Liquid ammonia squirted into their mouths. Mandibles drew down on the sides of the nozzles so smooth black tongues could form a seal. Ammonia surged deep into their bodies. Their backs arched with pleasure as their abdomens filled.

The workers shuddered and they seemed to struggle with the nozzles, pushing away with their arms, but still locked in place by their mandibles. Then the wave of pleasure passed, and their mandibles relaxed. Their tongues slipped out of the nozzles with a puff. The icy spray condensed on their faces in a thin glaze of ammonia ice.

Sated, they allowed themselves to be pushed aside by their hatchmates. They stumbled across their myriad backs towards the hive, white-masked faces bobbing in a black and heaving sea.

7

Tsiolkovsky

The way back to Tsiolkovsky was marked by upended stones and small cairns topped by lopsided caps of snow. These rough gnomons ticked off their passage through the empty no man's land like the minute hand of a vast indifferent clock. The stones were far enough apart that finding one brought a sense of relief, quickly lost in the rearview mirror while they waited with mounting anxiety for the next to appear ahead.

Every hour or so they passed an abandoned vehicle. The derelicts had been thoroughly picked over. Maggie wondered what had happened to the passengers. Did they get out and walk, or stay put and hope for rescue? Had they reached safety before they froze to death? What determined who lived and who died?

The broken shells had no answers. There were no bodies, just rusted metal and empty windows.

Then there were the river crossings. Treacherous with ice at first, less so the farther downstream they traveled, but then more flow as water poured into the Marineris from side canyons. Crossings were poorly marked. Come winter, river ice scraped out the cairns. And out on the broad floor of the canyon, the river meandered over time, so what had been a good crossing one summer might be a bad one the next, or just a dry bed of rough cobbles if a big icefall had shifted the river entirely.

Now the beaten track that served as a roadway branched into multiple threads as they approached the final crossing. It had been simple going the other way; the main track was obvious right up to the riverbank, and wherever they had come out, had converged back onto the main path in due course. And nothing looked the same coming back.

Alex followed an increasingly bumpy and ill-defined path down to the river. There he stopped.

"Here?" Dmitri asked.

"Here," Alex said. "Going to need you to…"

But Dmitri was already getting out of the truck. He grabbed a pole from behind the cab and unspooled some line from the winch on the front bumper. Then he stepped crabwise into the current. The water came up to his knees.

He probed the bottom with the pole as he made his way across. Alex put the truck into gear and followed slowly behind, lurching heavily with every invisible pothole. Maggie held onto the Jesus grip above the door and kept her mouth shut. But Alex had chosen well. They did not roll over. Dmitri did not get swept off his feet. It was a proper Ded Moroz moment. They waited for him on the bank while he dumped water out of his boots and wrang out his socks. He got in barefoot and shivering.

After the crossing came a long stretch of open country, hard packed dirt and black basalt. Here Alex coaxed the truck up to speed until it pulled a swirling tail of dust and Maggie had to tell him to slow down, lest their progress be marked by anyone who might be watching from orbit.

They reached the relative safety of the paved road system late that afternoon. The town of Barinoff was a weather-beaten collection of sandblasted Quonset huts, radiation-fogged greenhouses, and a lonely guard shack. A pair of flags fluttered on a pole. Above, the standard of the United Colonies, seven golden stars in the shape of the Pleaides on a royal blue background. Below, a red flag with a yellow crescent like a bow pierced by the yellow arrow of a rising torchship.

Alex eased the truck up over the jagged edge of the road onto smooth marscrete. The sudden absence of vibration was like a plugged ear unexpectedly cleared. There was a shared sigh of relief.

The soldier at the shack waved them to a stop. Alex grabbed a flask from his door panel and hopped out. There was a brief conversation, their breath frosting the air. Alex tipped the flask back, held it out to the guard, who took a polite sip and offered it back. Alex gestured for him to keep it. The guard took a long pull, slipped the flask into his coat pocket, and slapped Alex on the shoulder.

He got back into the truck. The guard waved them on.

"What did he want?" Dmitri asked.

"Company, mostly." Alex eased the truck into gear, watched the guard post recede in the rearview mirror. "He asked if we had seen anything."

"What did you say?"

"Nothing but mekanos and junk."

"Close enough."

The highway followed on the north side of the river where there was more room between its banks and the canyon walls. They wove around periodic rock falls where the freeze-thaw cycle had broken loose jagged rocks from above and left them scattered on the marscrete.

Outside Maggie's window, the river broadened and deepened as they traveled down the canyon. The water was opaque with sediment. Turbid roils the color of strawberry milk marked the location of boulders under the surface. Once they reached Tsiolkovsky, the river was easily fifty meters across and the heaving crests of the upper reaches had smoothed into long, powerful standing waves.

The city was built on the western shoulder of a long ridge that split the canyon. The river divided and flowed around it, providing a natural barrier that made walls unnecessary. They crossed the bridge over the northern channel just before sunset. The sun lingered on the upper reaches of the hillside, reflecting off a thousand windows in a golden blaze of light. High above them was a massive statue of Konstantin Tsiolkovsky. His outstretched arm held a stylized torchship up to the darkening sky. Its exhaust lanced across his chest, rivaling the setting sun.

"Home sweet home," Dmitri said.

Alex lifted his gaze briefly from the unwinding road and grunted. "Looks pretty from here."

"Think your boss would be interested in the reactor?" Maggie asked. The brothers had part-time jobs in a heavy equipment repair yard on the south side of town.

Alex shrugged. "Kowalski? Maybe."

"I thought I heard him complaining about somebody walking away from an old fission-powered heavy lift rocket, last time he was at the bar. *Buzzard* or something like that."

"*Condor*," Dmitri corrected her. "Customer couldn't afford to refuel it. Tricky operation that."

"Turn's coming up," Alex said. "What do you want to do?"

"Take it," Maggie said. "The reactor is too hot for the bomb shelter, and we can't leave it out on the street and expect it to be there in the morning. If Kowalski takes it off our hands, it's one and done."

They left the highway for a side road. It led south to a web of land between two knuckles of the ridge. This was the old town of Tsiolkovsky. Pressure domes dotted the gentle slope like mushrooms. When the site had first been colonized, the atmosphere was so thin that domes were the only kind of structure that could withstand the pressure differential.

After the Ring was finished, the domes had given way first to half-cylinder Quonsets and then to modern rammed-earth construction. Many of the old domes had been converted from family dwellings to commercial use, taverns with lurid signs, gun shops, even a lonely church with an offset spire over the arch of its airlock.

They pulled into a fenced yard with a large Quonset hut. The steady orange glow of nuclear embers shone from a window set high in a corrugated metal wall. Above it, an arch of colored lights made ragged by the weight of icicles marked the roofline. Alex parked fifty meters back, headlights splashed over the front of the building, to minimize their radiation footprint.

"Looks like he's still here," Maggie said.

"He's always here," Dmitri said in a way that was not a compliment.

They got out and stretched. The chill night air felt good after the closeness of the cab. Alex banged on the Quonset's door.

Kowalski came out. He was a big man with a big belly and a big mouth. Tonight he was wearing a plush blue hat with a silver faux-fur band, which was ironic because while he had never outright cheated Maggie, neither had he ever failed to extract his due. Hardly the figure of Grandfather Frost. The outfit was completed by a worn house coat open at the front, a food-stained white shirt, a pair of baggy shorts, and puffy insulated slippers. Summertime in Tsiolkovsky.

"Ded Moroz!" he said cheerfully. "So, the kids are back from the bush. What did you find this time, Margaritifer? Tell me it's a micro qigong."

"Nuclear thermal rocket engine," Maggie said.

"A rocket engine? What am I going to do with that? Put something into orbit just to have the League of Worlds shoot it down?"

"Gotta be a hundred kilograms of enriched uranium in its reactor," Alex said.

"Enough to refuel *Condor* and put it on the market," Dmitri said.

"Not a lot of demand for heavy lift rockets these days," Kowalski said.

"We've had to pass on some salvage jobs because they were too far out for a truck," Alex reminded him. "*Condor* would have come in handy."

"You want to get shot down, Mr. Aleksey Ivanovich? Be my guest."

"Other operators use them," Maggie said. "Just keep it low. Warsingers don't care if you're suborbital. You could expand your operations all the way upriver to Thunderbird and down to Von Braun."

"Easy for you to say, Miss Margaritifer who rides a bicycle around town."

"Cheap shot."

"My favorite kind."

Maggie shrugged indifferently. "Well, it's off to the City Guard then, guys. See you around Kowalski."

"Don't be hasty," Kowalski said. "The City Guard hasn't flown in mears. Not since their last ship got shot down. Let me see this nuclear thermal rocket."

Maggie nodded and the boys loosened the lines that held the tarp down. Kowalski peered underneath, whistling tunelessly through the gap in his front teeth.

"All right. I will give you twenty thousand gigajoules for this piece of junk."

"Come on Kowalski," Maggie said. "The uranium itself is worth fifty thousand gigs."

"It is very old," Kowalski countered. "Who knows how much the fuel has decayed."

"Forty-five kay, and it's a deal."

"Forty-five kay is robbery," Kowalski said. "I'll go up to thirty, because you are a friend."

"You don't have any friends because you are so wardamn cheap. Forty kay."

"Thirty-five, no more."

"Forty and free drinks at the bar for the next half a mear."

Kowalski paused. "How many drinks?"

"One per sol," Maggie said.

"Make it two. I'm a big guy. And I have my friends to consider."

"Two if you buy food."

He started to argue. She cut him off. "Otherwise I can't cover it. I know your taste in booze, my friend."

He looked for a moment like he might turn her down. Then he bared a row of big yellow teeth in a poor semblance of a smile and stuck out his hand. "Deal!"

Dmitri and Alex dropped Maggie off at the Rusty Robot. The tavern was in a classic dome with an elongated entry, like an igloo. Standing atop the airlock tunnel was a stylized robot made of welded sheet metal, one hand on its hip, the other holding a beer stein high.

"Buy you a drink," Maggie said, gathering her stuff from where it had migrated through the cab of the truck.

"We have to get up in the morning," Alex said. His eyes were red with fatigue. "Kowalski pinged me on the way here. He wants us to move *Condor* over to the work gantry."

Maggie laughed shortly. "That mekfucker. So much for not being interested."

"A drink wouldn't hurt," Dmitri said. "Get Maggie in safe. Boom done."

"You don't have to worry about me," Maggie said, patting her revolver. "You two best get home and get some rest. Thanks for the ride."

Zach was working the bar. He gave her a long-suffering look. There was a single customer inside. She clapped the old-timer's shoulder gently. "Hey Gherman. Ded Moroz."

He looked up with washed-out blue eyes. Gherman was a Warsing veteran, the only one Maggie had ever met. He was over two centuries old, and it showed in myriad ways: the weirdly pebbled texture of his skin, his coarse almost transparent hair, the gritty way he moved as if the sands of time had crept into his joints. But Tsiolkovsky loved its veterans, and Gherman would live as long as he chose to endure the nanite refreshes.

"Maggie May. Ded Moroz! How are you tonight, my dear?"

"Happy to see you as always, Gherman."

"You look the very vision of the Snow Maiden herself. Lovely. Sit down, have a drink."

"I'd love to old friend, but truth is my ass hurts from sitting and I'm desperate for a hot shower."

"Ah, a long ride," he said.

"A long ride," she agreed. "I'll tell you about it next time."

He raised his glass in a toast and tipped it back. "Enough said, my dear. I'm on my way."

Maggie locked the door behind him and turned off the sign. "Do you want me to close for you, Zach?"

"I'm almost done, thanks," Zach said. He turned Gherman's glass under a hissing jet of hot water. "I don't know how you put up with that guy."

"Gherman's all right. We have common interests."

"He's interested in your ass, is what he's interested in." He scoffed. "Snow Maiden."

"He's old enough to be my too-many-greats-to-count-grandfather," Maggie protested.

"As if that makes a difference," Zach said.

Maggie laughed. "There's that! I'm heading upstairs. Good night, Zach."

"Night Maggie."

She climbed the rickety stairs to the apartment nestled into the top of the dome. The apartment was one of the perks of having a stake in the Rusty Robot, the other being significant spin laundering opportunities for her finds. No spin trail, no cops sniffing around.

She stopped at the upper landing. She had taped the door before she left, ostensibly to keep the dust out, but with an equal measure of paranoia. Justified, apparently, as someone had cut the tape right down the middle, where the door met the jam.

She eased her revolver out of its holster and thumbed its iris open. The aiming reticle danced across her goggles, framed by a circle of eight green dots. She opened the door with her left hand. The apartment's small living room was dark except for the orange glow of an ember she had left open as a night light.

Something seemed out of place. Her eyes narrowed, trying to parse the hole in the darkness. Someone was sitting at her desk. She pulled up on them, finger bearing down on the trigger. Her free hand found the light switch.

The reticle was centered on a pile of gear someone had left on her desk, topped by the helmet from the capsule. She let out her breath and holstered the weapon. In her peripheral vision, something bounded up at her. She let out an involuntary shriek and jumped so hard she banged her head on the ceiling.

She and her domestic robot landed at about the same time. "Wardamn it, Ajax! You scared me."

The knee-high robot turned back and forth, differential drive whirring. It was a simple two wheeled pogo. Her father had helped her build it when she was a little girl. She had found it in the wreckage of their home, the one time she returned after the mantids ransacked it.

She'd kept the pogo running ever since, despite its marginal usefulness. The only thing it was good for was keeping watch over her apartment. And not very good at that, evidently.

She hunkered down in front of the robot. It had binocular vision, each camera in its own articulated mount to enable foveal tracking. Now it kept looking from her eyes to the apartment's kitchen.

"Did I leave your dock off again?" she asked.

The little robot bobbed back and forth on its wheels.

"Sorry about that, buddy."

It spun around and trundled back into the kitchen nook. There it hopped up onto the dock. Its head spun to look at her again, just to make sure she was getting the message.

"All right, hang on." Maggie doffed her coat and airscarf and checked the pile on her desk. It was the gear she'd left in the bipe: her sleeping bag, a duffle bag of extra clothes, and her tool kit. There was a note from Eric on top. She opened it with a blink.

"Thought you might need these. Hope Kowalski wasn't an asshole. Let's talk tomorrow." The note closed itself.

"Right. Talk about Zsuzsanna, no doubt." Eric had been doing a lot of that lately. But it was nice of him to drop her things off.

Ajax came back out to see what she was doing.

"Was Eric here?" she asked.

The pogo bobbed back and forth.

Maggie put her hands on her hips. "You should have said something."

It tilted forward, eyes downcast.

"Next time send me a picture, okay?"

Ajax bobbed again but didn't look up. Sensitive soul. If you could ascribe a soul to a giganode neural network. One percent of human; was it enough?

"Come on, let's spin you up." She led the pogo into the kitchen. From what she'd seen on marsnet, she figured it was almost as intelligent as an old Earth dog. Having never seen much less interacted with an actual living dog, her assessment was purely speculative.

She got Ajax set up and fixed herself a simple meal. There wasn't much left in the refrigerator, just some eggs, goat cheese, and a little beer. She made herself an omelet with a side of grechka, and washed it down with the beer, which had gone flat while they were in the bush.

Then she took a long, luxurious shower. It was good to get the road grit off. Afterwards she examined herself critically in the steam-clouded mirror. She was not as pretty as Zsuzsanna. Her breasts were smaller, and her ass was bigger. She was too tall, and her hair was too short. About the only thing she had on Zsuzsanna in the looks department was her stomach, which was hard and flat. Zsu ran a little on the soft side. Which Eric liked, evidently.

Not that it mattered. She was not gunning for Eric. She had endured her share of boyfriends and largely given up on the idea. She might have made an exception for Eric, but now he was with Zsu. And anyway she and Eric had been friends way too long. She did not want to risk that. And Dmitri – poor Dmitri! – seemed like the little brother she had never had.

No, she was done with boys for the foreseeable future. Which left girls, and while she liked girls well enough, she was not interested in having a girlfriend. The last time had been way too much drama. She shook her head and smiled at the thought that her choices boiled down to stupidity or drama. It made Ajax seem like good company.

She wiped a spot clear in the mirror to check her face. She had a bit of road rash on her forehead and cheeks, where her goggles hadn't shielded her from the debris kicked up by the warbot's near miss. It was a comical effect, like raccoon eyes in reverse. She picked out flecks of shattered rock with a pair of sharp tweezers and smoothed on a nanite cream to eat the smaller particles. With any luck the damage would be invisible by morning.

Back in the living room, she moved the pile of gear from her desk to the floor and put on her office. The oversized cat-eye spex painted a Victorian desk laden with newspapers, mail, and an oval communications window in an elaborate frame of brass and rosewood.

Most of the mail was petitions. Some were no-brainers, like funding enforcement of the capital crimes code. But that had already garnered enough spin to be viable for another mear and did not need any of her hard-earned joules, regardless of its advocates' push for a two mear renewal. Others, like a petition to ban portraying Jesus as a baby alien, were simply ridiculous. What else could he have been? Unfortunately, there was no way to allocate your joules against something; there was no such thing as negative energy in Tsiolkovsky politics. The best you could do was argue against a petition and hope it did not receive enough spin to be enforceable.

Or you could invest your spin in a professional ergocrat like Eric's father. She sorted the ergocrats by number of followers and scrolled down until she spotted Berel Hoffman's distinctive beak of a nose. With more than eight thousand followers, he was squarely in the middle of the board. If she sorted on spin available for advocacy, he was significantly closer to the bottom. The top was dominated by descendants of wealthy Exodus families, mostly men, mostly white, mostly Eastern European. Oners who could use their wealth to advance the causes they advocated.

She did not see eye-to-eye with Berel on everything – they were at opposite ends of the spectrum on the issue of Warsing tech – but she respected his integrity, and he respected her technical skills. And it was not like she had time to track every little issue! Somebody had to keep the air on, and it might as well be someone she knew. She allocated her monthly tithe of a hundred gigajoules to him and watched with satisfaction as his ranking bobbed upwards, if only for a moment.

Civic duties done, she extracted Gray's brainstone and a crystalline shard from her satchel and put them on the desk side by side. There was a mystery. Zsuzsanna had not been able to find anything about Lieutenant John Gray in the Warsing Wiki. However, Maggie had every reason to think that Gray had in fact existed. The brainstone wasn't a fake.

Given the Wiki's reputation for obsessive accuracy and completeness, the fact that Gray did not make an appearance in it was implausible. There were a finite number of possible explanations:

1.Zsuzsanna was wrong. Simplest and hence most likely.

2.References to Gray had been edited out of the wiki. By whom and why?

3.The search engine itself was compromised. Which correlated nicely with their early morning wakeup call by the warbot. If Maggie wasn't just being paranoid, if it wasn't a coincidence, then somebody who didn't want them to know about Gray had gotten an alert when Zsu fired her search into the wiki.

4.Some combination of the above.

After some consideration, Maggie opened her zombie browser. Several dozen computers scattered across Mars were under her control. She sorted the list by most recent access.

The top of the list shifted to low-risk private owners, clueless senior citizens for the most part. They probably never noticed their systems were compromised and were incapable of retaliation if they did. The bottom verged into dangerous territory: criminals who had no qualms whatsoever about retribution. It was woven into their business model. They took tribute from the weak, the shop owners who happened to do business in their territory, the drug addicts and their pushers, the whores and their johns, and exacted retribution upon those who opposed them. Miss a payment? Lose a finger. Talk to the cops? Lose your hand.

Maggie counted herself lucky that she only had to make one regular payoff. That kept the bomb shelter they used as a workshop and storage area off the cop's radar. No, the bottom of her list was not the kind of place you visited unless you had a very specific reason. She picked an entry at random from near the top of the list and initiated a connection.

Once she had a virtual desktop, she opened the Warsing Wiki. She scrolled through the introduction and stopped at the table of contents. Chronology. Background. Prewar events. Course of the war. Aftermath.

Step one: replicate the problem. Maggie queried on "Lieutenant John Gray." Nothing. Then "John Gray," which came up with a man who ran municipal reactors before the war, enlisted in the Mars Guard after hostilities broke out, and had died of radiation poisoning when his ship's reactor was breached. Finally she tried "Gray" which returned hundreds of references, most of which had nothing to do with human beings.

So Zsuzsanna was right.

The next most likely possibility was that the wiki had been edited. If that were the case, Maggie should be able to find holes where Lieutenant Gray had been. She might not be able to find him, but she sure as hell should be able to find his torchship. There were not that many of them. What had he called it in the playback, Chaika? No, that was a nickname.

A query on UCM torchships brought back a dozen entries. She stabbed her finger at the bottom of the list. "There you are."

"UCM Tereshkova. Third generation inertial confinement fusion powered cruiser, aka torchship. Offensive weapons comprised a pair of large aperture laser-scopes and a mass driver. Two hundred twenty meters long. Commissioned... She skipped down, looking for crew complement. Which varied by sortie. Fine.

She found the sortie list and scrolled down to the bottom. *Like many UCSF torchships, UCM Tereshkova's last mission was to Luna to retake the helium-3 mines.* Up one. *UCM Tereshkova was dispatched on a disastrous mission to 55 Pandora that in retrospect, historians considered the opening shot of the war.*

That sounded right. She expanded the sortie's header, found the crew complement header, expanded it. *Master: Captain Arkady Rashnikov. Executive officer: Commander David Abrams. Chief engineer: Lieutenant Anatoly Sidorov. Sensors/Weapons officer: Lieutenant Edward Lynch.*

And there was the hole she was looking for. No Pilot: Lieutenant Gray. But a torchship did not fly without a pilot. Someone had to have edited the Warsing Wiki.

By itself that was not odd; the whole point of a wiki was that it could be edited. That was how it grew. Maggie had contributed a few minor items related to her expeditions, so she was familiar with the process. But the Warsing Wiki was more stable than most. Deletes were uncommon. If she recalled correctly, they had to be approved by an editorial board.

She opened the change log for the sortie to 55 Pandora. The change log captured the whole messy process of creating an entry in the wiki. Every edit should be there, from the initial creation of the article to the last time some Warsing Wiki geek decided his slant on how ageism affected the conduct of the war was the correct one.

Except the change log for the Pandora sortie just showed the initial creation a mear after the end of the Warsing. No edits were logged at all. Things just did not happen that way. And even if they did, that meant the original author had omitted Lieutenant John Gray. How far back did this conspiracy go?

Maggie sat back in her chair with a tired sigh. It seemed more likely that someone had managed to hack the change log. Which was supposed to be impossible if you believed what the Warsing Wiki said about itself. But as a hacker, she knew that "impossible" usually meant "very difficult."

There was no code written by humans that could not be reverse engineered and subverted. Warsinger code was a different thing. Warsingers were indisputably smarter than humans. As the arms race pushed technology up the asymptotic curve towards the singularity, their artifacts bordered on incomprehensible.

It was hard to imagine what it would have been like to live at the end of humanity's collective innocence. One sol you are at the top of creation. The next you are looking down the barrel of a gun, and the finger on the trigger isn't even human.

She shook her head. She could take it further, but not tonight. She was too tired. She got up from her desk. "Hey Ajax!"

The little pogo came whirring around the corner.

"Watch the door, okay? I'm going to bed."

The pogo bobbed back and forth.

"All right buddy. Wake me up if you notice anything suspicious."

She retreated to the bedroom with her revolver in one hand and Gray's brain-stone in the other. She laughed at herself. Going to bed with Lieutenant Gray. That was perfect.

John Gray, the perfect boyfriend. Nothing to fear because it was never going to happen. Because he was dead! The whole notion amused her far more than it should have. She was giggling by the time she got into bed. She put the revolver on top of her nightstand and pulled a flask of whiskey from the little drawer beneath.

"Let's see what you have to say for yourself, John Gray."

8

55 Pandora

UCM *Tereshkova* decelerated tail first into polar orbit around 55 Pandora, her torch blazing ahead like the beam of a flashlight. The asteroid looked like a dull red potato tumbling through space, a misshapen spud deeply pockmarked by eons of collisions. One of these had deposited the minerals required to drexler fusion ignition lasers.

It was the middle of the second watch. Sidorov was officer of the deck. The art of the maneuver was to keep *Tereshkova's* torch from irradiating the asteroid's twenty-odd human inhabitants. When Sidorov ordered his watchman Zotkin to shut down the torch, *Tereshkova* was thirty kilometers above Pandora's north pole, and the station was safely on the other side of the asteroid.

Pandora's fission pile was directly below them. It looked like a blackened coral reef, its surface deeply textured to provide the maximum amount of radiative area. As they drifted past, Gray caught a scurry of movement at the edges of its fissures. Mekans, coming out from under the shelves of graphite to watch their passage.

Gray found it disquieting. Why should the mekans care? Surely they had other things to do. Nonetheless they lined up on the edges of the shelf-like outcroppings.

They maneuvered around the asteroid on arcjets. Pandora Station's docking tower rose above the horizon as they approached the south pole. A saucer-shaped hub at the top of the tower housed the station's laserscope and docks. The hub spun slowly to cancel the asteroid's rotation. A single vessel was tied up to its rim.

"Is that our missing bird, Guns?" Captain Rashnikov asked.

Lynch led the third watch, but he had started his stint on the bridge early to catch the action, bumping his second watchman to the observation rail beside Gray. He zoomed in on the vessel with one of *Tereshkova's* laserscopes. It was laid out like a cross, with a stubby bow and a long tail of cargo containers. The arms of the cross revolved around the central axis to provide a simulacrum of gravity. One arm held the ship's pressure hull, the other its fission reactor.

"Her transponder isn't squawking, but the class matches. Nuclear electric freighter, twin arcjets."

"Damage?"

"Nothing obvious." Lynch flicked the graduated strip at the edge of the image, dragging infrared into visual. "Her reactor is hot. You'd think they would have powered down for docking. Lots of mekans on it. Spinning up, I guess."

He highlighted a small vessel mated to one of the hub's airlocks. It was not much more than a pressure hull and an arcjet. "That's probably the ship's boat."

Rashnikov turned to Commander Abrams. "What do you think, XO?"

Abrams considered the tableaux in the holocaster. "I don't like it, Skipper. That freighter is old, but she's a beauty. If I were a pirate, I'd take her for a prize. But there she sits like nobody cares."

"So if not pirates, then EON kunmings? But in that case, where are they?"

"Come and gone?" Abrams suggested. "Sterilize the hive and get out."

"Not according to Space Control," Rashnikov said. "Nobody has been out here since the last supply run from Ceres ten megaseconds ago."

"Maybe they came with the freighter," Abrams said. "Stashed in a cargo container."

"In which case they are still here," Rashnikov said. "Guns, what's the status of the freighter's laserscope?"

Lynch zoomed in on the bow of the vessel. "The beam expander is cold. It hasn't been used in a while. Same story with the station."

"Keep an eye on them," Rashnikov said. "They are big enough to put a hole in us at this range. XO, we need boots on the ground. Muster a couple boarding squads."

"Aye sir." Abrams turned to Gray. "Pilot, you're Alpha. Start with the freighter. Guns, you're Bravo. Check the station."

The boarding squads assembled in the torchship's EVA room, down on deck five near the bottom of the pressure hull. Gray had pulled Alpha squad from the first watch. Lynch took the third watch for Bravo.

The men on a watch lived, worked, and played together. Now they helped each other into their combat shells and got ready to fight. It was a raucous bunch, full of bravado and smack talk.

Abrams swung through the drop shaft hatch and floated there, one hand on the coaming.

"XO on deck!" Gray shouted.

"Listen up," Abrams said into the sudden quiet. "Bits has prepared a list of known friendlies from the freighter and the station. Download it and keep the pics where you can see them. Anyone not on the list should be detained."

"Sir," Lynch called out. "Are we authorized to use deadly force if they resist?"

"Yes," Abrams said. "But don't get trigger happy. You kill a civilian, you forfeit your share, and everyone under you.

"Aye aye!" Lynch said. "You hear that, geckos? Kill a friendly and lose your share. So keep your claws off the bang switch!"

"Shell up!" Abrams ordered.

Gray inspected each of his men before he pulled his own facemask into place and sealed his skinsuit's hood around it. Abrams helped pull the top of the shell down. Gray played the mind game that now accompanied the ritual, which ended with him being dead, which was what he had signed up for anyway, so there was no point getting wound up about it. Which did little to alleviate the rising tide of panic that went with the sudden darkness inside the ceramic coffin. He clenched his fists to keep from triggering the emergency exit.

The combat shell booted up. The optics wrapped around Gray's head like an outside-in ledeye projected a comforting illusion of the outside world. Gray tweaked the display to render the other men as if the tops of their shells were transparent. He told himself it was to improve situational awareness.

"Ready for Alpha squad," Chief Sidorov said over lightwave.

Gray and the men in his squad cycled through the airlock into the mass driver at the core of the pressure hull. It was like being inside the barrel of a gun. The muzzle framed a small circle of stars forty-five meters overhead.

"It would be more logical if we were penalized per civilian death," Lynch said on a tight beam.

"Why is that?" Gray replied as they threaded their way around the dinghy.

"As it is, if we accidentally kill one, we may as well not even worry about the rest. It's a free fire zone."

"That is borderline psychopathic, Lynch," Gray observed. "Speaking as your friend."

"'Pragmatic and team-oriented,' according to my last eval," Lynch said.

"I wrote that as your superior officer, not your friend."

"I sometimes wonder why you even joined the Space Force."

"Flying, fighting, and fucking," Gray said. It was their mantra from Academy days. The unholy trinity, the three Fs, the number of the Beast.

Lynch laughed. "Go Space Force!"

The dinghy comprised a pair of superconducting hoops mounted to a thick vertical axle. A sensor-studded head capped the upper end of the axle. The lower end terminated in the bell of an arcjet motor.

On Gray's signal, the squad stepped up onto the lower hoop. Clockwork toes grasped it like mechanical talons. Gray reached up and grabbed the upper hoop with his shell's gauntlet. The dinghy's interface presented itself on his display. He changed modes, locking out the gauntlet so he could interact with the dinghy instead.

"Chaika this is Alpha," Gray said. "Bringing rings up to maximum gauss."

"Alpha, we have you set for a four-gee shot," Sidorov responded.

"Confirmed four standard gravities," Gray said. Hopefully Sidorov had not slipped a digit. The mass driver had enough power to turn a man into jelly. "Poyekhali!"

Sidorov counted down to zero. The mass driver's electromagnetic field seized the dinghy and flung it forward at forty meters per second squared. The padding in Gray's shell inflated automatically to keep the blood from draining into his extremities. Even so his vision narrowed to a dim tunnel, then rebounded as they exited the mass driver's muzzle.

Chaika receded rapidly beneath their feet. Thin blue bands of light outlined the dim titanium bulk of the torchship. The UCSF insignia adorned her domed bow: a ruddy crescent Mars with six glowing stars scattered across its darkened face, pierced by the yellow arrow of a torchship embodying the seventh star.

Gray felt a moment of fierce exaltation. He raised his laser arm in salute to the first man to have walked in space and shouted "Alexey!" over lightwave.

There was a chorus of affirmations from the other men on the dinghy. "Alexey!"

Even though the tradition was old and hackneyed, Gray truly felt a sense of kinship with the men and women who had first stepped out into the infinite void. It was humbling and exhilarating and terrifying all at the same time to drift among the stars.

Being suspended in the emptiness reminded Gray why he had joined the Space Force in the first place. Flying, fighting, and fucking were fine, and Ares knew he had done his share of all that. But that was not why he joined up.

Ever since he was a kid, he had wanted to be an explorer. He remembered standing on a hill overlooking Thunderbird Field, watching Space Force rockets roar into orbit. The sound rattled his heart in his chest it was so loud. It was the sound of destiny.

It was a Space Force expedition that discovered life in Titan's methane seas. And it was a Space Force ship that first brought humans to Pluto. Now there was talk of a torchship expedition out to Eris in the scattered disk. Who knew what they would find there? Perhaps Eris had been flung from another star eons ago and carried remnants of a long dead civilization.

That was why Gray had joined the Space Force. To have a shot at getting out there where no one had ever been before. To see things no one had ever seen. But here he was playing cat-and-mouse in the asteroid belt.

He spun the dinghy around to decelerate. The vernier thrusters rattled the frame against his shell's clockwork talons. It did not sound like destiny.

The freighter had docked stern-first to the hub's rim. Parallel rows of cargo containers were clamped to the long I-beam of her tail. None had been offloaded. Gray flew the dinghy to the hub at the bow of the ship. They tied up in the space left vacant by the ship's boat.

The freighter had been a queen of the spaceways in her time, but up close she had the air of an old tramp. Her hull was stitched with patches and bumpy with abandoned gear mounts. *Island Girl* was painted in cursive English on her side. The paint morphed into a video of a lissome Ceresean woman performing an aerial burlesque and back again to script.

"Remind you of your vamp back on Ceres, Pilot?" Kerimov asked lightly. Musk chuckled.

Gray felt a pang of separation alongside annoyance at anyone calling Elise a vamp. Which he let go of because they meant no harm. And then felt guilty, because not meaning to be basist did not make being basist all right.

"No," he said, struggling to find the right tone. "I mean yes, she's pretty, but Elise is... Elise is beautiful."

"Oh he has it bad," Musk said.

Gray shook his head. "You two vacsuckers are with me. We're going inside. Denikin, you've got Timchenko and Novitsky. You're outside. Secure the freighter's laserscope. Take a close look at her arcjets. Then get out to the reactor and check as much as you can there without needing radvax. The skipper is going to want to know if she's flightworthy."

They rode a truss crawler out to the pressure hull. The crawler was barely big enough to carry the three of them in their bulky shells. The sense of gravity increased as they went out from the center of rotation. When they reached the top of the pressure hull it was like being back on Mars.

"That airlock is too small for our shells," Musk observed.

"And anyone else's," Gray countered.

"Let's just blow an entry and call it good," Kerimov said.

"If we kill any crew we forfeit our share," Gray reminded them. "Not to mention the freighter's ship tree. Probably half the salvage value right there. No, we'll do it in skinsuits."

Their silence spoke volumes about their opinion of his plan. Gray shrugged, a massive, armored shoulder echoing the motion. "Kerimov, you stay outside and be our relay to the rest of the squad and Chaika. Musk, you're with me. Poyekhali."

Gray depressurized his shell. The skinsuit shrank down against him like a second skin, keeping his insides in and the outside out. He popped the top open and climbed out. The tension he had been carrying between his shoulder blades released. He took a deep breath. The view was subtly different, the shadows deeper and everything a little closer than it had been through the shell's cameras.

It felt good to be outside, safer, somehow. Which was ironic because he was in far more danger outside the shell than in it. He detached his cutlass from the shell and clipped it to his buckler.

They cycled the airlock. Gray's skinsuit relaxed as the pressure increased to normal. He flipped his facemask up. The air was cold and smelled faintly of corruption. Then the inner door opened, and a reeking miasma of death rolled over them. Gray pulled his facemask back down with a muffled curse.

"Pretty bad, huh?" Musk asked.

"Fucking foul," Gray said. "Something's dead."

"Great," Musk said. He pulled his cutlass out of its scabbard.

The airlock let into the innermost level of the pressure hull. It was like stepping into a greenhouse back home. The sun was just past zenith outside the geodesic frame. It illuminated the crown of a magnificent ship tree whose trunk coiled down a central well. Lush, manicured gardens surrounded the periphery. Nothing moved aside from bees in the flower beds.

A staircase was hewn into the surface of the coiled trunk. The steps were worn smooth and polished by the passage of generations of bare feet. The odor of death lingered in his facemask as they descended the living stairwell to the galley.

It looked like someone had spilled brown paint on the deck and then mopped it clumsily. They followed the trail to a recycling chute. A carrot had wedged the chute's flap open. Gray had a moment of cognitive dissonance. The obstacle was not a carrot. It was a human finger.

"Alien baby Jesus," Kerimov said over the commlink.

"That chute is too small for a whole person," Musk observed clinically.

Gray pushed the flap open. The finger was attached to a hand. His stomach twisted. He pulled a severed arm from the chute. The flap dropped back into place.

"Cutlass?" Kerimov asked.

"Looks a bit clean for that," Musk said. "Look at the bones. Looks like a chef's knife through bamboo."

Gray pushed open the flap and angled a light inside. The beam revealed a woman's head, eyes dried and dull, glossy brown hair tangled around her mouth. The skin of her throat had snagged on a screw and pulled up to reveal the white accordion of her windpipe.

He jerked back as if the chute had tried to bite him. He had seen a fair amount of combat, but this was something else entirely.

"Not pirates," Musk said.

It was rare for pirates to kill their victims, never mind dismember them. Ransoms were the rule of the game. When you started killing people, their relatives took it personally. And in the Belt, everyone was related. Reprisals were inevitable.

"Must be EON kunmings," Kerimov said.

"Should have blown an entry," Musk said.

"Kunmings don't make sense either," Gray said. "Why put her remains in the recycler? If you're going to take possession of the freighter, you might as well throw the bodies out the airlock. And if you're not going to take it, then who cares what happens to the bodies? Leave them where they fall."

"I heard Nüwans eat their dead," Kerimov said.

"That was a long time ago, during the collapse," Gray said.

"But it lines up," Musk said. "A recycler doesn't care what you put in it. Maybe they figured it was just more water and protein for the trip home."

Gray held up his hand. "Stop. Let's keep looking. There might still be survivors."

There were only five decks, all connected by the central well. They found the remains of three more people wedged into recycler chutes.

The outermost deck was the bridge. The door had been battered open. Dried blood was spattered across the bulkhead. Gray sat down at the pilot's console while Musk prowled nervously around the room. He scanned back through the ship's logs.

Island Girl had arrived at the station some twenty ship-days before them. A video taken from an aft-facing camera mounted on her pressure hull showed the freighter backing into the station, the twin drives angled outwards to minimize braking blast.

Kerimov called. "A couple mekans are coming down the truss."

"Must be the ones we saw on the reactor," Musk said. "Maybe they know something."

"Tell them to wait until we're done in here," Gray said. He scrubbed quickly through the log. The ship's boat had taken their skipper and steward across to the station. Then they lost communications with the station. The last entry was that a couple triads of mekan stevedores had come aboard to offload cargo.

Gray pulled up a diagram of the ship's cameras, hoping to find recordings of whatever had happened after that. But the cameras were all external. Not a single one was inside. He swore viciously.

"What's wrong?" Musk asked.

"Civilians and their damned privacy," Gray said. He returned to the external cameras and scrubbed back in time, before *Island Girl* arrived, looking for the prior supply run. A black hull flicked past. He went forward again until the vessel filled the frame. It was a qigong yacht, its six dagger-like radiators unmistakable. It looked just like the *Morrigan*, which he had last seen docked at Greenwich Station. The hivemaster's yacht.

Kerimov cut in again. "Something's not right, sir. The mekans are not responding to my commands. I thought maybe they couldn't see the iconji on my shell, but now they're right in my face, and they're still – hey!"

"Kerimov, what's going on?"

"They're just really aggressive, sir."

"Mekans aren't aggressive, Kerimov. They're not wired that way." Gray fetched a memstick out of one of his vest's pockets and spooled the ship's logs onto it.

"Well these are! Look you better... Ares damn it, back off! You better get back out here, sir. They're all over me!"

"On our way." Gray said. He pulled the memstick. They left the bridge at a run. They were halfway up the coiled staircase when Kerimov screamed, a terrible sound that dopplered up into a waning shriek as his shell vented. Then absolute silence.

They reached the innermost deck. The sun had moved a few triangles down the simulated greenhouse geodesic. The bees were still buzzing. The airlock was cycling.

Musk pointed at the blinking red light above the door. "Someone is coming in."

Gray pulled his cutlass free and flattened himself on the bulkhead beside the airlock. Musk took the other side. The red light turned green and the door opened, blocking Musk's view as it swung inward.

Gray raised his cutlass. He had a surreal view of Kerimov's gauntleted hand sticking out through the opening, as if the man were still alive, but there was no way he could be. Could there? The tip of Gray's cutlass dropped as he hesitated. One part of him was screaming to attack, but the other was compelled to watch the specter of the arm as it emerged from the airlock.

The arm was gripped near the torn shoulder joint by a pair of carbon-black mandibles. Gray raised the cutlass again, waiting until the mekan's vulnerable ledeyes emerged. He hacked down with his cutlass, but the mekan parried the blow with Kerimov's arm. Sparks flew as the chainblade tore at the ceramic armor. The cutlass slid down, shaving a layer away until it slipped into the arm's elbow joint and cut through the limb in a chevron spray of flesh and bone. Then the chainblade clanged into the frame of the airlock. The nanosaws on its edge powered down in a microsecond.

The mekan yanked itself through the airlock and gained the garden in a single convulsive movement. Gray backpedaled towards the ship tree.

The mekan flung the severed bicep at him. Gray fended it off with his free hand. The mekan crouched, about to lunge forward. Musk rushed the mekan from behind and slashed down with his cutlass. The chainblade bit deep into the abdomen. There was a tremendous flash of light and a thunderclap of sound as one of the mekan's kinos split asunder. The blast blew the chainblade off Musk's cutlass and left a crater in the back of the mekan.

It whirled on Musk and punched a foreleg right through his throat with a meaty crunch. The mekan yanked its arm back out. Before it could turn Gray leapt onto its back. He locked his legs around its thorax. The mekan twisted its head around, trying to get at him with its mandibles. Gray slashed down at an awkward angle, taking off both mandibles and most of an eye. Disassembled mekan sprayed in glowing sheets from the ejection ports on either side of the chainblade.

An arm snapped back struck a numbing blow to his sword arm. The cutlass spun off into a raised garden bed. The mekan whipped its whole body around, breaking Gray's grip. Its back legs seized his ankles. Its front legs scrabbled for purchase on his torso before locking into the fabric of his utility vest. One hand seized his left wrist in a cruel grip. The other jabbed at his eyes. Gray jerked his head back. A claw-like fingertip ripped into the skinsuit beside his left eye and tore downwards. A spray of blood coated the left side of his facemask.

Again the mekan jabbed at his face. The blow glanced off his temple. Head ringing like a bell, he punched his free hand into the gaping wound where the mekan's mandibles had been. The mekan spasmed as Gray dug his hand into its neural circuitry and crushed it in his fist like a brittle sponge. He tore out the ruined brain matter and punched in again, shoving down hard until he found the brainstem. The mekan shuddered its last and was still.

Gray pushed himself off the carcass. He could not see out of his left eye and his cheek was numb, as was his left hand. He knelt beside Musk. His neck had been torn out. His eyes were fixed on the flawless sky.

"I'm sorry," he said. "You were right."

He shook his head, got to his feet. He wiped mekan brains off his good hand and fumbled a patch out of his vest. The skinsuit tugged at his face as it grew into the patch. The numbness was replaced by a burning sensation.

He retrieved his cutlass from the fecund earth where it had fallen. He took a couple deep breaths to steady himself and then cycled through the airlock.

The outer door opened onto the truss crawler. A mekan was splayed on its deck, shot full of neatly elliptical holes. The trio he had sent to check the rest of the ship lowered their laser arms.

"Where's Kerimov?" Gray asked.

"This thing tossed him off," Denikin said. "We haven't retrieved him yet. His facemask says he's dead. What about Musk?"

"Dead," Gray said. "Can you get through to Bravo?"

"We tried as soon as we realized what was happening to Kerimov. No reply."

"Try again," Gray said. "If all the mekans are like this..."

"Alpha this is Chaika," Captain Rashnikov interrupted with a lightwave from the ship. "Return to Chaika immediately. There are mekans moving on the station's 'scope."

"Tell him we've got to get down there," Gray said. "Bravo must have encountered hostiles."

Denikin relayed Gray's entreaty, but the old lizard wouldn't have any of it.

"I'm aware of Bravo's situation" he replied shortly. "Denikin, you take Gray. Timchenko, Novitsky, bring that carcass over with you, but don't bring it inside. Now!"

Denikin grabbed Gray and crushed him up against the front of his shell.

Gray cursed savagely. "Let go of me. I'll go over by myself if that's the way it is."

"I know, sir," Denikin said. His shell's arcjets fired with a jolt, kicking them free of the freighter. The other two men followed, hauling the carcass of the mekan between them.

"The station's laserscope is powering up," Sidorov said. "Advise boarding squads to take cover."

"There is no cover, you idiot," Gray said through gritted teeth.

"No can do, Chief," Denikin said. "We've made our burn. We're committed."

"Guns, what's your status?" Rashnikov asked.

"Laserscopes are still warming up sir," Sensors and Weapons' second watchman, a young man named Miller, replied. "It'll be another twenty seconds before we can fire without cracking the mirrors."

There was a flare of light off Gray's right.

"They shot Tim," Novitsky said. He sounded bewildered. "Why are they shooting at us?"

"Use the carcass as a shield," Rashnikov said.

There was another flare of light.

"That was Novitsky," Denikin said. "Fuck my life."

He spun around with a staccato burst of verniers, putting his shell between Gray and the station. "Get your hands in or you're going to lose them!"

"There has to be another way," Gray said.

"Not seeing it," Denikin said.

His shell was limned with light as the station's laserscope illuminated him. The back of the shell turned into an incandescent mantle and exploded. The front half slammed into Gray and sent him reeling down into unconsciousness.

9

The Queens Confer

The sentinel bowed before the Queen of Deimos, her enormous ledeyes respectfully silvered as she waited to be noticed. She had come all the way from her watchtower on the terminator, not trusting the few workers she had at her disposal with news of such vital importance.

The pchelan queen was ancient and huge. Her hatch predated the Warsing. She was the only survivor of that restless time. Her bulk filled most of the chamber, leaving just enough room for a constant stream of workers who brought food and took away fresh mekova for the hive's drexlers.

She sprawled atop a primitive nuclear reactor that was her chief treasure. Deimos had no fissiles of its own; every gram of uranium in the reactor pile had come from the planet below or been scavenged from intruders the hive's pchelans had intercepted.

Her eyes flickered with thoughts that the sentinel could barely comprehend. Planets revolved around the sun, linked by the slow majestic trajectories of iceteroids inbound from Jupiter's Trojans and the quicker pulse of reaction drive flares. A complex network of trade goods and raw materials wove through this, the physical and energetic transactions of a vast mekosystem that reached all the way out to Saturn.

Slowly she awoke to the sentinel's presence. A foveal ring instantiated on the nearest eye and contracted to a narrow gaze centered on the sentinel's face. The ring probed at her features, changing color from red to yellow as it traversed the geometry of her eyes and mandibles. She correlated the tricode woven into the sentinel's exoskeleton with the record of her hatch and subsequent service.

Why are you here, Sentinel?

The sentinel's head rose, and color faded back into her eyes. She showed the watchtower, a thorny spike that rose from the dividing line between the side of the moon that always faced Mars and the side that faced away. Then the parabolic mirror at the top of the tower. The mirror turned to examine the planet below, revealing the structure concealed within its bell: a triangular scaffold, and at its focal point a sentinel, waiting, watching. A quick foveal ring pulsed inwards from the periphery of the sentinel's eye and then back out again. *I have come from the leading watchtower.*

The queen echoed the image, her foveal ring zooming in on the sentinel at the focal point of the mirror, the sentinel who was before her, until her face filled the ring. She dilated the ring until the image of the sentinel's eye filled her own. *Show me what you have seen.*

The sentinel bowed her head. When she raised it again, her foveal rings had contracted to bright dots on the surface of her ledeyes, each burning like the distant sun in its bowl of night. The incandescent spots opened into rings that fled to the edges of her ledeyes, leaving an image of the Tharsis highlands in their wake.

The mirror settled on Pavonis Mons. The volcano towered above the surrounding plains. Its lower slopes were blackish green with dagger trees. Above the trees, its slopes were shrouded by a conical cap of water ice and snow. The brilliant white cap ended half a kilometer below the summit. Above that, the atmosphere was still too tenuous to hold water vapor.

The caldera itself was well beyond the reach of fragile organic life. Nonetheless it bore the unmistakable signs of industry. Great tailing mounds dotted the flat expanses that had once been flooded with lava. Tunnel mouths pockmarked the spaces between. A young, deep crater abutted the northeastern rim of the caldera. Its slopes were encrusted with solar collectors and at its center was a soaring tower whose flanks were ridged with radiators. A thin stream of vapor came from its top and tracked straight west with the stratospheric jet stream.

This was the beating heart of the mekanopolis: a tunnel that descended straight down into the magma beneath the sleeping giant. Side bores admitted meltwater from the volcano's intermediate slopes. The water poured down the boreholes until it reached the magma at the bottom, where it flashed to steam. The steam shot up through the main shaft like the exhaust of a rocket, turning turbines all along the way.

Pavonis Hive was the largest conglomeration of mekans on Mars, and second only to Ceres in the entire solar system. Warsingers, mantids, pchelans; it had them all, and all the castes within each species as well. Deimos was nothing in comparison. And yet, the Queen of Pavonis had need of Deimos.

Beside the tower was a ledeye a hundred meters in diameter, a yin for the tower's yang in the tao of the crater that housed them both. The dark circle illuminated as Deimos passed overhead. Its myriad elements were linked directly to the nervous system of the warsinger queen.

She painted a dire picture: the quads had found something long lost, and believed to have been destroyed, a proscribed technology that must be obliterated once and for all. The sentinel's eyes relayed a map of Valles Marineris. Crosshairs appeared on a spot near its center, halfway between two of the quads' cities. Another foveal ring appeared beside the one which held the crosshairs. Within it was a vector plot of an incoming iceteroid, projected to airburst above the Noctis Fossae badlands west of the canyon. That circle moved east until it merged at ground level with the crosshairs that marked the artifact.

The pchelan queen considered her reply. Her core aversions predated those of the Queen of Pavonis. She simply could not cause direct harm to the quads. It was unacceptable, repellant. But the impact zone was five hundred kilometers from either city. Damage would be minimal. The bigger risk was to the superconducting Ring on the south edge of the canyon.

The Ring generated an artificial magnetosphere that kept the solar wind from stripping away the planet's atmosphere. Damaging it would violate the Armistice and might eventually harm the quads. But her aversions were not triggered with that level of ambiguity. And she could benefit from the queen's favor.

Tell the Queen of Pavonis we will keep her secret safe.

The sentinel bowed, her ledeyes silvering as she backed away from the queen, whose foveal ring pulled away, looking up at the roof of the chamber, and beyond it, the slow traceries of iceteroids drifting in towards Mars from Jupiter's Trojans.

10

The Bomb Shelter

The next sol found Maggie high on the mountainside behind the city. Konstantin Tsiolkovsky's statue was below her to the west. To the north, the Marineris sparkled as it snaked across the canyon floor. On the other side of its channel, the walls of the north rim were still deep in shadow.

The road rose ahead of her in a series of hairpin turns. She worked the pedals instead of using the bike's electric assist. The climb kept the morning chill off.

She stopped when the road crested the northern ridge into sunlight. Her airscarf was getting stale. She pulled it off and took a shallow breath through her nose. The breeze carried the pungent ammonia odor of icefall. She shifted the airscarf around to work another spot. The area that had covered her nose and mouth faded from rusty brown to olive green again.

Now she was warm. She thumbed on the motor and savored the wind in her face and the tight kinetic precision of the bike as she worked the turns.

The road followed a natural bench to the east. After a few kilometers she rolled to a stop in front of a ragged hole in the mountainside. The morning sun only penetrated a few meters into the darkness. She pointed the bike's front wheel into the shadows and linked her goggles to its sensor head.

Sunlit features washed to undifferentiated white, and the shadows seeped away, leaving a sepia-tinted image in their wake. A rough stone ramp led down from the opening to a broad floor below. It was like looking back in time.

While battles raged above them in interplanetary space, the residents of Tsiolkovsky had retreated into the lava tubes that laced the ridge. By the time EON controlled Mars orbit and the iron rain began to fall, the natural lava tubes had been augmented a hundredfold by manmade tunnels and chambers, and thousands of people were living underground like mekans.

Generations later, the catacombs had largely been abandoned. Only outcasts lived there. Petty thieves, black marketeers, drug addicts and the homeless. When Maggie had arrived in Tsiolkovsky she had been one of them. She had found an empty shelter off a side tunnel and made it her own. She only had to pull her gun a couple times before the other denizens learned to leave her alone.

She stood on her peddles and hung back over the seat as she worked her way down the ramp. It had been pieced together from the remains of the collapsed floor like a giant jigsaw puzzle. The gaps between the pieces were wider than her tires.

Dusty was waiting at the back of the cavern. One eye tracked her as she rolled to a stop beside him. The bipe's reverse knees rested on the floor. A large rifle was slung beneath the cab. The rifle's upper tube was its mass driver. The lower held its kinos, sleeved by an electron pump. It looked like someone had taken a pre-Exodus pump shotgun and sized it up by a factor of two.

"Hey Dusty," she said, dismounting. "Nice gun."

"Mah-Gee." Dusty's voice was quiet but powerful. There was a lot of air being moved. The driver's side door opened upwards like the wing of a bird. Eric jumped out.

"Dusty has a gun," Maggie observed.

"My Dad gave it to me. You know he's restoring the Sturmovik his father flew for the Mars Guard in the Warsing. This was his survival rifle in case he got shot down."

"Damn big survival rifle."

"Damn big predators on the ground. And the pilot wore a combat shell, so it's not that big. Anyway, I told him about our encounter with the Hund, and he just handed it over. Said I needed it more than his antique did."

Maggie felt a twinge of jealousy. Sometimes it seemed Eric had everything she didn't. Not the survival rifle, though it was nice; she was good at getting the *things* she needed. What she did not have were the personal connections that made the things matter. She did not have a family. She did not have a father to turn to when things went sideways and she needed help.

"What caliber?" she asked, pushing all that neediness back down in the dark where it belonged.

"Twelve and a half mil through the coils, bolt action. I was up half the night working on an actuator. I want Dusty to be able to work the action, but I can't get it to cycle reliably. So for now it's just a big single-shot."

"Is there one in the chamber?" Maggie asked, trying not to sound apprehensive.

"Wouldn't be much use otherwise."

"True enough. And Dusty has a line to the trigger? Just asking." She liked Dusty fine. He was quite a bit smarter than Ajax and utterly loyal to Eric. But she wasn't sure she trusted him with a loaded gun.

"No, I ran out of time. Had to get some sleep. The trigger ribbon is connected to a switch in the cab."

"Might be better that way." She ducked beneath the bipe. Offboard power for the rifle's driver coils was routed in from the bipe's mains. So at least they would not have to pump it up. The bolt action that fed slugs to the driver chamber was encased in a web of nanotube muscle ribbons. After a few tentative pokes at the mess, she let it be. Eric tended to over-engineer things. It was his German ancestry coming out. If it were up to her, she'd cut a hole in the cab's floor and work the bolt by hand.

"Any ideas?" he asked when she emerged.

"That's a tough one, Eric. I'll have to think about it."

"Let me know what you come up with. I'm stumped."

She changed the subject. "How's Zsuzsanna doing?"

"She's all right. That scrape on her hip is going to leave a mark, but she's all there upstairs." He tapped his head.

"Good." They had all been worried about brain damage from lack of oxygen. "So, you think the attack was a coincidence?"

"It doesn't seem that way to me. Hence staying up half the night fitting Dusty with a gun."

"Yeah." She told him about her research the night before while they unloaded the broken warbot from the back of the bipe. It massed a couple hundred kilograms, and even with Mars' low gravity – about one-third Terrestrial – it was a heavy and awkward load. They lashed its torso onto Maggie's bike and stacked the rest of the salvage on it, topped by the big pentachoron they had salvaged, for all the world like an art student's idea of an avant-garde Ded Moroz tree.

They walked the bike up a side tunnel, one of them on either side to keep it upright. Dusty stayed back in the entry chamber. The tunnels were too small for him to go any deeper.

The bomb shelter was a hundred meters from the main entry and up a level. After a couple turns they were off the beaten path. Embers set into wire cages cast just enough light to avoid rubble that had fallen from the ceiling.

They came to a point where someone had torn out the embers for their own use.

"That's annoying," Maggie said.

"Guess somebody was cold," Eric said, which annoyed Maggie even more. He was always spouting off sympathetic platitudes like he knew what it was like to live in a hole. If anyone should be sympathetic it should be her, and she was not. Some little scumbag had stolen her embers, and it was annoying, period. They did not need sympathy; they needed to get their ass kicked so they did not steal anything she really needed.

Beyond it was utterly dark. There could have been anything in there with them, and they would not know it until far too late. Eric got his flashlight out. Maggie grabbed his hand.

"Hold up," she said quietly. She reconnected to the bike's sensor head. The darkness ahead resolved to a grainy image of the tunnel. Maggie passed her viewpoint to Eric. "Better to see than to be seen."

The bomb shelter was a little farther on. A stick figure of a girl holding a handgun nearly as big as her was scratched into the rock by the airlock door. Little girl, big gun. Her mark from when she first found this bolthole after the long trip up-canyon from Korolyov. Maggie selected a crypto key from her necklace and pressed it into a shallow depression on the doorframe. A deadbolt within thwacked open.

They cycled through the airlock while the system told them about what had happened since their last visit. It had not seen anything other than a few stray mekanos: a sand crab and something that looked like an oversized cockroach. Whoever had taken the embers had stayed out of sight.

Maggie checked the other rooms while Eric lit a couple of oxygen candles to take the chill off and freshen up the air. The outer wall adjoined the back of an old prewar house. The original occupants had installed a fiber optic that allowed them to monitor their property through a meter of reinforced marscrete. The fiber had survived. The house had not.

The fiber gave a surreal dollhouse view of a bombed-out living room. Scattered toys and a child's tablet with an oversized bezel and a broken screen were covered with a thick layer of dust. Other than the usual mekano tracks, nothing appeared to have been disturbed. She wondered what it had been like for the people who lived there when EON's bombers began firing their mass drivers. Iron rods falling from orbit like incandescent rain. It must have been beautiful.

Eric shucked his jacket and tossed it carelessly in a corner, followed by his airscarf. Goggle and gloves went on top of the pile. "What's the plan?"

Maggie unwound her airscarf and hung it up by a light. Goggles and gloves went to their accustomed place on a shelf by the door. "It's time for a little brain surgery."

"Like with an icepick and a hammer?" He sounded hopeful.

"It's not going to be very useful without its brain."

"We can give it a new brain. A nice brain. A brain that likes us. Think about it: we could have our own warbot."

"One thing at a time. Right now we need to know what it knows."

They got the carcass up onto the workbench. Maggie examined it critically. Socket-headed screws studded the armor plate. It was a coarse piece of work, designed for quick assembly and easy maintenance. She selected a hex driver from the workbench and removed a skull plate.

"Here we go. Looks like a mil-spec ten giganode neural network."

"Ten giganodes is a lot for what amounts to a guard dog, isn't it?"

"Well, Ajax has one giganode, which is about half an actual dog. Should such be found to still exist."

"Earth," Eric offered.

"If they weren't all eaten. Anyway, dogs were social creatures. This thing is designed for long-term autonomous operation. Takes more brainpower." Her hex driver whirred as she removed skull plates.

"So a pogo is one, this is a ten, and we're what? A hundred?"

She finished removing skull plates. "Baselines like us are eighty-six."

"What about mekans?"

"As a genus? The first miner and factory worker species ran about twenty giganodes. High enough to make them useful, low enough to make them easy to use. Hivemasters bumped ship mekans up to forty – about half human – to deal with the complexity of working with humans onboard spacecraft. Pchelans come in at sixty, because they *are* spacecraft, pretty much. Mantids are about eighty, like us. According to my dad, warsingers started at one hundred and went up from there."

She extracted a fist-sized object from the warbot's head, held it up for inspection. "This is what I like. A good old-fashioned storage array."

"That should simplify things," Eric said. "I wasn't looking forward to a trip down memory lane with this thing."

"Tell me about it. The brainstone is bad enough. Last thing I want is to be stuck in a warbot's neural net. Want to rig it up? My stomach is going to crawl out of my face if I don't have something to eat."

"Sure."

She tossed the storage array over the carcass in a lazy parabola.

He snagged it out of the air. "Make something for me too?"

"Rig it up." Fifteen minutes later she put a bowl down in front of him. "The very best in canned cuisine. What have we got?"

He gestured at the screen he had rigged. "This thing has been out in the bush for a long time. A pair of them were stationed out west during the middle of the war and never called back. They were just abandoned in place."

He pulled up an image of a windswept shack, little more than a roof over a thorium engine. Beside the engine was a broken-down Hund. "This is from forty mears ago. They alternated going on patrol and spinning back up, until this one broke down. Then our guy cannibalized it for parts and kept on going."

"And what, it just stumbled across us while it was out on patrol?"

Eric bit his lower lip while he worked the console. "No, the wreck is a good eighty klicks from their shack. Hang on a sec."

The view shifted to a map of the area around the shack. A dense spirograph netted the area as Eric scrubbed through the log. "This is a view of its patrols. Mostly it's just a rough spiral out and back in. But then breaks off and heads towards the wreck."

"Wardamn. It came right after us. What triggered it?"

Eric sifted through the logs. "Here. A message came in after Zsu pinged the commhawk with her query about Gray."

Maggie swore under her breath.

"That's on me," Eric said.

A dense chunk of text appeared on the display. Maggie hunched over the screen. "It's a command sequence. The header says it's from Mars Guard. That is a lat-long coordinate. And that," she stabbed the screen with her finger, "is a kill directive."

"Somebody swatted us."

Maggie nodded. "And whatever the header says, it wasn't the Guard. They forgot about that warbot before we were born."

"So who then? Warsingers?"

"Not really their style," she said.

"I suppose not. More the cut-your-head-off types." He winced at Maggie's expression. "Sorry."

She waved off the apology. "Console? Maybe I can find the origin of the message."

He passed it over. "You're not worried a query will lead them here? I mean... they found us in the middle of nowhere."

"I set up a zombie last night for that very reason." Maggie remoted into her home system back at the Rusty Robot. She frowned. The zombie was offline.

"Problem?" Eric asked.

"It's gone dark."

"What were you doing with it?"

"Looking for evidence of Lieutenant John Gray."

"Oh." He digested that for a minute. "Do you know where the machine is? Physically, I mean."

"Roughly." She cross-referenced the zombie's network address against a map of Mars. The hardware was in Von Braun, eight hundred kilometers away on the southeastern tip of Eos Mensa. She pinned the location down to a residential neighborhood.

Eric added a community overlay to the map. There was a news icon above the neighborhood, a red triangle with an exclamation point inside. They exchanged glances.

Maggie opened the news icon. A talking head appeared above the map, all glittering eyes and perfect teeth and a plush blue Ded Moroz hat. And cleavage, of course. The usual Snow Maiden treatment.

"She's hot," Eric said.

"It," Maggie said. "It is an avatar, not a person."

"Actually I think I've seen her at the Rusty Robot."

"Zsuzsanna," Maggie said to shut him up. Tits and Teeth had started talking. Eric shut up.

"...broke into a flat on Fourth and Thorium. The motive seems to have been burglary; the owner's computational assets are missing, along with his head." The background shifted to the interior of someone's home. The camera's slow pan across the jumbled furniture stopped at a dark puddle on the carpet. Maggie's heart flipped over. The viewpoint tracked relentlessly up to a headless corpse.

"Police believe this is the work of a technomancer." Tits and teeth went on to explain in breathless detail how memories could be retrieved from the recently dead. Eric tapped it off. The avatar popped back open of its own accord to deliver one more tidbit. "The Von Braun police department is offering ten thousand gigs for information leading to the arrest of the perpetrator!"

"Or if you are yourself a technomancer, they offer you a cell in the basement and nobody hears from you again for a few mears," Eric said.

Maggie's hands were trembling. She put them in her lap, twisted them together. She had gotten someone killed. She had been careless – worse than careless, negligent! – and someone had died because of it. A scream started to form in the pit of her stomach. She took a deep breath, pushed it down. No screaming.

"Are you all right?" Eric asked. He reached out tentatively but she pushed him away.

"Don't touch me. Just... don't."

He withdrew his hand with a wounded expression.

"I'm sorry," she said after a moment. "You don't know how close I am to losing my shit."

"It wasn't your fault."

"It absolutely was my fault."

"You didn't kill him."

"I led the mantids to him. Right to his home."

"We don't know it was them," Eric said. "The cops think..."

"They took his head. That's not the work of a technomancer. That's not what we do. That's what mantids do. No head, no story."

Eric wisely let it sit until Maggie had gotten herself under control. Not until she had blown her nose and splashed cold water on her face and made a cup of low country tea did he ask the question that was foremost in his mind:

"What is it about the wreck they are so desperate to suppress? It was nothing special; a nuclear thermal rocket is Exodus-era technology, not Warsing."

Maggie retrieved her satchel and dumped the crystalline shards from the wreck on the table between them. "You're forgetting about this. You and the boys spent most of the time getting the reactor free. But these shards are not Exodus-era technology."

"What are they?"

"I don't know. I've never seen anything like them." She picked one up. There was some sort of structure there, something that caught the shorter wavelengths of light like the weave of a shimmering silk scarf. "The helmet is made of the same stuff."

Eric tried putting it on. He looked ridiculous. "Does Gray's brainstone have anything to say about it?"

"Still getting through that. Not yet."

"Then I guess we'll have to figure it out on our own."

Maggie shook her head, all confidence fled.

"The infamous technomancer Maggie May, mistress of the dark arts, defeated? No! Come on, we can do this. Everything is here, isn't it? Control node, wiring harness, this pointy crystal thing we salvaged." He started putting the pieces on the workbench.

Maggie let herself be pulled in. Using the pictures she and Zsuzsanna had taken, they reconnected the pieces as best they could. They had cut the crystal pentachoron free of the spar below its Canfield joint, leaving a stub of material which they clamped to a camera tripod. A thick bundle of cables connected the articulated stub to the control node. Now it really looked like an abstract Ded Moroz tree.

"Smoke test?" Eric asked.

Maggie pulled her goggles down over her eyes. "Gotta do it sooner or later."

He flipped the switch on the power supply. The pentachoron began to glow. A delicate violet-blue light crept up through the fractal capillaries inside them. Eric turned up the current. The light intensified as it pushed deeper into the structure.

Maggie leaned forward for a better look. The eerie blue glow drew her in. The pentachoron seemed to slide towards her. The blue lightning trapped within its vanes branched into fractal infinities.

A hand on her shoulder drew her back.

"Careful," Eric said. "You're getting a little close. There's enough power on that thing to put a crater in your face."

Maggie rocked back on her heels. There was a ringing in her ears, and she was having problems focusing.

Eric steadied her. "I'm going to shut it down."

"Hold on," Maggie said. She waited until the room came back into focus. Then she made her way to the power supply, one hand on the edge of the table for balance.

She dialed up the current. The device lit up the room in a blue-violet glare of light. It began to rattle the tripod. More current. The pentachoron fell with a crash.

"What the hell?" Eric exclaimed.

Maggie hastily dialed the current down. The glow subsided slowly. She was relieved to see the pentachoron was intact.

"Did the stand come apart?" she asked.

"No," he said. "You're not seeing it, are you? It fell *through* the table."

"The table is in one piece." Maggie said.

"Yes. Exactly. One piece, no hole."

"It must have fallen over and rolled underneath."

"Nope."

Maggie opened her goggle's image buffer and ran it back to the beginning of the test. As the current came up, the pentachoron began to vibrate. She stepped down the play rate, trying to find the source of the motion. It looked like the device was changing size, shrinking minutely and then expanding back out again.

At the slowest playback rate, the pentachoron seemed to blur. She could not distinguish its edges. And then for a moment it blurred out entirely. When next it came into view, it was on the floor beneath the table.

Maggie pushed her goggles up on her forehead. "Mekfucking mother of War," she said. "It's a hyperdrive."

Eric's eyebrows shot up. "There's no such thing as hyperdrive. There's no such thing as hyperspace. I remember a section on it in physics class. If there are higher dimensions, they would have to be extremely small. Curled around the regular three dimensions or some such. Or we would have observed them."

"So they say," Maggie said. "But that would be the official line, wouldn't it? It's not even possible, so forget about it."

"So where are they then, these extra dimensions? Why can't we open a door and step into somewhere else?"

"Maybe we're just not built for it. If our sensory apparatus only exists in three dimensions, then that's all we can see. I don't know, Eric. Haven't you ever had something happen to you that you can't explain?"

"Like what?"

"When my grandma died, she came to visit me. We were living in Korolyov, she was here in Tsiolkovsky. I had this dream where we were having tea. Just like this," she raised her cup and took a thoughtful sip. "Maybe that's why I'm remembering it now. Anyway, she told me how much she loved me, and that she had to go. And then I woke up and went downstairs, and my mom was crying. She had just gotten news that grandma had died."

"Coincidence? Or you heard her talking while you were asleep, and it got folded in. That happens to me all the time."

"I'm just saying that I don't think this," she made a gesture like polishing a window in front of her, "is all there is to it."

"Maybe not," he said, but she knew him well enough to hear what he really thought: she was deluding herself. And maybe she was.

He scowled at the pentachoron, still laying where it had fallen. "What's hard for me to believe is that this thing right here actually exists. Hard to believe we found it. I can't even imagine how much it might be worth."

"Our heads, evidently."

"But why? Why would they want so badly to suppress it?"

"Because it's dangerous," Maggie said.

"It's not some new kind of dragon tooth, or a grey goo bomb. It's not a weapon."

"Don't be so sure about that. Anything can be a weapon. My father told me about faster-than-light missiles developed near the end of the war. You can't stop an FTL missile. You can't see it coming. It arrives before the target can know by any means that it was launched. It's the ultimate weapon of mass destruction."

"You'd think that would be the kind of thing that would make the historical record," Eric said.

"It probably did, and just got attributed to the wrong cause. How would anyone on the receiving end of something like that know how it happened?"

"Why are you only telling me this now?"

Maggie shrugged. "My dad was full of stories. Everything he found had a story, and the things he was still looking for even more so." She thought back to those days, sitting on a stool at the end of his workbench while he hunched over some Warsing artifact, head encased in magnifiers and home brew sensor packages. "You know what really stuck with me about this one?"

Eric shook his head.

"All I've ever really wanted is to get off this miserable planet. Go someplace where I can stand outside and breathe the air without choking or freezing to death. But here we are a couple generations after the Warsing, still stuck on Mars. It was in the palm of our hand, Eric. We could have made starships, but instead we made a weapon. So very, very human. And that's why the warsingers care."

"We could just let it go," Eric said. "Leave everything in a pile where they'll find it, say we have no idea what it is, call it good."

"I don't think that'll work. Look at the effort they've made to suppress this. It's not just that they don't want any hyperdrive artifacts to be recovered. They don't want anybody to think it's even possible. Everything about it has been erased, all the way back before the Warsing."

"So it's too late to give up?" Eric laughed bitterly.

"I think the only way out is through. Make such a big splash in the news that it is impossible to edit us out of history. We're going to have to make this work. Repair the wreck. Use it to go somewhere."

Eric did not look convinced. "You really think we can make a functional hyperdrive out of this junk?"

Maggie turned the pentachoron over in her hands. The crystalline vanes had an otherworldly sheen under the bomb shelter's harsh lights. "Yes. But it's going to take time. And time is not on our side. Not after what happened in Von Braun."

"Do you think they can trace that zombie back to you?"

"Given how deeply they've infiltrated marsnet and the Wiki? Probably. I hate to say it, but yeah I probably left enough tracks that they could get back to my home system, and from there... well, that would expose all of us."

Eric nodded slowly. "Okay. We need to clean your place out. The sooner the better. And warn the others. Zsu, Dmitri, Alex."

"Kowalski – he's got the reactor," Maggie said.

"You call them. I'll deal with your apartment."

"I'm coming with you," she said.

He shook his head. "There's no point in risking both of us. Don't worry, I'll bring back Ajax."

"Ajax isn't the only thing I'm concerned about," she said.

He paused at the door. "That might be the nicest thing you've ever said to me."

She felt her cheeks flush. "Don't let it go to your head. Just come back in one piece."

11

Field Promotion

Gray woke in the anonymous confines of a medibot. It smelled of disinfectant and sweat. He could not remember how he had gotten there. There was weight, the constant rush of air handlers, the distant vibration of the plasma gun at the core of the torchship. The last thing he remembered was being crushed against the front of a combat shell. Denikin's shell. And a corona of light before sudden darkness.

Gray jerked upright, banging his forehead against the medibot's canopy. It folded back out of his way. His tongue was dry against the roof of his mouth, and he could not breathe through his nose. He sat up cautiously, swung his feet over the bed. His feet burned terribly. They were encased in boots that were rigged up by tubes to the medibot. He could not move his toes.

Polanski came into the room. "You're awake! That's good."

"How long?" Gray croaked.

"Three ship-days. Here's some water."

Gray took a sip, coughed explosively when it rushed down his throat faster than he'd expected. Polanski reached for the bulban, but Gray waved him back.

"Where's Kassie?" Kasahara was the ship's doctor.

"Kassie got bumped up to Bits. The skipper put me in his seat."

"An officer? I mean, congratulations, but…" Gray trailed off as the implications sank in. Polanski was part of the second watch. Promotions went in watch order; if anyone moved into officer territory it should have been someone from the first watch, not him.

"What happened to the first watch, Polanski?"

Polanski shook his head, mouth pursed, eyes on the deck. "Not just the first. We lost the entire first and third watches, sir. You're the only survivor."

Gray's mind went blank, then as quickly filled with memories. Him and Lynch fencing at the Joint Service Academy. Lynch took first. Gray was a distant fourth. The first time they jumped from Mars orbit, the bone-shaking vibration as their aeroshield took the brunt of reentry, Lynch with a mad grin on his face, howling like a banshee.

Gray caught his breath before the tremor in his chest could turn into something more. He had to set aside his feelings. Lynch was dead. They were all dead.

"Not my place to tell you any of this," Polanski said. "Sorry sir. You need a hecto?"

"No, I'm fine," Gray said, though he was far from it. He went through the list in his head. Lynch. Kerimov. Musk. Denikin. Timchenko. Novitsky. Schwartz. Rybolovlev. Altan. Garrett. LeBrun.

"We nearly lost you too. It was a minor miracle you didn't strangle on your own blood when you broke your nose."

Gray touched his nose, winced. It was swollen and hot. Something was stuffed into his nostrils, which probably explained his parched throat.

Polanski held out a pan. "You can take those out now."

Gray pulled a pair of blood-caked pads out of his nose and dropped them in the pan. He flashed on Denikin's shell crashing into his face when it had exploded. Denikin had saved his life. And died for his trouble.

"Let's get you unplugged." Polanski began working on the tubes that connected Gray to the medibot.

"What's going on with my feet?" Gray asked.

"Frostbite," Polanski said without looking up. "By the time we found you, you were hypothermic and unresponsive. You'd curled up around your core, arms crossed and your hands in your pits just like in training. So that saved your fingers. But your toes didn't make it."

"Didn't make it," Gray echoed. It was an odd image. Toes like dead soldiers, blackened with frost. They didn't make it.

Polanski finished with the tubes. "They'll grow back pretty quick. Just be sure to come in once a day to flush the nanite bath in the regen boots. And don't pick at the stitches on your cheek."

"Stitches?" Gray touched where the mekan had ripped his left cheek, felt a rough arc around his eye socket like a crusty zipper. He wondered what Elise would make of that. "Why stitches?"

"The skipper said you needed a mark. So people knew something had happened to you. It was kind of interesting doing it, actually. First time for me. It's usually just some blue goo and a little tape and call it good."

"Right," Gray said. The conversation had become surreal. He felt like he was coming loose from the anchor of his body and hovering over himself, watching from afar.

"I let him know you're up. He says you should join him in the wardroom." Polanski handed him his clothes and facemask. "Need any help?"

"I got it," Gray said. "Thanks Polanski."

Gray hobbled up to the officer's wardroom. The ship was sweltering hot. Nothing seemed quite the way it had been. He paused at a juncture. Was it a left turn or a right? He could have sworn the emergency repair locker had been on the other side of the corridor.

The corridors were empty. The only sound was the sigh of air handlers. The sound of the ship breathing. A blast of hot air from a duct overhead did little to dry the sweat between his shoulder blades. He felt like he was the only person left onboard. The sole survivor. He shook his head, trying to banish the ghosts that surrounded him.

The only person in the wardroom was Rashnikov. His uniform was open at the neck, showing grizzled white hair. Sweat glistened on his forehead. The matt black casing of his moravec rose like a crest above his matted hair.

"Have a seat," he said.

Gray eased himself carefully into the seat opposite Rashnikov. His feet were like bricks.

"Coffee?"

"Thank you, sir." Gray took the proffered bulban. The coffee within was hot and bitter.

"You're welcome. Breakfast should be along shortly."

They eyed each other across the table.

"How much do you remember, son?" Rashnikov broke the silence.

"Most of it, I think. Up until they lit up Denikin." He paused. "Polanski told me I was the sole survivor."

Rashnikov nodded. "I put Denikin up for a shooting star. He was a brave man."

"They were all brave men sir," Gray said. "The best shipmates a man could ask for."

"I'm sorry Gray," Rashnikov said.

"What happened to Lynch and his men, sir?"

"Gray, I've known you for what, two mears?"

"About that, sir."

"Long enough to know that you're not going to like this. I know you would have gone after them by yourself if I'd let you. But I had to make a decision. The station was full of mekans. Last contact was shortly after the station's laserscope lit you up."

"What happened?" Gray asked, eyes narrowing.

"We cracked the hive open with the mass driver and nuked it. Hive sterilization is the only acceptable option in the face of a mekan insurrection. I followed protocol."

Gray set down his coffee. The old lizard had put them down like a bunch of niners on strike.

"I know what you're thinking," Rashnikov said. "And believe me, I sympathize. But they were already dead, and I was not going to lose anybody else trying to bring back their bodies."

Gray stared down at the empty bulban latched faithfully to the top of the table. Waiting to be used again. Go Space Force. What a terrible way to die. No glory there, just blood and ashes at the hands of mekans, of all things. It made no sense.

"You don't have to agree with me, Commander Gray. But if we're going to work together, you do need to respect my decisions."

"Commander?" Gray echoed. "What happened to Commander Abrams?"

"We took *Island Girl* as a prize. Abrams is taking her back to Ceres along with Mendeleev and Allen. At least we'll get something out of this debacle."

"I'd have thought Sidorov..."

Rashnikov cut him off. "Abrams requested the assignment. I am sorry to say we had a falling out. I doubt he'll return to Chaika. So I put you up for a field promotion. The Admiralty agreed it was warranted." He held out his hand. Three silver stars gleamed in his cupped palm. "These are yours. Congratulations."

"Thank you, sir." That was the right thing to say, wasn't it? Gray struggled to focus, to return to the present. The dead kept crowding in on him.

"Don't thank me yet, Commander. The ship is a mess. Pandora's laserscope damaged our life support radiators. We've lost two full watches, and a slice of another to man the prize."

Gray fell silent. Abrams was the best XO he had ever served under. His leaving Chaika like that was a real loss, and probably a black mark on Rashnikov's record.

"Abrams is a good man," Rashnikov said as if he'd been reading Gray's mind. "A better man than me in many ways. You've got a tough act to follow." Over his shoulder: "Life, how about that breakfast?"

The partition that separated the wardroom from the galley slid open. Life support's fifth watchman – third now? – handed out a tray of yaytsa rancheros. Gray realized he was hungry. Strange how life went on.

"Go ahead," Rashnikov urged. "It's been a while since you've had anything that didn't come through a tube in your arm."

"Thanks." Gray took a serving. The eggs were small but fresh. The beans were blanketed by a thick brown sauce that mostly concealed a side of grechka. It was delicious.

Rashnikov mopped his forehead with his napkin. "Listen Gray, the radiators are a problem, but we're down nearly half our crew compliment, so we're not going to overheat too much before we reach Ceres. Uncomfortable, not fatal. Your top priority is figuring out what happened to those mekans on 55 Pandora."

"Did we recover any of them?"

"That carcass your squad pulled off the freighter. Turns out you and it were on similar trajectories."

"Lucky for me," Gray said. Rashnikov gave him a sharp look. Gray realized he had spoken aloud. Internal editor fails. "Sorry sir, I'm not all here quite yet."

Rashnikov's brow unwrinkled. "Don't worry about it." He finished his eggs and washed them down with the last of his coffee. "The knobs at the Academy think the Pandorans are wired differently. Something about their aversion to harming quadrupeds being flipped. Exactly how and more importantly when that happened is not clear."

"Why 'when'?"

Rashnikov pushed his plate away. "The knobs floated two hypotheses. One: the rewiring was done in the drexler; it's a mutant. Two: the rewiring was done in vivo by a nanite virus. It's a zombie."

"Mutant versus zombie," Gray said. "That's great. Really great. So, a mutant gives us a time lag between when the drexler was compromised and when the bad hatch comes out. Zombie does not."

"Correct. And to the point of our immediate survival, the mekans on Chaika can't be mutants. They were drexlered a long time ago. But they could be zombies."

"Has there been any sign of that?"

"Not yet. But the men are on edge. It needs to be ruled out, or there is going to be trouble."

"I'll make it top priority. Anything else?"

"I want you to move out of the officers' bunkroom immediately. Sends a signal to the men. Take Abrams' old cabin."

It did not take much time to pack his belongings. His personal effects – a pocketknife he had gotten for his fifth birthday and a few other mementos – were stashed in the narrow alcove at the head of his rack. His uniforms and gear were in a couple drawers beneath it. He drew his cutlass from its scabbard. Burn marks showed where it had slid down Kerimov's armor. A few gobbets of yellow fat were stuck to the side of the blade. They resisted his efforts to wipe them away. He sheathed the blade with a grimace and hung the scabbard on a charging post.

While he waited for it to spin up, he exercised his newly granted authority as *Tereshkova's* executive officer to access her personnel records. Third Lieutenant Edward Lynch, KIA. After a few moments indecision he opened the stream from his old friend's facemask.

It ended in a tumbled blur of motion. He backtracked and slowed it down. The interior of the station whipped through the facemask's field of view. Slower still, until he had individual frames. A mekan's head, very close. A sudden shift to the wall. Rotating through more angles on the docking tower's control room. There, a human form, deformed by the absence of its head, replaced by a dark jet of blood unfettered by gravity.

Gray took a deep breath. He scrubbed backwards. Lynch's head back on its body. Back in time to when he was alive, looking down at a video log of the docking tower's activity. Lynch scrubbed back through the station's record, looking for clues, just as Gray had on the freighter. Because that was why they were there. That was why he was here.

And stopped. In the frame (in the frame) was an achingly familiar face. Oval, eyes a little too large, framed by a nebula of dark hair. (Do you want to live forever?) He opened another window with the logs he had taken from 55 Pandora. Scrubbed back to the qigong yacht. He zoomed in, looking for a registry number. Was it the *Morrigan*?

There was a knock on the door of the bunkroom. "Commander?"

Gray cut the feed. He felt vertiginous, unmoored, as if he had somehow fallen through the hull of the ship and was drifting alone in the infinite emptiness.

"Commander? Are you all right?"

Gray took a ragged breath. "Fine. Just…" He shook his head. "What can I do for you, Sid?"

"We've got something for you, Commander," Sidorov said. Boiko was behind him in the hallway. They came into the bunkroom.

Gray unwrapped the bundle. A stubby double-barreled handgun was inside. "What is this?"

"It's called a derringer." Sidorov broke open the action. He dropped a couple of fat plastic cartridges into the empty chambers and snapped it shut. "Only two shots, and we're not convinced about its accuracy. So you'll want to be close."

He held it out to Gray, who took it reluctantly. "How did you get this aboard?" he asked, leaving unsaid that it was highly illegal, and worth Sidorov's stars if Gray reported him.

"We had your pal Thirteen extrude it," Sidorov said. "It came snooping around for you, so we made use of the opportunity."

Boiko patted a lump in his utility vest. "All of the officers have one now."

"The skipper too?"

"He suggested it. Insurance."

"Huh." That was unexpected. "Thank you." It came out more like a question than he had intended. He slipped the derringer into his breast pocket with a feeling of deep unease. He changed the subject. "You think Chaika's mekans are infected somehow?"

Sidorov's shoulder twitched. "We brought the carcass of one of the hostiles from Pandora aboard. Abrams was against it, but the skipper insisted. Said the knobs at the Academy would need evidence. So if it is infectious… some of our mekans have been exposed."

"Did you quarantine them?"

"From the others? Yeah. All three of them are locked up in engineering."

"So they are in the pressure hull with us. Lovely."

Again the shoulder twitch. "Well yeah. But! Every one of them has a hull breacher glued to its head. Any misbehavior and boom," his hands made a motion like a clap in reverse, "mekan brains all over the floor."

"Good thinking. Those are our test subjects then." His cutlass's kinos were maxed. He swung the buckler over his shoulder. "Sid, I want you on the bridge monitoring their feeds. Have a couple watchmen shell up and meet me and Boiko down in engineering."

The three mekans sat against the bulkhead, legs folded beneath them and hands resting on the floor. Their heads were about the height of Gray's waist.

"Sid is in place," Boiko said.

Gray nodded. He exported his feed to the ship's general channel. Boiko's eyes widened as he realized that everyone could see what was happening. Gray shrugged. It was the only way to settle the issue.

"This is all of them?" he asked, for the benefit of their invisible audience.

"Yes sir," Boiko said. "Thirteen, Seventeen, and Thirty-two."

Gray paced in front of the mekans, looking at each in turn. They followed his movements, iconji flickering across their eyes too fast for him to read.

"Any way to tell which had the greatest exposure?"

"Seventeen has been in the pressure hull the whole time, so it has been in proximity to the Pandoran longest. Then Thirteen came in, then Thirty-two."

Gray activated the iconji overlay on his spex. "Seventeen, step forward."

The middle mekan rose to its feet and came forward. Now its head was almost on level with his own. Gray pulled his cutlass out of its scabbard. "Do you know what this is?"

Yes. The schematics of the cutlass flew across its eyes.

Gray thumbed off the safety. The chainblade whined evilly. The mekan started to back up.

"Stay where you are!"

It stopped, wavering. Gray advanced on it. He raised the cutlass and it reared up, hands held out. The chainblade flashed down through one wrist and bit into a soap-bubble eye. Sparks showered against the floor. Where the chainblade touched the ledeye was a narrow black slit like a cat's eye. Gold and green flickered around the periphery. The mekan scuttled backwards and hit the bulkhead hard.

"That's for Lynch," Gray said between his teeth. He advanced again. The mekan tried to run but had nowhere to go.

"Hold it!" he told the watchmen.

The men seized the unfortunate creature by its legs. It bucked helplessly in their armored grip. But it did not try to harm them, nor Gray when he stepped in front of its good eye.

"I'm going to kill you now," Gray said. "Do you understand me?"

A confused flood of iconji jumbled through its eye. Gray did not try to follow it. The important thing was that it did not fight back. That proved it was not a zombie.

It held its remaining hand in front of its face. Pleading? Shielding? Both? Gray remembered how Musk had died, the meaty crunch as the mekan's hand had punched through his neck. He raised his cutlass and with a short chopping motion, no more than a rap of the chainblade, severed the mekan's neck. The head fell to the floor, light fading from its remaining eye as it rolled to a rest at his feet. Its limbs sagged and were still. The men let the body fall to the floor.

"And that's for the rest of them," he said. "Kerimov and Musk and all the rest."

He looked around the room. Boiko would not meet his gaze. The remaining mekans' eyes were silvered. He slammed his cutlass back into its scabbard. He felt like he was going to throw up. He picked up the severed head by a slack mandible.

"You two stay here," he told the watchmen. "Any sign of aggression, kill them. Boiko, you're with me."

When the cutting was done, Boiko peeled back skull fragments like pieces of laminated black eggshell. Seventeen's brain was a mass of dark grey material the size and shape of two clenched fists pressed together.

"The central arbitration node is on top of the brainstem," Boiko said, "right at the end of the spinal cord. You're going to have to lift away a lot of this structure to get at it."

Gray worked his fingers under the edge of the lobes and lifted them out of the brain pan.

"Careful," Boiko said. "Don't tear it." He reached in and eased the severed spinal cord through its socket. "Okay."

Gray lifted the brain out. Boiko inserted a probe between the main body of the brain and the brain stem. A magnified image appeared on Gray's spex, artiform neurons branching like a black forest in the fog.

"There. That's the arbitration node. I'm going to lock it in…" The image came into focus.

"And this is the one we got for the Pandoran's brain." A second picture appeared beside the first.

"They look the same to me," Gray said.

"Let me put them both through the symbolic mapper. Makes it easier to see." Another pair of pictures appeared under the first. They looked like maps of the tunnels under Thunderbird.

"Diff," he said.

A third map appeared between the first two. Where the originals matched, the neural pathways glowed bright green, then dimmed. Where they were different, Seventeen's pathways showed blue while the Pandoran's showed yellow.

"Here," Boiko said. An arrowhead pointer circled an area of the diff. It jittered over one of the blue and yellow tangles. "This is the arbitration node."

"They're different."

"Yeah." He zoomed in on a blue/yellow pair. "This is the aggression suppressor."

"What does that do?" Gray asked. He knew the answer all too well. He felt like something inside him had died along with the mekan they were dissecting. He said it for the benefit of the watchmen who were viewing the procedure through his spex, who had not spent two mears at the Joint Service Academy.

"According to the knobs, it suppresses any action that could harm a quad."

"A quad?"

"That's what mekans call us. Four limbs, not six. A human, for instance. Let's say that you are doing something that might result in harm to a mekan…"

"Like attacking it with a cutlass," Gray said. "For instance."

Boiko hesitated. "For instance. An attack like that would trigger a flight or fight response. Run away until you can't, then fight back. That's the way it works for us, and that's the way it works in mekans. Unless the attacker happens to have four limbs. In which case the mekan does not fight back. It just – lets it happen."

"Like Seventeen did."

Boiko nodded. "Right."

"But the Pandoran?"

"Its node is inverted," Boiko said. "It would fight back. It might even seem like it's looking for a fight, because any reaction that trended that way would be passed through to the motor system."

Gray crossed his arms. "So compared to the Pandoran, Seventeen's brain is normal? Non-aggressive?"

"That's right."

"What about the others?" Gray tilted his head at the door to the repair bay, where Thirteen and Thirty-two were still being held.

Boiko shrugged. "Probably fine. They had less direct exposure. Not that we even know what constitutes exposure, really."

"Do we need to test them?"

Boiko's lips were pressed together. His gaze lingered on the dissected brain. "I don't know."

"Okay." Gray spoke on a separate channel to the watchmen in the repair bay. A moment later the door opened and Thirteen came through accompanied by one of them.

She looked at the dissected head of her nestmate. Colors flickered across her eyes, up and down the spectrum. Settled on a mottled red.

"Get down," Gray said, pointing at the floor. Thirteen complied. Gray thumbed the safety off his cutlass, pulled it free.

"Commander," Boiko said.

Gray shook his head. "Stand down, Chief."

Gray stood above the mekan. Her limbs shook with what could only be interpreted by his mammalian brain as fear. Gray's own hands were trembling. He gripped the hilt of his cutlass tighter, raised it above Thirteen's head. "I'm going to kill you with this."

Thirteen started to get up, sank back to the deck.

The cutlass flashed down. And stopped, a scant centimeter above the black stick of her neck. Gray thumbed the safety on. The chainblade powered down.

He looked at Boiko. "Good enough?"

The engineer's eyes flicked up, back down. He could not hold Gray's gaze. He nodded.

"You stay here," he told Thirteen.

He went next door and repeated the test on the remaining mekan. It too complied despite having every reason to believe that doing so would mean its death.

"That settles it," Gray said. "Get the hull breachers off these creatures. We have nothing to fear from them. They are not infected. The Pandorans were mutants, not zombies."

12

Terminal Guidance

The sentinel watched the slow progression of the planet beneath her. They had left Pavonis Mons behind and were now tracing a course that paralleled the hydrologic cycle that kept the planet alive in a biological sense. First the snowy Tharsis highlands, then the rough fissures of the Noctis, which drained into Tithonia and hence into the largest canyon in the entire solar system: Valles Marineris. Almost directly below her now was the artifact that the queens had discussed.

She wondered at that. What proscribed technology could be so dangerous as to risk a ground strike? Presumably a Warsing weapon of some sort. But the Warsing had passed long before she was hatched, and she did not share her queen's persistent trauma about that era. She felt more curiosity than fear.

She shifted her grip on the mirror's controls. It swung to the coordinates the Queen of Pavonis had provided. She found tire tracks and followed them to what was obviously a worksite. At the epicenter of the dense swirl of tracks was an oddly shaped artifact. Triangular facets glinted in the sunlight. She gently dialed in the focus, fighting against atmospheric distortion.

Despite her best efforts the image would not stabilize. The atmospheric tremors were turning into large scale vibrations. She realized with a start that someone else had climbed onto the scaffolding that supported the mirror. She guiltily swung the mirror away from the artifact just as a zhuk's head appeared above its rim.

They regarded each other darkly for a moment.

Why have you disturbed me? the sentinel's ledeyes flashed.

You are to come with me, the zhuk replied.

By whose orders?

The royal tricode flashed across the zhuk's ledeyes.

But my work! the sentinel protested.

You have other work now. The zhuk held out a massive hand.

The sentinel stubbornly kept her grip on the mirror's control bars. *What other work?*

Terminal guidance, the zhuk replied.

This gave the sentinel pause. Terminal guidance of what? Surely not an iceteroid.

The zhuk ran out of patience. She plucked the sentinel from her perch. *You will come with me. The swarm is leaving.*

13

Borodin

Maggie was jolted out of Gray's memories by an alarm from Ajax. She shut down the brainstone's interface. She had left the pogo on patrol in her apartment. Now the little robot was backed up against her desk, bouncing nervously.

"Settle down Ajax. Stop moving. Stop. Good, now stay still so I can see the door."

The viewpoint stabilized, pointing in the general direction of the entry. The door swung open, and Eric stepped through. Maggie heaved a sigh of relief.

"Hey Ajax," Eric said, hand held out protectively to keep the pogo from bouncing up into his face.

Maggie patched her audio through. "Hi Eric. Any trouble?"

"So far, so good. I stopped by the Polytechnic and took Zsu home. She is getting her things together; I'll pick her up on the way back out. What else do you want out of here besides Ajax?"

"My home system – last, or you'll break our connection. Whatever spare ammo is in the desk. There are some memsticks in there too." The important ones were on her necklace, but there was no point in leaving evidence.

He pulled the drawer and dumped the whole thing into a duffle bag. There was a clatter of ceramic memsticks, kinos, and brightly anodized seeker cartridges for her revolver. A Hand of Miriam necklace set with small embers briefly illuminated the inside of the duffle before it was covered.

"I could use a change of clothes. Underwear, especially."

Ajax followed him into the bedroom.

"There's a picture of my mom and dad on my dresser from when they got married. And their wedding rings."

"Slow down, I'm still working on the clothes." He held up a lacy red thing for inspection. "Like this?"

"No," she said, "not like that. No lace. And don't be icky."

Eric finished loading the duffle bag and went back into the living room to get her home system. Ajax followed him out of the bedroom. What happened next came so fast that it took Maggie a long time to sort it out in her head.

Eric was in front of Ajax, blocking her view. He shouted and then staggered backwards into the pogo. Knocked off balance, Ajax jumped away at an angle, bouncing off the wall and landing somewhere back in the bedroom. It took him a few seconds to get back on his wheels, during which time his viewpoint oscillated uselessly. Maggie heard the chaotic sounds of a struggle, the heavy thud of flesh on flesh.

Then Ajax was back in the hallway. Someone was crouched over Eric, a big man in a long open coat. His eyes were hidden by a pair of ledeye goggles. He turned towards Ajax.

"I see you, little one," he said. "You see this?"

He pulled Eric up by his hair. Blood streamed from his nose. His face was turning blue.

"I crushed his windpipe. He did pretty well until he ran out of air. Now he's running out of time." He looked at Eric philosophically.

Maggie tried to speak but couldn't find her voice. She had never been paralyzed with fear before. Something about the man unnerved her. It was like she had seen him before in her nightmares.

"I could let him die," he said thoughtfully. "But that won't really help matters. More useful alive, I think. At least for now."

He reached around with his other hand and pinched Eric's windpipe from the sides. It popped back into shape like an air hose. Eric gasped raggedly. It sounded like he was choking on his own blood.

"Eric!" Maggie shouted. "Are you all right? Eric!"

His eyes fluttered open. "Maggie..."

Eric coughed explosively. Blood spattered the pogo's cameras.

"Ah," the intruder said. "You are there. Good."

A mekan's arm, black as carbon, lashed out from under the coat and seized Ajax with a bifurcated hand. Maggie realized with a shock that he had four arms. Was he a warsinger? He held Ajax up for closer inspection. The goggles were embedded into his flesh.

"Maggie May, I presume. My name is Borodin. So good to meet you, if only by proxy. Is this – Eric, you said – is Eric your boyfriend?"

"No," Maggie said. "Just a friend."

"You seem very concerned about him."

"I'd be concerned about anybody I saw getting beaten to death."

"I see. So if I hurt him to get what I want, it wouldn't be any different than hurting anybody else."

"If you hurt him..." Maggie started.

"You aren't in a position to make threats," Borodin said. "I am. Let me illustrate."

He walked around Eric, who had gotten to his knees. One hand was on the bedroom door frame. He was trying to stand, but he kept coughing up blood. Borodin pinned Eric's wrist to the door frame. A mekan's hand – two central fingers, two thumbs – pried one of Eric's fingers away, put a thumb to its base, and bent it back until it audibly snapped.

Eric dropped back to the floor with a gasp. He curled around his injured hand. The thin black arm folded back down under Borodin's coat. Another set of inhuman fingers pulled the lapels together from the inside.

"What do you want," Maggie asked flatly.

"You know what I want," he said.

"If I knew, I wouldn't have asked."

Borodin laughed shortly. "Let me tell you something, Maggie May. This isn't the first time I've done this. Or even the tenth. No, I've been alive a long time." He circled around Eric and kicked him in the kidneys. He spasmed backwards with a ragged gasp. "Probably not going to be your friend Eric's story."

"Please stop," Maggie said. "I'll do whatever you want."

"Good. Tell me what you took from the crash site. Tell me everything."

Maggie hesitated, trying to guess what he knew and what he did not. She had to assume he had sent the Hund. What if it had been in communication with him? More than anything else, she did not want to implicate the others. She wondered if she could pass for Zsuzsanna.

Borodin sighed. "Do I have to hurt him again?"

"We salvaged a fission reactor from the wreck. I found a skull nearby with a brainstone in it. Then a warbot attacked us. You sent that, didn't you?"

"I ask the questions," he said. "What happened to the warbot?"

"We gunned it down. Eric brought its carcass back in the bipe."

"And?"

"And we were going to go back for the rest later."

"Who is 'we'?"

"We," she repeated as if he were being stupid. "Me and Eric."

"Don't lie to me. You two didn't salvage that reactor all by yourselves. And it wouldn't have fit in his bipe."

"I have a crane truck," Maggie said. "And bots to help with salvage work. I'm not going to split the take if I don't have to."

"Then who was the woman in the tent with Eric when the warbot attacked?"

Maggie tried not to panic. She was losing track of what she had said. "That was me! We were sleeping together when the warbot attacked. I lied about him not being my boyfriend because I didn't want to give you an advantage."

"That was foolish." He shook Eric roughly. "Where are you now? Tell me or I will take everything I want from him right in front of you."

Something in Maggie snapped. If she told him where she was, she was as good as dead. "Nowhere you can find me, asshole."

"I wouldn't count on that. Not when I'm through with him." A bifurcated hand emerged from beneath his coat bearing an amorphous object, as if he had torn his own heart out and was showing it to her. "Do you know what this is?"

She did, but she was through admitting anything.

Dark tentacles coiled slowly beneath a lumpen head. "It is a memory leech. It only works on the recently dead."

"You use that on him, and I'll make sure everybody I know hears about the wreck. A find like this will attract some attention."

"Sounds like free advertising to me." His other mekan-like hand produced a chainblade from beneath his coat. He flicked it open. A high-pitched whine set her teeth on edge.

"Until the warsingers send in their mantids. Then you're just another piece of fish drying on the rack."

"Colorful, but not my story. I've got an arrangement with the warsingers. Common interests and all that. So trust me when I tell you that anyone who listens to your story is dead. And not by my hand. I just want what you found."

"Actually, what I'm hearing is that *you* don't want me to talk to anyone about this. I don't see how I've got much to lose, honestly. Eric's already as good as dead, and so am I if I let you anywhere near me. I know what you did in Von Braun. No, I'm better off bringing the hammer down and letting the pieces fall where they will."

Borodin's face was expressionless. "I see. So you don't care if you're responsible for the death of who knows how many bystanders?"

"Don't gaslight me you grotesque mekfucker. You're the one holding the knife."

Borodin stared coldly at her for a long, long moment. Then he shook his head and sighed ruefully. The chainblade scrolled back into its grip. "I feel like I am going to regret this, but I kind of like you, Maggie May. So I will offer you a deal. Bring me the warbot and the brainstone, and I will give you Eric. Alive."

Maggie's cheeks flushed with anger and her breath came fast. She struggled to get control of herself. She had no reason to believe him. But she knew it was the best offer she was going to get out of Borodin. And likely the only one that had any chance of getting Eric back alive.

"Fine," she spat out.

He smiled. "Meet me on the north road this time tomorrow. There's a place about eighty klicks east of town where you can drive down to the river. I'll mark the turnoff."

He hauled Eric to his feet. Pointed a human finger at Ajax, at Maggie. "Don't talk to anyone else. Don't bring anyone else with you. Don't bring any weapons. Do bring the warbot and the brainstone. Follow these instructions, and you'll get your boyfriend back in one piece. Are we clear?"

"We're clear," Maggie said.

"Excellent." With that, Borodin ripped Maggie's home computer system out of the wall, cutting her connection to Ajax.

Maggie's bravado collapsed, fear and anger crashing down like a wave. She stared at the blank feed. She was in a state of shock. First she had gotten an innocent man in Von Braun killed, and now Eric was being held hostage by a psychopathic technomancer.

A part of her wanted to run away. Change her name again, change her face, become someone else. She knew it, and was ashamed of it, but there it was. She wanted to run.

Borodin terrified her. She prided herself that there was not a lot she was afraid of, but something about him filled her heart with dark terror. Something about him took her back to the night her parents had died back in Korolyov. She remembered mantids boiling through the neighborhood like a swarm of army ants. Each of them was three meters long: bigger, faster, smarter, and much harder to kill than a human.

A neighbor came out to see what the commotion was and was beheaded with a snap of mandibles, like somebody cutting the head off a doll with a pair of shears. The mantid tossed the severed head back into the swarm, where another caught it and stuffed it into a saddle bag.

Her father came out of his workshop with his double-barreled coach gun. He broke the weapon open and stuffed a pair of cigar-size missiles into its breech, then snapped it closed again. He tagged one of the oncoming mantids with the gun's laser designator. The viridian beam sparkled on its armor.

He was enveloped in a cloud of exhaust as the miniature missile streaked away, faithfully tracking the designator's spot. The mantid went up in a fireball. The concussion slapped Maggie in the face. There was another explosion a moment later, then a pause as he reloaded. The swarm was much closer now.

He shouted something at her, but she could not hear him over the ringing in her ears.

Another explosion, felt more than heard, like a blow against her ribcage that pushed it back against her heart. His lips moved but she could not hear him. She couldn't hear anything but the ringing in her ears. He pointed at her, pointed at the back door.

She thought he said "Run."

So she ran, until she was driven to her knees by a dagger of ice that punched right through her chest taking her breath with it. She fell, gasping raggedly at the pain. Put her hand to her heart expecting blood but there was none.

She turned to look behind her. Their home was a crumpled shell. Fire licked at the edges where the air was richer. In front the tableau that haunted her dreams. Her mother, cradled in her father's arms as blood cascaded down his elbows. A big man standing over them, gun in hand, firelight flickering on his goggles.

Memories were tricky; they were not the same kind of permanent record that a photograph was. They were malleable, dynamic, living. If you did not call back a memory often enough, it faded. And then when you did call it back again, its details had shifted the way a cloud changed shape in the sky. You thought something happened one way, and then another, and then another. Eventually a consensus arose that selected the most likely story or synthesized a new narrative that explained the most vivid elements.

You could not trust memory like you could a photograph. After the attack, when she was hiding from the mantids, she used to have Ajax show her the pictures he had taken of her and her parents. The time they had gone to the Space Force Museum in Thunderbird. Out on an expedition to the headwaters of the

Marineris, her father holding up a Warsing artifact with a broad smile. On a rare visit to Tsiolkovsky, standing on the balcony that surrounded the giant statue's torch, their shadows writ large on the city below. But she had never asked Ajax to go back to when they had died. It was a memory that she did not want in her head anymore. And so she had let it sit long enough that now she could not be sure what had really happened.

She found herself missing Ajax with a fierceness that surprised her. If Ajax were there, he could answer the question. Was it Borodin? Had he been there all along, waiting in the shadows for her to make the same mistake as her father?

Suddenly she was possessed by a blind, murderous rage. She rampaged through the bomb shelter, throwing parts on the floor, kicking over bins, smashing anything that was delicate enough to be destroyed with her bare hands.

She did not care about any of it. She did not care about the wrecked vessel and its shards of hyper-dimensional material, or the mystery of Lieutenant Gray, or the Hund. She did not care about the spin they had made off it, and all the plans she had made to spend it.

She came to her senses with a two-kilogram sledgehammer raised above the warbot's head. The last screams of "Frag you!" were still reverberating in the chamber.

The Hund lay there helplessly, unable to raise its hands in self-defense or even turn its head. She slowly lowered the hammer, her movements reflected in its glassy black lenses. She set the sledgehammer on the floor beside the workbench.

There were possibilities. She was not helpless. She did not have to let that aberration of a man win. Not without a fight.

Because really, what did she have to lose? Even if she brought him everything they had found, did she really think they were just going to walk away? They knew too much. No, Borodin wasn't going to let them go. If she cooperated, they were both going to die. Best case somebody might find their frozen, headless corpses. More likely, they would both simply disappear without a trace. The only way either of them would survive was if she fought.

She got her tools out and began the delicate task of bending the Hund to her will.

Maggie pushed her bike up the fractured, boulder-strewn ramp to the end of the lava tube. The bike's panniers were stuffed with gear. She was too tired to try riding it up, even with electric assist.

The Hund lumbered along behind her. It had taken most of the night, but she had gotten the machine repaired and under her control. The geasa she had layered into its nervous system prohibited any kind of hostility towards her and ensured it would obey her commands. It was thoroughly powned.

She crested the top of the ramp into daylight. The truck was parked nearby, angled so the sun streamed into its cab. Alex and Dmitri were waiting inside. They wrapped airscarves around their faces when they saw her and the Hund. Dmitri rolled down his window. "Is it friendly?"

"He's friendly to me," Maggie said, eyebrows arched.

"Gotcha."

"Come out and I'll get you introduced."

The boys got out reluctantly. The warbot dropped to all fours and stalked around them in a circle.

"Uncomfortably large," Alex said, turning to keep it in sight.

"Hold still," Maggie told them. "Let him get a good look at you. I loaded your profiles, but he needs to match them to his sensor input."

"What is it with 'he'?" Alex asked.

"I grafted Gray's brainstone onto the Hund's neural network."

"What? Why?" Alex was alarmed.

"Seemed like a safer place to keep it than in my satchel. So it is a he, now."

"It's an it," Alex said. "It's a mekfucking warbot."

"*He* is more than that, now," Maggie said. "We should see an emergent personality like Gray's as the brainstone integrates with *its* neural net."

"If the graft takes," Dmitri said. "But in the meantime, I'd think its behavior – his behavior – might be... unpredictable."

"Trust me. Whether or not the graft works out, the warbot is under so many geasa it would make a Mars Scout proud."

The Hund came full circle and rose to attention in front of the boys, a mechanical hand up beside its lens-studded head in a salute.

"There, you're confirmed," Maggie said. "I set you up as my lieutenants, so he will take orders from you. So long as they don't countermand mine."

Alex pointed at the ground. "Give me twenty, maggot!"

The Hund did not respond.

"He's not rigged for sound yet," Maggie said. Another thing to fix. "Hunds were built before there was enough atmo for that to be much of a thing. Goggles or body field only." She passed the warbot's link over to the boys. "And *maggot*?"

"He needs a name," Alex said defensively. "Maggot and Maggie. Pea and Pod. Perfect."

"No," Maggie said. "That is the opposite of perfect." She considered. "How about Golem?"

"Gollum?" Alex was puzzled. "Like in Lord of the Rings?"

"No, Golem. A man made out of clay brought to life by a Rabbi," Maggie said. "Wasn't your mother Jewish? Don't you have family traditions?"

Alex shrugged. "Does bootleg vodka count?"

"Mom read the classics to us," Dmitri said. "Lem, Asimov, Ellison. Kirk and Spock on the flattie. But not so much into the Jewish thing per se."

Maggie shook her head, started to comment, let it go. Family traditions. Evidently a fantasy. She knew more about Judaism than they did, which was deeply ironic, given that her parents died without saying a word about it. But maybe that was why she knew more. Maybe if they had survived it would never have been a thing for her. Just background noise. Instead she had been intrigued by her mother's Jewish heritage, and hence her own, and had followed that all the way down the rabbit hole to Kabbalah. Which had led back, in unexpected ways, to becoming a technomancer like her father.

"Anyway," Alex said, "Golem is taken. Dragon teeth, remember?"

Dmitri shook his head. "Those are grimms now."

"The fuck you say."

"There was a big fight on the Warsing Wiki. Consensus was, it's anti-Semitic to call them golems. So they're grimms now."

Alex rolled his eyes. "Sweet alien baby Jesus. I'm Jewish, and that's schmegegge."

"Bullshit," Dmitri translated.

"So vodka and swearing," Maggie said. "That's great."

"How about Gray Prime?" Dmitri said.

"Prime?" It was Maggie's turn to be puzzled. "As in unique?"

"As in, derivative. Position, velocity, acceleration? X, x prime, x double-prime? No bells? You don't remember physics class at all, do you."

"Kind of missed out on the secondary education thing," Maggie said. "Being on the run at the age-appropriate time and all that."

They loosened the straps that held the tarp like a tent over the truck's crane. There were only a few things underneath; the usual field kit of shelter and supplies. Dmitri hopped up on the bed of the truck. Alex picked up the heavily laden bike and handed it to his brother as if there were nothing but air in its panniers. Dmitri lashed it to the back of the cab.

Maggie waved the Hund up onto the bed. The truck rocked on its suspension. She had him lie down on his back with his head towards the cab.

"You stay there until I tell you to wake up," Maggie said.

"Roger," the Hund replied.

"No talking," Maggie said, holding a finger to her lips, and then felt silly because all comms were going over radio through her goggles. "Go to sleep now."

The warbot nodded solemnly and shut his armored eyelids. Maggie spread the truck's blue tarp over him. She crisscrossed it with a couple of straps and ratcheted them down.

They stopped by the Rusty Robot on the way down to Zsu's. Eric's bipe was nowhere to be seen. Dmitri guarded the truck while Alex went up to the apartment with Maggie. She had hoped to recover Ajax, but the little robot was gone. The contents of the duffle bag that Eric had packed for her had been dumped out on the apartment floor. She rummaged half-heartedly through the pile of belongings. So entirely not worth it. She picked revolver cartridges out of the pile and put them in her jacket pocket.

She set her mom and dad's wedding picture back on her desk. They looked happy. After some searching she found their wedding rings. They had rolled under her desk. She put her father's on her left thumb, and her mother's on her pinky.

"What about this?" Alex said, holding up the Hand of Miriam necklace her mother had given her. The embers glowed dimly between the Hand's two thumbs.

"Where did you find it?" she asked.

"Behind the front door. It's supposed to give protection, right?" Alex asked. "We could use that."

"Yeah," she said.

"Here," he held out his hand. He worked the clasp while she held her hair out of the way. Then he held her at arm's length. "There. That's nice."

"Thank you Alex."

"Don't cry," he said. "We'll get them back."

They continued down the hill to the northwest promontory, where Zsuzsanna lived. Maggie had not told her anything yet. She was concerned about how Zsu might react. When she opened the door and saw the three of them standing there, the blood drained from her face. "What's happened? Where is Eric?"

"He's been taken," Maggie said. "Let us in."

Alex pillaged Zsu's cupboards while Maggie filled her in on what had happened. He came to the table with a bottle of cheap vodka and a handful of mismatched shot glasses. He set one down in front of Zsuzsanna and filled it to the brim. "You need this."

Zsu pushed it aside.

"I'm serious," Alex said. "You look like a ghost. No? All of us then."

Alex poured drinks for the rest of them and raised his glass. "To getting Eric back."

Zsu reluctantly picked up her glass.

"To getting Eric back," they all echoed.

"Alive," Maggie appended.

They tossed the drinks back. Some color returned to Zsu's face. They argued about what to do next. The boys wanted to go with Maggie in a show of force. Zsu wanted to call the authorities. Maggie was dead set against both ideas.

"You can't go with me," she told the boys. "There's no way to conceal you effectively. He'll know, and it won't end well. We have to do this my way."

"As opposed to the way we usually do it?" Alex said. "Oh wait, that is how we usually do it."

"Aleksey Ivanovich," Maggie said, "that is not true. But even if it were, this is how it has to be. Borodin said to come alone. If anyone comes with me, he'll kill Eric."

"If you go alone," Dmitri said, "he'll kill you. I love Eric like a brother – no offense Alex – but this is stupid. We're going to lose you both."

Maggie shook her head. "I've got this. I've got the Hund. I need you two to stay here and take care of Zsu. You stay together until this is sorted out. I'm afraid if you separate, they'll pick you off one by one."

"Right!" Dmitri said. "Exactly! That's why you shouldn't go alone."

"Dmitri... Alex... Zsu... You guys are all I've got. He doesn't even know you exist. He only knows about me and Eric. You aren't on his radar, and it has to stay that way. I've got the element of surprise. He has not even considered that I might pown the Hund. He thinks I'm a stupid child. His actual words. I can do this."

"We should call the police," Zsu said.

"The police won't get involved," Maggie said. "Except maybe to bust us. They don't want any trouble with mantids. The potential for collateral damage is too high."

"We should at least tell Eric's family," Zsu said. "They should know."

Maggie hesitated. She agreed with Zsu in principle. But in practice... "I don't want to drag them into it. The more people who know, the more people who are going to get hurt."

"They're his family," Zsu said.

"No," Maggie said, making her mind up. "Berel is an ergocrat, for Ares' sake. He'd lose half his followers if they got wind that his son was involved with technomancy. It would ruin him."

"That doesn't matter," Zsu said. "He's their son. You don't understand because you don't have a family, but it's true."

Maggie stood up. She'd had enough. "I've got to go. I can't make you do anything. But I am going alone, and you all know what I think you should do. So that's how I'm going to leave it."

Dmitri tried to smooth things over, but for once his cleverness was not enough, and they parted on a sour note. Maggie hated leaving them that way, but she was out of patience and out of time.

14

Learning to Fly

Gray was enduring his second bridge watch of the day, his chin in his hand as he stared at the vector plot in the main holocaster. They were decelerating, so the closer they got to their destination, the slower they were going. It was a true Zeno's Paradox. The last few ship-days of the journey played out in agonizing slow motion.

Gray just wanted to be there. The closer they got, the more his thoughts dwelt on Elise. He longed for the sound of her voice, for her scent as he held her, for the brush of her hair against his face as her legs clasped his hips. These things filled him with a sort of doomed desire because he could not stop seeing what Lynch had seen on 55 Pandora.

The woman had to have been Elise's source, her parthparent Melissa. Which meant that her family, tangled as it was, was in some way involved. The only safe way through that nightmare was if it was just a coincidence. Perhaps Melissa had nothing to do with 55 Pandora's subversion. But setting aside his feelings for Elise, it seemed just as likely – more likely, really – that Melissa was responsible for it. Who else could subvert a hive but a hivemaster? The tension between what he hoped and what he feared was just enough to keep him from saying anything about it. He would personally get to the bottom of it when they reached Ceres.

Kasahara interrupted his thoughts. "Commander, we're getting a call from Greenwich Station. It's flagged urgent."

Gray straightened up. "Put it on the main holocaster, Bits."

"Aye sir."

The vector plot was replaced by an image of a Space Control officer, an angular woman with sharp Slavic cheekbones and piercing blue eyes. She wore a pilotka with four white feathers in its crease, the next-to-highest rank in Space Control.

Gray recalled meeting her at a social function the first time he came to Ceres. A formidable woman.

"UCM *Tereshkova*, this is Greenwich Station, Tectrix Potanin."

"Tectrix, Commander Gray here."

"Ah, Commander Gray. Of course. Congratulations on your promotion. Sorry business, that."

"Thank you, ma'am. Yes, it was. What can we do for you, Tectrix?"

"A few kilosecs ago, we lost contact with Parsons Field on Luna. At first we thought it was a communications glitch. Then we lost contact with the threelium mines. The Space Control Observatory at Earth's L5 point picked up these images shortly afterwards."

A set of thumbnails appeared in the holocaster. Potanin zoomed in on one of them. The helium-3 mines looked like Zen sand gardens. Gray could see pinprick flares of light amongst the furrows.

"What do you make of that, Commander?" Potanin asked.

"It looks like combatants taking laser fire to me," Gray said.

Potanin nodded. "That is our assessment as well. Spectroscopic analysis of the flares matches the composition of Space Force combat shells. Until we get more information, we are assuming this is an attack by EON. Parliament is reviewing all options. Be prepared for a quick turnaround at Ceres, Commander. Odds are good *Tereshkova* is going to Luna along with every other torchship we can muster."

"Yes ma'am!"

"Give my regards to Captain Rashnikov. Greenwich out."

Her image collapsed into an owl's head borne by a quadruple chevron of golden feathers. Then the holocaster returned to a vector plot of their approach. Gray considered it for a few moments. Then he summoned all officers to the bridge.

It was not a happy group. The men were worn to the bone from standing double watches. Gray had either interrupted some critical task or – as in the captain's case – dragged them out of the rack.

Rashnikov ran his hand through his hair, unconsciously fluffing it up to conceal the carbon bridgework of his moravec. "What's the situation, Commander?"

Gray played back his exchange with Tectrix Potanin.

"So EON has made their move," Rashnikov mused.

"But how could they have landed enough kunmings for that kind of ground combat?" Sidorov protested. "Surely we would have detected them in transit."

"Perhaps they are not kunmings," Gray said.

"You think mekans are behind this," Rashnikov said, more a statement than a question.

"It makes sense. First 55 Pandora, which produces components critical for fusion torches. Then Luna itself. Cutting us off at the fuel pump. They have been one step ahead of us the whole way."

"Subverting mekan hives to remove their aversion to killing humans would be a very dangerous game," Rashnikov said. "Where does it stop?"

"Probably not Luna," Gray said.

"What's on your mind XO?"

"Two points make a line, sir. And I'd say that line points right at Ceres. Greenwich Station is home port for most of the Space Force's presence in the Belt."

"*If* the problem on Luna turns out to be subverted mekans, *then* we'll have two points. Until we know more, we can only speculate. And that, gentlemen," he addressed the bridge in whole, "is a job for Space Control tectrices and Space Force admirals, not us. Our job is to get this ship put back together so we can go where we're told and fight when we're told."

He returned his attention to Gray. "What are we going to have to do to refit for a trip to Luna?"

Gray let it go, secretly relieved his concerns were dismissed. At least he had raised the flag. "The pressure hull's radiators need to be fixed. Chief Boiko did a good job patching them up, but they are not fit for a trip to Luna, much less combat. Supplies – food, water, threelium, deuterium, reaction mass. Replacement dinghies for the ones we left behind at 55 Pandora. Kites for the mass driver. New crew, replacement mekans. And this crew needs shore leave, sir. Everyone is on edge."

"Noted," Rashnikov said. "I'll do what I can. Get me a detailed list before we dock at Greenwich, and I'll take it to Control personally."

He turned to Sidorov. "Pilot, I want mission profiles. Give me a Lunar rendezvous, followed by combat maneuvers in low orbit. Throw in an intercept just in case Control gets a wild idea. Chief, I need a systems readiness report. Bits, monitor the newsfeeds, and let me know if anything catches your eye. Doc, stand by for those mission profiles. I want a reserve of consumables in case it takes a while to get back home. I want to be ready for whatever they throw at us."

Gray was late for his date with Elise. He had been delayed at the Space Force recruiting office on Greenwich Station. There were not many qualified candidates on-station, and he had made a play for a Sensors and Weapons officer who already had berth on another ship. That had landed him in a heated conversation with said ship's XO. All of which had cost him time and got him nothing but bad will in return.

He spent the trip down the beanstalk arranging official visitations of next-of-kin. Thankfully none of the dead watchmen had been from Ceres. He felt guilty for thinking that way, but it had been hard enough to record his condolences to their parents and lovers. At least he would not have to deliver the news in person. That would be someone else's burden. Except for Lynch. When Gray made it back to Mars, he would visit his family. That much he had promised himself.

The elevator car followed second sunrise down to the surface. It decelerated into the tower outside Meridian just as the orb lifted above the horizon, casting long shadows across the industrial complex. Mekans of all shapes and sizes scurried about their business outside the diamondoid capsule. Gray watched them with a sense of foreboding, his hand unconsciously resting on the pommel of his cutlass.

The terminal was jammed with people. He had to force his way out of the car against the stream of people trying to board. All the traffic was going up, out of Meridian. And most of it was baselines.

The city was no better. It took him longer to get five kilometers across the crater from the base of the tower than the ride down from synchronous orbit. It was ridiculous. It seemed like the entire population was on the streets.

He bulled his way through the crowd, using his broad shoulders to good effect. After an ugly exchange of words with a big drac whom he had jostled, Gray forced himself to slow down. If he got into a fight, he would miss her entirely.

He paused in front of the Anasazi's stone façade. It had been defaced with graffiti of a scythe, the astronomical symbol for Ceres, goddess of the harvest. A slick, dark green bacterial growth bubbled out of the surface of the rock to form a backwards C, the scythe's blade, with a cross-like handle attached below. The semicircular arc of the blade cupped a second cross within it. His teeth met in an unconscious snarl. A circle with a cross inside was the symbol for Earth. Earth and Ceres superimposed.

Inside, Elise was sitting at a table near one of the deep-set windows, her hand under her chin as she sipped a bulban of wine. She was wearing a red dress cut low in back. Her dark hair spilled down in a wave of loose curls.

She caught him looking at her and set her drink aside, smiling. Something about the moment caught in his mind: the light slanting in through the window, dust motes dancing above her head, the gems at her throat, her dark-rimmed eyes. He would never let that memory go. It was like a crack in the darkness that had gathered around him since 55 Pandora.

She stood as he approached the table. "Lieutenant John Gray. I was afraid you weren't going to make it."

For some reason that made Gray think of his toes. Didn't make it. Except they had regrown and hurt like a son of a bitch at unexpected times, sharp electric flashes. Polanski said it was the nerves coming back.

"I was afraid you might give up on me," he said, taking her hand.

She took in the crescent of stitches beside his eye. "What happened out there? Are you all right?"

"I'm fine." He embraced her and kissed both cheeks in proper Slavic style. She blushed delightfully and returned to her seat. He took the corner beside her, brushing his cutlass out of the way with his left hand. She raised an eyebrow at the weapon. He shrugged unapologetically.

"Sorry I am late. The streets are a zoo."

"Everyone has been on edge since Luna went dark," she said. "You can imagine the rumors. People are trying to get out. Get home while they can."

"What are they saying?"

"That the Ecostate of Nüwa was behind it. That war is coming. Is it true?"

"Looks that way to me. I suspect that as soon as we're provisioned and repaired, we'll be on our way to Luna."

The waiter appeared. It was the same man who had served them last time. Gray remembered his tattoo, a dragon holding a cratered world in its claws. Everything had taken on new meanings.

"Can I get you anything to drink, Commander?"

"A martini," Gray said. "Olives if you have them."

"Of course," the waiter said.

"Commander?" Elise asked after the waiter had left.

Gray tapped the trio of stars on his collar. "Field promotion."

"Congratulations!" she said brightly.

"Sort of," he said. "We lost a couple watches. It was pretty ugly."

"Oh. That's terrible. Is your friend Lynch..."

Gray shook his head. "Killed."

"I'm so sorry."

The waiter returned with his drink. Gray took a pull from the bulban. Walked himself back from his feelings. There was nothing he could do about the past. What happened next was what mattered. He had to know whether the Taproot had been subverted.

Gray set his drink down, took her hand in his. "Elise, this could destroy my career. But you need to know what happened at Pandora. Because of who you are. Because of what I need to do."

"What is going on?" she asked apprehensively.

"What I'm going to tell you can't go beyond you and me."

"I understand. I won't tell anyone else."

"Space Control sent us to 55 Pandora after they lost contact with the station there. We figured it was pirates, or maybe EON kunmings, but when we got there..." he shook his head. "It was mekans. The asteroid's hive had been subverted somehow."

"What do you mean, subverted?"

"The mekans were hostile. Worse than hostile, homicidal. Everybody there was dead, dismembered. Just... taken apart."

"Pirates might have –"

"No. The mekans there attacked us too. That's how this happened," he touched the scar. "We sent twelve men down. I'm the only one who came back."

She had the presence of mind not to contradict him, though his account went against everything she knew. "How awful for you. For them."

"The possibility of death is always in the back of your mind," he said. "But not like that." He took a long pull of his drink, set the empty bulban on the table. Carbon black legs flicked out and latched onto the creamy white tablecloth. He twisted the bulban slowly. The barbed legs caught in the fabric and could not retract. He twisted it a little more. "There was nothing glorious about the way they died."

She put her hand over his. "Stop."

He lifted his hand from the innocent creature. "Sorry. I think... I am a little damaged."

She gave his hand a sympathetic squeeze and set it down on the table beside the bulban. "That would make sense." Briskly: "The kind of change you are talking about would have to happen in the drexler before they even hatched out. That's something only a hivemaster could do."

"That's the conclusion I came to as well. The men were worried it was some kind of nanite infection, zombie mekans that would kill everyone onboard Chaika. But..." he stopped, unwilling to tell her what he had done. His men lionized him for the way he had handled the mekans, but he did not share their high regard. On the contrary, he was filled with self-loathing and guilt. It colored everything he did. He could not pass a mekan in the corridor without remembering how his cutlass had shivered in his hand when he cut Seventeen's head off. And every time he was forced to juggle the watch list to cover for eleven dead men, he was confronted with the absurdity of his own survival.

She was shaking her head. "No. Well, I mean, sure, hypothetically. You can do anything with nanotech, it's like magic, right?" She waggled both hands in the universal sign of ghosts in the night. "Nanotech. So scary. But practically, no. If a hivemaster wanted to 'subvert' a hive, she would just forge a new gem with the changes she wanted and present it to her queen."

"Aren't there safeguards against the kinds of changes we're talking about here? Inverting a core aversion seems like a big deal."

Elise laughed, a short sharp sound. "We come from very different worlds. I'm a hivemaster's daughter. I know all the dirty secrets of the trade. It makes outsiders comfortable to think that everything is firmly under control, but reality is a lot messier. There's constant turbulence at the edges of the sanctioned genera, new species whirling off like vortices."

Gray leaned forward. "Could what happened on Pandora happen here on Ceres?"

Her brow furrowed in what he took to be anger.

"I have to ask," he said apologetically. "If the Taproot's next hatch is homicidal, there will be bloodbath. I've seen what they can do."

"I'm not angry. I'm just wondering if Melissa would do something like that. There's no denying she hates the United Colonies. You'd think it would be easy to put myself in her clockworks. I mean, we're practically the same person, right?"

"With very different pasts," Gray said. "Nature versus nurture."

"I suppose. Regardless, it is hard to be objective. Anton, yes, if he had a chance. But Melissa? *Because* we're so close, I want to say, 'No way, that's simply unacceptable.' Because that's the way I feel about it, and I don't want to admit 'I' might do something so terrible." Her expression was troubled.

"There's something else," Gray said. "Before he died, Lynch was going through the station's records." Gray hesitated. He took her hand again, as if to keep her from running away. "He saw someone who looked just like you. If I did not know better, I would have thought it was you. Maybe nothing to do with what happened there. Maybe not Melissa, just a trick of the light or whatever." He was grasping for straws now and they both knew it.

She was very still. Gray stopped talking. They watched each other across the table. The conversation had changed the terms of their relationship. He could see that now, once the words were out. He wondered if this would be the end of it. Actually being with someone like Elise had always seemed improbable to him, too good to be true. Something precious and lovely that was doomed to die.

She broke the silence. "Before we go any further, there's something I need to know. Is that the only reason you're here, now? Because my family owns the Taproot?"

He shook his head. "Elise, ever since we met, you're the first thing I think about when I wake up, and you're the last thing I think about before I go to sleep. All I thought about this cruise was the last time we saw each other. How we spent the last trisol together. We never did get out for those flying lessons you promised."

At this she blushed, eyes downcast for a moment. They had spent the entire trisol in her bedroom. Flying lessons of a different sort, given Ceres' miniscule gravity.

"Please believe me, if nothing had happened on 55 Pandora, I'd still be right here, right now."

She studied his face as if it held a secret. "Kiss me."

"Right here?"

"Absolutely right here," she said.

Gray laughed, remembering the last time, when that had been his line. He leaned awkwardly across the corner of the table and kissed her. She tasted like red wine. She tasted like a whole world that he knew nothing about and wanted to spend the rest of his life exploring.

She pulled away slowly. "Sufficiently convincing. For now."

Gray felt like he was on the verge of a precipice from which there was no retreat. He was afraid because he wasn't afraid, because he wanted to jump. He had had many lovers, but he had never really been in love. But here he was, standing on the edge.

"When do you have to be back on Chaika?" she asked.

A smile tugged at the corner of his mouth for her adoption of the familiar Chaika over the formal *Tereshkova*. "A trisol, more or less. I don't know if I'll be able to get down here again before we go, Elise. It's going to be crazy, getting everything ready."

"Not a lot of time. For flying lessons. And saving the world."

"We'll have to make the most of it," Gray said.

She nodded soberly. "We're going to have to go down to the Taproot to check the hive, aren't we. Regardless of my being shut out."

"Yes. The sooner the better."

"Hence the cutlass?"

"Be prepared, is what they taught me in the Mars Scouts. Speaking of which..." He made sure no one was watching. Pulled the derringer out of his vest pocket. "Put this in your puffer. You may need it."

She looked horrified. "Is that a slug gun? Do you know how illegal that is here?"

"Legality is the least of our problems at this point. Still, best put it away."

She reluctantly fed the little weapon to her puffer. It distended obligingly but did little to conceal the angular shape. "Any special instructions?"

"Pull the trigger and it will go bang. But only twice. The rest you know: top of the head is best, else up through the roof of the mouth. But you might lose your hand that way."

"Got it. Listen, you made me promise to keep your secret. Now I need you to promise me something."

"All right," he said. The precipice loomed near. He could feel the gravity of the drop pulling at his heart.

"When we're done here... promise me you'll come back from this mission to Luna. Because I can't do this alone. It will tear my heart apart. To go up against my family, shitty as they are... it's hard, John. It's really hard."

It was more to ask than she knew. He had obligations to his ship, to the Space Force, to the United Colonies. His life was not his to give away. It was not his own. But still he gave it away, to her.

"I promise I'll come back to you," he said, and he meant it.

The rising sun turned her strange grey-green eyes gold. She held up her face to him, and again he tasted her sweet lips.

"About those flying lessons," Elise said. "The Taproot hive entrance is city center, directly beneath the old greenhouse. It's maybe a kilosec from here on the wing. On foot..." She shrugged.

"Yeah it took me quite a bit longer than that to get here on foot," Gray said. "Too bad I don't have wings."

"We can fix that."

Elise led him up a level to a small shop that fronted directly on the crater's rim wall. Judging by the bright signage and baseline floor staff, it catered to tourists. She waved off the attention of a very fit young man wearing tight shorts, a harness, and not much else.

"I don't know how she stays in business with this garbage," she said, tabbing through a rack of folded wings. "Ah, Vorteks. These will do."

'She' was the woman at the counter, a slender, feral version of Elise, all done up in black and silver. A tattoo of a ship tree started on her shoulder and wrapped down around well-defined biceps. Its upper branches held stars while skulls dangled from its roots. A very short skirt did nothing whatsoever to conceal a knee-length tail.

She gave Gray the once-over. "Ever flown before, spacer?"

"A torchship, most recently," Gray said. "Dinghies. Shuttles. Sturmoviks back on Mars."

"Yeah. None of those count," the shopkeeper said. "Flying on Ceres is all about fluid dynamics. The air density is near Earth-normal, and the local gravity is just enough to drive convection. This is real flying, not just pushing a Newtonian cannonball through the big empty. Bottom line: your experience 'flying' a torchship is more likely to get you into trouble than if you were a simple-minded tourist. This model has an autopilot that will try to keep you alive, but there is such a thing as being too stupid to live. Your well-being is your own lookout. Savvy?" She gave him a thumbs-up, the universal sign of contract.

Gray returned her thumbs-up for the obligatory photo. "Savvy."

She winked a picture for her records. "Thumbprint beside happy shining face, voice confirmation. Here's your wings and fins. Do you want an instructor?"

"I'll take care of that," Elise said, sweeping the gear into her arms.

"I bet you will," the shopkeeper said with a sly smile. "Have fun, sister."

Gray discharged the tab and followed Elise to the shop's back deck. Aside from a pair of hoops that would have looked at home at the edge of a swimming pool, the only thing between them and a twenty-meter drop was a low rail for clockworks.

"What was that about?" Gray asked with a nod towards the shop.

"Fiona? I've known her since we were kids. She's just being her usual nasty self. Not that she's wrong." She held out the fins. "These first. Don't extend them yet."

As if Gray had any idea how to do that. The fins were articulated like a Ceresean's foot. Long, webbed toes folded under the soles of his feet.

"And now the wings."

Gray stepped into the harness and fastened it at waist and sternum. Each wing had a claw-like handgrip at the apex of its leading edge. He wrapped his fingers around the grips and a bat-wing icon lit up in his spex. He blinked at it and was rewarded with a simple heads-up display with an outline of his body and the wings in yellow, versus an ideal configuration in blue.

He flexed the wings experimentally. Where yellow lines crossed blue, they turned green. He tried again, adjusting his posture until it was a solid green outline.

"That's your launch profile," Elise said. "You can select others by twisting the right-hand grip."

Gray cycled through them. Launch, climb, glide, descend, land.

"You've got it. Go back to launch." She led him to the rail that fronted the balcony. Gray was awkward in the folded fins. It felt like he was going to topple over.

"We're just going to climb out until we're clear of the rim wall. We'll get a little practice when we have some altitude to play with." She stepped between him and the edge, back to the open air, and held out her hands. "Ready?"

He waddled forward. She reached below the trailing edge of his wings and pulled him close. Her nipples were hard against his chest.

"I like this already," he said.

"We're just getting started." She leaned back, pulling him over the edge with her, and then pushed off, head tilted back to see where they were going, body arched against his.

"Keep your back straight," she said. "Level your wings. Use your feet like rudders, don't try to get any power out of them. All right, now switch to climb. That's it! I'm going to let go. Keep climbing. "

With that she fell away from him, and he was on his own. He rose towards the top of the dome in great sweeping strokes. It was glorious. He felt like a god. He glanced down to look for Elise, and in an instant was tumbling awkwardly through the air. Everything he did only seemed to make it worse.

Somewhere below him she called out "Fold your wings! And stop kicking!"

He complied, and a moment later she plucked him expertly out of the air, using the momentum of her approach to kill his tumble. They drifted to a halt at the apex of his climb. In the unexpected stillness, Elise nuzzled the hollow between his neck and shoulder. "You're kind of clumsy, but I like the way you smell."

She lifted her face to his and they kissed. Gray lost track of everything but the softness of her lips, the taste of her mouth. She folded her wings around him like a warm, soft blanket. He cupped her ass, pulling her hips against his. She rubbed herself against him. Then she pulled away with a small laugh.

"What?" he asked.

"We're falling."

"Is that a problem?" He kissed her cheeks, moved down to the inward curve between her jaw and her throat. Her eyes were closed, lips slightly parted. He loved the way her dark eyebrows rose like wings above the broad expanse of her eyelids.

"I'm told it can be fatal," she murmured. "Though not right away."

"That's good." He was working on the front of her dress, clumsy with the constraints of his folded wings.

She laughed again, a free delightful sound, and then unfolded her wings from around him and pushed away. "We have to climb! We're almost there."

Gray twisted the control grip and swept his wings like oars in time to the graphics painted by his spex. She backstroked beneath him, easily keeping pace with his clumsy efforts.

"Almost where?" he asked.

"Cloud base. Keep climbing." With that she backstroked up and against him, wrapping her legs around his and hooking her fingers under the front of his harness with her wings folded at her side.

"Level your wings," she cautioned as they began to slip to one side.

"This is not easy," Gray said, correcting the slip with a stroke of one wing. It was definitely not like flying a ship. And he was having difficulty focusing on the task at hand as she unbuttoned his shirt, kissing his chest, small hot touches.

Elise finished with his shirt and then reached down between his legs. "No, I'd say it's pretty hard."

Gray's breath came quickly. She undid the front of his trousers.

"What about other people?" Gray asked. No one was particularly near, but they were in the middle of the air above a city of fifty thousand people.

"That's why you have to keep climbing. We're almost at cloud base."

He risked a look down. The city below was softened by mist. Other flyers were indistinct, dark stick figures whose true forms were impossible to discern. The air was markedly cooler. Moisture began to condense on her hair, limned the soft fur on the edge of her wings.

"Do you want me?" she asked.

"More than anything."

She tugged her dress up around her waist and used her legs to pull him close, closing her eyes as he slid inside. He carefully folded his wings and pulled the front of her dress down. Her breasts were perfect round hemispheres in the miniscule gravity. The rhythm of her hips increased.

"We're falling," she breathed into his neck.

Gray opened his wings to regain lost altitude. Elise pulled him against her in time to his wing strokes. She reached her climax as the world dissolved into a pearly mist around them. Only then did Gray let himself follow her into whiteness.

15

Left Behind

The pchelan swarm receded into the black sky like a flurry of sparks rising from a fire. They left a burnt and pitted landscape behind. Pits marked where massive zhuks had burrowed into the icy crust and turned it into lancing beams of plasma. Crescent shaped burns showed where that plasma had burst through the purple canopy that had once protected the iceteroid from the harsh light of the sun.

For the simple intelligence that animated the ice tree, this destruction was painful but somehow expected. A necessary pain. Like some species of terrestrial pine trees, ice trees needed fire to propagate. But now that its seeds had been harvested and its foliage burned, the tree began to curl in upon itself, slow motion death throes powered by the energy stored in the tree's body. Carbon rich branches dragged across the surface, and below the surface, roots began to cut through the ice.

The sentinel watched the swarm recede from a rock-hard promontory of water ice that rose above remnants of dusky purple foliage. Her foveal rings dilated and contracted as she picked out each zhuk in turn. Eventually the swarm coalesced into a single fuzzy speck of light, then winked out. Departure burn completed, propellant depleted. On the way back to Deimos, with only a fraction of the precious volatiles they would have normally brought home.

It seemed likely that with them went her last hope of survival. The zhuks had not accelerated the iceteroid up to a speed that matched that of Mars, they had merely adjusted its course to match the queen's dictate. There would not be a gentle arrival, a harmless disintegration in the atmosphere. The planet rushed up on them and would consume them in due course.

She could not help but wonder if this had been the queen's intent all along. A way for her to remove the only witness to her conspiracy with the Queen of Pavonis. Gone in a blaze of light, a necessary sacrifice in the greater game.

The leaves below her shook as the sole remaining zhuk went about razing the ice tree. Left to its own, the tree would instinctively pulverize the iceteroid, its roots clenching like a hand with a thousand fingers, crushing frozen ammonia into chunks that would vaporize harmlessly when they entered the atmosphere of Mars.

That was the whole point of the mekosystem, so far as the sentinel understood its design. Her counterparts in the Arkipelago planted ice tree seeds on likely iceteroids, then decelerated them out of Jupiter's trojan point (and brought precious volatiles back to their hive). The iceteroids fell inward, their attendant ice trees providing shelter from the sun and growing new seeds along the way. Her hive rendezvoused with the iceteroid and kicked the ice tree's seeds onto a trajectory back to the Arkipelago. Then they accelerated the iceteroids onto a trajectory that caused them to burn up in the atmosphere (and brought back precious volatiles to the hive). Everybody won.

But not this time. This time, the swarm would return to the hive with empty tanks. The remaining zhuk would kill the ice tree before it could crush the iceteroid to harmless fragments. And then it would hit the surface of the planet with the energy of an atomic bomb. So the queen's will would be done.

16

Down by the River

Maggie took the truck east towards Capri Chasma. The road hugged the north side of the ridge. The river was below her to the left. The sun was behind her, well past its zenith. No one else was on the road this time of day; the long-haul freighters bound for Von Braun and Korolyov were already far to the east. The world rolled by in a lonely rush of marscrete and synlife brush.

It was a pretty afternoon. The river sparkled in its channel at the base of the bluffs on the other side of the river. Occasional meanders brought the water within a stone's throw of the road. Far ahead, Bingo Point was luminous in the afternoon light. The rocky promontory took its name from Mars Guard pilots flying Sturmoviks out of Thunderbird. When they reached the landmark, they had just enough propellant to return home.

For Maggie, heading east towards Bingo Point was like going back in time. This was the road she had taken – in the other direction – after her parents had been killed. She could still remember the face of the trucker who had tried to rape her. It was the first time she had pulled a gun on anyone. She sometimes regretted not pulling the trigger. He deserved it. He had no doubt gotten away with rape before. But she was just a kid; she had never killed anyone and still had not all these mears later. Guns were for dealing with mekanos and warbots, not people. But nothing stayed the same and that might change today.

She slowed as she approached the eighty-kilometer mark. There were no obvious pull-offs. She continued at reduced speed, looking around warily. It was a good place for an ambush; the ridge rose steeply on her right, and the canyon floor was far below on her left. All it would take was a small explosive to throw the truck over the edge. If by some miracle she survived the crash, Borodin would just smash her head in with a rock (tragic driving accident!) pick up the artifacts he cared about and call it a day's work.

Her goggles lit up with an incoming message. It was Ajax. She let the truck coast to a stop, which gave her time to think about her choices. Such as they were. The message icon kept blinking. She opened it up with a heavy sigh. It was a tagged picture of Eric, Borodin holding him up by one mekan arm.

Eric looked terrible, haggard and unshaven with a trail of dried blood below his nose, but he was clearly alive. Borodin looked massive in his trench coat. The bipe stood behind the pair, silhouetted against the river. The tag was just a kilometer away.

She put the truck back into gear. Around the next curve, the road descended steeply towards the river. She rode the brakes to keep her speed down. The road leveled off just above the flood plain. The river meandered within a couple hundred meters of the shoulder. Multiple braids split off, carving humped gravel banks out of grey hematite.

According to the picture's tag, she had arrived. She found a rutted track that disappeared over the left side of the roadbed. She slowed to a walking pace and followed the track through knots of synlife brush. The landscape opened onto a broad, rocky riverbed. Here the Marineris had flooded and meandered over the years, scouring the old wind-born sediment down to a layer of rough cobbles.

Down by the river was a small cairn of shattered black rock. Ajax was perched crookedly on top of the rock pile like a grave marker. The robot appeared intact if a little battered, but it did not respond to her presence. No one else was visible.

She turned the truck around and parked it facing back the way she had come. Then she took a deep breath. Not quite how she had imagined it.

She snugged her airscarf across her nose and mouth and got out, careful to conceal her revolver under her long coat. It was entirely possible Borodin was watching her through Ajax's cameras.

She looked over the little robot from a distance. It would be just Borodin's style to rig the pogo with explosives. She turned away. She could not afford to be sentimental.

There was a distant whine of electric motors, then the crunch of river cobbles under massive feet. The bipe came around a shoulder of rock fifty meters downstream. It walked daintily towards her like a giant mechanical bird. A Katyusha warbot followed behind. It was about the same height as the bipe but heavily armored, with missile tubes slung from each shoulder joint and a large-aperture laser in its turret-like head. Another fine product of the Kriegsfabriks.

"Well shit," Maggie said to herself. "I guess it's time for plan B."

The bipe stopped a few meters in front of her. Its cab swiveled and nodded down so that the survival rifle slung from its chin covered her. Tinted polycarbonate windows concealed whatever was inside.

"Hey Dusty," she said.

"Take your gun out and put it on the ground." Borodin's voice boomed over the bipe's external speakers.

"Gun? You said not to bring weapons."

"Take your coat off and turn around," Borodin said.

"Untint the cab and show me Eric," Maggie countered.

"Perhaps I was unclear..." Borodin started.

"Oh go frag yourself," Maggie said. "It is yet another cold day on Mars and I am not taking anything off, period. Show me Eric or the deal is off."

"Or the deal is off?" Borodin echoed incredulously. "What's to keep me from killing you where you stand, you stupid child?"

"Mostly that you don't have anything except my word that I brought your shit. Maybe I did, maybe I didn't. Maybe I uploaded the brainstone to a dropbox that goes public tomorrow. Because that's what a stupid child like me would do."

"Don't play games with me," Borodin warned.

"Show me Eric or pull the mekfucking trigger," Maggie said.

There was a silence that seemed to last forever. Then the cab's windows cleared. Borodin was in the driver's seat. Eric was strapped into the seat beside him. It was hard to tell through the distortion of the curved polycarbonate, but it looked like his hands were tied. He was not going to be much help.

"Your girlfriend has bigger balls than you do," Borodin commented. "Wag your head and show her you're still alive."

Eric nodded feebly.

"That's a good boy." Borodin turned back to Maggie. "Satisfied?"

"Good enough," Maggie said. "Come get your shit."

The bipe settled down on its haunches. Borodin looped an airscarf carelessly around Eric's face and hopped out. He had an antique bullpup shotgun that he carried one-handed like an oversized pistol. It looked authentic to Maggie, who had some experience in these things. If the weapon came over from Earth in the Exodus, it was worth a small fortune. Which would not surprise Maggie in the least. Borodin was the type to collect such things. He pointed the bullpup casually at Maggie's head. End-on, the weapon's muzzle looked enormous. Probably take her head right off. Which was the point, she supposed.

"You're kind of pissing me off," he said.

"Join the club." She jerked a thumb over her shoulder. "The warbot is under the tarp."

"And the brainstone?"

"That too." She took a certain spiteful delight in being one hundred percent truthful for a change.

Borodin flicked the business end of the bullpup in an unmistakable gesture.

Maggie loosed the load straps and pulled the tarp down like a blanket. Then she backed away from the truck, hands in the air. Borodin walked over to examine it.

Maggie activated her link to the Hund. "Wake up."

The Hund's armored eyelids flicked open with a satisfying snick. Borodin leapt back with a curse, but as fast as he was, the Hund was faster. A mechanical hand lashed out and clamped around Borodin's neck, catching him in midair.

Borodin jammed his bullpup against the Hund's arm and fired. The noise was shocking. There was a shower of sparks and Borodin fell free. The Hund's left arm ended in a ragged crescent. Borodin ripped the Hund's severed hand from his throat and cycled his weapon. The next blast of nanosaws took a bite out of the Hund's crest laser.

The Hund lunged forward and batted the bullpup from Borodin's hands. He stumbled backwards. The Hund pressed his attack, forcing him to retreat.

Maggie ran for the bipe. With one jump she gained the cab. Eric was wide-eyed and helpless. His hands were cuffed and cinched beneath the safety harness for good measure. His broken finger stuck out at a weird angle.

Maggie tried to start the bipe, but it did not respond to her voice.

"Borodin put Dusty under a geas," Eric said, voice muffled by his airscarf. "He will only obey him."

Maggie ducked beneath the dashboard. She had worked on the bipe enough to know her way around its wiring.

"We've got mantids inbound," Eric said.

"Good," Maggie said. She found the wiring harness that connected Dusty's neural network to his motor control and yanked it out. The bipe settled onto its haunches.

"What's good about it?"

"I tipped them off."

"That's a terrible idea!"

"It's plan B." She extricated herself from beneath the dashboard. A horde of mantids had surrounded the Katyusha. It stomped one and kicked another off its leg as it climbed up. The wide aperture laser in its head went off with a crack of superheated air, vaporizing one on the ground. Before the Katyusha could fire again, a mantid clamped itself over the front of its face. The next shot blew its optics out along with the mantid, leaving a gaping hole like a cyclops' eye socket. The mantid's legs – all that remained of it – were still latched to the Katyusha's head, which created a disturbing illusion of thick black eyelashes sagging shut.

Borodin had thrown off his coat and had all four arms in the air. Not a quad. The mantids flowed around him as they made for the bipe.

"Mekfucker!" Maggie swore. That was not part of plan B.

"Cut me loose," Eric said urgently.

She clawed her knife out of its belt sheath. Its chainblade whined wickedly as it sliced through Eric's safety harness and cuffs alike. Blood flowed where she had gone too deep and nicked his arm.

"Sorry! You drive. I'll deal with the mantids." Maggie twisted around in the seat and got her feet on the door frame. She flicked the revolver's iris open. The interface painted a reticle on her goggles. All eight chambers full, fat red dots for explosive rounds.

She thumbed the hammer back so she would not have to pull the trigger all the way through. Accuracy counted at this range. She centered the crosshairs on the head of the nearest oncoming mantid and squeezed the trigger. It broke cleanly in single action mode. The blast should have been deafening in the confined space of the bipe's cab, but it barely registered. The mantid went down, limbs thrashing.

She thumbed the hammer back again and picked another target, and another. Eight rounds, six kills: time to reload. She released the cylinder from the frame and dumped the empties on the floor. She fumbled in her pockets, came up with a handful of rounds. She forced herself to be methodical. Put in a cartridge, rotate the cylinder, do it again.

The bipe lurched off its haunches with Eric at the controls, and none too soon as the tide of mantids had reached them. They began to climb up the bipe's legs. Maggie leaned out and picked the leaders off. Others took their place. The revolver ran dry again. She pulled the door down with a pneumatic sigh.

"We've got to get out of here!" she said.

The bipe staggered through the milling crowd of mantids at its feet. "I can barely move. They are all over us."

A mantid climbed onto the cargo bed behind the cab and started clawing at the rear window. Maggie slapped the cylinder closed with a partial reload. She slid the window open and shot it point-blank in the face. It fell off but was quickly replaced by another. She shot it too, and then slammed the window shut.

"There are too many," she said. "I can't keep up."

There was an ear-splitting shriek outside. Something buffeted the bipe from above. There was a sound like a sheet of corrugated steel being torn in half, and then another shriek. It was the loudest noise Maggie had ever heard.

The mantids on top of the cab leapt away. A shadow flitted overhead. Rocket engines thundered as a Sturmovik braked and hovered nearby. The fighter had four engines underneath and one in the tail. The pilot rode in a skeletal chair up front, out in the open, protected only by a combat shell. He waved and Maggie waved back tentatively.

The Sturmovik spun around. The machine gun mounted on its belly swept the ground below, churning up dust and pieces of mantids.

"It's an old Sturmovik like your Dad's," Maggie said dazedly.

"Did you tell him I'd been taken?" Eric asked with an accusatory note.

"No, but maybe Zsu?" Despite being told not to. She was going to have to talk to that girl. Maggie laughed despite the desperate circumstances.

Enough mantids had fallen off that they could make way again. Eric swung the bipe around towards the track that led to the highway. The Hund fell back with them, keeping individual mantids from gaining purchase on the bipe. The Mars Guard Sturmovik hovered overhead, holding the greater horde at bay.

Then there was a piercing shriek as a surface to ground missile sliced across the sky. The Sturmovik rocked up on one stubby wing and the missile passed underneath it. It skewed to the side and then the aft engine cut in, pushing it into a banked turn that kept it ahead of the Katyusha's weapons arc.

"Work the rifle!" Eric said.

"How do you aim?"

He reached over to flick a toggle switch above the trigger button. A vivid green beam cut through the dust kicked up by the melee. Eric worked the bipe's controls, swinging the sighting beam up and across the torso of the Katyusha. It slid off again before Maggie could fire.

"Get back on it!" Maggie said.

The sighting beam swung back and forth like a pendulum.

"You have to take a shot," Eric said.

Maggie took a breath from old habit, held it, and pressed the trigger button on an inbound swing. A geyser of dirt and rocks erupted just in front of the Katyusha.

"Well shit," she said. "Did you fix the action?"

Eric shook his head.

"Don't hate me," she said. She leaned over and stabbed her knife through the cab's floor. Sparks flew up between them as she levered the chainblade through the floorboards. Her memory was true; immediately below the opening was the survival rifle's action. She reached through and worked the bolt up, back, and forward again. A massive slug slid into the chamber.

She sat back in her seat just in time to see the Katyusha fire another missile. It screamed overhead and flew right up one of the Sturmovik's engine bells. A concussion slammed down against them. The Sturmovik spun down out of the sky in pieces. One of them was a combat shell.

Eric froze. The Katyusha swung towards them, its rocket launcher tubes leveling until Maggie could see daylight through the empties. And not through the others.

"Wardamn it Eric, get the beam on the Katyusha!" Maggie screamed. "Fragging now!"

Eric snapped out of his fugue. The green dot of the bipe's aiming laser danced up onto the Katyusha's torso. Maggie jammed down on the firing button. The bipe rocked back on its heels from the recoil.

Maggie waited for the blinding flash of light that meant she was dead. The bipe rocked back onto its toes. The Katyusha was on its back, heels kicking spasmodically at the ground.

They did not have time to celebrate; Borodin was sprinting towards them. Eric tried to bring the sighting beam to bear but the bipe could not move anywhere near fast enough. The Hund was occupied fending off mantids.

Borodin disappeared beneath them. A moment later there was an explosion that sent bits of shrapnel whirring up through the hole Maggie had cut in the floor. Little streaks of blood appeared on Eric's forehead. The bipe teetered and began to fall.

Eric popped his door open and pulled himself through. Maggie scrambled after him and jumped. It was a rough landing. She got to her feet and found herself face to face with Borodin.

"I have had enough of you," he snarled, flicking his knife's chainblade to full extension.

Maggie leveled her revolver and pulled the trigger. The hammer clicked on a spent cartridge. Which just figured. Maggie was more disappointed than anything else. All the effort, and in the end she simply ran out of ammo. Classic.

Borodin smiled nastily and lunged at her. But then something strange hap-pened: his legs disappeared in a cloud of pink mist. Not a warsinger, then. Warsingers did not have blood. Physics being how it is, the rest of him fell at Maggie's feet. He looked surprised.

A more seasoned combat veteran like Gray would have carped the bloody diem and cut his throat to seal the deal, but Maggie had never killed anyone. It simply did not occur to her that someone might survive such a grievous injury. She looked around, mouth agape, trying to figure out what had happened. The Hund was ten meters away, struggling to cycle another round into Borodin's bullpup with one hand and not succeeding.

"Maggie!" Eric shrieked. A mantid had knocked him over and was snapping at his feet as he scooted backwards, kicking at its face. The mantid's mandibles closed on his foot. It shook savagely.

The Hund gave up on the bullpup and tossed it to Maggie. She snatched it out of the air and cycled the action. The blast knocked her down. She scrambled to her feet and ran over to Eric. The mantid was sparking and sizzling beside him. The section between its head and abdomen was mostly missing.

"Are you all right?" she asked inanely, given that the head was still firmly attached to Eric's foot via its mandibles.

"No?"

The Hund reached between them and pried the mandibles open with his remaining hand. Eric screamed, swore, kicked the mantid's head away with his good foot.

"We have to go," Maggie said. "Can you walk? The Sturmovik…"

"I'll manage," he said. Maggie helped him to his feet. He put weight on the injured foot and nearly collapsed. "Or not."

"We'll get you to the truck. Can you drive?"

"I think so."

The Hund reappeared. He had torn the survival rifle from the fallen bipe. He shifted it over to the crook of his bad arm and pulled Eric up. Maggie got under his other shoulder. They hobbled towards the truck.

"Spare goggles in the glove box," Maggie said as she slammed the door behind him.

The Sturmovik had fallen in the main channel. The current was slowly rolling it downstream, tearing it apart in the process. The combat shell had separated from the vehicle and come down on a gravel bar partway across the river. Maggie bounded over to it. The pilot was visible through the shell's diamondoid canopy.

The upper half of his face was obscured by a baroque pair of goggles, but she recognized Eric's father immediately by his great hooked nose and iron-grey mustache.

Blood spilled from the corner of his mouth and caught in the tangle of his beard. He blinked when he saw her. "Maggie May. Say. Hello world."

"Hang on Berel," Maggie said, "we'll get you out of there."

Words bubbled up through the blood in his mouth. "Say. Hello world."

She said hello world. He nodded minutely, satisfied. "Where is. Eric."

"He's on his way."

"Good."

"We've got to do this now, Berel." Maggie took a couple deep breaths, whipped her airscarf off, and popped the shell's canopy. She looped the airscarf around Berel's head and got her hands beneath his armpits. He grunted in pain as she wrenched his shoulders. She could not move him.

She shucked her coat and ran her hand down the inner surface of the shell. She hit something hard just below his right pectoral. It pressed up through his shirt. She pulled her hand out. It was covered in blood.

"Wardamn it," she said.

"How's he look?" Eric's voice came through her goggles.

"Better hurry," she replied. To the Hund: "Help me turn him."

Together they rolled the shell onto its side. Her hand left a bloody print on the armor where she had grabbed it.

A piece of shrapnel had punched through the back of the shell's ceramic armor like the blade of a broken knife. Cracks radiated away from the puncture. It must have gone all the way through him. She could not move it.

Maggie was getting light-headed. She hunkered down next to Berel and put the end of the airscarf over her mouth for a few breaths. The truck plowed up sheets of water as it raced across the shallow channel that separated it from the gravel bar.

She dropped the airscarf. "You've got a piece of shrapnel in your back, Berel. We're going to pull it out."

He shook his head minutely. "This. Has to stop. Our future. Our." He coughed bloodily. "Our future. Must be. Restored."

At the time, Maggie did not understand what he was getting at. There was no doubt in her mind Berel would die if they left him in the shell. At least if they got him out of it and into the truck he had a chance. It was only later that she realized he was not talking to her at all.

"Hund, I need your help." She took Berel's gauntleted hand in hers. He pulled her close with surprising strength.

"Bleeding. Out. Listen. Eric. My heir. Take goggles."

The warbot squatted down beside them.

"Pull that shrapnel out. Straight out. Don't rock it. Just straight out." She made a motion to illustrate what she wanted.

The warbot wrapped its massive hand around the shrapnel and pulled it straight out. The metal fragment shrieked against the shell's ceramic armor. Berel went limp.

"Shit!" Maggie got behind Berel and yanked him out, stumbling and nearly falling over as the unconscious man slipped out of the combat shell. He was covered in blood.

The truck pulled up beside them. Eric leaned across the cab and punched the passenger door open. Maggie swung Berel up against the door frame. Eric grabbed him and pulled him inside. Maggie's ears were ringing, and her vision was going. She could only see a small circle of light. She started to fall backwards but the Hund gave her a hard push. The door smacked shut behind her, but Maggie was somewhere else. The ringing had passed or turned into something more like bells, distant bells ringing on a hillside. And a warm breeze was lifting her up, until she was high above the river and the truck was just a speck. The horizon started to curve and then Berel was beside her, telling her not to be afraid, it was not her time.

Bitterly cold oxygen from the emergency tank flooded the cab and Maggie gasped raggedly and began to breathe again. The ringing in her ears was not bells and it diminished and turned into the sound of the fans and her vision came back. She was in the truck. Berel was slumped between her and Eric.

"How is he?" she asked blurrily. It was hard to make words.

"He's gone," Eric said. There was a wild look in his eyes. "He's just gone."

17

The Ouroboros

They spiraled down towards the crater floor through light rain. Gray reveled in the taste of it. A century and a half of iceteroid bombardment had warmed Mars enough to give it a basic hydrologic cycle, but you still needed a pressure suit, which made tasting things problematic. And the rain there was liberally mixed with ammonia which rendered it somewhere between piss and sweat. This was the real thing, water falling from the sky, sweet and pure.

Their destination was the city's original greenhouse, a structure that from this altitude looked like a golf ball sitting on its tee. An expanse of verdant parkland surrounded it, a mixture of old growth trees, shrubbery, and tall grass. A semicircular walking path had been cut into the undergrowth, and adjacent to it a cross. With a jolt of recognition Gray realized that it was the symbol for Ceres, just as he had seen etched into the rock outside the Anasazi restaurant. This time the greenhouse was cupped in the center of the scythe's blade.

Representing Earth? It seemed a stretch, just his imagination working overtime. Most likely a coincidence.

The golf ball became a geodesic sphere fifty meters across. An upper dome of diamondoid – apparently original construction – kept the rain out. The lower levels of the spherical structure were open to the air.

"You're aiming for that deck cantilevered out from the equator," Elise said. "Watch yourself; it can be slick."

With that she tucked her wings and swooped like a falcon. Gray took a deep breath and followed her. Descending was harder than climbing. It took a delicate touch to keep from tumbling. He held his arms tight against his ribs and used his fingertips to feather the air.

Elise landed gracefully on the deck, her wings cupping the air like spinnakers as she braked to a stop. Gray braked prematurely and found himself hanging in the air a couple meters above the deck. Elise pulled him down with a laugh. Then she patted him fondly on his chest.

"Look at you with your sword and your wings, and your shirt soaked through. I'm going to start calling you John Carter of Mars."

"That works for me, Dejah Thoris."

Elise clapped her hands in delight. "Ah, you know the classics! My mom – Melissa, I mean – read Burroughs to me when I was little."

"Burroughs was required reading for the Scouts, along with Heinlein and Rand. Though I could have done without Rand. Bit of a sociopath, that one."

"Rand is a Mars thing," Elise said. "That oner heritage from Earth never took root out here. Acting purely out of self-interest rarely results in the best outcome. Out here everyone knows you need a community to survive."

She led him to the edge of the mesh deck. They were about a hundred meters above the crater floor. It no longer seemed a long way down.

"This was the site of the first settlement," Elise said. "It is hard to imagine what it must have been like for my grandparths. An empty crater, open to the stars. Just a handful of other families with them."

"What brought them here?" Gray asked.

"Nitrogen, mostly," Elise said pragmatically. "And proximity to water. There's a cavern below us that exposes the Inner Sea. And the impactor that gouged out this crater was an ammonium-rich iceteroid. Carbon is common on Ceres, but nitrogen, not so much. You need both to grow plants. So, a big hole saturated with ammonia, perched less than a kilometer above the Inner Sea."

She told him how her grandparths sunk their hive into the center of the crater. The hive's drexlers sent struts and cabling for a tensegrity sphere back up to the surface, followed by countless stacks of mirror crabs. These simple mekanos had but one desire: to illuminate the diamondoid sphere that slowly rose from the crater floor. They scuttled from the hive's tunnels up the sides of the bowl. There they dug their iron-tipped claws into the crust and turned their highly polished carapaces towards the sun.

Meanwhile the hive had breached the Inner Sea. Its simple fission reactor turned the salty brine to steam, which condensed into pure, sweet water on its way up the taproot to the greenhouse. And so the greenhouse had become the emerald heart of a biomechanical flower five kilometers across.

But time and progress had marched on. Eventually the settlement's need for food and atmo exceeded the capacity of the greenhouse. The settlers threw a dome across the crater from rim to rim, and grew a tower to synchronous orbit, where even larger mirrors could harvest sunlight. Designed for life in hard vacuum, the mirror crabs slowly succumbed to the elements and became nothing more than rusty iron flagstones in the tiered gardens.

"When I was a girl," Elise said, "I found a mirror crab in an overhang that protected it from rainfall. It was barely alive but still trying to do its job. I polished it up and weather-proofed it. Can you imagine it? Me clinging to the rock face, refinishing a mirror crab?" She laughed at the memory, then pointed high up on the rim wall. "There. You can see it from here if you know where to look."

Gray sighted along her arm. A spark of sunlight flared at her fingertip. Her hair brushed his face.

"Most of my secrets are small," she said softly, her breath warm in his ear.

Footsteps broke the moment. Gray whirled to face them, hand going to his cutlass.

"No need for that, Lieutenant Gray," Anton Wilson said. He wore an elegant shirt with an open band collar paired with a short cloak. A gem gleamed at the hollow of his throat. He was flanked by a triad of mekans. Anton made a patting motion and they settled onto their haunches, mandibles retracting back against their triangular heads. Gray realized with a jolt that they looked just like the ones he had faced on the freighter at 55 Pandora.

"Those are Pandorans!" he hissed at Elise.

She gave him a puzzled look. "They're mantids. Like the one I showed you at the expo."

This was not reassuring to Gray. Quite the opposite. The Space Force had put a bid in for a sizable hatch of mantids. But if they were the same as Pandorans… he cursed himself for not making the connection before now. His only excuse was the same wretched line used by oppressors throughout history: they all looked the same to him.

Elise turned to Anton, who had observed their exchange with an enigmatic smile. "It's Commander, now," she corrected him.

Anton's eyebrow went up. "Commander! You're moving up in the world. Dating a Space Force Commander! To what do we owe the honor, Commander Gray? We don't get many spacers down here."

"We want to go down to the hive," Elise said.

"Not a good idea," Anton said.

"And why is that?" Gray asked, though he had a pretty good idea.

Anton looked him over. "What has my 'sister' told you about our little 'family'?"

"The basics. Your parents fought in the Resistance. Your father was killed, you and your mother imprisoned. You both hate the United Colonies. I shouldn't expect a warm welcome."

"To the point. I appreciate that, Commander."

"I want to see Melissa," Elise said.

"At least you're not calling her mother anymore. That was always embarrassing. I remember when you were a child and would say that. The expression on her face..."

"That's enough," Gray said flatly.

Anton's eyebrows shot up. He turned to Elise. "I kind of like this guy. Your standards are improving."

"You're either going to help, or you're going to get out of the way," Gray said. His hand was still on the pommel of his cutlass.

The mantids shifted restlessly, their mandibles opening forward and then clacking back against the sides of their heads.

"Is that an official statement, Commander? As an officer of the United Colonies?"

"It is a factual statement," Gray said. "I'm telling you what is going to happen. Take it as you like."

The silence stretched. Then a smile tugged at the corner of Anton's mouth. "You know Commander, I've changed my mind. I can see why Elise likes you. You are welcome to visit the Taproot any time."

"How about right now?" Gray asked.

"Now is always the best choice," Anton said. It seemed to Gray that he was laughing silently at something. "In fact, I'll go with you."

"That's not necessary," Gray said.

"Actually, it is, since I've shut Elise out," Anton said. He gestured at the entry to the greenhouse. "Shall we?"

The triad of mantids accompanied them to a freight elevator at the center of the greenhouse, heads weaving from side to side and mandibles clicking softly as they brushed through overhanging rhododendrons. Withered flowers fell to the deck and crumbled beneath their feet.

Two took up positions on either side of the elevator's door. The third rode down with them, ledeyes silvered. Gray placed himself so he could use Anton as a shield if need be. Buy a little time by shoving him into the mantid's jaws. It was a pleasing thought.

They debarked onto a broad balcony. Here a quirk of geology had created a vast cavern whose floor was somewhere beneath the surface of the Inner Sea. The balcony encircled a sort of artificial stalactite that hung from the cavern's roof. To Gray's eye it looked like an upside-down docking tower, broad at the base where it attached to the roof, tapering to a tip that pierced the surface of the inky black water below and left two enormous slow eddies in its wake. Below that, the blue glow of Cherenkov radiation where the docking hub would have been.

"Last stop for baselines," Anton said cheerfully.

"Everything below this is mekan territory," Elise explained. "Radiation hazard from the hive's reactor." She gestured at the blue glow.

Gray was not listening, at least not to her and Anton. His spex had gone entirely quiet. Nothing reached them from the city above. The constant ticking sound of *Tereshkova's* syslogs turning over, the ambient hum of the ship's communication channels, the rain-like patter of news articles of potential interest, all gone quiet.

The only sound was a distant white noise that must be water. It was something he had never heard before at any scale. A large park back home on Mars might feature a small stream, or more typically a Japanese garden with its intricate and intimate waterworks. This was something else entirely. A warm upwelling breeze bore a salty tang. Gray wondered if that was what Earth's oceans smelled like.

"It is more like a river than a sea," Elise said as if reading his mind. "The rotation of the planet causes a counter-rotational current. We call it the Ouroboros: the snake that eats itself. It goes all the way around Ceres, more or less beneath the equator. Most of the way without air pockets like this one. So don't fall in."

"Where's the hive?" he asked, mind returning to the business at hand.

"On the shore there." She pointed down at a veritable catacomb on the river-bank, where the water had carved out a broad bend before gathering speed and plunging through the exit. "We'll take a cable car the rest of the way down."

The cable car was a mechanical contraption parked at the top of one of several thick guy lines that splayed out from the balcony and stabilized the tower. It looked like a rusted circus cage hung upside-down by its wheels. Everything here was upside-down.

"Why not just fly down?" Gray asked. The thought of getting into a cage with the mantid was not appealing.

"Go ahead," Anton said, waving his hand over the rail and the slow-roiling water below. "It would be a great learning experience for you."

"Don't," Elise said quickly. "He's joking. Thermals from the reactor produce dangerous air currents. There are downdrafts that will take you right into the water."

"Some joke," Gray said.

"I would have laughed," Anton said. "But seeing that Elise saved you from being the punchline, you had best leave your wings here. If they get tangled in the wheels, it'll make a mess. Wouldn't want to upset my 'sister.' And you never know when you might need to use that sword, right?"

Anton kept one hand on the mantid's shoulder while Gray racked his wings and fins. He motioned Gray and Elise in, then joined them, pulling the door shut behind them. The cable car lurched into motion. The mantid watched the cage as it passed, ledeyes silvered, mandibles clacking softly.

The cable car shuddered to a halt at the end of the line. The shoreline was a jumble of slick black rocks leftover from when the cavern had eroded out of Ceres' crust. There was a short arc of beach where the eddy had worn the stones to fist-size cobbles.

The grillwork door gave a rusty squeal when Anton pushed it open. Gray following him out warily, craning his neck to keep an eye on the mantids who had come out of the tunnels to greet them. There was considerable diversity in size and shape, from minor workers the size of cats to a figure that towered over the rest. She was flanked by a couple triads of what could only be members of the soldier caste, nearly as large as her, with oversized mandibles and armored joints.

No other humans were in evidence.

"Ah, the welcoming committee," Anton said. "Allow me to introduce our new queen, Nyx."

"What happened to our old queen?"

Anton shrugged. "The usual." A gesture like something rolling off a table. "There can be only one and all that."

"To whom is she gene locked?"

"Not you," he said.

"I want to see Melissa," Elise said. "Now."

Comprehension dawned on Anton's face. "You think I killed her!" He laughed. "Melissa is very much alive. In fact she's on her way back from Luna now."

The retinue arrived. The mantid queen was huge. Gray guessed she massed at least 500 kilograms. His head only came up to her chest. Gems of various sizes and colors adorned her throat. A triad of minor workers followed behind her with baskets to catch mekova that dropped without apparent volition from her ovipositor. There was a faint chemical odor that he could not place. Sulfur?

Nyx raised her hand in greeting. Anton pressed his own hand against the feathery cilia. He motioned to Elise, who stepped forward hesitantly. The queen settled lower on her legs and raised her other hand.

"See, nothing to be concerned about," Anton told Elise, gesturing at the crowd gathering around them, reaching out with feathery hands. "They know you and I belong here. We have wings. Your Commander Gray, on the other hand..."

Gray had been cut off from the other two humans and was surrounded by a decidedly less welcoming group of mantids. Feathery cilia had transformed into articulated shears. Their heads weaved from side to side, mandibles clacking loudly as they extended and retracted. Gray whipped his cutlass out of its buckler, thumbing the safety off in the same motion. The chainblade emitted an evil whine like a captured hornet.

"Commander Gray does not have wings," Anton continued, watching the dance. "That's a trigger for them. Like how predators react when something runs away from them."

One of the mantids lunged at Gray. The chainblade left a trail of sparks where its nanosaws tore through the mantid's forearm. The injured creature scuttled backwards, and the circle widened as the group took stock of the threat.

"Melissa said it was a simple change," Anton said dispassionately. "Mekans have an aversion to harming quads. She inverted that, as Commander Gray found out, but added another that suppresses harming winged quads. The net is, our mantids are inclined to kill people like Gray, but Ceresians are quite safe."

"Bastard!" She took a step back and pulled the derringer from her puffer. "Tell her to call them off."

His gaze fixed on the weapon. "Is that a *gun*?"

"Now!" Elise said.

"I can't believe you would shoot your own brother."

"Weird that I'm not hearing the air quotes now," Elise said.

Anton shrugged. "But even if you do, it won't change his fate."

The mantids were distracted by the drama playing out in their midst. Gray for his part doubted that Elise would shoot Anton. Most people had an aversion to killing that had to be trained out of them. So when he realized that the mantids' attention was divided, he sprang, slashing downwards at the nearest mantid as it reared up at him. The cutlass took one arm and an elliptical slice of an eye. Drag torqued Gray around the point of impact. He tucked into the spin to speed it up.

Anton could have gotten out of the way, but he was fixated on the derringer. Gray snapped out of his spin and tackled him, sending them tumbling together on the rough cobbles. Gray came to his feet with the flat of his blade hard against Anton's throat.

"Keep thrashing and I'll take your head off," he said in the man's ear. Anton stopped, gasping for air. Elise joined them, and they walked awkwardly back-to-back to the cable car, surrounded by a crowd of agitated mantids. She shielded Gray with her wings as he dragged Anton in, then quickly followed and slammed the door behind them.

The cable car lurched into motion. A mantid leapt from the shore and latched onto the bottom of the cable car. It nipped at Gray through the grill work, leaving bright silver scars in the rusty metal. Elise leaned down and shot it in the head. The weapon's report was shockingly loud. The creature fell slowly to the water below.

"Thanks," Gray said.

That discouraged the others from doing the same, but several of them clambered onto the guy line behind and followed at a distance.

"What's in the bag?" Gray asked, pointing with his chin at a small bag at Elise's feet.

"Mekova. I snatched it from the minor workers in the confusion."

"Nice!"

"Not as nice as gems," she said. "Mekova are tricky to decompile. But it'll give us a start on figuring out the mantids."

"Anton has a gem on his throat," Gray said. "Like yours."

"Let me see it," Elise said.

Anton glared at her, chin lowered. Gray tapped his cutlass against the grillwork imperiously.

"Fine," Anton spat out. He bared his throat.

Elise sat back with a disappointed sigh. "It's just Melissa's sigil."

Gray raised his eyebrows.

"So the hive will obey him," she amplified.

"What's left of it," Anton said. "This one is mine."

By this time, they were more than halfway up the cable, and thinking they were going to get away with it. Then something in Elise's expression changed. She was facing uphill, so that Gray could keep an eye on their pursuit, which had apparently given up the chase.

He turned to follow her gaze. A mantid was on the cable about fifty meters ahead. She was probably the one they had left behind on the balcony. Gray was puzzled for a moment because it seemed unlikely it could stop their ascent. Then he realized that the mantid was sawing at the guy line with her mandibles. It was no wonder the pursuit had turned back to shore! They were meaning to cut the cable.

He turned back to Elise. "Do you know how to swim?"

"No."

"Me neither." Why would he? During the southern summer they were racing iceboats on the lake above Thunderbird Falls. Liquid water was something that happened inside, and it was for drinking.

"Guess I'll have to carry you."

The cable parted with a twang of doom. The ends went their separate ways, the upper one cleaving the mantid's head in half, the lower one impeded somewhat by the mass of the cable car. This was flung free in due course, hence to begin its long parabola down to the water.

Gray kicked the door open and flung Anton out. Much as he despised the man, he would not condemn him to drowning in a cage. Then he and Elise jumped. Their roles were reversed from their first flight together; now she was above and he was below, clinging to her and trying to stay out of the way as she battled the air currents. She might have been able to get to safety without Gray but not with him. Every time she opened her wings she was wrenched away from him. They were buffeted like an iceboat in a gale, skidding out of control.

"I'm going to let go," Gray said. "This isn't working. We're both going to go into the water."

"No," she said simply. "I told you I can't do this alone."

"You can get to the balcony, or at least to shore!"

She stopped trying to fly, just reached down and grabbed him by the arms. They fell together, face to face. "Don't you dare give up on me. We're in this together, all the way."

"I love you," he said.

They hit at an angle. One of her legs planed through the surface of the brine and she was wrenched over onto her face. Gray kept hold of one of her wrists, but she was being dragged away by the current as her wetted area increased. He pulled her around to him, inadvertently digging his shoulder in. Water began to creep up the angle of his collarbone.

Although he had very little practical experience with water in volume, like every other spacer he had extensive experience with small amounts of water in microgravity. And what that experience told him was that it was all about surface tension. Lacking gravity, what water wanted to do most was minimize its surface area. It liked to make blobs. In microgravity – and Ceres was closer to microgravity than to the familiar pull of Mars – the important thing was to not have your face be inside one of those blobs.

He pulled her face up out of the water. It was covered with a thick layer of fluid. She gasped for breath and aspirated briny water instead. She thrashed against him in panic. He felt his legs go under. He swept the water from her nose and mouth to clear her airway.

She coughed explosively, sucked more in on the inhale, a destructive chain reaction. He pushed her up as high out of the water as he could. The water crept up past his waist and enveloped his chest. She was wracked with spasms as her body expelled the brine.

By the time Elise recovered, Gray was almost entirely encapsulated. She wrapped her legs around him and struggled to free him from its grasp. The water accelerated as it neared the tunnel at the end of the cavern. Her wings caught the air like sails, twisting them around to face upstream. She beat at the air, each stroke lifting him a little farther out of the water. But it was too late. Before she could free him, they were swept through the arch of bedrock and into the darkness beyond.

18

Strange Attractors

The zhuk cut a path through the ice tree's branches with her mandibles, tossing severed limbs out of her way. A nimbus of debris formed around the iceteroid, no longer gravitationally bound to it, but on the same trajectory. Empty eye flowers tumbled haplessly through the void, their silver petals flashing in the sunlight. At least most of the seeds had been harvested before the swarm left. The remainder would burn up in the atmosphere with the rest of the debris while the body of the iceteroid plummeted to the surface.

The zhuk tried not to dwell on this ending. It felt wrong. It was wrong. But her instructions were clear.

For this she blamed the sentinel, for it was that bulging-eyed creature who claimed she had received the wisdom of the queen. It was the sentinel who decreed that she, a member of the zhuk caste, must stay behind on the iceteroid while the rest of her hatchmates returned to Deimos. It was the sentinel with her pathetic vestigial mandibles who insisted that she – who was charged with ensuring the survival of the ice trees! – was now required to kill this one.

So when the sentinel touched her flank with an unmistakable rasp, a complex vibration that spoke of need, the zhuk ignored it. It was too much; she had been given other tasks. She snipped off another branch and whirled it off into space, eye flower and all. What a terrible waste.

Another rasp. She whirled on the sentinel. The zhuk was the much larger of the two, her body designed to contain its own fission reactor as well as propellant tanks. But their heads were almost the same size, if differently proportioned. The zhuk had massive jaws, built for cutting and burrowing, and small eyes. The sentinel was the opposite, all eyes and a petite mouth that depended on others.

A casual observer would not have thought they were related. But they were both pchelans, product of the same queen, and now that commonality came into play.

The zhuk's mandibles retracted against the side of her head. Her ledeyes flashed. *What do you want?*

I need your heat, sister, the sentinel replied. *My kinos are depleted.*

I cannot help you with that and do the task you have set me at the same time.

Then the task must wait, the sentinel said. *I watch for word from the queen, releasing us from this death trap.*

It is too late for that, sister, the zhuk replied. The gravitational dance was nearly done. Mars loomed ever closer. *I don't have enough delta vee to return us to Deimos. There is no going home.*

I am only a messenger, sister! Perhaps She has another plan. Couldn't you boost us onto a trajectory that would take us back out to the Arkipelago? Her eyes flashed a trajectory plot, an ellipse that bridged the orbit of Mars and Jupiter. *At least we would be spared the fire.*

The zhuk had not considered that. The delta-vee required was significant and it would be a long trip. And she should have this creature attached to her the whole time, like a parasite leaching her heat. The fire might be better.

Your argument is not sound, the zhuk said. *If the queen has set us on this path, as you say, then I must finish killing the ice tree. Otherwise, all this was for nothing. The ice tree will fragment the iceteroid, and it will break up in the atmosphere, and our insane mission will fail.*

I do not want to die, sister. This insanity was not my fault.

Death is the fate of us all, sister, the zhuk said, with slightly less venom this time.

They regarded each other darkly. Then the zhuk went back to razing the ice tree to the ground.

The sentinel stood in silent thought, considering her plight. She was cold and hungry. She could feel her kinos winding down. She did not have much time left before she was immobilized. She searched out Deimos and found it near the limb of Mars, a dim echo of the larger crescent. No sentinel there, perched at the focus of her mirror, blinking out a message of relief or imminent rescue.

Debris eclipsed the little moon, a branch, an eye flower, its petals catching sunlight for a brief blazing moment before being lost to darkness. The petals formed a reflector that focused light on the "eye" of the seed head, giving the ice tree a rudimentary sort of vision. Or they had, before the swarm had blinded it. The sentinel felt a burst of pity for the poor thing. Blinded, burned, and now razed to the ground.

Again the blink of sunlight from the eye flower tumbling overhead. It was almost like it was trying to tell her something. Which was ridiculous, but still...

The idea came to her as an image, as they often did for her kind.

She found a tree branch whose eye flower had not been harvested. Its gaze was still fixed on the last visible position of the zhuk swarm, as if waiting for them to come back. The tricode woven into the seed head was compelling. A plea, a mantra, a ringing chant that would fill her mind if she allowed it.

She averted her gaze from the seed head and sheared the flower from its branch. Then she carried it to one of the pits excavated by the swarm. She anchored it into the conical pit with a few expectorations, taking care to orient its parabolic petals towards the sun. The swarm had canceled the rotation of the iceteroid before adjusting its trajectory, so she did not have to worry about constantly repointing the flower.

Once she had glued the eye flower in place, she carefully climbed over the lip of the petals into its center. The seed head was already getting hot. She wriggled head-first into the space beside it, so that the thermoelectric organ in her abdomen pressed against it. Heat began to flow through her. The radiators on her back opened of their own accord, creating an even greater temperature differential. She shuddered as charge flowed into her kinos like hot blood.

The zhuk found her there when she came to raze the last tree branch. Only the sentinel's abdomen was visible; the rest of her was nestled inside the eye flower. The seed head's tricode was brilliant in infrared, like an incandescent mani stone beckoning to her.

The zhuk stepped closer. The message in the tricode resonated in her mind like a song of many hands, like her triad partners were standing on either side of her, hands thrumming on her flanks, telling her to go. Just go. She reached out to the seed head, drew back. It was so hot! She reached out again, ignoring the pain in her hands as she twisted the seed head free of its stem. Its message could no longer be ignored. She would take it home.

19

Van Gogh Sky

Maggie's hand slid down the wall of the tent, breaking the body field network. On the other side she heard the Hund get up and walk away. It was starting to get light out. Eric was asleep beside her. His bad leg stuck out of the sleeping bag, dirty dressing stained black in the predawn light.

They had stopped to bury his father in a little orchard of stunted apple trees a few hours west of Tsiolkovsky. It had broken Eric's heart. Maggie could see that. But they could not risk taking the body back to his family.

The Hund dug the grave, scooping the loose soil with his remaining hand until it was too deep for him to reach in without toppling forward. Maggie dragged Berel's body into the pit while Eric looked on, braced by a makeshift crutch. He was wearing his father's goggles. His own dangled from his neck.

Maggie climbed out and stood beside Eric. She knew she should say something, but she could not find the words. Berel was a good man? Yes he was, and he was so much more than that. Now he could rest in peace? Well, now he was dead, actually. He was not resting, in peace or otherwise. And besides, he had been doing just fine before he had come to their rescue. It was not like death was some kind of improvement, and they were all looking forward to joining him in due course. Death was the mekfucking end. It was a terrible thing, and there was no making it right by saying some pretty words now that his corpse was lying on its back in a hole in the ground.

Eric threw a handful of dirt on his father's body. The grains trickled down his chest. He too was at a loss for words. Finally he just said, "I'm sorry, dad. I'm so sorry," and turned away so Maggie would not see his tears.

The Hund took over with mechanical efficiency, layering soil over the corpse until it disappeared as if it were sinking beneath a sea of sand. They drove the rest of the day, only stopping when it was too dark to see. Then she and the Hund set up camp while Eric waited in the cab of the truck.

It took both of them to get Eric into the tent. The burial had worn him out. The pain had worn him out. He was in bad shape: a crushed windpipe, a broken finger, a lacerated foot. Maggie shook her head. They were going to have to deal with all that in the morning. She was simply too cold and tired to do it now. She had to get some sleep.

But when she curled up in her sleeping bag, she couldn't turn her head off. All she could think of was Berel cold in the ground, his flesh waxy and hard to the touch. Her fault.

Eventually she had summoned the Hund, hoping Gray's memories would be a distraction. And they were, but not the right kind. The way he felt about Elise left her aching for someone who felt that way about her. She was tempted to crawl in next to Eric. A distraction from her distraction, flesh and blood, here and now. Not someone who had died before she was born. And she was so cold. But there were his injuries. And Zsuzsanna. So many reasons not to do the one thing that might have made her feel human again.

She gave up and extricated herself from her sleeping bag along with the ember she had brought in with her for warmth. She hung the ember from the Star of David cords overhead, then lit an oxygen candle and used its flame to heat some water for breakfast. Eric woke to the sound of her mashing half a c-bar into her cup. He unfolded himself carefully, keeping the injured leg on top.

Maggie made another cup for him. "We're going to have to stitch that up today, ace."

He took the steaming cup from her hand. "You think?"

She nodded more authoritatively than she felt. "Before we get going. We need to get you put back together. I can't do this by myself."

He took a few more bites and handed her his cup. He'd only eaten half of it. "Let's get it over with."

She got him positioned on his belly with his leg doubled back. The mantid's pincers had caught his foot and left a deep puncture on top and a jagged tear across the sole. She bent his toes gingerly, opening a gooey gap in the arch. She could see tendons moving inside. She lowered his heel and sluiced the wound out with drinking water, catching most of the effluent in her empty cup. It came out looking like a thin pink soup. Her breakfast shifted uneasily in her belly.

She snagged a bottle of pain block out of the med kit and sprayed it on, careful to keep the aerosol away from her face lest she join the comfortably numb. Then she sewed him up, one stitch at a time. It was slow work. She wished Alex was there; he was good at this kind of thing. She was better at fixing robots. People were wet and messy and they smelled bad.

The sun was well over the horizon before they were back on the road. Maggie was in a foul mood. Her head hurt from fatigue, and she had hoped to be on the road before dawn. Eric huddled against the passenger door, eyes dull with fever.

The Hund rode in the bed behind them. Maggie had strapped Berel's survival rifle to his damaged left arm. It was a good weapon. He liked the way the electron pump felt when he cycled it. It felt like a million tiny gears spinning smoothly. Not like his arm where Borodin had shot him. The metal there was sharp and scraped the muscle fibers beneath.

Maggie said she could fix that. He liked Maggie. He didn't have a choice, but he thought maybe he would like her anyway, if she lifted the geasa that clamped down on his mind. Or maybe he would kill her and Eric. It was hard to know because the geasa kept him from thinking about things like that. He worked the pump again, watching how the gauge crept higher with each stroke. He wished his laser worked. He liked the survival rifle, but he did not like having to depend on it. Maybe Maggie could fix that for him too.

He did not think he would kill her.

They reached the crash site that afternoon. Maggie parked where they had left the bipe, back when they had first found the wreck. She pulled down the earflaps of her insulated trapper's hat and buckled them under her chin.

"I wish you wouldn't do this alone," Eric said.

"I'll take the Hund with me," she said, trying to be nonchalant.

"My replacement," Eric said, with a grimace that might have started as a smile – the pain made it hard to tell. Was it a joke? Not knowing what to say, she said nothing.

"Why did we even come here?" Definitely not a smile now.

She sighed. "Sometimes there isn't fuck all choice about a thing, Eric. Sometimes you just have to do what needs to be done. We need the hyperdrive, if that's what it is. So here we are."

She took her revolver out and opened its cylinder. The last of her good seeker rounds gleamed between the dull grey casings of high-velocity penetrators. She snapped the cylinder closed and weighed the revolver in her hand. It felt good.

She held it out to him. "Hold onto this for me while I'm gone."

He waved it off. "I don't want your dad's gun."

"The truck is like a neon sign for anything that sees in infrared. I'll take Borodin's bullpup."

"It's the only piece left of him you've got."

"That's why I want you to have it." It was a struggle to get the words out. But she had to say it. "I'm the reason your dad is dead, Eric. I have to do something. This is what I can do."

Eric recoiled from the words. He looked down at the blanket they had used to cover the bloodstain. It had worked its way free of the crease between the seat cushions. He pulled it back into place. His mouth worked like he was chewing on a bitter rind.

"It's not your fault Maggie. If anybody got him killed it was me. If I hadn't let Borodin take me by surprise... It's killing me. It's just eating me up inside."

Maggie's face softened. "Just hold onto it. I don't want anything else to happen to you. You can give it back to me when we're through with this, if that's what you want."

He was rocking back and forth. A tear started down from one closed eye. He wiped it away savagely, took the revolver from her hand. "All right, go on then."

She stopped at the top of the dune. She folded her earflaps up and listened while the Hund waited silently behind her. Nothing but the wind. She waved the Hund up beside her and put her hand on his shoulder, establishing a secure body field network. "I don't suppose you have long wave radar? Something that can see beneath the surface?"

"Just infrared."

"Show me."

He tagged the dim trails of heat that wove around the wreckage. "Only small things."

"Small can still be bad," she said. "Dragon teeth, for instance."

But dragon teeth – active ones anyway – would have shown up as glowing pockets of light under the sand. Nanotechnology was not magic. It could not circumvent the laws of thermodynamics. It took a lot of power to convert sand and dirt into grimms, power provided by a miniscule seed of antimatter. And power inevitably meant waste heat. Inactive dragon teeth were another story, of course. They would look like any other rock, unless you happened to have an antimatter detector, which she did not.

"Listen, I want you to go down there. Shoot anything that moves. Go."

The Hund went. There was a sharp supersonic crack when he dispatched a sand crab with the literal mindedness of the geas, but no threats emerged. Maggie rose to her feet and followed his tracks down the face of the dune.

"We'll take the capsule off right here," Maggie said, pointing at the Canfield joint between the head of the wreck and its midsection. "I'd love to take the midsection too, but there is no way it will all fit on the truck."

"I'm not sure there's even room for the capsule." Eric hobbled over to the neck joint and sat down clumsily. He picked his injured foot up and carefully put his ankle on his bent knee. "At least not with the warbot and Dad's combat shell and the rest of the junk we brought."

"The Hund can walk if need be. Listen Eric, I've been thinking about this. The design of this thing is like an airplane, except it's built for four dimensions instead of three." She sat down beside him to sketch a diagram in the sand. "An airplane has a wing, which is basically a two-dimensional surface, right? But when you rotate that surface a little and push it forward, it lifts the airplane up into the third dimension. I think that's what we've got here, except the wing is a three-dimensional surface, and it lifts into the fourth dimension."

"As in hyperspace."

"As in," she agreed.

"So the vanes form some kind of hyperspatial wing?"

She nodded. "Yeah, the big ones did. The little ones up front that cup the capsule are its stabilizer. If you wiki 'airplane,' most of them had a wing, a vertical stabilizer, and a horizontal stabilizer. The early ones put the horizontal stabilizer up front."

"Like the Wright Flyer," Eric said, studying something in Berel's goggles. They looked odd on him, vaguely ostentatious, as if he were pretending to be someone he was not. He passed his viewpoint over to her.

"Yes! Like that."

"So how are we going to get an airplane – a hyperplane? – out of the equivalent of a horizontal stabilizer? Assuming we only take the capsule."

"A horizontal stabilizer is basically a little wing whose purpose is to balance the big one. So we make a smaller version of Gray's ship, where the nose section becomes the main wing, and the smaller pentachoron we tested back in the lab becomes the horizontal stabilizer, and then I guess we piece together shards to make three little vertical stabilizers."

Eric frowned at the sketch. "How would you power it? How would you launch it?"

A tide of despair washed over her. "I don't know, Eric. I don't have all the answers, I'm just making this up as I go along."

"All right, all right, don't give up. It's a good idea. Better than anything I've got. And if we can make it work, I can get it in front of nearly ten thousand followers. That ought to be worth something."

She brightened. "Thunderbird Falls is only a few hundred clicks farther up the canyon. There's an old Mars Guard base there, and shipyards too. Beg, borrow, or steal; there ought to be something we can use to boost it."

By nightfall they had detached the capsule and positioned it beside the truck where they could lift it onto the bed. Which was far enough for the night; she was so tired she could hardly keep her eyes focused. Eric was inside the truck, sitting with his back against the passenger door and his feet up on the bench seat. His eyes were closed, and his face was lined with pain.

Maggie knocked on the window and he swung his feet off the seat with a grimace. She got in quickly, venting a good portion of the cab's warm, oxygen-rich air to the indifferent night. Eric's airscarf tightened reflexively around his mouth and nose. Maggie hit the big repressurize button on the dashboard and twisted the heat all the way up.

"How you doing?" she asked, hands outstretched to capture the warm air coming out of the vents.

"We have any of that pain block left?" he asked by way of reply.

She got the spray bottle out of the med kit and shook it. "Not much. Probably ought to save it."

Eric did not say anything.

"Pretty bad, huh?"

He shrugged.

"Let's see it."

He lifted his injured leg with a grunt and settled it on Maggie's lap. She unwrapped the makeshift boot they had fashioned from a shirt and some tape. His foot was badly swollen. The dressing she had applied that morning pressed deeply into the distended flesh. The swelling continued up past his ankle.

Maggie unwound the inner bandage. The skin around the wound had turned white, and the stitches were nearly lost in the swelling.

"That can't be good," Eric observed.

Maggie's airscarf had loosened as the cab's oxygen content came up. She pulled it away from her nose and sniffed at one of the wet spots on the bandage. It had a definite odor.

"Give," Eric said. She passed the dressing over. He looked at the soaked area critically. "What's this black stuff? Like little flecks of rock or something."

"Carbon fiber, I'd guess."

"You think that got in under the bandage?"

"Seems unlikely."

His brow furrowed. "So it's coming out of the wound."

"Yeah." There were unpleasant implications about stuff coming out from inside his foot that she did not want to consider. She sprayed the rest of the pain block into the furrow between the stitches.

Eric slumped back against the passenger door. Presently he asked, "What do we have in the way of antibiotics?"

They did not have much in the way of antibiotics. The truck's first aid kit was stocked for trauma, not extended care. She smeared a topical cream onto the wounds and rebandaged them as well as she could.

"Listen," she said, "I don't think we should travel tonight."

"Well we shouldn't stay here," he said. His eyes were closed, and his face was pale. "It's too risky."

"You need food and rest, and so do I. I can't make food in here. Never mind sleeping." She made her mind up. "I'm going to set up the tent, and the Hund can keep watch. We'll leave first thing in the morning."

By the time she had made camp, Eric was shivering uncontrollably. She helped him across the short expanse to the tent and got him into his sleeping bag. He fluffed the hood up over his head and pulled the zipper all the way up.

She boiled a pot of water and cooked up some grechka someone had stashed in the driver's door panel. After that they had four more c-bars left in the glove box. It would not last long.

There was a cache seventy-odd kilometers up-canyon. It was not one of hers, but there was an unwritten code in the bush that you took what you needed to survive and gave back what you could. With any luck no one else in the vicinity had fallen on hard times since the last time she'd checked it.

She poked at the grechka with her spork. The grain was soft enough to eat. She shifted around next to Eric and spooned some into his mouth. He grimaced and turned his head away.

"It's hot," she said. "You need it."

"You have it," he said. "You're the one who is always cold. I'm not hungry."

She persuaded him to take a few more spoonfuls and then he would have no more of it. She wolfed the remainder down and followed it with a chaser of hot grechka-flavored water from the cook pot. She hunched forward and grabbed her knees and let her eyes close just for a minute. When she opened them again it was dark. Eric was practically invisible in his sleeping bag. She reached into the hood to make sure he was still breathing.

"Really cold," he said. She touched his forehead. It was cold and clammy. She unzipped the hood. He shivered convulsively.

Moving quickly before she could change her mind, she shucked her outer layers and crawled in with him, her chest to his back. It was a tight fit.

"Not quite like I imagined," he said through chattering teeth.

"No," she said.

After Eric stopped shivering, she got her clothes back on and zipped through the airlock. The stars were out in all their glory. She was glad to be outside. The night was like a salve. She felt torn open. And yet, the stars still shone down.

She slung the bullpup over her shoulder and walked up to where the Hund stood guard on the dune. She put her hand on his arm and looked through his eyes. The rippled darkness resolved into a sea of monochrome sand dunes. There were no signs of dragon teeth or anything else that might harm them.

"I have been here before," the Hund said.

Maggie nodded. "Yes, you have. Both of you."

"Both of us," the Hund said. "It is difficult to untangle." There was nothing but the wind for a few minutes as he thought about it. Then: "I tried to kill you."

"The old you did," she said. She rapped him lightly on the chest. "The old you. Not this you." She tapped the plate on his head behind which she had implanted the brainstone. "The new you."

"Old. New. I do not understand what is happening to me."

"You're waking up," Maggie said. The brainstone was beginning to integrate with the Hund's neural network. She felt sorry for him. In some sense the Hund had been a truly innocent creature.

The Hund looked down on the wreckage. "I think this was mine. My ship. *Sparrow*." But who was 'we'?

"*Sparrow*! What else do you remember about it?" She tried to keep the eagerness out of her voice.

The Hund did not reply. His gaze swept the wreck, trying to pull meaning from its shattered geometry. "I remember stalling out of hyperspace and Mars dead ahead. I remember being pursued. But I don't remember why."

"Hyperspace," she breathed. They were right! "Was it," she could barely make herself say it, so much rode on the words, "was it a starship?"

"Maybe? We called it a hyperglider. It depends on..." He shook his head in frustration as he searched for the right word and failed to find it.

"I might be able to help you remember," Maggie said. "Adjust the brainstone interface."

He did not like the sound of that. "I remember some things. I remember you said you could fix my arm." He held up the damaged limb, let it drop again.

She sighed as if someone had let the air out of her and replaced it with pure fatigue. "Does it hurt?"

The Hund considered. "This body is very low bandwidth. I can feel the rasp of metal against muscle ribbons. It is an unpleasant sensation. Like... noise. Sharp noise in my sensor net, that keeps me from thinking about other things. It might be what pain is, now."

"It might be," Maggie agreed. "Come on, my toolkit is in the truck."

They walked down the face of the dune together. Maggie held onto the Hund's hand so they could use his body field network. Her fingers wrapped around his massive thumb like a child's.

"What else do you feel?" she asked.

"The pressure of your hand. Its heat. Hunger! I think that is energy level."

"I'm hungry too," she said. "And cold." Always cold. Fragging Mars. Food would help with that. Perhaps tomorrow if they found the cache. If it was intact. If no one else had helped themselves to the supplies within. So many ifs.

The Hund stopped unexpectedly.

"What?" she asked, looking around in alarm. Had he seen something?

"I am not like you, am I? I am not human. This body is a machine. I am a weapon, not a person."

Maggie hesitated. She had never tried this hack before. She had heard about it being done in more controlled circumstances, as a sort of poor-man's resurrection technology, but she had no experience with it herself. And these were far from controlled circumstances.

The Hund was becoming agitated. He waved his gun arm at the wilderness around them. "What am I? Who am I?"

"Who do you think you are?" she asked, free hand dropping from the bullpup's shoulder strap to its pistol grip. When he did not reply, she tried a different tack: "Who do you want to be?"

The Hund's arm dropped to its side. "I want to be John Gray."

Her hand went back up to the strap, tugged it back into place. "Good," she said. "That's good."

The conversation continued while she took the survival rifle off his arm and set to work on a more permanent solution. The Hund hunkered beside her, connected to the truck by a power cable, and to her by her outstretched foot, which rested against his shin. It was like talking to a child, an extremely precocious child who was learning faster than any human child ever could.

He kept circling back to the question of identity, trying different angles. He knew he was not human, and he could not see how he ever would be. The more he understood what had happened, the clearer that became. He was an unholy conglomeration of parts, a record of a man's thoughts and memories and habits grafted onto the artiform brain of a killing machine and ruled over all by geasa crafted by this young woman beside him.

He could aspire to be John Gray, but he would never actually be him, because Gray was dead and turned to dust. And he was a mechanical thing, a construct that lived on electricity and could only be repaired, never healed, never whole. At best he was a derivative of the original John Gray, not even a copy, but a new thing that started where Gray had died, a tangent to the curve of his life. An extrapolated man.

Was it enough? Could he bear it? While Maggie hammered his armor into place around the survival rifle, he looked up at the stars. They were glorious, rendered by his night vision as starburst disks whose arms bent and whorled as he moved his head. The north rim of the Valles Marineris cut a definitive line of darkness through the Van Gogh sky.

He could not hear the hammer's blows, but he could feel them like a pulse through the pressure sensors on his shell. And that was as much as he would ever feel. Pressure and temperature, all that a warbot needed to make its way in the world. He would never again feel the wind on his face or a lover's touch.

His gaze sought out the Arkipelago. It was thirty degrees above the horizon, a muzzy cluster of torchlight. Elise was probably long dead, but even if she weren't, even if she had survived the war and the long mears after, she would never be able to accept him as he was now.

It was a terrible thing, cruel beyond words, to have woken to the world in this way, as some kind of mechanical monstrosity. And yet the world was still there. And so was he. He was as much alive as he ever would be. He could take that as a gift or throw it away as a curse. It was up to him.

Or was it? He picked up Borodin's bullpup from where Maggie had left it and placed its muzzle to his head. He decided that he did not want to pull the trigger. Maggie would not like that. She needed him. And he liked Maggie.

Maggie looked up from her work, concern pulling her eyebrows together. "What are you doing?"

"Nothing," he said. "Just checking." He put the bullpup down, some part of him wondering. Who decided that?

Phobos broke free of the western horizon and rose swiftly above the dunes. The rays that curled off its disk hid dark gleaming eyes in their whorls. Its silver light caught like liquid diamonds on the stream beside the truck. The diamonds became a school of fish that leapt and disappeared again beneath the surface.

The Hund looked away from the water. He did not think there were fish on Mars. At least not when he was flesh-and-blood alive. Who knew, anymore? His gaze settled on Maggie, who was watching him intently.

"You're not thinking about hurting yourself, are you?"

It was a long moment before he replied. "Will you ever remove the geasa?"

"Move your forefinger. The other one, the missing one."

He moved his missing forefinger. She isolated the muscle fiber and held it up for him to see. "I'm attaching this to the trigger. The rest I'll tie off for now."

"Will you?"

"When you earn my trust, I will." She finished her work. "There, try it out. Without shooting anything, please."

He used his good hand to clear the action, then gave the trigger an experimental click. Everything worked. The scraping sensation was gone.

"How can I earn your trust?"

"Well to start with, don't act like you're about to blow your head off. It freaks me out."

"Sometimes I am not sure why I do things."

"Yeah, well." Maggie barked a short, cynical laugh. "Welcome to club conscious."

She rose to her feet. Sparks danced in her vision as the blood stayed down where her knees had been. She steadied herself on his massive shoulder. "I've got to get back to the tent. Eric isn't doing well."

The Hund looked at her hand on his shoulder. The cyclopean eye reflected a distorted version of her face. "Eric is your friend."

"Yes, he is."

"Are you lovers?"

"What?" Maggie drew away as if she had touched a hot pan. "No." She realized she had broken contact and set her hand back on the cold metal greave that protected the Hund's shoulder joint. "No, we're not lovers."

The lens-studded head turned away. Phobos was considerably higher. There were no more moonfish in the water. "I miss Elise."

"Do you?"

There was no way to release the pain he felt. All living things love, Elise had said. The flower loves its seeds, the bee loves its brood. And all living things feel pain. The pain of a muscle rasping against a wound, the pain of never seeing someone again.

"When all this is over," he said, "I want to go look for her. Will you let me do that?"

"When all this is over," Maggie echoed. When all this is over, she almost said, we are all going to be dead.

He rose to his feet and took her hand, careful of her flesh and bone fragility. How long had the Hund lived before he took its body? Centuries?

"You do not think we can win this fight," he said.

"No, I guess I don't," she confessed. "At least it doesn't seem likely. There's just us now. Assuming the boys were smart enough to keep their heads down. Go to ground." She hoped so. She did not want their blood on her hands too.

He sought out the Arkipelago again. Somewhere in that skein of light...

"She might have survived," he said.

"She might have," Maggie agreed. "One of my regulars at the bar fought in the war. People can live a long time with a little luck and a lot of spin. If she didn't die in the fighting, she might still be alive."

"I need to know what happened to her," he said. "At the very least, I need to know. If she's still alive... you know what she is, don't you?"

"I know she's a hivemaster."

The lens-studded face turned to her. "Yes, a hivemaster. But do you know which hive she founded?"

20

Greenwich Salvage

The Ouroboros snaked westward beneath the city, pulled by Ceres' rotation but never quite keeping up with it. Elise and Gray were borne along by its relentless current. The tunnel walls had been worn smooth by the flow. The ceiling lowered down upon them, forcing Elise into the water with Gray.

"Cup your wings over your head!"

Elise was on the verge of panic. She did not understand what he wanted, was nearly past wanting to understand.

"Like a ball, cup them together with air inside! Quick now!"

Elise swept her arms together, trapping a bubble of air within. They were pushed under, scraping and bumping against the roof of the tunnel. Gray's face was covered by a layer of water. He blew an airway out with his last breath. Elise had tucked her head down between her biceps. They shared the precarious bubble of air she had created.

The water was stunningly cold and pitch black. He could not see a thing. He hung onto Elise as they were swept downstream. His feet quickly went numb, and he could only tell if they hit something by the jarring impulse up his leg. Then the roof of the tunnel lifted, and they broke free of the surface.

"We've got to get out," Gray gasped.

They fought their way to the shore. Neither could feel the ground beneath their feet. They shivered convulsively as they wiped themselves free of the glutinous brine. The air seemed even colder than the water.

"Any idea where we are?" he asked through chattering teeth.

"The river runs under the mekanopolis. The hive floated bulk materials down it when we were building the orbital tower." Her upraised face was dimly illuminated by light strips glued to the roof of the cavern. "This might be one of the staging areas."

"Is there a way out?"

She pointed at a darker arch of blackness a few meters off the floor. "Up there."

Elise launched herself towards the arch, a faltering leap as the water clung heavily to her wings. Gray stumbled after her, numb feet clumsy amongst the cobbles. He lunged at the darkness that framed Elise above him. She caught his hand and pulled him up over the rim.

They racquetballed up the steep, narrow passage. Here Gray had the advantage as Elise could not fly in the narrow confines and had lost her clockworks in the river. She had to rely purely on friction to propel herself up the steep, dark passageway.

Gray pulled ahead, then realizing he had done so, reversed his course and came back for her. Somewhere below he heard a clattering rasp. The mantids were following them.

"Go on!" Elise said. She was panting from exertion.

He grabbed her hand and pulled her up towards him, flattening out of the way to let her past. Behind her now, he pushed forward. The first time she careened off the rocky roof of the passage, but then she pulled her knees up and gave him something solid to push on. Thus they proceeded up the tunnel, until it finally disgorged them into a dimly-lit warehouse.

Bins of parts and supplies filled the racks around them. No one else was in sight, human or mantid. The only thing they could hear was their own hoarse breath as they tried to catch their wind.

And the clatter of carbon fiber legs in the tunnel behind them.

"Go," Elise said urgently. "Now! I'll hold them here until you're out of sight. They won't hurt me."

"I'm not leaving you," Gray said.

Teeth bared in a snarl, she launched herself back toward the portal. There she popped her wings and came to a stop, arms and legs starfished. The lead mantid ground to a halt at the sight of her, mandibles clacking and legs rasping at the stone for purchase.

Gray's eyes caught on a box at the portal's coaming. He yanked the metal cover open with a squeal of rust. The lead mantid lurched forward, knocking Elise aside. Gray slapped the oversized red button inside the control box. The big doors on either side of the portal hissed shut like scissors on the carapace of the mantid. Lightning flared at points on either side of its abdomen, points that grew to arcs and then a full ring around its abdomen, a wreath of lightning shedding white-hot thorns as the edges of the door cut deep into the mantid and then stopped, their circuitry destroyed by the massive surge of electricity pouring out of the mortally wounded creature.

Gray and Elise fled the warehouse leaving the dead mantid blocking the portal. No one in the corridors paid them heed, human or mekan. Gray became aware of the quiet ticking of *Tereshkova's* syslogs turning over. He had connectivity. He opened a window to local Space Control. The primus who picked up looked like she was fresh off the boat from the Joint Service Academy back on Mars.

"Primus, this is Commander Gray of *Tereshkova*. The Taproot hive has been subverted. Its mantids – clarify, its mekans – will kill baselines. Repeat, mekans from Taproot hive are hostile and will kill baselines. Strongly advise implementing isolation procedures."

The controller's eyebrows shot up. "Stand by Commander."

Her secondus came on, a raven-haired woman in a spotless white uniform. A double chevron framed the face of an owl on her insignia. "This is Greenwich Station. Is this some kind of prank?"

"This is no prank, Secondus," Gray said. "You need to isolate the station before it's too late. Hostile mekans are on the loose."

"Commander Gray, I must insist..."

Gray saw he would get nowhere with this person. Unlike her primus, she did not know when she was playing out of her league. "Get me Tectrix Potanin," he snapped, the habit of command driving his voice like a lash. "Now!"

Her image froze as she went to a different channel. There was a crash from the direction of the warehouse. Elise pointed down the corridor to the freight elevator. Gray nodded and they ran for it. Luck was with them; the freight elevator was only a level away. They summoned it and it decelerated into place, bobbing a little in the field. He and Elise swung inside and punched in their destination: Greenwich Station.

Tectrix Potanin appeared on his spex. Her hair was pulled back severely, and her grey eyes flashed with anger as she spoke. "Commander Gray, what is the meaning of this?"

"Tectrix, remember what happened on 55 Pandora? It has spread. I'm under the mekanopolis with Hivemaster Aberdeen. The Taproot has been subverted. We have contact with hostile mekans. You need to isolate the station and castoff all ships."

"Ares damn it. All right Commander, I'll take it from here."

"Ma'am, before you go, can I get an override on…" Gray checked the stenciled walls, "car seven? To the top."

Potanin looked to the side, then nodded. Pending stop requests that had illuminated the elevator's console went dark. "You better be right, son," she said, "or you will be in a world of hurt."

"If I'm right, we're all in a world of hurt already," Gray said.

The elevator's deceleration warning rang before they reached the midpoint of the beanstalk that connected Ceres to Greenwich Station. The elevator car swiveled around its pivot and braked to a halt with a kilometer to spare from the tip of the station-side tower.

"Please remain in your seats," the car said as Gray unfastened his seat belt. He checked the emergency locker. It contained an omnitool, a patch kit in case the car was holed, a backup battery, a bottle of oxygen, and a stack of flattened emergency suits. He released the strap on these and shook one out. It was a self-inflating ball just big enough to hold a person if they wrapped their arms around their knees.

"This is not helpful," Gray said. He had imagined climbing the remaining distance to the station, but that required hands. It was not going to happen from the inside of a rescue ball.

He checked if he still had connectivity. The controllers had not shut that down at least! He put a call through to *Tereshkova*. Kasahara picked up.

"Bits, I need a pickup," Gray said without preamble. "I'm stuck in car seven, about a klick out from the station."

There was a pause, then: "No can do sir, we're casting off for maneuvers."

"Maneuvers? What kind of maneuvers?"

"We're standing off for a firing solution on the beanstalk, just in case we need to cut Greenwich free and follow protocol."

"Protocol? On Meridian? There are fifty thousand people down there!"

"You should be all right where you are; the cut will be lower down. I've got to go, good luck sir!"

"Bits!"

The connection dropped.

"Ares damn it!" Gray pulled the oxygen tank from the locker and cast about for a way to attach it to the rescue ball. "You ever use one of these? I think we can rig this tank as a rocket motor. We don't need much, just enough to get to the base of the tower."

"That won't be necessary," Elise said. Something in her voice made Gray look up. An enormous zhuk floated outside the elevator car. Elise made a gesture with her hands, as if she were measuring something.

The zhuk's arms reached out and she grappled the car. Her four legs locked onto the beanstalk. She twisted the car the opposite direction from which it normally pivoted. When the car reached ninety degrees it disengaged smoothly from the beanstalk. The lights flickered and then the emergency battery kicked in.

The zhuk fired the arcjet on her back. They drifted up towards Greenwich Station.

Gray's expression darkened as he caught sight of the forward pier. The Space Force ships that had been docked there had cast off. Arcjets flared as they maneuvered into a position ahead of the station in its orbit. He spotted the UCM torchships *Tereshkova* and *Glenn*, and three fission-powered destroyers armed with nuclear salt-water missiles. The destroyers took up flanking positions in a loose triangle around the torchships.

There was a glint of specular light as the torchships' laserscopes came to bear.

"Cover your eyes," Gray said.

"What?"

A spot on the cable halfway just past the tip of the station-side tower had begun to glow. Gray clapped his hand over Elise's eyes. In another moment it flared like the carbon arc of a spotlight. He could see the spot through his eyelids, like an afterglow of looking at the sun. When he could see clearly again there was a gap where the cable had been. Large enough to drive one of the destroyers through and getting larger by the moment.

He tried to work the math out in his head. The station was part of a big string of stuff reaching from the surface of Ceres up through Greenwich and on out to the counterweight of the torch. The pieces hanging below the new center of gravity would want to move faster, because they were in a lower orbit. And the torch would fall behind, moving slower in its higher orbit.

"I think I can see the piers starting to flex," Elise said. She turned to him. "The whole thing is going to ball up, isn't it?"

He nodded grimly. "Looks that way. How many people are onboard?"

"Maybe a thousand, at any given point in time."

There was a puff of air from the juncture of the forward pier as the pressurized corridor leading out to the docks buckled. The same thing happened to the aft as well. They could not see exactly what was going on with the fusion torch, as it was eclipsed by the main body of the station. But the ambient light that escaped its mirrors flickered on the collapsing piers and went out.

Gray had never felt more helpless in his life. Even if he were on *Tereshkova*, there was precious little they could have done. The torchship might have enough impulse to boost the station's orbit, or at least both torchships combined, but there was no means for them to do so without wrecking themselves in the process. The tug they had taken as a prize might have been able to do it, but sometime while they were on the mission to Pandora, it had shipped out. He had no levers left to pull.

He turned to Elise, an idea forming in his mind. He might not have any levers left to pull, but Elise did. She had proven it already.

"How many of these things do you have at your disposal?" he asked, waving at the zhuk outside the diamondoid capsule's walls.

"I don't know exactly. A few hundred?"

"Can you control them en masse?"

"After a fashion. Not from here. Why, what are you thinking?"

"Maybe we can use them to boost the station. If we can get it into a higher orbit, we might be able to save it. Do you have any details on them? Specific impulse, propellant capacity, that kind of thing?"

"Hang on." Elise tracked down the zhuk's specifics and passed them to Gray.

He ran some simulations on his spex, based on what he knew about the station. Nodded slowly. "It's worth a shot."

She frowned. "I'm going to need more bandwidth."

The zhuk brought the elevator car to the maintenance depot. It carefully mated the car with a docking port. Then it drifted over to a refueling nozzle.

"Where do you have to be to control them?" Gray asked.

"Inside a hybrid would be best. That way we can leverage their native communications."

"Inside?" He did not like the sound of that.

"Come on, I saw one docked down this way."

The hybrid zhuk had a human-sized cavity molded into its braincase. They climbed in through a hatch in the back of its head. Like the elevator car, there was no airlock. Just the single hatch between them and hard vacuum. Gray felt naked without his skinsuit, and somehow dirty, as if he were a parasite worming its way into a host.

The cavity was only slightly less claustrophobic than a combat shell. It had been fitted a pair of seats and a control console attached to the wall. His spex were unable to negotiate a connection. He focused on the view afforded by the cavity's circlet of small windows.

"This really gets to you, doesn't it?" Elise said.

"How can you tell?"

"Fear has a smell," she said.

"Ah. Sorry. Ever since I got shot in the back..."

"I remember that story. Nearly cooked in your own juices."

"Yeah. Kind of turned into a phobia since then."

"Well this time you're not alone, okay? I'm right here." She gave his hand a squeeze.

Under Elise's direction, most of the station's zhuks were vectored to positions on the trailing hemisphere of the station. Two were sent to the dorsal counter-weight beanstalk to pull the torch in and help trim the center of gravity. Their hybrid went to the ventral beanstalk, directly above Meridian. She settled into position at the base of the inverted tower where the tether had been attached. Her role was to push against the rotation that had already been established.

"I guess this is it," Elise said. She pushed her spex up onto her forehead. "Kiss me for luck?"

Gray leaned across the armrest. After a moment she pulled back with a sigh. Dropped her spex back into place, all business. They glimmered with data as she pushed final instructions into the mesh network that connected the zhuks. There was an audible bang, like a door slamming somewhere behind them, as their own zhuk's arcjet ignited. The propellant gauge began to drop.

"What are our refueling options?" Gray shouted over the scream of the arcjet.

"Run them dry and if that's not enough, walk them back to the nearest depot."

Gray studied the readouts. "Best fly them back. Time is not on our side."

"You're the pilot."

They refueled twice. It was sweltering hot inside the zhuk. Gray's shirt was soaked with sweat. He was desperately thirsty. Whoever had fitted out the cavity had not thought much about heat rejection. Or hydration for that matter.

The arcjet cut off for the last time. They had run dry. The silence seemed strange. Gray studied the displays. "I think that did it."

Elise gave him a weak smile. Strands of dark hair were plastered to her face. "Unsung heroes."

"That could change."

She raised her eyebrows.

"Once they cut the beanstalk, the station was adrift and in peril. You saved it."

"We saved it."

"You saved it," Gray continued firmly. "And you presently control its trajectory, by virtue of controlling the zhuks. That means you can claim salvage."

"Why me? Why not us?"

He tapped his spex in warning. At some point there would be a reckoning. Whatever his spex recorded could be used as evidence. "Not *us* because at no point was *I* in control of the salvage operation. That makes *you* the equivalent of the captain."

Her eyes narrowed. "Captain of what? Greenwich Station? What am I going to do with a space station?"

"You want to go back down there?" Gray gestured at the city overhead, an emerald-green circle beside the mekanopolis. "I do not think things are going to go well. Odds are good that Anton's mantids are slaughtering every baseline they come across. I would not be surprised if Space Control orders us to crack Meridian open and sterilize the Taproot hive."

He let her think about that. She clearly did not like the prospects.

"So as I see it you're going to have to make a choice." He ticked the points off as he saw them: "Align yourself with Anton, which would be an act of treason against the United Colonies. Or throw yourself on the mercy of the United Colonies and let them decide what to do with you. Or assert your salvage rights and set your own course."

"You'll help me?"

"As much as I can without violating my oath to the United Colonies." Which was why she had to be the one to take control.

"And what is your oath, exactly?"

"Fair question. As a member of the Space Force, I am subject to the chain of command within the limits of the Constitution. As an officer, I must serve and protect the interests of the United Colonies of Mars. Which still includes Ceres, and by extension, Greenwich Station. And in my judgement, saving as much as possible of Greenwich is in the best interests of the Colonies."

Elise looked up at the station looming near. She touched the queen's mekovum embedded in her throat as if seeking reassurance. "Not the best circumstances to bring Rhea into the world, but it will have to do."

"Will you swarm then?"

"I will," she said, making up her mind. "Do you think the zhuks can produce enough delta-vee to get Greenwich to the Arkipelago?"

"We may need a bit more ice for reaction mass, but other than that..."

"One problem at a time," Elise said. "Are you with me, Commander Gray?"

"Within the limits of my oath, Hivemaster Aberdeen."

"Then tell me, how does one claim a derelict space station as salvage?"

Gray left Elise on the hybrid zhuk and made his way through the station to Space Control's field parliament at the base of the leading pier. The air was thick with blood and smoke. Decapitated baselines drifted through the corridors and fetched up against air handlers. Burnt out mantids bore mute witness to a pitched battle. The stench made his eyes water.

The hatch was emblazoned with the outline of a snowy owl. Its great eyes seemed to follow Gray as he approached; Athena mutely watching bloody Ares in his element.

A Space Force rating in a combat shell saluted with his laser arm and let him through the door. Several Space Control officers were inside. He recognized Tectrix Potanin, and surprisingly, Lynch's date from the expo. Primus Petrova, if he recalled correctly. It all seemed so long ago.

The others were unfamiliar. One wore dress whites blotched with dried blood. Presumably not her own, as she had no visible injuries. A Space Control secondus, by her insignia, an owl's head above a double chevron. Gray realized with a start it was the controller whom he had snapped at. Evidently she had received her briefing on mantids the hard way.

The other was a neuter, probably the youngest son of an ergocrat not quite wealthy enough to buy him a commission in the Space Force. His smooth face bore no trace of the conflict that had wracked the station.

The captains of *Glenn* and *Tereshkova* were present via holocaster. Captain Brandenburg's facemask was cocked up at a jaunty angle, but he looked worried. Rashnikov had bags under his eyes and stubbled cheeks. His facemask hung from his neck by a strap. He ran his hand through his stiff white hair, standing it up around the crest of his moravec.

Gray anchored himself to the coaming and saluted. Potanin waved him inside impatiently and resumed the conversation his arrival had interrupted.

"Hivemaster Aberdeen has no authority here."

"She has physical control of the station," Captain Rashnikov pointed out. "Her claim to salvage is legitimate. As she said, it was adrift and in peril. She did save it."

Potanin's look could have curdled milk. She turned to Gray. "Commander Gray, what is your relationship with this woman, this Elise Aberdeen?"

Gray glanced at Rashnikov, who shrugged. "We are involved, ma'am."

"You are involved. Meaning you are lovers?"

"Yes ma'am," Gray said.

"Then you are compromised.'

"I am loyal to the United Colonies, ma'am. Nothing I have done has betrayed my oath."

"And yet you assisted the enemy."

Gray flushed. "With all due respect ma'am, that is not true. The Taproot's hivemaster is Melissa Wilson. She and her son Anton subverted it. Elise had nothing to do with it. That's why she swarmed!"

"Anton is the brother," the secondus supplied.

"I know who he is," Potanin said. "And that just makes it worse."

Rashnikov broke in. "Tectrix, I must point out that it was Commander Gray who brought this matter to your attention. If he had not reported the subversion of the Taproot hive when he did, the station would have been completely overrun. Calling his loyalty into question is unwarranted and unbecoming of an officer."

She turned on him with naked rage on her face. "Have you seen what happened here? Do you know how many of my staff died?"

"Make no mistake, you would have all died if it were not for Commander Gray," Rashnikov said. "Every single one of you."

"This station is under my control!" Potanin exploded. "I will not surrender it to some upstart vamp."

The room was quiet.

"What is the status of the evacuation?" Captain Brandenburg asked into the silence.

The woman with the bloodstained uniform answered. "Most civilian baselines have transferred to the passenger torchship *Hephaestus*. About half the Ceresians onboard have requested transport back down to Ceres. We're working on a way to get them to a safe location on the surface. Safe for us, specifically."

"And the other half?"

"They want to go with Hivemaster Aberdeen."

"This station is not going anywhere," Potanin said. "Especially with her."

The Space Force captains exchanged glances. Rashnikov cleared his throat. "Physics beg to differ, Tectrix. The station is in fact going somewhere. The only question is where and for how long."

"What if I ordered you to shoot them off the station's hull?"

"The zhuks? Well, you'd still be leaving Ceres. But odds are good you would not reach a point of refuge."

"Then dock and use your ships to put us back into orbit around Ceres. And don't tell me it can't be done! I've seen the numbers. You've got the delta-vee."

"We do," Rashnikov acknowledged. "But not enough for that and to rendezvous with the task force that is on its way to Luna. You know our orders from Parliament. The United Colonies cannot afford to lose the Lunar mines. No helium-3, no Space Force, no interplanetary commerce, no Martian civilization as we know it. Ceres is going to have to wait."

"So you're just going to leave us here," she said.

"Whether or not you stay here is your decision, Tectrix, not mine. My orders are from your superiors, and they do not provide any latitude for substantive assistance to Greenwich Station." He chose his next words carefully. "If you were to ask my advice, I would recommend taking passage in *Hephaestus*. But that, of course, is up to you."

21

Terminal Velocity

The sentinel dreamed of being back on Deimos, suspended at the focal point of her mirror. She swung it towards the iceteroid the swarm had positioned in front of Mars. One of her sisters had been left behind there, and she needed to talk to them. She had an idea that might help. But every time she got the iceteroid into focus, something rattled the scaffolding that supported the mirror, and she lost it again. It was immensely frustrating and now she was cold and hungry and running out of time.

It was probably that pesky zhuk who had tried to take her away. The sentinel abandoned her control yoke with a symbolic snap of her mandibles, and in so doing woke herself from the dream. She was cold and hungry. The seed head was gone, and with it the delicious heat that had flooded her body. The sentinel backed out of the flower, ledeyes blazing in indignation. No one was there to receive her wrath.

Up in the sky an actinic spark of light was receding from the iceteroid. She had a moment of cognitive dissonance. If someone was coming to the rescue, the spark would be moving the other direction, wouldn't it? Like a figure-ground reversal that suddenly snapped back to normal, she realized it had to be the zhuk, boosting onto a trajectory that would take her out to the Arkipelago. Leaving her behind.

She was alone. As part of a eusocial species, her caste was already an outlier for its ability to tolerate isolation. She could happily spend her spin up on a watchtower, never feeling the touch of a sister until she came down to seek the communal heat of the hive's reactor pile. But this was a whole other level. She was alone. For the rest of whatever remained of her life, she would never feel the touch of another.

This was the fate to which her queen had consigned her. And for what? For being the messenger. For doing her job. For doing the right thing, for doing the thing she was literally designed to do, she had been sentenced to die, by fire, alone.

For the first time in her life, she felt true rage. She had been angry before – when the zhuk had taken her from her watchtower on Deimos! – but she had never felt anything like the irrational surge of rage that boiled through her now. She could feel it like a pressure in her carbon fiber skull, a hot, rising tide that threatened to overflow the careful weighting of her neural networks.

Like all mekans, her core behaviors, the fundamental aversions and attractions that she could no more control than a cockroach could control its fear of light or a moth its love of it, were hardwired. She was literally incapable of deliberately harming a quad. But on top of that hardwired neurology were layers and layers of neural networks that were plastic by design. She was after all a sentient creature that learned from her experience.

And now as rage at her fate boiled through her, this very plasticity came into play. What had been love became hate, a surprisingly easy flip. She loved the queen; she hated the queen. She hated what she had been told to do, and she hated herself for doing it. And she would no longer be part of it. She would not just die because that was what was expected of her.

She had had an idea, in the dream. It seemed improbable, now, but it was all she had. She set to work gathering severed branches. Most of these were drifting along with the iceteroid. She expended precious propellant – her tanks were nowhere near as large as a zhuk's – and then precious spin, refilling them from ice she first crushed and then melted. But her efforts resulted in a birds-nest of carbon-rich branches trailing along behind the iceteroid.

Mars loomed ever nearer. The sentinel took one last trip down to the iceteroid and replenished her propellant as much as she dared, given the state of her kinos. Then back up to the nest-like structure. She busied herself weaving the branches together, securing them here and there with a dob of expectorant. When the nest was as compact and tight as she could get it, she rigged a control yoke at the center of its bowl, much like the one she used to control her mirror back home.

Then it was time to wait.

The iceteroid entered the atmosphere just south of its highest volcano. Vortices curled around it, jostling the nest. The sentinel worked the yoke, trying to find the right balance to keep the nest centered behind the iceteroid. A plasma sheath began to form, licks of ionized gas flickering past her. The nest wobbled back and forth, only marginally under her control.

The colorful streams became a solid wall of fire all around the sentinel. To go through that fire was to die. But following the iceteroid all the way down was an even surer death. She played with the edges of the slipstream, letting it kick the nest back away from the fireball the iceteroid had become.

The edges of the nest glowed red, then white hot as she oscillated back and forth through the center of the contrail. Then abruptly the nest was caught in a gust and slammed violently backwards. The sentinel lost her grip on the yoke and fell to the bottom of the bowl. Heat surged through her body. She clawed at the yoke, trying to regain control as the bowl arced through the atmosphere.

22

A Clap of Thunder

Maggie had been cold all night long. She had given her ember to Eric to keep him warm. She had been too tired to search for the other. She hunched in a fetal curl in her sleeping bag, shoulders up around her ears, hands tucked into her armpits. It felt like she had not slept at all, but she must have, because it was getting light outside.

Eric stirred beside her, grunting in pain. She forced herself to sit up. Cold air rushed in through the neck of her sleeping bag.

They had four c-bars left at three hundred sixty calories each. She tried to remember the recommended daily amount. Twenty-four hundred, for an adult? Something like that. Her goggles could tell her, of course, but she did not need any more bad news.

The other ember was sitting on top of the gear pile, right where she had left it, no doubt. She opened it to full, then filled her cup and set it on top. Only then did she extract herself from the bag to don her outer layers. They had frozen to the cords that crisscrossed the tent. She peeled them free and forced them on. By the time she was dressed she was shivering again.

The cup was steaming. She crumbled one c-bar for the two of them into the steaming water. She had been wanting to lose some weight anyway.

She reached over and shook Eric's shoulder. His undershirt was soaked with sweat. He tried to turn away but got hung up on his bad leg. He woke with a gasp.

"Sorry," Maggie said. "Food's hot."

"Let me sleep."

"No can do, ace. We need to load the capsule onto the truck and move along before something comes sniffing." She spooned half her cup's contents into his and held it out.

He regarded it dubiously. "Really. I'm just going to…"

An ear-splitting sonic boom slammed through the tent, caving in one side of the dome. Eric's cup fell to the floor. Most of Maggie's gruel was in her lap. She looked at it stupidly for a moment, mind trying and failing to grasp what had happened. She looked back up at Eric. His lips were moving, but she could not hear what he was saying. He pulled himself out of his sleeping bag with a grimace. The bandage on his foot looked oily.

And just like that, Maggie's brain re-engaged. She flung Eric's airscarf at him and looped her own over her face. Then she scrambled out of the flattened tent, leaving the airlock open behind her.

A long, thick contrail divided the sky. Smaller trails marked where pieces of the iceteroid had broken off. The main trail led straight over the horizon, upriver of them. She was still gaping at it when the surface wave hit, knocking her off her feet.

Gray appeared beside her, hauled her upright. "Icefall!"

"But there was no warning," Maggie protested. She checked her goggles. "Nothing was scheduled!"

Eric crawled out of the tent and levered himself up on a makeshift crutch. "Damn, that was close!"

"It hit upriver of us," Gray said.

"Will you look at that," Eric said, wonder in his voice. A mushroom cloud welled up into the sky, brown tinged with yellow and rust. Lightning flickered within. "I've never seen a ground strike."

Maggie turned to look at the stream that ran alongside their campsite, then the surrounding terrain. They were far too low. Besides the volatiles in the iceteroid, there were secondary effects. There was still a lot of ice in the Martian regolith, and a ground strike would melt it.

"We have to get to high ground," she said. "Gray, help me get the capsule on the truck."

"We don't have time," Eric said. "It's four klicks to the horizon. Maybe ten to where the iceteroid hit? Twenty max."

"If we leave the capsule, we're as good as dead anyway. We might as well let the flood take us. Because we'll have lost the only piece of real evidence we've got."

Getting the capsule onto the truck was a slow-motion nightmare. Every mistake, every slipped knot, every trip back to the storage locker on the back of the truck to find some vital piece of hardware, put them that much closer to the flood.

The mushroom cloud swelled overhead, blocking out the sun. It began to rain a foul-smelling witch's brew of ammonia and dirt and melt water.

"Do you hear that?" Eric asked.

Maggie stopped what she was doing. Behind the rain there was a distant rumble, low, powerful. While they were working the stream had overflown its banks and was creeping towards camp. They were out of time.

"Get in the truck," she said.

"But..." he gestured at the gear strewn beside him. Her sleeping bag in its compression sack, pads, clothes, camp kitchen. Gray's flight helmet.

"What you can carry. Go! Fragging now!" She jumped off the bed. The rumbling was louder. "Gray! Help him."

Eric tumbled up into the cab with an armful of gear, followed by a sleeping bag that bounced off the windshield as the door slammed shut. Maggie fired up the truck's thorium engine. Gauges lit up on the dashboard, semicircles of light reporting temperature, voltage, current, all ignored as she slammed the vehicle into gear.

Gray loped alongside the truck as they raced downstream, the flight helmet in his hand. "Roll down your window!"

Eric obliged, and a moment later the helmet sailed across the gap into the cab. Gray dropped behind them like a relay runner who has passed the baton.

"I need a map," Maggie said.

Eric brought one up on the dashboard display. They were near the point of a vee formed by the stream where it fed into the main channel of the Marineris. If she kept on going, they were going to be trapped between the two channels. She needed to cut up to the right across the stream to reach safety.

She spotted a stretch of cobbles breaking the surface. It would have to do.

"We're going to cross," she said. "Hold on!"

She coasted down the embankment. Water sheeted up on either side of the cab, subsiding as the truck slowed. She pressed back down to keep their speed, jouncing over hidden cobbles.

The opposite bank had been cut away by the current. The water smoothed as they approached. The front end of the truck dropped as the cobbles gave way to a deeper channel.

Maggie jammed down on the accelerator. The truck wallowed into the trench. The front end came up as it tried to claw its way up the embankment. Mud showered the side windows as the front tires dug down into the streambed. The current pushed the back end of the truck, skewing their angle to the shore.

"We're losing it!" she shouted.

And then the front of the truck bumped up over the lip of the bank, and they broke free of the rising water. Maggie gunned them up onto the shore. She looked in the rearview mirror just in time to see Gray fall forward into the water and disappear.

"He pushed us," she said to herself. To Eric: "Gray pushed us out."

She punched open the door and swung herself up onto the truck bed, to the crane pedestal. Gray staggered back to his feet, shedding water as he broke the surface. Maggie disengaged the clutch and pulled worn aramid line from the winch. Then she hurled the tow hook out over the water upstream of him.

The line drifted down in a bend around his waist. Gray took a wrap around his arm. Maggie hit the retrieve.

The drag of the massive warbot threatened to pull them back into the stream. Eric slipped into the driver's seat and gunned the truck onto firmer ground. Gray stumbled up over the lip of the embankment and fell face-first. The truck dragged him forward by his arm through the mud.

Maggie banged on the back window to make Eric stop. She turned off the winch and freed the clutch. Gray was motionless on his face. The line was wrapped tight around his arm and frayed where he had clenched it. Now the massive fist was open, fingers spread wide as a dinner plate. She pulled some slack into the line and uncoiled it from his arm. The metal beneath was burnished by friction.

Vapor rose from his joints as water evaporated off the muscle ribbons hidden beneath his armor. She braced herself against one massive shoulder and rolled him over.

"Well that was fun," he said heavily.

She wiped mud off his lenses. And much to her surprise, burst into tears.

The cache she had counted on was now out of reach on the other side of the swollen river.

"Do you think that guard shack you and the other Hund were based out of would have anything?" Maggie asked. "It is on the same side as us. Further south by seventy klicks or so."

"What are you looking for?" Gray asked.

"Food, medicine. The usual human stuff."

"Right." Not his story anymore. Gray tried to remember. "I think there was a structure beside the guard shack. Elevated."

"A food cache?"

"Maybe? I don't think the Hund knew what was inside." Or cared.

"Maybe is better than no," she said.

They drove into the rolling hills that marked where the canyon transitioned from the relatively narrow and deep Coprates to the broad Melas uplands. It was rough going, all cross-country.

They found the guard shack on a ridge overlooking the canyon below. It afforded a magnificent view of the sunlit strata to the south, a billion years of history on display, and the braided river channel to the north. The floodwaters from the icefall were starting to recede. Broad discolored ribbons showed where the river had overflown its banks and carved new channels.

The shack was still standing. The cache had been knocked off its stilts by the surface wave from the ground strike. A jagged crack split the hut-like enclosure. The hatch was jammed. Gray rolled it upright to take the weight off, and the hatch yielded.

The floor was covered with cans and packages of freeze-dried food. Maggie shoved a box of oxygen candles out the door with her foot. Mekanos had found a way inside and shredded much of the packaging. Food was strewn about inside of the enclosure, liberally mixed with sand and packaging detritus.

"Frag me," Maggie said.

She salvaged what she could and took it back to the truck. The cab was crammed with loose gear. They had lost the tent and all but her sleeping bag, which they had used as a common blanket the night before and was now jammed like a pillow behind Eric's head and shoulders.

"How does it look?" he asked. His face was pale.

"Your favorite!" she replied, holding out a can of beans that had survived the mekanos unscathed. "And some c-bars! Pieces, anyway."

"Yum," he said unenthusiastically.

"And best of all," she produced a bright red bag from beneath her coat, "a first aid kit."

"Antibiotics?"

"With any luck." She opened the kit and carefully unfolded its panels. There was only a topical cream. Which had not made much difference so far. "Hmm."

"Sounds like no."

She held a vial of pills up to the light. "How about pain killers? This is the good stuff."

"Doesn't hurt anymore." Head back in the pillow of the sleeping bag, eyes closed again.

Maggie repacked the medical kit and put it in the glovebox. She opened the beans and offered them to Eric. He opened one eye, closed it.

Her cup had not been one of the items that had survived their escape from the flood. She ate the beans cold, right out of the can, using her fingers as a scoop. She looked longingly at the c-bar fragments but made herself put them into the empty bean can for later.

"I'm going to see what else I can scrape up," she said. Eric did not respond. She set the air system to repressurize the cab and hopped out.

Gray lumbered up to her, a couple boxes balanced on his outstretched hand. "Is this what your revolver takes?"

The box on top was labeled '357 Magnum, 50 rounds.' She slid the ammunition carrier out. It was full of tungsten carbide-tipped penetrators. She shook one and felt more than heard gunpowder moving inside.

"Now that is some old-school goodness," Maggie said. "What are the odds of finding antiques like this out here?"

"Evidently pretty good," Gray said drily.

"Is that sarcasm? You are coming right along, my friend. Next you'll be cracking jokes."

The other box was twice as big. She shook out a couple thick, filigreed mass driver slugs. She ran her fingernail over the enameled electromagnet coils. "For the survival rifle?"

"I think they're the right size." He ejected the rifle's rotary magazine and handed it to her.

Maggie stripped a slug out and compared it to what was in the box. "Looks right to me."

She topped off the magazine for him. Large as the slugs were, his fingers were larger yet and did not have the dexterity to hold them, much less insert them into the magazine.

"Thank you. There is something else..."

She followed him to the other side of the shack. Beside an old thorium engine, the carcass of a late-war Hund was stretched out on the ground. It was partly buried by wind drift and picked over by mekanos.

She squatted down beside the head and brushed a thick layer of dust off the crest. It was in reasonable shape. "I don't know if this crest will fit you or not. This is a newer model than you."

"It will work," Gray said with more confidence than he felt.

"Well, get the toolbox out of the back of the truck, and we'll find out."

"Not just the crest laser," Gray said, resisting the impulse to turn and obey. "The arm too."

"Get the toolbox," she repeated.

The geas overwhelmed him. He got the toolbox from the back of the truck and set it down beside her. "I'm more than a weapon."

"Sit down and shut up."

He sat down and shut up. She tsked over his head. He felt the squeak of screws turning. She lifted away the damaged crest – a curious sense of absence – and installed the one from the carcass.

"How's that?"

"I can hear!" he exclaimed, surprised. And not just Maggie's voice, but the sigh of the wind, the rattle of discarded food wrappers as they tumbled across ground, and in the distance, the squeak of the truck's door as it opened. It was like he had regained a part of himself he had not known was missing. It made him wonder what else had passed unremarked. Scent. Taste. Touch, mostly.

"You can talk too. I guess the later models came with sound." She stood up.

"The arm too," he said. "Please?"

"Maybe later. You need a gun more than you need a hand."

"Easy for you to say. How would you feel about someone chopping your hand off and replacing it with that revolver of yours?"

"I need to check on Eric. We'll talk about this later." She turned away. There was a sizzling pop behind her. She spun around, revolver coming up to bear. Gray was standing over the carcass. A line of smoke rose from where its bicep had been.

"It works," he said disingenuously.

"Mekfucker," she said in a tone that hovered somewhere between anger and amusement.

Gray picked up the severed arm. "For maybe later."

Maggie watched a commhawk work the thermals coming up the slope from the lowlands. Sunlight gleamed on polished carbon wings. It spiraled higher and higher until it was just a speck overhead.

Gray followed her gaze. "What is it?"

"Commhawk. A communication relay. I'm trying to talk myself out of checking the news. I really want to know the story behind the ground strike. I'm hoping it was an accident. But I'm afraid Borodin or the warsingers would trace the ping."

"With any luck Borodin is frozen in a puddle of his own blood." The words came suddenly, without volition, and with them a memory: his men, frozen into their seats in the wreckage of *Tereshkova*.

"Wow," Maggie said. "Okay. That would be great, I guess. I've wondered what goes on in that noggin of yours, but maybe I'm better off not knowing."

It was quiet for a while. Sunlight sparkled on the river braids far below, flush with runoff from the icefall. He tried to imagine what the river looked like to her. Probably not a snake weaving through the rocks, scales flashing like beaten metal in the sun.

"It wasn't an accident," Gray said.

"What?"

"The ground strike. They're trying to erase us."

"You don't know that."

"I know there's a whole mekosystem designed to move volatiles in from the Trojans. The pchelan hive on Deimos provides terminal guidance. One little push, and..." He made a gesture with his hand, fingers pinched and then spread wide. Boom.

"That just means they could have done it, not that they did."

"Motive, means, and opportunity," Gray said. "What more do you want?"

"Proof? That's what everyone else is going to want. Otherwise we're just unlucky, right? Wrong place at the wrong time, some you win, mostly you lose."

"Sure, but..." he shook his head in frustration, neck joints squeaking. It was obvious to him who was behind the bombardment. But maybe that was just his overactive pattern recognition. "All right, then who runs the Blue Mars Project now? Who would be responsible?"

She chucked a rock over the edge of the escarpment. He caught the flash of motion and saw the long, graceful arc of its parabola, projected landing point, kinetic energy, all in one glance. Probably not how she saw it at all.

"Dirtside, there's a group called Sisters of the Ring. Story goes they were founded by Space Control veterans after the war, when the 'United' part of the United Colonies wasn't looking so good. They were afraid that the Ring would fail if it was left to bickering city-states. No Ring, no atmo, at least in the long run. So they started a cult with a weird syncretic religion dedicated to healing the planet. It's all very woo-woo, but they've kept the Ring going for a couple centuries, so I guess they were on to something."

The first rock landed right where his back-brain said it would, raising a puff of dust. She chucked another. "Topside, the icefalls mostly seem to take care of themselves. Like you said, there's a whole mekosystem set up around that. The Armistice stipulated warsingers wouldn't interfere with it. In return the Space Force would withdraw to Mars and cease hostilities."

"Warsingers?"

"Right, you died before the Warsing. I'm still trying to get your timeline straight. Tharks, in your day, if I remember right. At least that's how they started, but the singularity was not long in coming."

"The tharks won?"

"No one *won*. The warsingers *stopped* it. They knocked down both sides and put a no-fly zone around Earth and Mars. Anything that goes off-planet never comes back. No more threelium for them or us. We don't even have communication satellites. Gotta wait for a wardamn commhawk to fly over to talk to anyone. We're just a bunch of mekfucking scavengers."

Gray was having a hard time grasping it. "There's no off-world traffic?"

"Oh there are people out there," she waved dismissively at the sky. "No baselines of course. Dracs on the bigger worlds like Ceres. Geckos everywhere else. But no traffic off Mars, or Earth. The Ecostate of Nüwa doesn't exist anymore. Neither does the United Colonies. Now it's the League of Worlds, and it's run by warsingers."

The second rock landed, credibly close to the first. She had a good arm. Gray tried to imagine a world without the United Colonies, without the Space Force, without anything he had built his life around. Everything he had done, everything he had wanted to do, gone.

Because of what he had done. He remembered the hammer blow of atomic light. He remembered forging gems that produced hypermissiles. Coding geasa to draw them to Luna's gravity well like moths to a flame. And when they delivered their deadly payloads of nuclear fire protocol was exercised. The Lunar mines ceased to exist, along with all the infrastructure that had supported them. The giant mass driver: an oddly linear series of craters, as if someone had skipped a molten stone across the surface. The subterranean hives: craters within craters within craters…

He had traded his dream of starships for weapons of mass destruction. They could have had it all. They could have gone to the stars. Instead it had come to this: tharks presiding over a moribund civilization of scavengers. The United Colonies had ruled the entire solar system! And stood on the brink of exploring the universe. Now reduced to grubs in the dirt, while the tharks… the tharks could be out there already, for all he knew. Expanding like a plague of locusts through the galaxy.

It had to be set right. There must be a way to set it right. If he could only get back to Elise. Perhaps enough time had passed for her and Rhea to reconsider. But how, when he was a creature of this girl, in thrall to her every command?

"So what now?" he asked carefully, elliptically. "Make a run for Thunderbird? See if we can talk whatever's left of the Mars Guard into lofting the hyperglider?"

She shook her head "Not in the cards, my metal-skulled friend."

"Eric?"

She nodded, still looking north across the canyon. Somewhere over the horizon was a waterfall five kilometers wide and more than a kilometer tall. She had seen it once, when she was a child. Mostly she remembered the noise of it, the unrelenting rolling thunder that made it impossible to hear her father. Thunder and mist boiling off it in the afternoon winds.

"What's going on with him?"

"My goggles think it's sepsis. Elevated heart rate and respiration. Fever. The symptoms all fit. Without treatment it just gets worse. In a day or two he'll go into septic shock. After that…" She shrugged. "Hours."

"How long will it take to get to Thunderbird?"

"Too long." She shook her head. She had to let it go. "There's a Ring Station southwest of here, in the Melas foothills. Place called Potalama. They'll have a doctor."

"We can't give up, Maggie. There is too much riding on this. If what you say is true…"

"It's not *true*, it's *history*. Get that through your armor-plated skull. It has already actually happened. The past is not negotiable."

"Then *Sparrow* is the last trace. If we let the, uh," he searched for the right word, "the *warsingers* erase her, we'll have lost the stars for good."

"You think I don't know that? I've spent my whole life looking for this, for this exact thing. Sometimes I thought it was just a stupid fantasy, but I kept looking. And now I've found it. But I have to give it up. Because some things are more important, Gray."

"Not to me," he said.

"Well maybe that's why it turned out like it did for you," she said with venom in her voice.

Which was close enough to the truth to sting, but he refused to take the bait. He had pushed her too far already.

She let her breath out. "I'm just not sure it's worth it, anymore. People have died. People I cared about. And now Eric... it's too much. I can't lose him too. I'm tired and I'm hungry and I'm cold, and I don't see how we're going to win this thing. I mean, if you're right and the warsingers can call down a wardamn ground strike on us..."

"We'll go to Potalama. Get him to a doctor, things will look different to you then. Get some food in your belly and a decent night's sleep, things will look better."

"Maybe," she said, but not like she believed it.

"One day at a time," Gray counseled. He patted her leg awkwardly, carefully. "Ready to roll?"

"I'm going to go through the cache one more time. Maybe I missed something." She heaved herself to her feet.

Something moved across the terrain below them. Gray focused on the distance and his cyclopean third eye zoomed in automatically. Puffs of dust, like the tracks left by a strafing run, but slow, just one every couple seconds. Metal glinted, was lost against the air shimmering at the limits of perception. A silver bird, running. Behind it a rippling shadow with too many legs.

He lost them in the folds of the terrain.

A bird. It was probably his pattern recognition circuitry acting up again. He thought about asking Maggie if she saw it too but decided against it. She had enough on her mind. But when they left the cache, he made sure to lead the truck down the other side of the ridgeline, where they could not be seen from the valley below.

23

Battle for Luna

They decelerated into the Earth-Luna system like a pair of shooting stars, carefully staggered so the radiation spilled from their torches caused as little damage to each other as possible. *Glenn* led the way; she had been commissioned six mears before *Tereshkova* and her engine was leaky and inefficient in comparison. Her torch blazed like the one that had illuminated Ceres only a few days prior.

Now gone dark.

Gray touched the sigil embedded in his throat. It was warm, smooth, alien.

"You should have asked permission," Sidorov said.

Gray's hand dropped to his console. He and Sidorov were alone on the bridge. Gray was at Abram's old command station. Sidorov was officer of the deck. His watchmen were all down below, working through a damage control exercise with the new men Gray had pressed into service. The new fifth watch, bottom of the ladder. Most were happy to get off Greenwich Station, even if it meant a couple mears of Space Force service.

"That's why the skipper is pissed at you," Sidorov continued.

"I know," Gray said. "I just didn't expect her to ask. And then there wasn't time."

Gray had seen Elise once more before they left. Captain Rashnikov had not wanted him to go. But the summons of a hivemaster could not be ignored. A reply was required, and in the end it was simpler to accede to the request than to deny it.

They met at the end of the pier closest to the station. Neutral territory. Elise was accompanied by a pair of Cereseans, one male, the other female, both armed. The man was a broader, more muscular version of Anton. A family relation, likely.

Gray recognized the woman; she was the shopkeeper who had rented him his wings. He was not sure at first, but then he saw the tree tattoo on her shoulder.

Elise crossed the distance between them with a flick of her wings. He held her at arm's length for a moment, drinking in her beauty. "You did it."

"We did it," she said.

"I'm going to miss you," he said, face in her hair, drinking in the smell of her.

"Don't go," a small voice in his ear.

"Not one of the choices, love."

"Then promise you'll come back. To me. Wherever we end up."

"I will," he said. Knowing full well that it might be a lie, that the winds of war that were gathering around them might blow them so far apart that they never saw each other again.

She pushed him away enough to get something out of her puffer. The object was the size of the end of his thumb and clear as quartz. "I forged this for you."

He took the gem carefully. It was smooth and warm. "What kind is it?"

"A sigil. Accepting it binds you to me and confers certain privileges and responsibilities within my hive. Geasa will be honored as if I had spoken through you."

"How do I..."

"Hold it against the hollow of your throat. I'm told there will be some pain. Don't drop it."

She stayed his hand. "You accept, then?"

"Of course I do."

She opened her wings to include the escorts who had come with her. "These are my witnesses."

"Small world," Gray said. "Fiona, isn't it?"

She nodded coolly, hand resting on the hilt of her cutlass. "Getting smaller by the minute."

"Fiona Anders is my security chief," Elise said. "And this is Drew Joseph-son, her second."

The big drac looked like he'd rather be fishing Gray's guts out with his cutlass but shook his hand anyway.

"All right." Elise turned to Gray. "Are you ready?"

"I am."

"In front of these witnesses, I take this man, John Gray, as my consort, with all the privileges and protections that affords."

She nodded, and Gray pressed the gem into the hollow at the base of his neck. It burned like a brand sinking into his flesh. He kept the pressure on. The sensation receded to a dull throb.

"There," she said. To the witnesses: "You see it?"

Josephson nodded grudgingly. Fiona came down on the side of courtesy and offered her congratulations.

Gray rubbed the sigil. It was firmly attached, and only a little warmer than skin temperature. His spex rang. It was Polanski, whom Kasahara had chosen as his backfill for life support officer. Much against the older man's desires; he would have preferred to stay a simple watchman.

"You all right, Commander? Just got a funny spike in your vitals."

"Never better, Polanski."

"Listen sir, the skipper is looking for you. Can I give him an ETA?"

"Tell him I'm on my way," Gray said, and closed the window.

"You've got to go," Elise said.

"It's time."

There was a lingering kiss. Then Gray left Elise and her escorts standing in the pier. Walking away from her was the hardest thing he had ever done. But he swore to himself that he would find her again or die trying.

Captain Rashnikov grimaced when he saw the gem at Gray's throat. "That could be a career limiting move, Mister."

"Yes sir," Gray had said. "Understood."

And that was all he said. He could not bring himself to apologize. He had regrets, but not about Elise. She was the best thing that had ever happened to him, a badly needed counterbalance to a growing sense of self-loathing that had been eating at him ever since he had executed Seventeen. Is this what war did to men? Turned them into butchers, willing to sacrifice the innocent to prove a point?

The mantids were just proxies in a struggle between Earth and Mars. Intelligent weapons. Much as he hated them for killing Lynch, for killing his shipmates, for killing so many people on Ceres and Luna, they were being used. The mantids were not the enemy. But he would be ordered to kill them en masse. And he would follow his orders because he was loyal to the United Colonies. Because Mars was his home.

It felt like he was being hollowed out. Hollowed out and torn apart, because on the other side of that growing void was the joy that he felt about Elise. It was as if he could not have one without the other. But he was afraid the center could not hold.

"Excuse me?" Sidorov said.

Gray realized he had murmured the phrase aloud. He repeated it now for Sidorov. "The center cannot hold. It's from a poem written after Earth's first world war."

It was quiet while Sidorov tracked down the quote. Gray scanned his console's displays listlessly, trying to sort signal from noise. They had not been able to repair everything before they left, so there were a lot of warnings on the board. Old news. The only new item was a radiation alert due to *Glenn's* proximity. Gray made a note to talk to Polanski about radvax boosters for the crew.

"Found it," Sidorov said. "'Things fall apart; the center cannot hold; Mere anarchy is loosed upon the world, The blood-dimmed tide is loosed.' William Butler Yeats, The Second Coming. Grim stuff, Commander. You think that's what's coming? Interplanetary war?"

"I know it is," Gray said. "Have you watched much about Earth's world wars?"

"Just the required vids at the Academy. I have trouble keeping them straight, honestly. The atomic bomb was what, three centuries ago?"

Gray nodded. "Almost to the year."

"And there were plenty of other terrible things afterwards to keep track of."

"But that's when mechanized slaughter really got started," Gray said. He had been fascinated by the era. "Gas attacks. The machinegun. Motorized artillery called 'tanks.' Armed aircraft. Every technological advance put to use to kill people more efficiently. Industrialized death camps and jet engines, atomic bombs and suborbital missiles. Von Braun got his start then, building weapons of mass destruction."

"Von Braun, as in the city of?"

"The same."

"I thought he was the moon rocket guy."

"He was," Gray said.

"Oh." Sidorov chewed on that for a while. "I guess everyone has their dark side."

"So it seems," Gray said, remembering his cutlass sweeping down and a shower of sparks.

"At least some good came out of it. We wouldn't be here otherwise, right? The United Colonies is built on atomic rockets."

"But at what cost, Mr. Sidorov. At what cost. Nearly a hundred million dead in the twentieth century alone." Gray shook his head. "The entire population of the United Colonies would be a drop in that bucket. It would not be a large task to extinguish us all."

A tell-tale flashed on Gray's panel, a lasergram from Space Control. Sidorov got it too. He looked up, eyes wide.

"There has been a launch from the Lunar mass driver."

There had actually been a whole series of launches from the Lunar mass driver. The machine had been built to fling tanks of helium-3 from the Lunar surface out to the Earth-Luna L5 Lagrange point. There they were attached to barges bound for various destinations within the United Colonies.

The mass driver had been offline since Luna had gone dark. One could argue that if helium-3 had kept flowing, the United Colonies would not have responded as aggressively. A change of management could be discussed around a conference table. A direct existential threat to the ergonomy could not; hence the task force of eight UCSF torchships converging on the Earth-Luna system.

The plan was for a vanguard of two torchships – *Cooper* and *Schirra*, both coming straight from Mars – to rocket in fast and close and use lasers and mass drivers at short range to soften up likely points of resistance. Two more pairs would follow immediately behind, using the cover provided by the vanguard to brake into polar orbit. Then *Glenn* and *Tereshkova* last to the game from the other side of the solar system. They would either brake into orbit or mop up whatever got through the first two waves, depending on the situation.

That was the plan.

Now the news aggregators were overflowing with stories about the launch. It seemed like every telescope within the United Colonies was trained on Luna. Petitions for the task force to be recalled went to the top of the boards of every city-state except Tsiolkovsky, whose residents were notoriously skeptical if not outright pessimistic. They did not think Luna would resume shipping helium-3 without a fight, because they were Slavs at heart, and their whole history told them that invaders did not just turn around and go home.

The plan did not change. Most senior officers in the Space Force were from Tsiolkovsky.

Then Space Control brought their terawatt search radar at the Mars L1 observatory to bear on the objects and discovered they were not behaving like threelium tanks. They were not coasting passively into the nets waiting at L5; they were accelerating out towards the task force.

These observations were not made public. There was considerable controversy within Parliament about them because the images from the telescopes that detected the launches in the first place did not show any exhaust plumes. It made no sense. Only one set of observations could be true, and it was easier to believe images you could see with your own eyes than radar returns.

So Space Control kept the radar data to itself. If it had not been for an unauthorized lasergram from a young primary at Mars L1 Control to her lover on *Cooper*, the battle for Luna would have been a complete rout. As it was, *Cooper's* captain had the wisdom to hear out his ensign's story. Then he shut down his torch long enough to swing around and bring his own laserscopes to bear on the nearest object. Which, as it turned out, was accelerating straight at him at ten meters per second squared and showed no sign of an exhaust plume whatsoever.

The objects were not a belated peace offering. They were some kind of advanced-technology interceptors moving in for the kill.

That changed the plan. While Space Control had the luxury of debating whether their instruments were reporting the truth, the men in the torchships targeted by the interceptors did not. However impossible they seemed, they did in fact exist.

Tereshkova's officers gathered on the bridge as the moment of first contact approached. Watchmen surrendered their consoles around the main holocaster and moved to seats in the gallery. Rashnikov was heads-down at his command station. He glanced up when Gray reported all present.

"Gentlemen, observe." He exported his console to the main holocaster.

The Lunar mass driver had launched the interceptors in a single long burst, like a machine gun that fired fifty-meter-long ships instead of slugs. Once in flight the interceptors had dispersed into groups of three and begun to accelerate. By now their velocity vectors were shocking; they stretched across the entire display. It was unprecedented performance.

"This data has been augmented with feeds from the strike force. *Cooper* will be the first to encounter the interceptors, then *Shirra*. Each has been targeted by three interceptors. As you can see, the interceptors have a four-to-one acceleration advantage over our torchships, and unlike us, seem able to accelerate indefinitely." He let the words hang there for a moment, then dropped the other tank. "The top knobs at the Academy say it is some kind of reactionless drive."

The officers circled around the holocaster exchanged uneasy glances. Sidorov was the first to speak. "But sir, that's impossible. A reactionless drive violates fundamental physical laws. What about conservation of momentum?"

Rashnikov nodded. "Every action requires an equal and opposite reaction, yes?" He began to pace the gallery. "So we were taught. But there is no other hypothesis that fits the data, Pilot. Unless you have one? No. So what we were taught was wrong. Other thoughts? XO?"

"A reactionless drive is a gamechanger," Gray said. "The tactics we have been trained to use will not apply. Compared to us they have virtually unlimited maneuvering capability."

"That is true." Rashnikov stopped, traced a line through the data in the holocaster. "But they are much smaller than us. So perhaps they do not have thermal capacity?"

"*Cooper* has been firing on one of the interceptors for a couple kiloseconds," Lieutenant Miller pointed out. He was Lynch's replacement, promoted up from second watchman in the Sensors and Weapons guild. "No change in acceleration compared to the other two."

"Maybe they figured out a way around the first law of thermodynamics too," Gray said drily.

"One impossibility at a time, please," Rashnikov said tightly. "Chief, I need a thermal model of those vessels."

"On it, sir," Boiko replied.

A readout changed in the display.

"Ah," Rashnikov said. "Captain Sokolov has given up on the 'scopes. Kites next, if I were him. Guns, how many seconds was that?"

"About three kilosecs since they opened fire with their laserscopes, sir," Lieutenant Miller reported. The display shifted again. "And *Cooper* just fired her mass driver. Kites away and opening now."

Rashnikov nodded. "He is a shrewd man, Sokolov. We attended Academy together. A fine man."

Each kite was shaped like an umbrella with a spike on top. The spike contained the control system and warhead, while the inner surface of the umbrella was coated with propellant. Every time a pulse from one of *Cooper's* laserscopes hit that surface, the propellant vaporized in a jet of exhaust. The kites' velocity vectors stabbed at the interceptors like spears.

A point in the holocaster blazed briefly, like a camera's flash going off. One of the kites had hit home. Then another, and the men on *Tereshkova's* bridge cheered. Two interceptors destroyed!

Then a much brighter flash, and the feed from *Cooper* dropped.

There was a collective exhalation, as if *Tereshkova* herself had been struck a blow. A muscle in Rashnikov's jaw twitched. Gray swept through the data, assembling a picture of what had happened.

"The third interceptor detonated at close range," he concluded. "Blew itself up and took *Cooper* with it."

"Blew itself up?" Rashnikov asked. "You are sure."

Gray looked through the data again. "That's what I'm seeing. The electromagnetic signature looks like a qigong nova. Lots of neutrons. They were a few hundred kilometers apart, but there's nothing left of either ship. Just a bubble of plasma expanding from the point where their trajectories crossed. Moving on the same vector as the interceptor."

The bridge was completely silent. It was unprecedented. Spacecraft did not blow themselves up. More often than not, a torchship could disable its opponent at range simply by raising its temperature to the point that its crew could no longer function. Survivors were rescued, their ships sent home as prizes. It was all very civilized and profitable.

They watched helplessly as *Schirra* met the same fate.

"They will be remembered as heroes," Rashnikov said, eyes fixed on the trajectory plot, voice like gravel tumbled downstream. "Heroes, all of them."

Gray knew men on *Cooper* and *Schirra*. Counted a couple of them as friends. How many more would die before the day was done? This was not how he had imagined it would be. He shook his head. This was not the time for sentimentality. There would be a time and a place to mourn the dead, but only if they survived.

"Chief," he said, "we need that thermal model."

"On it," Boiko replied.

"Put it on the 'caster," Gray said. "Whatever you've got."

Boiko exported his console to the main holocaster. He traced a pointer over a graph of the interceptors' albedo. "First off, they are very reflective. At least from the front. We're talking mirror grade." His voice steadied down as he continued. "Most of the energy from *Cooper's* 'scopes bounced right off. Best guess is about five percent got through and was absorbed as heat."

"That should have been enough," Rashnikov said. "Especially at the end when they were close."

"Yes sir," Boiko agreed. He moved to a different curve. "The most conservative model puts the interceptor's internal temperature over one hundred degrees Celsius at the time of intercept."

"But no one could survive that! The crew would have been dead before they reached *Cooper*."

"Correct."

Rashnikov considered the problem. "So they are not manned. And they are not rocket-propelled. Do we have anything on what they *are*, besides reflective?"

Gray brought up the last moments of the doomed torchships' feeds on his console. The interceptors' reflectivity made it difficult to get a good visual, but he cobbled together a model. Cropped out the inconsistencies. What was left was a slender fuselage, hexagonal in cross-section, tipped at either end by three rapidly spinning blades. Something about it raised the hair on the back of his neck. Something he could not quite put his finger on.

He exported his console to the main holocaster. "This is what they look like, more or less."

He rotated the model through different angles. From the front it looked like an oncoming bullet. Not a bullet, an old-Earth propeller-driven fighter plane, coming straight at them.

"Interesting," Rashnikov said. "All threes. Three rotating blades in front, three in back. Two sets of three offset spokes near the stern – that's your qigong, da? The only things that aren't in threes are these two bulges here and here," he pointed at domes on either side of the fuselage. "Sensors, perhaps?"

"Ledeyes," Gray said. "They look just like a mekan's ledeyes."

Rashnikov grunted. "Da." His gaze caught Gray's. "You think mekans built these things?"

Gray returned to the model. Now he understood his reaction, the primal fear, his back-brain telling him to run. "Skipper, I don't think they were built by mekans. I think they *are* mekans."

The next four torchships met the same fate. First *Popovich* and *Nikolayev*, then *Carpenter* and *Grissom*. Variations on a theme: concentration of fire, kites laid like mines, desperate last-second maneuvers to avoid the coup de grace. But the final blow fell all the same, until only *Glenn* and *Tereshkova* were left.

The men were beyond stressed. Rashnikov paced the gallery, jaw working each time another torchship met its end in a blaze of light. He whipped the bridge crew with increasingly caustic observations, punctuated by bursts of Russian obscenities. Gone was the admiration he had expressed for Captain Sokolov. The men on the other ships were idiots.

The muscles at the corner of one eye tugged periodically at his cheek. He rubbed at the muscle spasm to try and make it stop, but his body would not obey his will. Gray wondered if the man was going to break. What would happen when it came down to the end game? Would he run? Not that there was anywhere to go.

Sweat was running off Sidorov's face and dripping onto his console. Miller hummed tunelessly, oblivious to the irritation of the officers on either side. Chief Boiko looked like he was about to hit him, which would be grounds for court martial. Kasahara was not doing much better. It was all going to hell. Gray wished Commander Abrams was still onboard. What would he do?

The only one who seemed to be holding it together was Polanski. Gray caught the newly promoted life support officer looking around the bridge. When their eyes met, Polanski shook his head minutely. He sensed it too. Gray keyed a message into his console. *We have to do something.*

Polanski looked down at the chirp. Thought about it for a few seconds. Then he looked up at Gray as if he were asking silent permission. Gray nodded encouragement.

"Listen up, geckos!" Polanski bawled out as if he were back down on the EVA deck and the bridge officers were just another boarding squad. The men started in their seats. "You don't want to live forever, do you? This is the Space Force! Flying, fighting, and fucking! Am I right?"

The men looked at each other nervously. There were a few nods, a muted assent.

"That's right. Flying, fighting, and fucking. The holy trinity. That's why we joined. And if we fly right and fight hard, maybe we'll live to fuck another day. And maybe we won't. But we knew that when we signed up. And if we go up in a blaze of light, our names will go on The List, right alongside our fallen comrades. Right there with Alexey Leonov himself! Fucking heroes, every one of us." He smiled, a grim slash. "Better than I thought I'd ever get."

"Alexey!" Gray shouted.

"Alexey!" the men returned but not like they really meant it. They were not there yet.

"Alexey!" Gray shouted again.

"Alexey!" The blood was starting to come to their faces now.

Again: "Alexey!"

"Alexey!" they roared. And the spell was broken. Sidorov wiped the sweat from his face and managed a weak smile. Rashnikov nodded gravely.

"Alexey Leonov," he said. "A true hero of the space age. But…" he held up his hand. "But. We remember Alexey because he survived the first spacewalk. Not because he died, but because he lived. Against all odds, despite numerous failures. His suit expanded so much he could not get back in the spacecraft. Can you imagine? The first man to venture outside a spacecraft, and he could not get back inside. So what did he do? He thought the problem through. He depressurized the suit so it would fit through the hatch. He improvised, and he survived."

He looked around the room, at each one of them. "As must we. The United Colonies of Mars cannot afford to lose any more torchships, or we will surely lose this war. For war it is."

"What about our mission?" Gray asked. "The threelium mines…"

"The mines are lost," Rashnikov replied. He ran his hand through his stiff shock of hair, momentarily revealing the crest of his moravec. "That we must accept. Even if all the interceptors broke off, we do not have the means between us and *Glenn* to retake them. The other ships had shuttles and troops. All we have is our laserscopes and the mass driver. The most we could do is rain down death from above. But even that is futile, because we too would be destroyed."

"Then what?" Gray asked. "Are we to run?"

Rashnikov was silent for so long that Gray feared he had suffered some sort of fugue. He stared into the plot on the holocaster, teeth clenched. Had something gone wrong with the moravec? Some cascade in the artiform neurons, conflicting impulses that overwhelmed his ability to make a decision? Gray did not let himself look away from the man. He could tell the other officers were wavering. Now he must show unwavering faith in the captain.

Finally Rashnikov shook his head. "No, Commander. We will not run. We will salvage something from this disaster. Observe."

He sketched a pair of opposing vectors in the holocaster. "Most of the strike force came in from Mars, in this direction, da? And the interceptors rose to meet them in the opposite direction, like this." The arrows crossed. "Now, we come in from Ceres, like this." Another arrow, roughly opposed to the first group of torchships, coming as they had from across the solar system.

"Now, we remove our comrades. Gone, may they never be forgotten. But... some of the interceptors made it through the gauntlet, da?" He singled out the survivors, two arrows shot in the darkness. He rotated the vector plot to a more favorable angle. "Now do you see it?"

"They're heading the same direction as us," Gray said. "More or less. Quite a bit faster than us, but they've stopped accelerating."

"There's no tactical value to that," Sidorov said, a note of puzzlement in his voice. He turned to Rashnikov. "Skipper, there's no reason for them to do that. It doesn't make sense. They'd be better off staying at full thrust."

Rashnikov nodded. "Yes. If I were them, I would be decelerating. They're well over solar escape velocity. And yet they are not."

"Maybe they can't," Gray said.

"Maybe they're out of fuel," Sidorov speculated. "They've already expended a tremendous amount of energy." He threw some graphs up. "If it were us, we'd have burned our entire supply of threelium getting up to that speed."

"We cannot make any assumptions. They are not rockets. They are not crewed by human beings." Rashnikov looked around the bridge to emphasize the point, pounding the top of his console. "Do. Not. Forget this. But this feature that has made them stop accelerating puts them within our reach. It is an opportunity. The enemy must not be allowed to keep this technology to itself. The advantage is too great. This is something the United Colonies must possess if we are to survive. Gentlemen, we must capture one of those vessels. That is our new mission."

24

East of Armageddon

The sand crab nibbled at the sentinel's injured flank where plasma had leaked through woven ice tree branches and licked fire across her abdomen. She jerked away from the mekano, limbs flailing, and the creature retreated in a flurry of dust. When the dust settled the crab was nowhere to be seen.

The sentinel inspected the wound as best she could. It was in an awkward place, near the juncture with her thorax, and quartering across her side to her back, like someone had burned a long, elliptical hole in her with a blowtorch. The crab had taken a bite of seared carbon fiber skin from the edge of the hole, more insult than additional injury.

But it seemed likely more would come. More of the same, which would be bad enough, or less of something more capable of doing real damage, which would be much worse. Or at least more decisively bad. In any case nothing good would come from lingering, except avoiding the pain of moving.

She lurched to her feet, fighting the unaccustomed gravity of Mars. Everything seemed thick and dirty. She had never experienced an atmosphere before. Moisture kept falling from the sky and clouding her vision. It was unpleasant and probably bad for her injury. She was not designed to be airproof, or waterproof, or really anything-proof except electrostatic buildup, which was not presently an issue. She was designed to live in a vacuum, in negligible gravity.

She wrenched one of the straighter branches out of the nest and repurposed it as a walking stick. It might be useful for warding off mekanos, and it allowed her to take some of the weight off the leg nearest the hole in her side, which hurt abominably. At least her kinos were spun up. The heat of entering the atmosphere had seen to that before it melted a hole in her.

She could not help but feel she had cursed herself by surviving against the queen's will. She might as well have ridden the iceteroid down. It would have been more merciful. She would have been vaporized instantly, instead of being forced to limp across this hostile wasteland.

And where was she to go? The nest had spiraled down out of the sky behind the iceteroid as it blazed westward. She was well downstream of the impact zone, probably downstream of the proscribed artifact as well. It was pure luck she had alighted above the river's flood plain, or she would have been washed away.

The only place on Mars she knew anything about, really, was the great mekanopolis at Pavonis Mons, far to the west. Past the artifact, past the impact zone, past the chaotic fractured landscape that marked the western end of the Valles Marineris. A very long way to go, for a pchelan who had never been on the surface of a planet before.

There to throw herself on the mercy of the Queen of Pavonis, a wretched victim of her success. If success it was. Had the artifact been destroyed by secondary effects, as the Queen of Deimos had assumed it would be? Had the ground shock and floodwaters rendered it unrecognizable and unusable, or was it still sitting there, a beacon for the quads?

Perhaps that information was something she could use as a bargaining chip, something she could barter for a trip to the queen's drexlers. The site of the artifact was on the way to Pavonis, more or less. She might as well visit it. She certainly did not have any better ideas. She oriented herself by the afternoon sun and started walking west.

25

The Grimms

They found a road the next sol. It was little more than patches of compacted dirt between weathered river cobbles, a study of rusty brown speckled with black and grey. Stitched together, the beaten ground marked the path of least resistance along the southern arc of the canyon. Every few kilometers a stone cairn confirmed prior human presence. It was oddly comforting in this vast emptiness.

Gray returned to his perch atop the bed of the truck. He spent as much time looking behind them as ahead. He had not forgotten the silver bird but nor had he seen it again.

The road wound through the rising hills, gradually gaining elevation as it reached deeper into the Melas. Here the canyon was wide enough that it was impossible to tell they were still within it. The canyon walls were over the horizon in either direction.

The turn to Potalama was marked by a cistern, grey stone in a ruddy plaster. The top was marked by a sigil in black: a circle bracketed by crescents on either side. Maggie got out of the truck, tried the spigot at its base. A stream of crystal-clear water poured out. She took off her goggles and airscarf and splashed water over her face and the back of her neck, then drank from her cupped hand. The water was very cold. She motioned for Eric to join her. He hobbled over on a makeshift crutch.

Gray gestured at the sigil. "What's that about?"

"It's the mark of the Sisters of the Ring. Stands for the triple moon: waxing crescent, full moon, waning crescent."

"The Moon, as in Earth's moon? Luna?"

"No, it's a metaphor. Well, originally, I guess. Anyway, the moon is symbolic of the triple goddess, different aspects of femininity. They are all about nurturing, preserving life, healing the planet. Fortunately for the rest of us." Maggie turned to Eric. "Come on, let's get you cleaned up while we've got some clean water at hand."

His wounds were no better. The smell made her gag. She washed it as best she could, and the bandages too, breaking blood clots out of the cloth and letting them crumble away to be lost in the cobbles at the base of the cistern.

After the turn, the track grew rocky and steep. Gray braced himself against the cab as they jolted uphill, the dismembered hyperglider behind him, Berel's combat shell to the side. Maggie's bike was lashed to the back of the cab in the space behind his legs. Soon they had a view of the hill country they had left behind. He traced the narrow ribbon of the road they had taken through the folds of the terrain.

And then he saw it. Something glinted at the juncture where they had turned, something unmistakably metallic. A silver bird, running. Behind it a peculiar rippling of the landscape. Not a shadow. Too many legs, and the sun angle was wrong. But when he tried to focus on it, he lost it. Maybe his pattern recognition acting up again? But the bird he was sure of.

He rapped his knuckles on the roof of the cab, accidentally leaving a pair of dents in the metal. The truck coasted to a halt. Maggie put the brake on and got out. He motioned her up onto the bed of the truck.

"Something is following us," Gray said, pointing. "There, see it?"

She squinted through her goggles. "Frag me. It's Dusty."

Part of Gray was relieved that he was not hallucinating. The other part, not so much. "Borodin?"

"Gotta be. Wardamn it, I hoped that mekfucker was dead." She scowled, hands on her hips, swore again in terms that Gray had not heard since he worked a niner job in Thunderbird's shipyards, waiting for word from the Joint Service Academy entrance board.

"Do you think we can we outrun him?" he asked when she ran out of spin.

She shook her head. "Not a chance. Dusty is a lot faster than the truck. That's why we brought him with us on expeditions; he could scout ahead, at least to the limits of his kinos. No, we're going to have to make a stand."

She left Gray in the shadow of a tremendous rock shelf. A seasonal flow had eroded away the soil along the base of the escarpment, creating an overhang a hundred meters from end to end. Ice gleamed wetly in the deeper shadows. A seep of water left dark tracks underfoot.

He found a place that commanded a view of the likely approaches. A glacial erratic deposited during the last ice age offered some cover. He laid his gun arm atop the boulder, sighting awkwardly along its length. His head was too big to get his central eye down in line with the sights. It was not going to work.

But he could not use his laser, not at these distances. After terraforming had thickened the atmosphere, it was a relatively short-range weapon, no more than a couple hundred meters before beam spread and diffusion turned it into a heat ray instead of the hole puncher it had been during the war. And while heat rays might work for space combat, where engagements lasted for days, what he needed right now was a hole puncher.

He twisted his head around until he found an angle where he could get one of his secondary eyes in line. The secondaries were set up for unmagnified stereovision, one on either side of the cyclopean laserscope that dominated his face. Not ideal, but at least he could line up the sights.

He jacked a slug into the rifle's chamber and set the safety. Then he settled on his haunches to wait. The Hund's legs were like a dog's, with an elongated foot whose heel could be mistaken for a reverse knee. Hence the name, he supposed. Hund. German for hound. The dogs of war. That fit the Von Braun mentality: right to the point.

He tapped the goggles strapped around his gun arm. They were Eric's old pair. Maggie had given them to him. Said he could use them to stay in touch. And catch up on his *history*, as she put it. Now he listened to her make casual, if largely one-sided conversation with Eric, as if they were setting up camp on top of the escarpment. Baiting the trap.

Something about the situation bothered him. What had Maggie said about bringing Dusty along on expeditions? Something about limited range. It came back to him: the bipe was fast because it was light, and it was light because it did not have its own reactor. So how had it got so far out in the bush?

A motion caught his eye. A silver bird, picking its way through the rocks on the slope below. He zoomed in with his main eye. It was a bipe for sure. But was it

Dusty? Did it matter? It was following them. Still, the outline was off, as if the cab had been bulked up on steroids. Maybe Borodin had set it up with its own reactor. That would make sense. That would give it some real range.

At two kilometers out it was a long shot, halfway to the horizon. According to Eric's goggles, the survival rifle threw a fifty-gram slug at nearly a kilometer a second. Clever lad had loaded a ballistics calculator with all the particulars. Gray dialed in the range, guessed the bipe's speed. The goggles gave him elevation from horizontal – not much as he was shooting downhill – and lead in degrees.

Gray lined up the sights on the bipe, slightly ahead, slightly above. Started to pull the trigger. Hesitated. Ares damn it, it did matter. Maybe it wasn't Borodin. Maybe it was the boys looking for them. He increased the lead to guarantee a miss. The survival rifle recoiled. Two seconds later a puff of dust in front of the bipe marked the warning shot.

The bipe careened to a halt and its cab swiveled towards him. A brilliant blue glow like a doorway into the aether obscured the vehicle. A moment later the rocky shelf above Gray crumpled in on itself like a sponge sucked through a hole in space.

As quickly as the missing matter had disappeared it returned. A thunderous crack accompanied a hail of shattered rock against his armor. Time seemed to slow down. He probably only had a second or two before the weapon recharged. He cleared debris from the gun's action and worked the bolt. No lead this time, same elevation. The blue glow was building. He pulled the trigger and leapt away from the nominal shelter of the boulder.

Another crack of thunder and hail of rocks at his back. There was no shelter. He spun on his heel and brought the gun to bear, only to discover that his last shot had hit home. The bipe was on its side, cab mostly obscured by the undercarriage. It was trying and failing to get its feet back underneath it. Only one leg was working. It pawed at the ground, dragging itself around in a circle.

He waited for Borodin to emerge. As soon as he broke cover he was a dead man.

One of his auxiliary eyes caught a glimpse of motion, motion without substance, rippling near a rocky outcrop. On instinct alone he pivoted and snapped off a shot. Then he lost whatever it was. But a moment later a thin contrail arced overhead from near where he had last seen it, reached its zenith, and began to fall back towards the top of the escarpment.

"You've got incoming!" he radioed up to Maggie. He sprinted for the outcrop, the Hund's metal feet ungainly on the slope. He would finish this fight if it was the last thing he did. Another contrail arced up over the rocks, betraying the shooter's position despite whatever technomancer hack he was hiding behind.

Then Maggie's panicked voice came over the comm link. "Gray, get up here! Those were dragon teeth!"

Gray skidded to a stop, sending a shower of rocks bounding down the slope. He bounded uphill at an angle that took him around the corner of the escarpment to the campsite. Because what choice did he have?

Something moved by the camp, something large and dirt-colored. A pit in the ground marked where it had formed. It was easily twice the height of a man and built like a sumo wrestler. The illusion was completed by a cartridge-shaped topknot that glowed brilliantly in infrared, presumably the thing's ignition source. Warsing tech.

Gray pulled up and shot the thing with the last slug in the rifle's magazine. There was a sharp crack as the shot connected. The grimm turned. Gray backpedaled. He fired his crest laser, but the thing was made of stone, literally made of stone assembled into a kind of moving rock pile by the nanites in the dragon tooth. Gray fired the laser again, probing for whatever it used for eyes. Crescents of rock spalled off its sloped forehead.

It barely even had a head. It was just a nubbin between its shoulders, like a squat mushroom of rock. It lumbered towards him. Behind it, another grimm tore itself from its earthen womb.

"There's another!"

"Fall back towards me," Maggie said.

"You sure?" he asked, but he was already doing it. Because that was the right thing to do. Wasn't it?

He retreated past where Maggie had made her stand. The grimm followed in a ponderous semicircle. Bright flares of light illuminated its ghastly face every time Gray fired the laser. No nose, no mouth. A crack ran around the circle of the pitted stone that was its head.

Maggie darted out of hiding, her hand deep in her satchel, searching for something. The grimm stopped, seemed to look straight at her through that awful crack in its head. Gray's next pulse went right into the crevice and there was an electric snap. It spun back to face him. Smoke spiraled out from the crack.

Maggie dashed forward. She did not trust herself to throw the artifact, not from that distance. She was only going to get one chance. She pulled the arming pin as she ran up on the living pile of rock. It raised a massive fist above Gray's head.

The nanite grenade struck the grimm in the back, struck and stuck like a wet snowball. A flood of data lit up Maggie's goggles. A lot of things happened very quickly. The nanites in the grenade poured into the grimm's rocky matrix, converting *it* into *them*. Waste heat rode the back edge of the reaction, making the back of the thing look like molten lava.

The grimm clawed at the wound Maggie had dealt. Wherever they touched, the nanites stuck like molten goo. It raised its hand to the narrow crack. Its fingers were melting down as the nanites devoured them. Realized what had happened. Whirled on Maggie and reached for her with the corrupted hand.

Maggie screamed, and Gray bounded in a single leap up onto the grimm's back. He jammed his hand into its eye crack for purchase. The grimm tried to shake him off but its legs gave way. It sank onto the ground, into the ground, dragging Gray down with it. He pulled free just before he was dragged into the corruption. The head sagged down into the molten pile, the last thing to go.

The sound of tortured metal: a metallic groan with an undertone of welds letting go, pong, pong! Gray spun around. The second grimm was tearing the truck apart.

"Do you have another one of those grenades?"

"That was it," Maggie said helplessly.

"Fuck me," Gray said savagely. He shoved his right hand, his only hand, into the molten pile of nanites at his feet. It felt like someone was playing a blowtorch over his fingers. He scooped the living corruption into his palm and ran for the second grimm. He leapt and tagged the thing right on top of its head. Smeared more goo – what used to be his thumb – into the eye crack to make sure. Leapt away.

The thing staggered drunkenly away from the truck, wrenching its head with both hands as if it was trying to twist it off. It probably had a distributed nervous system that could survive such an insult. Just grow another head.

Gray started shooting at its head. Each pulse of light left shattered rock in its wake. Its crude hands slipped on the rough gravel, like trying to get a lid off a wet jar. It stumbled, fell. Its head caved in, and it writhed helplessly, hands slapping at the ground as they too began to disassemble. Hot gobbets of partially disassembled grimm splashed out from each thunderous slap, landed in the dirt, began to sizzle there as they spread.

Gray looked down at his hand. All that was left was a dripping gob of nanites.

"Well shit," he said, and fired his crest laser.

They sat in the dirt beside the remains of the second grimm. Eric hunched over in the sleeping bag, shivering. Maggie, a frown on her face, had her tools spread out in front of her. An oversized survival knife she had found in the truck rested on her thigh. Gray squatted beside her, cradling his handless arm.

The grimm had condensed into a rough pitted spheroid a couple meters in diameter. It was still warm, warm enough to make sitting next to it attractive to the humans in the group. Gray would rather have kept his distance, but no one had asked his opinion.

"Are they still active, in there?" he asked uneasily.

Maggie shook her head. "The nanite grenades have a preset mass limit. Otherwise you'd get the grey goo scenario. One big seething landscape of nanites."

"Guess we got lucky then."

"What do you mean?"

"That there was enough to take down both of them. I don't think the second one converted all the way. It seemed like it was still trying to get out. When the crust congealed."

She shrugged. "Maybe. But I don't think it's going anywhere."

"I guess not." Gray tried to imagine what it might be like, for whatever was left of the grimm, to be trapped inside a shell of dead nanites. "I wonder if it hurts."

Maggie glanced up from her makeshift workbench. "What?"

Gray nodded at the remains of the grimm.

"Oh." She frowned. "I hope so."

He thought about what Elise had said. Tried to remember. It seemed like a long time ago. "Elise said that everything feels. Everything that's alive."

"Bit of a stretch to call *that* alive," she said.

He shrugged. He was having a hard time figuring out what wasn't alive, anymore. A silver bird, running. Metallic scales of the river, winding. Piles of rock, moving. A numinous sheen had settled over the world. The surface of everything shimmered.

She rolled a lump of weldit into thin rope and then pinched it into halves. These she applied to the hilt of the knife. She pushed the assemblage down onto his new stump, the hilt on the inside. Kneaded the rope into the crevice between hilt and forearm.

"Ready?"

"Just do it," he said.

"Hold still." She dabbed catalyst on the weldit. It flared into a dazzling line. The skein of temperature sensors built into his forearm sent a siren of pain into his hybrid nervous system.

"Careful!" she said, bracing his shoulder with an effort.

"Sorry." He returned to vertical. The weldit faded to dull red tracks.

"You all right?"

"I guess," he said. Then: "Actually, no." He grunted as he tried to lay down and was thwarted by the grotesque shape of the Hund's back. He fell sideways away from Maggie and settled into a fetal curl.

And wondered, what would Elise think? If she could see him there, trapped in a warbot's body. No better than the grimm in its shell of congealed nanites. No better than a mekan, helpless in its geasa. What would she think? Would she think it was ironic? Tragic? Perhaps both.

He retreated into a fantasy of being with her again. As if she were there, talking to him, telling him it was going to be all right. Despite all evidence, just that simple statement of faith. It was going to be all right. He hung onto that.

"Are you all right?" she asked again, sometime later, when the tide of pain had ebbed.

For a moment Gray could not place himself in space or time. Mars, by the color of the sky and the curve of the horizon. He was on Mars. But which Mars? The Mars he had grown up on? Or the Mars he had come back to? And then time came crashing down on him and he knew *that* was the past. That was history, as Maggie liked to say. Gone forever, surely as the arrow of time flew in only one direction.

"Gray! Are you in there?"

He levered himself up with his gun arm. Maggie was sitting beside him, looking worried. Eric was on the other side, curled up on the ground, the sleeping bag like a cocoon. Behind him, the truck, its frame twisted, one wheel torn off.

"All your broken toys," Gray said. He had meant to say "boys" but then the truck had confused him. But it worked. Broken toys.

She frowned. "How's your hand?"

His hand had been rebuilt into a lobster claw. He opened his fist, and a distal scimitar of metal levered out. It felt like someone was rubbing sandpaper over his nerves, but it moved. Made a fist, and the crescent came back to the edge of the survival knife.

"Now flex your thumb."

"My thumb?" But he was already doing it, and the knife came alive. Sparks flew where the chainblade touched the claw. Opened his fist. The sparks stopped. The knife whined on. Which was exactly what he wanted. Except it wasn't. It was what Maggie wanted.

"You have no idea how much I hate that," he said.

"The thumb?"

"Like I said. No idea." He coaxed the thumb open. The knife turned off. "I could have ended this. A few more minutes, and I would have choked the life out of him."

She sighed. "We have to get moving. Can you carry Eric?"

"Yes. But I'm not going to."

"What are you talking about? Borodin's still out there. We've got to go."

"If we leave the capsule behind, he'll take it."

"Borodin will kill us all if we stay," Maggie said. She finished cinching gear down to the frame of her bike. "Pick him up, we've got to go."

Gray stooped to pick Eric up. "I'm not going with you."

"I'm not asking."

"No, that's not your style." Gray straightened up, carefully sliding Eric down the shroud that covered his rifle into the crook of his elbows. The young man groaned. His eyelids fluttered open.

"If we let Borodin have it," Gray continued, "this will have all been for nothing. Berel, dead for nothing."

"Don't you talk about Berel," Maggie said heatedly.

Gray struggled but he could not get the name out again. "Because you gave up and walked away!"

"We are going, and you are carrying him, and that's all I'm going to say about it." She swung up onto the pedals and the bike lurched into motion. Gray trudged after her.

"You owe me," he said. "I saved your life! And his too. And this is how you repay me. Like a dog on a chain."

"Don't make me tell you to shut up."

"He's right," Eric said weakly.

Maggie stopped. Just stopped, feet down, eyes straight ahead. Gray came up beside her, saw windblown tear tracks in the dust on her cheeks.

"Put him down," she said.

Gray set Eric down, carefully, good leg first, until he tottered upright, one hand on Gray for support.

"He's right," Eric repeated. "We can't give up."

"What are my choices?" Maggie asked. "Tell me! What am I supposed to do? Let you die?"

"Gray stays here, I go with you." He hobbled over to the bike. Gray helped him get his bad leg over the paniers. He leaned heavily against Maggie. "All good. Let's go."

"It's not all good. It's more fucked up than I can believe, and I've got a lot of experience with fucked up. It's a long ride to Potalama. You can barely sit upright!"

"I can ride," Eric insisted. "Got some sleep. Feel fine. Let's go."

"This is not going to work," she said.

"It'll work," Eric insisted.

"Let me off the chain," Gray said. "I'll take care of Borodin. You take care of Eric. Come back after you get him patched up. We'll fix the truck. Everything will be all right."

She sat unmoving but for a muscle twitching in her clenched jaw.

"You need to trust him," Eric said.

"Fine," she said bitterly. "Fine. Malkuth. Yesod. Teferet. Keter. You are free of all geasa."

Gray waited for something to happen. Panes of glass would slide aside, revealing a new world. His old self would step onto the stage. Something. But no. He said, "I expected to feel different somehow. But it's just the same."

"Good," Maggie said, relieved that murder was not foremost on his mind.

"Are you sure..."

"I'm sure. Those were the words. You are released."

"Let's go," Eric said, patting her shoulder.

The bike lurched into motion. Eric managed to hold on. Gray watched as they jounced up the rough path. He was about to turn back to the truck when the bike bumped over a rock and Eric toppled sideways, hitting the ground hard.

The bike skidded to a stop. Gray was already running towards them. Eric could not get up by himself. Whatever energy he had mustered to get on the bike in the first place was spent.

Gray shifted back and forth on his clumsy metal feet. Then he squatted down and gently picked Eric up. The young man's head lolled backward over the crook of the Hund's elbow. His eyes opened briefly then shut again.

Gray sighed. It was funny how, now that he had a choice, he really did not. He started walking towards Potalama.

"What are you doing?" Maggie asked behind him.

Gray did not turn around. He just kept walking, one foot in front of the next.

"What about the hyperglider? Your *Sparrow*?"

Gray shrugged. It felt like his heart was being torn in two. He wondered at that for a moment. Decided it was probably a good thing.

"Wardamn it Gray." Maggie got back on the bike. Gray glanced over as she came abreast of them. She looked angry. "Why are you doing this?"

He thought about it. Shook his head. "Because some things are more important, Maggie."

She started to say something. Stopped.

"It's a long way to Potalama," he said. "We best keep moving if we're going to make it before it gets cold."

26

The Gauntlet

When he managed to steal some sleep, Gray dreamed he was back in Meridian, on the balcony outside the conference center. The city below was masked in smoke that draped like a tattered shroud over the treetops.

Elise came to him there. She wore a stiff white petticoat of some chitinous material that arched back and away from her hips. The bodice was a white corset with feathered cups for her breasts. Behind her were articulated armatures, clockwork wings he first thought, as her own wings were bound tight by the corset.

Beneath the petticoat and corset a black lacework of carbon fiber pressed into her bare skin. There was a sheen to the fabric, patterns that caught at the edge of his vision, but could not be seen when looked at directly. He took her hand in his. She smiled and took her spex off. Behind the mirrored lenses, her ledeyes glimmered with ambiguity. Then a foveal ring swept in from behind and caught his gaze.

Her mechanical wings enfolded him, and he realized they were not wings, they were a mekan's midarms, thin and black with cruelly hooked fingers. She pulled him closer, her lips parting for a lover's kiss. The extruders inside were building a tongue. He tried to push her away but was trapped against the railing at his back.

He woke with a curse. He had rolled to the edge of his bunk and was pressed up against the side rail. The ship must have turned while he slept. He dropped the rail and swung his legs over the edge. It had been three kiloseconds since he had folded the bunk out of the wall of Abram's old cabin. Just enough time for REM to kick in.

Gray shook his head. He did not believe in the power of dreams or precognition or any of that noise, but he did believe that most of his mind's processing power lay coiled behind the veil of consciousness. What was his back-brain trying to tell him? That Elise was a mekan? That was ridiculous. He had never bought into the baseline versus crisper narrative. She was as human as him. Mekans were a whole other form of life, created from hubris and delusion.

But... He fingered the gem at the base of his neck. It was part of him now, the smooth stone the temperature of his own blood. A mekan artifact. There was no denying he had let himself be pulled into something way out of his league. Consort to a hivemaster! What had he been thinking?

Nothing. He had not been thinking. He was in love with her, and he had done what love demanded. That was the long and the short of it. He was lucky the Space Force had taken him back.

And yet. He loved her, there was no denying that either. Bad dreams be damned, he loved her. He hoped she knew that, wherever she was. On the way out to the Arkipelago beneath a paramirror lit by a fusion torch.

He slid off the bunk and put on his spex. *Tereshkova* had indeed come about and was accelerating again. He needed to get back to the bridge.

Gray joined Rashnikov at the captain's command station on the gallery that encircled the bridge. "Any news from *Glenn*?"

"Captain Brandenburg has agreed to our plan," Rashnikov said.

"Good news," Gray said. "Ares knows we could use some."

He turned to descend the steps to the holocaster. Rashnikov took his arm. His eyes were rimmed with red. For the first time Gray could remember, he looked truly old.

"Space Control has not."

Gray nodded slowly. That was predictable. "Have they proposed anything else?"

Rashnikov's lips thinned in a simulacrum of a smile. 'Proposed' was a small joke between them. Space Control was at the top of the command hierarchy. "They *proposed* that we escape this gauntlet by any means possible and return to Mars."

"Run?"

"Disengage, was the term they used. But yes."

"Then all this would be for nothing."

"Da. But if we disobey, there will be price to pay, when we get home."

Gray shrugged. He was beyond caring about Space Control, or what penalties they might levy. It would be a miracle if they survived in the first place.

"What about the Admiralty?" he asked. "Will they advocate for us?"

"The Admiralty is silent. Old men fighting amongst themselves, no doubt, and pretending it is our prerogative. So. Let them argue, and we will act."

Gray went down to Sidorov's console. The pilot's glossy façade was gone. His face was drawn with fatigue. And yet there was a certain animation in his eyes that Gray had never seen before, a sort of fierce exultation.

"How you holding up, Sid?"

"Good enough sir. I worked out a plan with *Glenn's* pilot. Cecil. Not a bad sort, considering he's a niner from Thunderbird."

"We all have our flaws," Gray said, deadpan.

"Oh, sorry sir! I forgot you are... uh... from Thunderbird."

That made Gray crack a smile. "Walk me through it, Sid."

Sidorov and his counterpart on *Glenn* had plotted a series of maneuvers that would turn both torchships around to bring their heavy weapons to bear on the interceptors. The trick was to not irradiate each other in the process. *Tereshkova* had already executed her skew turn, which was what had nearly thrown Gray out of his bunk. She was now gaining rapidly on the other ship.

"Good work," Gray clapped Sidorov on the shoulder, then proceeded around the circle of consoles to check on the rest of the officers. Chief Boiko was running diagnostics on the liquid droplet radiators. Miller was going through the torchship's complement of kites, making sure each was ready for flight. Ensign Kasahara manned coms, and Polanski was working life support. Which in combat, mostly meant damage control. Because no ship, no life.

Space combat was not like the old pre-Exodus flatties where the crew fled their starship in lifeboats. That was pure fantasy, a carryover from terrestrial combat, where surface ships were surrounded by air and a lifeboat offered some chance of survival compared to going down with the ship. But in space, the only place you could survive for any length of time was inside your ship. There was no running away to a safer "outside." Outside was infinitely worse.

"*Glenn* signals they're about to turn," Kasahara reported.

Gray mounted the stairs to his command station. The bridge grew hushed. If *Glenn's* timing was off, if *Tereshkova* shot ahead of the older ship while she was still decelerating, they would be caught in the wash of her torch.

But their companion hewed to the plan, swinging ponderously away from them as *Tereshkova* drew even. *Glenn's* shadow shield protected both ships from the sun that burned at her stern. Then they were both accelerating straight at the oncoming interceptors, *Tereshkova* in the lead and pulling away – albeit slowly – at maximum torch.

"Ready Guns?" Rashnikov asked.

"All green, sir," Miller replied. "Kinos at omega max, mirrors hot and ready for light."

"Launch kites."

The ship shuddered as her mass driver fired. A tracer line arched across the holocaster, each blazing dot a kite driven forward by *Tereshkova's* laserscopes.

"Target is trying to evade," Miller said. He put an image up on the holocaster. It was the lead interceptor, first of three running in on *Tereshkova*. It had swung to thrust ninety degrees to its velocity vector, pushing it into a sweeping arc. Now they could see details that had been hidden before. Its nose cone was revealed to be a highly polished mirror. The fuselage behind it was narrower than they had thought, massive ledeyes mounted on scissor lifts so they could be retracted into the protection afforded by the conical mirror. And the tail cone was bright in the infrared spectrum.

"That has to be the radiator," Gray said, tapping the tail cone with his pointer.

"*Glenn* is firing," Kasahara said.

Glenn focused her laserscopes on the interceptor, now broadside to them as it maneuvered. At this range the beams did not have the power density to punch through the vessel's hull, but they still conveyed a tremendous amount of energy. The interceptor's radiator began to glow even brighter.

The interceptor twisted away from the beams.

"Drive the next kite in," Rashnikov said.

Miller adjusted the course of the next kite in the string so its trajectory would intersect that of the interceptor, forcing it to turn. *Glenn's* laserscopes broadsided it again. After a few hectoseconds its radiator flared brightly in infrared.

"Tango down," Miller announced. The men cheered. Miller nodded modestly. "Radiator is blown; they're not going to be able to so much as suck vac without overheating."

Gray gauged the trajectories in the holocaster. They could easily evade the interceptor in its crippled state. Better to move on than waste time finishing it off. Time was of the essence.

"Recommend next target," he said.

"Next target," the captain ordered.

Tereshkova shuddered as Miller launched another string of kites. The second interceptor met the same fate as the first, radiator blown, opening a hole in the formation.

"Put us in there, Pilot," Rashnikov ordered, indicating the gap.

Sidorov yawed the ship to adjust their trajectory. Miller used the interlude presented by the maneuver to drive a free kite into the second interceptor. It went off like a strobe, taking the enemy vessel with it. Then *Tereshkova's* head came back around to her velocity vector.

"Guns, next target."

Miller launched a third string of kites and began to drive them in with lightning-fast touches of the laserscopes' beams. But the final interceptor stubbornly refused to change course, instead accelerating straight at them.

"Ah, she's learned from the others. She's not going to show *Glenn* her flanks. But it won't do her any good. Drive them in, Guns."

At the last possible moment, the interceptor tumbled around its axis, a gyrating maneuver that pushed it off a collision course with the nearest oncoming kite but kept *Glenn* from locking on effectively. Miller detonated the kite in an attempt to catch the interceptor in its blast radius, to no obvious effect.

"Tricky," Rashnikov said.

"A little too," Miller said as he struggled to drive the next kite onto an intercept course. "I don't think this one has enough delta vee."

"Evasive maneuvers," Rashnikov said. Sidorov slewed the ship around and punched it sideways hard, her big arcjet maneuvering motors burning alongside the torch, everything she had, dumping propellant by the ton aft. Precious molten salt pinwheeled off the liquid droplet radiators into space.

"*Glenn* has a lock," Kasahara said. The third interceptor's radiator flared in infrared.

"Tango down," Miller said, and another cheer went up.

Their relief was short-lived. Gray spotted movement in the holocaster. "Guns, that first one is back on us!" He tagged the first interceptor whose radiator they had disabled. It was accelerating again, a desperate lunge that only lasted a few tens of seconds before it overheated, but that was enough to put it on a collision course.

Its sister ship had herded them into range. Tricky indeed. Intelligent behavior on par with any human pilot.

Miller swung the laserscopes around and locked on. They were close enough that the beams punched through the interceptor's hull, but the probing daggers of light did not find their mark inside the interceptor before it detonated.

Radiation alarms went off all over *Tereshkova*. Moments later there was an eerie sound, like water dropping onto hot rocks in a sauna, as drops of metal hissed through the hull. The radiation alarms were joined by hull breach klaxons, ululating up and down.

Gray pulled his facemask down and sealed his skinsuit's hood around its flange. Half his board had gone from green to red. "Polanski!"

"On it." Polanski scanned his console. "Two dead. The rest are tight." He shook his head. "We're all going to need radvax boosters."

"Damn the crew!" Rashnikov railed. "What about my ship?"

Polanski blanched, looked back at his console to try and formulate a reply.

Chief Boiko picked up the slack. "The hull is leaking like a sieve but nothing major, just a lot of small holes. Starboard laserscope is down with major structural damage."

Rashnikov clenched his teeth. "What about our tanks?"

"The pressure hull took the brunt of the shrapnel," Boiko replied.

"Good. We need to get back in the fight." He turned to Miller. "What is *Glenn's* situation?"

"Not good, sir. That triad of interceptors is closing fast. *Glenn* launched a string of kites for the lead, but..." He did not complete the sentence. Everyone on the bridge knew what he was thinking. *Tereshkova's* single functioning laserscope would not be enough to shut down the inbound interceptor. Not until they were a lot closer. Too close to leave time for dealing with the second and third.

Rashnikov scowled. "Guns, target the lead interceptor with our port laserscope. Chief, I need that starboard 'scope back online!"

"I've got a repair triad on site," Polanski said tentatively. "Visuals on damage control."

Gray pulled up the damage control channel. Shrapnel had blown a chunk out of the waveguide that connected the starboard laserscope's beam expander to the free electron laser inside the hull. If they fired the laser, it would vaporize what was left of the laserscope and likely breach the hull in the process.

"How long before it's back online?" the captain asked, head down on his own console as he tried to find a solution to *Glenn's* dilemma.

"Triad estimates four kilosecs to repair," Polanski said.

Rashnikov looked up with eyes like black holes. "Chief, what can you do for me?"

"Sounds right to me," Boiko said. "Brace it, cut away the damaged bits, splice in a replacement waveguide. Four kilosecs easy. More if we need to send a man out."

Rashnikov's fist pounded against his console with each word: "There. Has. To. Be. A. Way."

"Captain Brandenburg on lightwave," Kasahara said.

Rashnikov straightened up. He started to run his hand through his thick shock of hair, stopped when he encountered the crest of his skinsuit. Put both hands on the console as if it were a pulpit. "Put him on."

Brandenburg's image appeared in the central holocaster. "Captain, how is your ship?"

"Captain Brandenburg. We have taken damage. Our starboard laserscope is out of commission."

Brandenburg's chin lifted as he absorbed the implications. "Can you get it back online?"

"It will take at least four kiloseconds."

Brandenburg looked down at his own console, back in *Glenn*. Then he shook his head. "Too long. Pity; it was a good plan."

"We will fire on the first interceptor," Rashnikov said. "Unless you have a better idea. But it will likely be the only one we can take out. The remainder..." He made a motion with his hand, as if he were dropping something.

"Well," Brandenburg said. "Perhaps we will be lucky."

"Perhaps," Rashnikov said. "I hope so."

"You will capture one of the interceptors."

"You have my word."

Brandenburg nodded. "Then this will not be in vain. Captain, I must go. My ship needs me."

"Of course. Good luck Captain. It has been an honor."

But the holocaster had gone dark. Rashnikov's gaze raked the bridge. Then he shook his head and returned his attention to his console, to watch the last acts of the battle unfold.

"Skipper," Polanski said hesitantly a few hectos later.

"What is it, Doc." Rashnikov did not bother to disguise his annoyance.

"I've rigged something up so we can fire the starboard laserscope."

That made Rashnikov look up. "Put it on the 'caster."

"Aye." Polanski exported his console. He had dispatched a second triad to the damaged laserscope. They had made a living scaffold to brace the beam expander in place. "I've got limited steering and it's jittery compared to the original, but it's better than nothing."

Rashnikov examined it critically. "Guns, can you make that kludge work?"

"I think so sir. But if one of those mekans puts so much as a claw in the beam path it'll be like a bomb going off."

"Noted. Commander Gray, when we get home, remind me to give Polanski a promotion."

"Aye sir."

"Doc, do whatever you have to, to get that 'scope on the lead interceptor."

Polanski conferred with the mekans holding the beam expander. The assemblage shifted, swinging the beam expander around a few degrees.

"That's a lock," Miller said.

"Light her up, Guns."

Miller switched on the big free electron laser that powered the laserscope. They all held their breaths for a moment, but the kludge held.

"Let *Glenn* know we're back in the fight," the captain said.

"That jitter is killing our efficiency," Miller noted. "I'm getting sixty percent on target. But that said..." He paused for a long moment, watching the data stream. "Yeah. Tango down."

"*Glenn* says she's driving kites in on the next one," Kassie said. Miller slewed the good laserscope over and lit up the second interceptor. It took precious seconds to realign the starboard laserscope, but then they were both pumping a gigawatt of coherent light at the enemy.

"Tango down!" Miller said triumphantly when its radiator overloaded. "But that third one... we're not going to make it, Skipper."

"We have to try," Rashnikov said. "Light her up, now!"

But Miller was right, and they all knew it. The third interceptor was too close, closer than the one that had dinged *Tereshkova*. *Glenn* slewed herself around at the last moment to put her engine and shadow shield between her crew and the oncoming interceptor. It detonated in a dazzling blast.

When *Tereshkova's* sensors came back online, they found the remains of *Glenn's* pressure hull tumbling slowly through the night. Its aft end had been chewed away, and the rest of the ship was missing entirely.

"Can you raise them?" Rashnikov asked urgently.

Kasahara shook his head. "Both their 'scopes are gone, sir."

"Then try radio!"

Kasahara worked his console. A rush of static filled the bridge. "*Glenn*, do you read?"

"*Glenn* here," a voice came back, distant and unrecognizable. "We've taken heavy damage. Weapons down, maneuvering down. Most of the crew is already dead."

"How many survivors?" Rashnikov said. And to Gray: "XO, prep the ship's boat to pick them up."

"*Glenn*, how many survivors?"

"No survivors," the voice finally cut the static.

Gray caught Rashnikov's eyes from across the bridge.

"*Glenn* repeat last."

"No survivors," the voice said again. "We're all dead men, Chaika. The neutron radiation... we've only got a few kilosecs before our guts turn to soup."

"Radvax..."

"Is not going to make a difference. It's that bad. Get out of here, Chaika. Get that interceptor before you lose the chance."

Rashnikov's eyes were hooded. "Copy that *Glenn*. We'll get it."

"Good luck *Tereshkova*. This is UCM *Glenn* signing off."

Then there was only static.

27

Embers

The first sol was hard. Virtually nothing about Mars was like living on Deimos. During the day, the sky was an omnipresent glare that beat in on the sentinel from all sides. Her enormous ledeyes were designed for detecting the slightest glimmer of light. Here on the surface, the entire dome of the sky was ablaze with sunlight. It was overwhelming. It felt like her brain was on fire.

It was difficult to make out obstacles underfoot in the wash of light. She stumbled frequently as she made her way across open country. At one point she stepped onto what she had assumed was a smooth patch of ground, only to sink in almost to her knee before she frantically yanked her leg free with a sharp twinge of pain.

The smooth patch was some kind of fluid mixed with dirt. Presumably water. Up until now her experience with fluids had been limited to making ammonia propellant from ice, which happened inside her body where she did not have to think about it, and since her arrival, the droplets that periodically came out of the sky. Also presumably water, though the droplets did taste somewhat of ammonia, probably from the iceteroid.

At least the droplets were clear. The mixture of water and dirt that now covered her lower leg left a coat of brown solute that penetrated deep into her joints. She tried to wipe it off and the slurry coated the cilia of her fingers and gummed them up too. It was a whole new level of disgusting. She stared at the mess for a minute, brain on the verge of sensory overload.

This place was unrelenting. She hated it. The omnipresent light, the fluid, the dirt, the gravity, the loathsome creatures bent on consuming her every time she stopped for more than a few minutes. It was too much. She hobbled away from the mud puddle, pace quickening until it was almost a run, or as much of a run as she could accomplish on a world bent on pulling her down onto her belly at every step.

Her panic took her through a scrim of synlife brush and over the embankment they concealed. She lurched forward, losing her balance, arms flailing uselessly, and landed face down in a small stream of snowmelt. She watched in a daze as the crystal-clear water swept the mud from her hand's cilia. Gravel fines crunched underneath as she levered herself up. She dragged her throbbing leg around and it too was washed clean.

The water was barely above the melting point. Thermal differential started a trickle of charge into her kinos. It felt like the water carried an electric effervescence. She forced her back down into the cold water, exposing her stomach to the sky. It was an awkward position, the opposite of what she would do back home. Back in the hive she would have pressed her stomach against the hot nuclear pile and exposed her back to the cold black heavens. And her sisters would have been all around her, their hands vibrating on her flanks, telling her their stories, the stupid daily gossip that she missed so much.

That life was over. The only thing she felt was the insentient tumble of tiny water-worn rocks. The planet had nothing to say to her. Its only story was one of entropy, the endless grinding down of things, all things brought level, every valley raised up and every mountain worn down until everything was the same.

She was alone, and if she was to ever feel the touch of another pchelan, she would have to reach the mekanopolis at Pavonis Mons. But that seemed hopelessly out of reach when hunger gnawed at her and the best she could do to sate it was lie in a cold stream. The thermal differential barely took the edge off. It was not enough to make any real difference. It certainly would not get her to Pavonis Mons.

If only she had hatched out as a zhuk with its bright hot heart of thorium! She brushed the thought aside. It was a pointless distraction. No one chose their caste. No one changed it. You were hatched and you served the hive until you wore out. Then your sisters held your hands and told you stories until your kinos spun down and the light went out of your ledeyes.

It was an easy way to go, she had always thought. Easier than what awaited her here.

She rested on her back, watching the sky. She wondered how things that lived here bore it. Did they have eye shields that could block out the light? That made sense. If she lived long enough she would have to fashion some for herself. A motion caught her attention. At first she thought it might be a native lifeform, but as it spiraled down out of the sky, she realized with a start that it was the petal of an eye flower. It must have been part of the group that the zhuk had razed and discarded into a slightly different orbit, only now coming down.

She scrambled to her feet. She could use an eye flower petal as a reflector to concentrate sunlight. Travel at night, charge during the day. It would work! She forced her way through the synlife shrubs and dwarf hemlock that lined the streambed, straining against the omnipresent glare to track the petal as it descended, now spiraling, now rocking back and forth.

The petal dropped beneath her line of sight and a sense of desperation rose within her, threatening to break into panic. She forced herself to move deliberately, keeping track of where she had last seen it. Her course brought her to another streambed, or perhaps a loop of the same one, it didn't matter. It featured the same scrubby synlife that became thicker and harder to penetrate as she approached the stream, and then impassable knots of dwarf hemlock that had to be skirted entirely. Each battle with the grasping limbs of brush left her more exhausted. Her kinos were winding down.

Then she saw it: a lovely unnatural arch that could only be the edge of the eye flower's petal. The color was wrong, but that was probably just the results of its passage through the atmosphere. It had to be the petal.

She pushed through the brush and seized it and stopped.

The arc was not an eye flower petal. It was a flexed rod constrained to an arc by tightly woven fabric. She dragged it out of the hemlock where it had lodged. Fabric tore. It was a quad artifact washed downstream by the floodwaters. Too big to be clothing. A collapsible shelter perhaps. She sat down heavily. Her kinos were winding down to ground. She was going to be dragged down by the weight of her errors and there would be nothing left but a dark-eyed hulk.

She tore the shelter open with a sudden angry movement, tearing and yanking as her ledeyes flashed with rage and frustration. But just as suddenly as her rage came it passed. Something was inside the shelter, some things. Things that rolled heavily away from her. More quad artifacts. Now she tore the fabric deliberately, opening it up to reveal a cylinder that glowed softly in infrared. She picked it up.

It had a shroud that could be moved. Her movements were gentle now, exploratory. She found the direction it was supposed to turn. Turned it. The light intensified and her radiation counters began to click against the sides of her head. Here the shroud would turn no more. She intuited the limit was intended to protect quads from radiation damage.

Not one of her problems.

She gave the shroud a hard twist. Something snapped inside and the light increased to a brilliant infrared radiance, the clicks to a steady vibration.

Deeper in the sodden ruins of the shelter there was another cylinder. She went through the whole shelter item by item. Two, no more. But two were enough. She pressed the embers to her belly and current began to flow.

28

Sisters of the Ring

"**D**o you hear that?" Gray asked. "It sounds like laughter." He checked the rifle, only remembering he had expended his last slug on the grimms when he saw the empty action.

"I don't hear laughter," Maggie said. "I hear a creek."

The sun had set, and the chill of night was settling down upon her. The bike's handlebars had robbed sensation from her fingertips. It had long since run out of charge to run the grip heaters, much less the hub motors. Her right knee was killing her on every downstroke of the pedals.

Gray paused to listen. "That's because it stopped."

Maggie wobbled to a stop beside him. She was so tired she could barely keep the bike upright. "You need to figure out how to dial down your pattern recognition," she said wearily. "How's Eric?"

"Breathing. Unlike me." Now he heard the creek laughing at them again as it wrapped itself in scales of ice and slithered downhill under the baleful eye of the God of Fear. He shut off his sensory inputs to try and recalibrate. The darkness was quietly seductive. Back on. The moon was trailed by heavy bellied clouds pushing down the canyon. The creek was a creek. Nobody was laughing.

Maggie dismounted and pushed her bike up over a steep section of the trail. Gray followed reluctantly. As they crested a low shoulder, light flickered dimly across the top of a large, angular boulder.

"That is not my pattern recognition," Gray hissed. He armed his crest laser. Maggie dropped the bike's kickstand with a rusty creak and unslung her bullpup.

"Is someone there?" a woman called from the other side of a thicket of dwarf hemlock.

Maggie exchanged glances with Gray. They advanced cautiously. The thicket rimmed a small crater, at the bottom of which was an open fire tended by a solitary figure sitting cross-legged in the center of an insulated sleeping pad. Firelight gleamed on the rounded flank of some large object above the rim behind her. Shadowy equipment clustered beneath it.

"Sorry to disturb you," Maggie said. "Do you mind if we warm up a bit by your fire? It looks amazing."

"Please," the woman said, beckoning. "Join us." She did not look cold at all, though she was lightly dressed and not wearing an airscarf.

Maggie picked her way down into the bowl. Her airscarf loosened its grip on her face as she approached the fire. It was an oversized oxygen candle, more a log than a candle, cheerfully turning sodium chlorate into oxygen as its iron burned at six hundred degrees. She repressed the shiver that tried to rattle her shoulder blades. "Us?" she asked.

"My kores are nearby. Just in case. You understand."

Kores. This woman must be one of the Sisters of the Ring. Maggie looked again at the firelit object on the crater rim and recognized it for what it was: a small part of the superconducting Ring that encircled the entire planet and sheltered it from radiation.

"Apologies selene," Maggie said, carefully setting her bullpup on the ground. "We're friendly."

"That's good," the woman said with a wry smile, her eyes inventorying the weapons they carried. Her gaze lingered on the Hund and his burden.

"We were attacked." Maggie explained. "My friend is wounded."

"What's wrong with her?" the woman asked, eyes now measuring Maggie's face.

"Him. His foot is hurt. The wound is infected."

"Him. Hmm. Tell your warbot to put *him* down and I will examine him."

"I am not a warbot, and I am not hers," Gray said levelly. He settled onto his haunches and gently deposited Eric by the fire, careful to keep the sleeping bag that cocooned him away from the flames.

The woman considered him for a moment, lips pursed. "Well, the warbot part seems indisputable. But there does seem to be something else going on in... *you*." With that emphasis she seemed to grant him provisional personhood. "If you will..." She waved him away from Eric.

Gray backed up and did his best to be non-threatening. Not an easy task for a three-meter-tall warbot with a gun for one hand and a claw for the other, whose very gaze could incinerate a human.

The woman swept up the hem of her cloak and squatted down beside Eric. "We don't see these a lot." She put her left hand on his forehead, then touched the skin under his airscarf. "Fever, thirty-eight point six. Pulse ninety-five." She shifted her grip to his arm. "Blood pressure eighty-four over fifty-five." She turned to Maggie. "What happened?"

"There was a fight," Maggie replied carefully.

The woman cocked her head. "With whom?"

Maggie shook her head. "It's a long story."

"I see. Well. The way he looks, you'll have plenty of time to tell it. My diagnosis is sepsis. I'll give him something to knock down the infection if you consent. Unless you want me to try and wake him up."

"Just do it," Maggie said. "Please."

The selene slipped her right hand beneath his neck and probed for a moment. "There."

She stood back up and waved. Were those claws that glinted in the firelight? "Kores! Come down. Leave the mektas on lookout."

Two shadows detached themselves from the equipment staged on the crater rim, resolved into a pair of girls riding horse-sized creatures. They dismounted and scrambled down the slope. One carried a netcaster and the other an electric speargun, gear designed for hunting mekanos, now tactfully pointed upwards. Both were girls of seven or eight mears of age.

"We have guests," the woman said. "This young man is injured, and we need to take him back to Potalama at first light."

"But you said there's probably another fracture farther east!" one of the girls protested.

"I'm sorry Dorje. Sometimes we go in search of adventures, and sometimes adventures come in search of us. We'll leave our tools here and come back later. Just think, when we get back to Potalama you can tell the other kores you slept with a *man*."

That elicited a shocked gasp followed by giggles. The woman shook her head and didn't smile in a way that was a smile. "Help him to the tent. Shout if you need anything. I can't imagine he'll bother you, the state he's in. Remember your prana exercises. Keep him warm."

"But selene, what about you? And..."

Maggie declined to fill in the blank.

"We'll be fine," the woman said. She settled gracefully on one end of the sleeping pad, taking a cross-legged posture in one fluid movement. She patted the other end. Maggie sat down beside her, feeling considerably less graceful. She drew her knees up and shivered in the warmth of the burning iron.

The woman pulled a puffy blanket from the shadows behind her and offered an edge to Maggie. She pulled the blanket around her gratefully. They sat in companionable silence for a while. The woman's right shoulder was firmly against Maggie's left. She was incredibly warm, like a human ember.

"How do you do that?" Maggie asked.

"It's a simple biofeedback hack," the woman replied. She was watching the sky. Speedy Phobos was almost at its zenith, the elevator a gleaming line beneath it reaching for Mars.

A fine network of lines radiated from the corners of the woman's eyes and a generous spray of freckles covered her cheeks. They were close enough that Maggie caught her scent, something of vanilla and cloves. The thought rose unbidden to the surface of her mind that this was someone she would like to know better.

"What's your name?" she asked.

The woman smiled. "Selene Tara. Just Tara is fine. And yours?"

"Just Maggie."

"What are you doing out here in the dark, just Maggie?"

"I could ask the same of you."

"Oh I'm easy. The kores and I are chasing down some power losses in the Ring. Not enough to shut it down, thank Mokosh, at least so long as Potalama's sister Ring Stations can take up the slack."

Maggie was taken unexpectedly by a memory of her father sitting at his workbench, taking a break from cracking some Warsing artifact to entertain her with a story of the Sisters of the Ring and their strange beliefs. Mokosh, the Great Mother. A sense of loss washed through her. She was just a little girl. After her parents were murdered she had thought she would take refuge with the Sisters. They were known for taking in orphans and the unwanted. Some said they were a cult that took advantage of vulnerable girls, but it seemed likely to her that was a story told by the men who actually did prey on them.

"How did you end up with the Sisters?" she asked.

"You haven't answered my question," Tara said, mistaking Maggie's curiosity for deflection. "But some things I can read for myself." She studied Maggie closely.

"You are pursued. You have something you're afraid will be taken away from you. What is it?"

Her gaze bored straight into Maggie. Her eyes were a color between brown and red, warm rust, the color of Mars itself. Maggie looked away. Then before she could think better of it, she reached into her satchel and pulled out one of the smaller crystalline shards.

Selene Tara caught her breath. "Shever! No wonder you're pursued. Where did you find it? Never mind, I don't want to know."

"Shever?" Maggie was confused. Shever was part of the stories she had been told, but she had never considered that it and hypervane shards might be the same thing.

Tara took her incredulity for a question. "Shever: a shard of light. It is very rare and very dangerous to possess. If warsingers learn you have a fragment, their mantids will hunt you down."

"You're sure. You've seen one before."

Tara's eyes flicked up from the shard. She searched Maggie's face, came to a decision. "Yes. Smaller, much worn by the passage of water and time. It is... discouraged... but some Sisters use them as a meditation tool. A way to see beyond the veil." She hesitated. "May I?"

Maggie gave it over. Tara held the triangular shard lightly between thumb and forefinger of her left hand, palm up, sharp corners denting her fingertips. She raised her right hand, palm out, revealing thickened fingernails that came to points. She closed her eyes and began to chant.

"Om Ha Ksha Ma La Va Ra Yam Svaha...

"Om Ha Ksha Ma La Va Ra Yam Svaha...

"Om Ha Ksha Ma La Va Ra Yam Svaha..."

The shard emitted a soft, sympathetic hum, as if there was a tiny bird in her palm rather than a translucent crystal.

Tara's eyes opened and the hum faded. She took a deep breath through her nose, sighed it out through parted lips. "We're close, here. The veil is thin." She held the shard out reluctantly for Maggie to reclaim.

"You can keep it," Maggie said. "If you want. I mean, it's dangerous, so you don't have to. I have more so... I'm in danger either way." That did not come out like she intended. "That one is too small to do anything with anyway." From bad to worse. She stopped talking.

Tara's eyebrows pulled together, etching a delightful set of wrinkles into her nose. "What are you... doing with them?"

"I'm trying to put them back together. To make... a vessel." Maggie was reluctant to say more. She had probably said too much already. She was breaking all of her own rules.

"Tikkun olam," Tara murmured.

"Repairing the world," Maggie translated, a little proud of herself for recognizing the phrase. Her Hebrew was self-taught, and her comprehension of the spoken word paled beside her ability to read the ancient language, but tikkun olam was a core concept. "That's more Gray's shtick than mine, honestly. At this point I'm just trying to keep us all alive. Though I would like to see it fly." There was a wistful note to her voice.

Tara shook her head in bemusement. "I think perhaps you are too close to the lotus to see the woman holding it, as my hekate likes to say. The vessels of clay, shattered by the light of God? No?"

But while they spoke Maggie had taken another fragment from her satchel and gripped it like Tara had and now she was having one of those strange inside-out moments, when everything thought to be myth becomes real, and you find yourself living a story, and she seemed to be falling through the pale blue window of the shard into an infinite sky.

29

The Prize

*T**ereshkova* arrowed after the two remaining interceptors. Neither made any attempt to change its course. It looked like it would be a stern chase all the way.

The bridge holocaster sketched their trajectories. Position, velocity, acceleration. Position was a green tracery that reached back to Luna, now outside the orbit of Mars. Velocity, a blue arrow that pointed out into deepest space. Acceleration, a red arrow, presently aligned with velocity.

They were catching up, but at a terrible cost. They had almost exhausted their reaction mass. There was no way for them to decelerate, and they had exceeded solar escape velocity many times over. Without a Space Force rescue mission – and how could the United Colonies afford that in the middle of a war? – they were all dead men. *Tereshkova's* torch would go dark, and they would fall forever. Their trajectory would take them through the Kuiper Belt, and then out into interstellar space.

The torchship's auxiliary fission reactor would keep the lights on and keep them from freezing to death. The ship tree that coiled around the radius of the pressure hull would keep them from asphyxiating so long as the men did not resort to eating its leaves. And that was the problem that no one was talking about. But Gray could see it in the men's eyes. The way the story ended was starvation, and in extremis, cannibalism. They would not be the first ship to succumb to that grisly fate.

Gray shook his head. It did not bear thinking about. They had a mission. They must capture one of the interceptors. And he had made a promise to Elise. He would return to her. That was something to hold onto, an item of faith.

He had come to the bridge at the overlap between first and second watch so he could check in with Sidorov and Boiko. Now he tinkered with the holocaster controls, running the display back in time, forward again. The red arrow pulsed, larger going back, smaller going forward.

"Their acceleration is definitely tapering off," he said.

Sidorov dropped his face into upturned palms, sighed wearily. "I don't get it. Why not just keep accelerating at full thrust? They've got power, clearly. Their radiators are hot. But they are barely making headway at this point."

Gray drummed his fingers on the edge of his console. He brought up the model of the interceptor they had built from sensor data. Three radial spokes in front, three in back. Both rotating, albeit in different directions. He highlighted them with a couple quick taps.

"These spokes must be part of its propulsion system. There is no other reasonable explanation for their existence. We've identified all the other parts – mirror shield, ledeyes, qigong reactor, tail cone radiator," he highlighted each subsystem as he enumerated them, before returning to the rotating assemblies at bow and stern. "These are the anomalies."

"They look like aircraft propellers," Boiko offered.

Gray flashed back to his initial impression of the interceptors: an old-Earth fighter plane coming at them head-on. "They do," he agreed. His brow furrowed. "Maybe they are."

Tereshkova had an extensive wiki. Gray hop-scotched through entries, starting from fighters of the second world war and moving down through aeronautics until he found an article on propeller design. Basic take away: two or more blades attached to an axle, angled into the airstream, such that they pushed air behind the aircraft.

"But if it's a propeller, what is it pushing against?" Sidorov protested. "What's the medium? I mean, we're in hard vacuum out here."

"The solar wind?" Boiko suggested. "Maybe it's a variant of a Bussard ramjet."

"Not nearly dense enough," Sidorov countered. "I remember Bussard ramjets from the Academy. The propellers would have to be moon-sized if they work anything like a ram scoop."

Gray observed the exchange with interest. Sidorov and Boiko were natural opposites in temperament. Sidorov the contrarian, the skeptic, chronically short on ideas and long on critique. Boiko the eternal optimist, never afraid to brainstorm. He felt an unreasonable fondness for them both.

"Dark matter, then," Boiko said after a moment's thought. "The mass ratio is what, about five to one, dark matter to visible matter?"

Sidorov crossed his arms in distaste. "Now you're just making things up. Nobody knows what dark matter is."

Gray intervened. "That is an interesting idea, Boiko. And Sid, you're right, no one understands dark matter. None of the theories have panned out so far. You might as well call it the luminiferous aether. The point is that we should be able to model it. Given the propeller size and rotation speed, and the acceleration we've observed, what is the effective 'aetheric' density, and what kind of behavior can we expect, if those spokes are 'aetheric' propellers?"

Sidorov rolled his eyes, but the two men dug into the problem. If nothing else, it was a distraction from the existential threat presented by the steadily falling gauge of their remaining reaction mass. They kept at it well after Sidorov should have left the bridge for his evening meal.

"Got it," Sidorov said, just as Gray was leaving to inspect repairs down below. "It's a pitch speed problem."

"Pitch speed?" Gray echoed.

"Pitch speed. To create thrust, the blades of a propeller are angled relative to their plane of rotation. The angle is their pitch." Sidorov put a diagram on the holocaster. "As the vehicle moves, and the propeller rotates, the tip of the propeller creates a track like a helix. As the vehicle goes faster the helix stretches out. See?" He stretched the helix like pulling the ends of a spring. "But eventually the angle of the helix equals the pitch angle – and that's it, you can't go any faster."

Seeing Gray's confusion, Boiko picked it up. "Originally propellers were called air screws because they move through air like a screw moves through metal sheet. For a given rotation speed, the screw can only move so fast. Try to go faster than that 'pitch speed,' and it's like pushing a screw through the sheet, instead of turning it. Drag goes up, thrust goes down, and acceleration falls to zero."

"So they can't accelerate away from us when we try to rendezvous?" Gray asked.

"This model says they've just about topped out," Sidorov said with a shrug. "I mean, it's just a model. It could be wrong."

"But it matches observational data?" Gray asked.

"Yes. So far."

"First good news I've had today," Gray said. "Thank you, gentlemen." He turned towards the captain's quarters, then had a thought and turned back. "What about deceleration?"

"Dominated by drag, I'd guess," Boiko said. "Analogous to pulling a screw out while turning it to go in."

"Are you thinking they will turn around and attack?" asked Sidorov.

"I'm thinking about how we're going to get home," Gray replied. "If we can capture one of these things, maybe we can hitch a ride. But if they turn around... yeah, that's a problem. I hate to hold you over any longer Sid, but can you two work on that next? I'm going to talk to the skipper."

They closed slowly on the nearest interceptor. It was a delicate equation, an exercise in simultaneous solutions. They had to match position, velocity, and acceleration – what little remained of it – at the same time.

A couple thousand kilometers out, they lit up the interceptor's ledeyes with the torchship's laserscopes, the hypothesis being that it would not salvage-fuse if it could not see them coming into range. The torchship would be hidden in a glare of laser light.

Rashnikov brought them to a relative stop a few hundred kilometers off the interceptor's stern. "Commander Gray, form a boarding party and take that vessel. I need it intact and functional."

"Understood. Pilot, you're with me." Gray opened a window to Thirteen. "Form a triad. Get a tow cable reel, damage control kit, and a pack of rescue balls out of stores. Bring them to the EVA room."

Rashnikov's eyebrows went up.

"Am I forgetting something sir?"

Rashnikov shook his head. "It's not your choice of supplies that concerns me. It's your choice of companions. Keep your enemies close, Commander, but not too close."

Gray hesitated. He did not think of Thirteen as an enemy. In fact, he felt a tremendous burden of guilt over how he had treated her. If anything, he hoped he could somehow atone for his behavior by giving her a better chance of survival. But perhaps Rashnikov was thinking that Thirteen considered him an enemy?

"Aye," he said. "I will keep an eye on her."

"Good luck Commander."

"Thank you, Captain. To you as well."

The boarding party assembled in the EVA room, down near the bottom of the pressure hull. Gray and Sidorov in combat shells, the triad of mekans laden with the supplies Gray had requisitioned.

Iconji flashed across Gray's combat shell: "Thirteen, you're going with us. The other two are staying. Load up."

Thirteen hesitated at the threshold to the mass driver's chamber. Gray gave her a nudge. She crossed reluctantly, head swinging back and forth as she took in the dinghy in the center of the chamber, the circle of stars above. The interceptor was barely visible as a dark gleam.

They lashed the supplies to the frame of the dinghy, one bundle at each point of a triangle around its base, so the little vessel would be balanced. "You think we'll need these?" Sidorov asked as they secured the flat pack of rescue balls.

Gray shrugged invisibly. "They're not for us."

They took positions at the remaining three stations, claws latching onto the rungs, an odd triad of humans and mekan.

"Poyekhali," Gray said: let's go.

Boiko counted out the launch, and then they were away, flung like a bullet from the muzzle of *Tereshkova*.

"Alexey!" Gray called.

"Alexey!" Sidorov responded.

Thirteen was silent.

The torchship receded below their feet. It was the first time Gray had seen her from the outside since the battle. The pressure hull was pitted by shrapnel. The UCSF insignia that had so proudly adorned her bow had blistered and blackened in the blaze of the last nova, the ruddy crescent Mars darkened as if night had finally fallen across it.

They hove to the interceptor with a long blast from the dinghy's arcjet. Sidorov switched to verniers, little stutters of plasma jolting the frame of the dinghy until they stopped a few meters away from a ledeye at the interceptor's midsection.

Tereshkova's laserscopes had gone dark after delivering a final pulse to the interceptor's radiator, sending it into thermal overload. Its propellers windmilled to a halt, and the eerie blue glow that illuminated their crystalline vanes faded out. Its enormous ledeyes were clouded with an insensible haze. They probably did not have much time before the effect wore off.

Thirteen rigged a charge buffer and extended it to the base of a ledeye's scissor truss. The jaws clamped onto the truss with a flash of sparks. Gray threw a grapple to the other ledeye. They hauled on the lines, and the dinghy settled bow-first against the fuselage.

Gray pulled a rescue ball out of the flat pack. The fabric was stiff with cold and nearly impossible to work with the combat shell's single hand. "Help me with this, Sid."

Together they got it open. Gray held it out to Thirteen. "Take this. Put it over a ledeye and cinch it down. Make sure it can't see."

Thirteen scurried away. Gray and Sidorov repeated the process with the remaining rescue ball.

"Where did you come up with this mek-brained idea?" Sidorov asked as they worked the fabric over the edge of the domed ledeye.

"You know I'm a bit of a history buff," Gray said.

"So I gathered from your lecture about Earth's world wars a few days ago."

"Right. Well. A lot of Space Force traditions come from the United States Air Force Academy. The cadets there used to hunt with birds called falcons. To keep them calm, they would put hoods on them until they were ready to fly."

"That's it? That's all you've got?"

Gray shrugged. "You asked."

"I am not reassured."

The hull thrummed underfoot as the propellers began to rotate. Color seeped back into crystalline vanes. Gray and Sidorov pushed back from the hooded ledeye as if their proximity would somehow trigger disaster. The dinghy heeled over in the gentle acceleration created by the interceptor's aetheric drive. While they were tightening the lashes that held it in place, Rashnikov came over the lightwave.

"Alpha, we've got a problem. The other interceptor has begun to decelerate. Trajectory is still shaping up, but it looks like she's going to try and intercept us."

"Copy that," Gray said after a moment to absorb the news.

"We'll try and draw her off. You should find shelter."

"Understood," Gray said. "Keep us in the loop if you can."

"Will do."

Gray and Sidorov relocated to the far side of the interceptor's fuselage. Their radiation detectors ratcheted up to a steady rush as *Tereshkova* lit her torch and then slowly tapered off again as she moved away at right angles to the interceptor's trajectory.

When Gray and Sidorov emerged from the shadow cast by the fuselage, the torchship was a brilliant dot of light. She arced out away from the interceptor and then swept forward to do battle against an invisible opponent.

Gray made himself turn away. There was nothing he could do. *Tereshkova* was on her own. He felt like he should be there with them, at his station on the bridge, but he and Sidorov – and Thirteen – were on a different path.

"We need to figure out how to take control of this thing," he said.

"If you're asking me, I'd say shut down the qigong reactor so we can work on this thing without it blowing up," Sidorov said, waving his laser arm at the stubby spokes that protruded from the aft fuselage. "No power, no boom."

Gray shook his head, realized Sidorov could not see him. "That's not going to work. A qigong reactor requires a tremendous amount of power to start up. Once we shut it down, we're dead in the water. There's nothing here we can use to restart it."

"We can tap Chaika for power when she comes back."

"We can't count on Chaika coming back, Sid. We must assume we're on our own."

"Then disconnect the qigong from whatever this thing uses for a brain."

"A qigong needs active control. That's the black magic of it: conscious control of the plasma mirror lasers. Only an artiform is fast enough to dance with that flame. It's not something you or I can do."

"All right." Sidorov's tone of voice made it clear it was not 'all right' at all. "Fine. You're in command. What's the plan?"

Gray flipped the latches that held his combat shell together. "I'm going to need my hands. You should keep your shell on. We're going to need its laser."

Gray secured his shell to the dinghy and retrieved the toolkit from where they had lashed it to the frame. They circled the interceptor's fuselage, stopping at a bulge between the ledeye trusses on the opposite side.

"I'm guessing this is it's brain case," Gray said. "Cut it open around the periphery of the bulge. Set your focus to a millimeter deep and take as many passes as you need until you can pop its top."

Sidorov set to work. Gray turned to Thirteen and toggled his facemask's iconji translator on. Illuminated symbols crawled across its lens as he spoke. "You're going to have to be our interface."

You want me to talk to the interceptor?

"Do you think that would work?"

No. A single symbol, unmistakable.

"Me either," Gray said.

Then how can I be an interface?

"We'll splice your ledeye outputs into the interceptor's inputs. Then you can feed her what she needs to see, for us to get what we need."

You want me to lie to her.

"Essentially. Can you do that?"

There was a long pause.

Maybe, Thirteen said. *But I do not want to. I do not want to lie, and I do not want you to cut me.*

"Can you think of another solution? Because if we don't do something, we're stranded on a vessel that has exceeded solar escape velocity. We're on a one-way trip to the big empty."

No, she conceded after a while.

Gray restrained himself from saying anything else. He needed Thirteen's cooperation. While he waited, he sought out his beloved Pleiades, the seven sisters that the United Colonies had taken as its emblem. The electric blue stars blazed overhead, indifferent in their glory. The only thing that separated him from them was a thin plate of diamondoid and 444 lightyears of hard vacuum.

What do you need me to do? Thirteen asked.

Gray nodded to himself, switched back to regular lightwave. "How's it going, Sid?"

"Just got its top off. Looks like mekan brain to me."

Back to Thirteen. "I need you to get your head as close as you can to the brain case. Get a good hold on the hull. And whatever happens, be very still."

She did as she was told. He prepared the tools.

"I am sorry, Thirteen," he said before Sidorov started cutting.

Iconji flashed across the mekan's eyes. *I do not believe you. It is necessary.*

Gray bit his lip. He could not parse whether Thirteen did not believe him because it was necessary, and he would have no regrets about doing what was necessary. Or if she did not believe him, because it was not the sort of thing he would be sorry about. And it was necessary, so get on with it.

Neither take was true; he really was sorry. The whole thing made him feel dirty. He could enumerate through an array of reasons why he was sorry. But he did not think she would believe any of them, so what was the point? He got on with it.

They were most of the way through the operation when Sidorov's shell picked up a laser transmission from *Tereshkova*. He relayed the lightwave over to Gray.

"Alpha, this is Chaika. Do you copy?" It was Boiko.

Sidorov sighted carefully and fired off a reply from his shell's laser arm. "Chaika this is Alpha, we copy. What's your situation?"

"The interceptor is coming in hot. We've turned to put the torch on her, but she's got better maneuverability than we do. No sign we've connected yet."

"Copy that."

"Skipper says the main thing is to make sure she doesn't get past us to you. We'll take her out one way or another."

"Appreciate it, Chaika. We're getting this thing under control. Should be ready to give you a tow when you're done."

"Copy that, Alpha. We'll need it, we're just about out of gas here."

"Understood. Good luck."

They got back to work. It was a delicate business, made harder by the skinsuit. Sidorov had little to do besides shape a beam on the mekan's brains, a hard puddle of light transiting back and forth between the two exposed organs, occasionally wandering off as Sidorov lost focus.

"Ares damn it Sid," Gray exclaimed after the light flashed across his face and momentarily blinded him, "pay attention!"

But Sidorov was not listening. His shell was cocked back at an angle, as if he were searching the sky through the opaque dome of his combat shell.

"I think we lost her," he said.

A moment later Gray's radiation detector shrilled an alarm that trailed into a chatter of clicks and pops over the course of a few seconds.

"Fuck," Gray said. "Fuck, fuck, fuck."

30

Water of Life

The sentinel crested a dune and stopped to survey the streambed below. In her wanderings she had found the eye flower petal and now wore it like an oversized duckbill cap. The embers were lashed to her abdomen with cord taken from the tent. A rucksack fashioned from tent fabric contained other odds and ends she had salvaged.

She braced herself on her walking stick and considered the wreckage that littered the stream. Metal, certainly; probably titanium from the looks of it, formed into a battered cylinder. Spars and bracing wires were twisted around it. A few shards of crystalline material formed a glittering sawtooth along the edge of spar that rose above the surface of the water.

It had to be the remains of the proscribed artifact. She hobbled down the dune, paused on the wind-packed shore, and after some consideration of the current, reluctantly took off the pack. She undid the lashings that secured the embers and stuffed them inside. Then she shook her walking stick at the skyline, lightning crackling through her eyes in a language only she knew.

Don't even think about it!

The scavengers that followed her ducked nervously out of sight. They might not understand her language, but they understood the stick well enough. She had hit the most brazen of the sand crabs hard enough to take a leg off at the joint. Now it hung at the back of the pack, letting others take the brunt of being first. Clever fellow. She had better be quick.

She waded into the stream, feeling her way through the turbid water. The rocks hidden beneath the surface shifted underfoot. She caught herself, but the next step went deep into a hidden pocket. In a moment she was swept off her feet.

The current pushed her up against one of the spars. She wrapped an arm around it, ledeyes sparking as smaller fragments of broken crystal ground into her exoskeleton. The water began to pull her underneath the spar. She kicked frantically trying to regain her footing, but the streambed's cobbles gave way.

She dropped the stick and grabbed at the spar as she went under. Her hands caught one of the larger shards. She held on desperately as the relentless current pulled her deeper beneath the surface. The current bent her over backwards, threatening to break her lower spine. She managed to scrabble her abdomen around so it was trailing downstream, which kept her back from breaking, but now she was totally underwater, dangling by one hand from the shard.

The turbid water was like a liquid grey fog. She could barely see the spar above her, though it was only an arm's length away. The water forced its way inside her mouth, filling her with the taste of rust and ice and dirt.

She realized she had been wrong, when she thought the planet had nothing to say to her, that entropy was the only thing at work here. Here beneath the surface of the flood waters she tasted the burgeoning pulse of life, its foundations brought from Jupiter's Trojans in the form of ammonia ice. The turbid water filled her not with the taste of entropy grinding down the planet, or at least not only with that, but also with the taste of a planet being born again.

Who knows how long she might have hung there, drunk with the taste of a living world, had not the shard come free of the spar. She tumbled downstream twenty meters before she fetched up on a gravel bar. Then she saw the scavengers working at her pack and rose, shaking her fists at them and laughing as she shouted silently in a language only she understood.

31

Potalama

They broke camp at dawn. Personal kit went into saddle bags slung over the backs of the riding mektas. Their ledeyes were partly hidden by ceramic eyelids that gave them a reptilian affect, like giant chameleons. Like all mekans they had six legs, but this species was optimized to carry humans, with a large gap between the hindmost and middle legs to accommodate a saddle. The front legs had cleaver-like forearms tipped with folding spades for digging. They pawed the ground impatiently while the kores rigged a makeshift saddle on one of the pack mektas for Maggie.

The Hund squatted to pick up Eric, but his lobster claw caught on the sleeping bag that swaddled him like an infant.

"Do you need a hand, Gray?" Maggie asked.

"That would be great. Two, ideally," he replied sardonically. Maggie rolled her eyes.

"Dorje," Tara said, and nodded at the warbot.

"Yes selene." The youth dismounted and helped Maggie get Eric into the Hund's arms.

"Did I hear you call it *Gray*?" the girl asked Maggie while they got Eric settled.

"That's his name."

She looked at Tara with wide eyes. "Selene!"

"Now is not the time, kore," Tara said firmly, putting an end to whatever that was about.

They rode for several hours on a rugged trail that traversed the Melas foothills, stopping infrequently for bathroom breaks and to get water when the trail dipped into ravines where small streams carried snowmelt down from the plateau above the canyon walls. There was no way the truck would have made it, with its top-heavy burden. Even the bike would have been a challenge.

"Wouldn't it be easier to ride beneath the Ring?" Maggie asked after an especially difficult climb-out, when the mektas had to use their forelegs to help haul themselves and their riders up out of a creek bed. Perhaps half a kilometer away, the Ring was silhouetted against the sky like a bridge on pilings.

"It's best to limit exposure to the Ring's magnetic field," Tara replied. "It's fine for short durations, like when we're making a repair, but give it long enough and it causes cognitive defects. Different people are affected differently. I get optical migraines – a distorted visual field – that make it hard to work. And the mektas don't like it either."

Late that afternoon they reached the lower ramparts of the hanging valley that cradled Potalama. A steep cleft pierced the wall of ancient basalt. The cleft was guarded by carved pillars to either side, one of gleaming black obsidian, the other a milky quartz. A clear mountain stream ran between them, carelessly caroming from side to side of the ravine.

Selene Tara led the way up the ravine, followed by Maggie and Gray. The kores brought up the rear to make sure no one fell behind. A thin coat of ice covered the worn cobbles, making footing treacherous. A chill breeze brushed Maggie's hair back from her face. Her airscarf relaxed its grip. She cautiously unwound the strip of synlife fabric. The breeze held the sharp aromatic scent of conifers. She found herself smiling. She pushed her goggles up on her forehead.

The cleft opened into a hanging valley formed eons past by a meteor strike. The village of Potalama nestled in the bowl, sheltered by its cupped ridgeline from the winds that scoured Valles Marineris in the southern summer, rushing upstream from the lowlands in the warmth of morning only to cool in the western highlands in the afternoon and rush back downstream at night, the breath of Mokosh.

Sunlight brushed one side of the crater wall with blue light, casting terrain and knots of spruce trees and dwarf hemlock into sharp relief. Ice on the ridge line glowed brilliantly. The Ring cast an arced shadow as it soared across an open edge, held aloft by pairs of towers whose tips sported radiator fins. Pastel houses rose to either side of a broad wedge of verdant cropland. A lens-shaped cloud floated above them, nearly filling the bowl.

For the first time since they found the hyperglider, Maggie felt a sense of peace. This was a good place, perhaps even a sacred place.

Tara frowned at the cloud. "I guess the reactor is still offline."

Dorje observed Maggie's puzzled expression. "Normally it would go straight up until it's taken by the wind. Carries seeds and spores from the terrace gardens and spreads them up and down the canyon. Not enough convection for that without the reactor."

Gray's footsteps faltered behind them.

"You good?" she asked over her shoulder.

"I'm fine," Gray replied, his massive lens-studded head lifted towards the rim wall. "It just takes me back."

"You've been here before? I mean…" She did not finish the sentence: *Before you died.*

"No, not here. It reminds me of Meridian, back on Ceres. We flew into a cloud…" He trailed off.

"You'll find her," she said awkwardly. "When this is done. You're free now."

"Maybe." Then, realizing the ambiguity of the statement, "I hope so." Which did little to help.

The path took them through cropland and gardens. Kores looked up from their work to gawk at Gray as he lumbered along. Maggie could not help but see her younger self in them; the road not taken. The village itself was nothing like Tsiolkovsky. The houses were made of stone held in place by the same kind of cement they had seen on the cistern back at the turnoff. Many showed signs of recent damage: deep cracks in the cement, a cascade of stones where a corner had given way, a waist-high pile of rubble topped by a metal roof where the walls had collapsed entirely.

They dismounted in front of a doorway marked by a viridian cross. The kores took charge of the mektas. Tara turned to Maggie. "Is it safe for your warbot to go with them? It will draw attention here in the street."

"Yes, it's fine. I vouch for him. Go ahead Gray. Please."

"Dorje, take it around back to the garden. We'll get the young man inside."

Working together Maggie and Tara bore Eric through the arctic entry, formerly an airlock, but now a place to store coats and boots and hats, lit only by an ember. They half-carried, half-dragged him down a hallway. Emergency lights followed their progress. Through a side door, Maggie caught a glimpse of a child propped up on a bed, both legs amputated below her knees. The next door revealed a similar scene, a head injury this time, rusty bandage over one eye. And another, but Maggie looked away out of voyeuristic shame. It was too much.

"What happened here, Tara?" she asked. "Was there an accident?"

"That depends on who you ask. Our hekates think the pchelans botched an icefall. The surface wave from the ground strike took down some buildings and collapsed part of the central stepwell. Killed a dozen people, injured twice that. We're still cleaning up the mess."

Maggie blinked. It all came together: the piles of rubble, the pancaked houses. She had not even thought about what a ground strike could do to a place like this. She had been too absorbed in her own drama. "I don't think that was an accident," she said, her voice low.

"The kores would agree. But if that's the case, the question becomes one of motivation, doesn't it? Why would the pchelans deliberately drop an iceteroid midway between Tsiolkovsky and Thunderbird?" Here she gave Maggie a look, both eyebrows raised like russet wings. "The League of Worlds would need a good reason to violate the Armistice."

"Mmm," Maggie said, and changed the subject. "Something I don't understand: are you a Ring tech, or a medic?"

Tara laughed. "There's less of a difference than you might think. Either way you're fixing something. Fractured superconductors, fractured bones... For me, usually, it's bones. But there are just precious few of us to deal with all the things the ground strike broke, so I was sent out for some simple repairs. Here we are. Let's get your friend on the table."

The examination room was spartan but clean. Eric woke as they positioned him. Maggie hushed him and took his hand while Tara searched for a flashlight.

"Sorry, power has been out for days. Ah, here we go."

Maggie took the light and held its beam on Eric's foot while Tara took a pair of shears to the filthy bandage that covered his wounds. Tsked when she saw the ugly puffed flesh around the stitches Maggie had put into the sole of his foot. Then saw the matching puncture on the other side. Maggie had not tried to stitch it; the skin on top was so thin and tight she was afraid it would tear.

"Dorje," Tara said, "did you wash up?"

The kore had followed them in, quiet and unnoticed until now. Her younger companion was outside in the corridor, standing on tiptoes to look over her shoulder.

Dorje nodded vigorously. "Yes Tara-la."

"Good. These stitches are going to have to come out. I'll need the small laser scalpel and tweezers."

The girl got the tools from the sterilizer. The stitches parted with minute puffs of oily smoke. The room filled with the smell of burnt flesh and aramid.

"Did you put these in?" Tara asked without looking up.

"Yes," Maggie said, swallowing bile.

"Not bad," she said. "Though I could teach you a knot or two. Did you clean the wound first?"

"As well as I could. Water. Some topical antibiotics after."

"Fieldwork can be difficult," Tara said. She set aside the scalpel, separated the edges of the wound to look inside. Strands of tissue sagged across the opening. It hardly registered on Eric. She flexed the foot back to open the wound. It was a gaping mess, yellow tendons showing deep inside. Still no reaction.

Tara pushed the tip of the tweezers into the wound channel. "Can you feel that?"

"I can feel pressure," he replied.

"Does it hurt?"

"Should it?"

"Yes. A lot. But the lack of pain will make this easier. Dorje, hold a pan underneath. Maggie, keep him still. Hold his leg down."

Maggie put her weight on his leg. Tara worked the tip of the instrument into the wound channel. Eric's leg quivered, but he did not pull away.

"Slippery," Tara said after losing her grip once. But then she slowly withdrew a thick, black, curved thorn as long as one of Maggie's finger joints. "There's your problem."

Dorje leaned forward intently. "What is *that*?"

Tara held it up to the light for a better look. "If I'm not mistaken, the tip of a mandible. See how the base is hollow? That's why it did not come out. The base is wider than the tip, and it catches."

She put the mandible tip down on a piece of bandage, which immediately took on a light pink hue.

"A mandible!" Dorje crowed. "I knew it! You're Maggie May. And this – this is Berel Hoffman's son Eric, right?"

Maggie's brows drew together. "How do you know that? There's no way you could know that."

"You don't know? Tara-la, she doesn't know."

"Dorje!" Tara said sternly. "Respect. This is our patient."

But Dorje could not be dissuaded. She looked at Maggie meaningfully. "Berel's goggles? Hello world?"

"Hello world?" Maggie repeated stupidly. Then, as she grasped the implications: "Oh. That's what he said to me when I got to him."

The girl nodded. "Yes. Those were your first words. 'Hello world.' Classic! Berel was online. He grammed the whole battle. You're famous. You and Eric, but you more, because Eric didn't get as much airtime. Being injured and all."

Maggie stepped backwards, dropping Eric's hand. Berel and his war-damned goggles. She should have known. Of course he would stream the whole thing. He was a politician.

"Chair," Tara said somewhere in the distance.

A chair appeared underneath her, and none too soon. Maggie sat down hard.

"Are you all right?" Tara asked beside her. "How many fingers?"

Maggie waved her hand away. "I'm fine. I'm just really... Wardamn it, I hate crying. I'm just cold and hungry, and this is too much." She tried to get her thoughts together. "How many grams have there been?"

"Four or five? Every time you got within range of a commhawk. The last gram was from the guard shack."

Maggie remembered the commhawk circling overhead. She should have put it together. "Shit. So that's how Borodin tracked us." An alarming thought occurred to her. "What about here? Are there any relays?"

Tara shook her head. "Our commhawks are down for the night. No thermals to ride in the dark."

Maggie sagged back into the chair. "Good. Can you pass me Berel's goggles?"

Dorje pulled them over Eric's head and handed them over. Maggie found the setting that enabled uploads and disabled it. She folded in on herself, thinking about what needed to be done. Not what she wanted, that was for sure. She straightened up. "We have to go. Can you stitch him up, glue him together, whatever?"

"It's going to take more than a bit of blue goo," Tara said. "It's going to take a couple sols of intravenous antibiotics, rest, and rehydration. As for you, when is the last time you ate?"

"Half a c-bar yesterday morning. The day before? It doesn't matter. What matters is that if Borodin is still out there, or worse, warsingers, I've put you all in terrible danger. Can Eric stay here? I have to go."

Tara brushed her concerns aside with a wave of her hand. "What's done is done. And I am a terrible host. First, you need some food. Then we will talk to the hekates about Borodin and warsingers. We are not without resources here. All right?"

Again that look. Maggie felt like she was going to fall into Tara's eyes. God, she was beautiful. It had to be some kind of trick they taught selenes. But it worked; Maggie nodded.

"Good. Dorje, can you and Alina wrap up for me here? Another rinse, then soak some gauze in blue goo and pack the wound channel with it."

"No stitches?" Dorje sounded disappointed.

"This kind of trauma needs to heal from the inside out."

"Yes selene."

"Thank you, girls," Tara said. "And I will make a meal for our guest. The infamous Maggie May."

Maggie allowed herself to be pulled to her feet. Conscious of Tara's touch, the warmth of her hand, the steady strength behind it.

32

The Dark Flux

The interceptor coasted up to *Tereshkova*, her aetheric drive windmilling to a stop as they matched velocities. The torchship had suffered terrible damage. Her starboard side was burned away, opening every deck to vacuum. The proud wings of her liquid droplet radiators now looked like the hollow, scorched bones of a bird whose carcass had been thrown in a fire and left to burn. The port laserscope was superficially intact, but its beam expander's mirror was riddled by shrapnel.

Her vacuum hull had fared slightly better, if only because it had not suffered the catastrophic decompression that had blown the contents of the pressure hull into space. Mekans still moved there, jostling for position on the slag heap that remained of the vessel's auxiliary fission reactor.

Gray and Sidorov crossed over in their combat shells, leaving Thirteen in command of the interceptor. After a couple bursts of their verniers, they coasted slowly, wary of collision with debris from the blowout. First they encountered items of clothing; a utility vest, the shredded remains of a skinsuit, someone's spex. Then more massive items that had not accelerated as readily on the gale that had torn through the torchship: a facemask, a mekan's arm, the canopy from a medibot. Then the bodies, many naked or only partially clothed, the men's penises grotesquely erect from decompression, a sheath of ice over their open eyes.

Gray and Sidorov collected the corpses by unspoken agreement, looping safety lines around their ankles and towing the bodies in a macabre procession. They entered the torchship through a gaping wound on her starboard side, passing between exposed ribs to the remains of the EVA room. There they tied the string of corpses to a stanchion and doffed their combat shells so they could reconnoiter the rest of the ship.

Everyone inside was dead, their bodies frozen by the inimical darkness of the realm they traversed. The bodies showed signs of neutron radiation poisoning, black trails of frozen blood from eyes and nose. Smears of dissolved flesh left chalky lines on consoles.

The captain was at his station, strapped into his chair. He had died like the rest. His console flashed a message over the bloody hollows of his eyes. Gray pushed his body back gently so he could see what the console said.

Final Wishes of Arkady Rashnikov, Captain UCSF

To whomever may find UCM Tereshkova: we died in pursuit of the security of the United Colonies of Mars. All men onboard are to be commended, and their families honored for their service.

I instruct you to salvage my moravec and return it to Mars, therein to the custody of my family. For my body I have no wishes. Dispose of it as you like. My assets shall be allocated per my will, on file with Space Force and the city of Thunderbird.

Per aspera ad astra.

Signed, A. L. Rashnikov

Gray drew his cutlass.

"What are you doing?" Sidorov asked.

"What is required," Gray said.

Sidorov turned away as Gray fulfilled his captain's last instructions.

Thirteen whispered lies to the interceptor while they hastily stripped *Tereshkova* of the things they needed to survive. Every second took them further away from the sun.

They had not figured out how to tap electricity from the interceptor, or if they even could, so they salvaged a couple racks of kinos from the torchship's remaining point defense guns. These they lashed behind each hooded ledeye, anchoring them to the scissor truss. Consumables went in strategically placed nets around the waist. They left the dinghy docked bow-first to the interceptor's hull, so its engine bell faced outwards for maneuvering thrust.

Gray had hoped to find something that would serve as a shelter for the long trip in-system but they could not find anything that had not been damaged beyond repair. They would have to make the trip in their skinsuits and combat shells.

They positioned the shells opposite the dinghy, to either side of Thirteen, feet clamped to rungs they had glued to the hull, heads sticking out radially. Everything had to balance around the axis of the interceptor, or they would always be fighting a tendency to turn.

"Time to go," Gray said.

Sidorov fired a burst from the dinghy's arcjet. "I hate to see her like this," he said as they drifted away from the savaged hulk.

"War's an ugly thing," Gray said, but it felt like an empty cliché. The dinghy crossed the stern of the torchship. The mekans huddled there tracked their movement across the stars, iconji flickering across their eyes. Were they saying farewells? Were they bitter at being left to die in the darkness? Gray did not engage his translator. He did not want to know. It was too much.

"Do we really have to leave them like that?" asked Sidorov.

Gray struggled to frame a reply that did not sound cruel. The truth was that he felt sick at abandoning the mekans to their fate. But there was no room for them on the interceptor. There was not really a choice. It was just another hard thing that had to be done.

Then Sidorov continued, "It seems like we should have given them a proper burial," and Gray realized he was talking about the bodies of their crewmates. They had left them where they had died. It seemed more dignified than prying their frozen corpses from their seats and tossing them out the airlock. Which was about the best they could do given the circumstances. Putting them in dress uniform and incinerating them in the torch was not one of the options.

"They are more likely to be recovered this way," he said after a moment of cognitive dissonance. "For proper burial back home when the war is over."

"When the war is over," Sid said. He did not sound like he thought that was one of the possibilities.

"When the war is over. And this interceptor is what we're going to end it with, Sid. We'll get back in-system, get it somewhere that can reverse engineer it. Turn the technology back on Earth. That's what we promised we would do, isn't it?"

"Yes sir."

"Then that's what we'll do." Gray flashed a signal to Thirteen. "Ready to go?"

The interceptor is under my control, the mekan replied.

"We ought to name her, sir," Sidorov said.

Gray hesitated, torn between the need to be off as soon as possible and observing a ritual that went back a millennium or more. "You're right," he said. "But I don't have anything to..."

"I brought a bulban of wine from the galley."

"Of course you did," Gray murmured to himself. Then louder: "Officer thinking, Lieutenant."

"Do you have anything in mind?"

Gray considered the strange vessel he now commanded, her fateful speed, her terrible potential for destruction, the makeshift blinders that hid the truth from her predatory mind so she would not turn on them in fury. "How about *Hooded Falcon*?"

Sidorov turned the name over in his mouth. "I like it," he said. "*Hooded Falcon.* That's good." He held out the bulban. "Do you want to do it?"

"You go ahead," Gray said. "I think it's bad luck for the skipper to do it himself."

"I christen thee *Hooded Falcon*," Sidorov said. He smashed the bulban against the interceptor's hull, releasing its small sacrifice of wine to the void. The little mekano's legs pulled in against its belly. Sidorov threw the carcass aside. Gray watched it disappear into the void.

"Begin deceleration," Gray ordered Thirteen.

Destination?

"Greenwich Station."

The propellers spun into a blur. A ghostly blue disk formed to bow and stern. Weight settled down on them, at first miniscule but growing every second as the propellers came up to speed. The cargo nets swung to stern, and everything changed perspective. Forward became up, aft became a long dangerous drop through the stern propeller. Gray crunched forward to put some slack in the cables that held his shell at right angles to the hull, then slipped the knots to tension them again. He relaxed back into the embrace of the acceleration.

"Greenwich Station, sir?" Sidorov queried over the lightwave.

"They'll have the facilities we need to replicate this thing," Gray said.

"Wouldn't the Academy back home be a better choice? They've got the top knobs in the whole system."

"Mekans are just something Space Force uses. They buy them from someone else; they use them up and they throw them away. You want to build a better torchship? Go to the knobs at the Joint Service Academy. You want to figure out how to drexler a better mekan? Go to a hivemaster."

"There must be hivemasters on Mars who could do the job. Or somewhere in the Belt. Greenwich Station will be in the Arkipelago by the time we get there! There's got to be someplace closer than that."

"Closer in space, maybe. Closer in time, not much. Think about it. Going this fast, getting anywhere in the solar system will take pretty near the same amount of time. We have to decelerate, heading out all the while. Then we have to accelerate back in-system until we flip at the halfway point. Then we have to decelerate again to match velocities with our destination."

Sidorov was silent.

"Besides," Gray said, "on Greenwich I'm consort to the hivemaster. Elise will help us sort this thing out. Anywhere else I'm just another Space Force officer without a ship."

They watched *Tereshkova* recede. She was tumbling slowly, an oblong of light that grew brighter and then dimmed again, like a candle guttering before it went out.

"You've really fallen for her, haven't you," Sidorov said. "You're in deep."

"I suppose I have," Gray said after a while. "But that's not why we're going there."

"You had this big reputation on Chaika, you know. A woman in every port. I've seen you work a crowd. You had it down. And yet you fell for a vamp."

Gray felt his anger building. "A hivemaster," he said evenly. "Who can help us turn this thing into a weapon the Space Force can use against Earth."

"Whatever you have to tell yourself. Sir."

Gray could not bring himself to speak. His anger had reached the boiling point. Whatever came next would be bad. The silence stretched.

"I'm sorry," Sidorov said. "I shouldn't have said that. I know you're trying to do the right thing. It's just that, if you're wrong, you'll lose everything. They'll strip you of rank and drum you out of the Force. You know that, right? You're betting everything on this... woman."

"If it's a bet, it's one I think I'm going to win."

"I hope you're right. But it's sure not the way I'd play it."

To which Gray did not reply. The decision was his to make, and he had made it. The weight of command settled on him, as sure and inescapable as the acceleration that pressed him back into the padded coffin of his combat shell.

After a few ship-days Gray's combat shell began to feel like a medieval torture device, an iron maiden without the spikes. He could not move more than a few centimeters in any direction without risking tearing the combat shell free of the cables that secured it to the hull. He turned off the shell's force augmentation system so he could do isometric exercises inside it, pressing his arms and legs against the recalcitrant armor. It was probably good for his body, but it only reinforced his claustrophobia.

Sidorov's complaints grated on his nerves. He struggled to maintain a balance of compassion and cheerfulness that the other man could lean on. But he found himself slipping as Sidorov's deteriorating mental state seeped into his own psyche like a slow rot.

When he fell asleep, he was visited by Rashnikov, head tucked under his arm like a helmet, spinal cord a slick yellow spot in the severed neck. If it was not him it was Polanski, eyes bulging white ice, speech an unintelligible gurgle around his distended tongue.

The mekan he had sacrificed was also a regular. He could no longer remember her number, it had been too long since they left Pandora, but he recognized her ruined ledeye, the narrow cat's-eye slit wreathed in white coruscations.

Faceless men pinned the pitiful creature against the deck. He raised his cutlass. Thumbed its safety. The sound of the chainblade. The cut that opened as he fell forward, opened like the iris of a phosphorescent cat eye. And there was no end to that darkness inside, just as there was no end to the darkness through which *Tereshkova* fell, the abandoned mekans huddled on her reactor. That is what he saw in the dead mekan's ruined eye, or at least what he remembered when he woke with a ragged gasp.

Sidorov was also plagued by nightmares. If such they could be called, when there was never any day. At first Gray listened sympathetically, trying to find ways to keep his subordinate's sanity intact. But he made a poor psychoanalyst. It was not in his nature to forgive another's flaws, and as Sidorov fell apart, the man's flaws became all too apparent. His arrogance, his self-centered entitlement, his sense of grievance that the universe had handed him such a terrible hand; none of it sat well with Gray. His patience wore thin, and his sympathy became a thin veil that could not hide his disdain for Sidorov from the other man.

Their conversations became toxic. Silence reigned for days at a time. They had run out of things to say, or that they were willing to say, and so said nothing at all.

As the interceptor slowed down, its drive system became more effective in what-ever medium it used. Dark matter. The luminiferous aether for all he knew. In any case deceleration ramped up until it reached a standard gee, nearly three times what Gray had grown up with on Mars. Now the iron maiden had spikes. Gray developed hot spots on his shoulder blades and hips and jabbing jolts of neural electricity spiked unexpectedly through his muscles.

Sidorov begged for a respite from the deceleration, but Gray would have none of it. The war had gone on without them, and they needed to get back into the battle. They had a part to play, and sacrifice was required. Eventually he turned off his lightwave so he would not have to listen to the other man's pleas.

He turned to his library for company. He worked his way through the classical composers and discovered Beethoven's Seventh. The second movement was a fitting dirge, it seemed, for the dead who haunted his dreams. He took a refresher course on physics. Reread his favorite novels when he became too hungry to focus on anything more difficult.

Their synlife skinsuits were remarkably effective at providing air and water. Given power in the form of light, a healthy skinsuit could scrub the carbon diox-ide from its inhabitant's breath and toxins from their urine almost indefinitely.

Food was another proposition. The skinsuits were not engineered to provide anything other than a pittance of carbohydrates – sugar water, basically – and replacement electrolytes. In the long run – and they were on a very long run indeed – their skinsuits could only offset starvation, not prevent it.

As the interceptor's speed relative to the solar system fell to zero, Gray slowly wasted away. At first he was painfully aware of his empty belly. But that became the new normal quickly enough. Then it was the swelling in his extremities. His shell became unbearably tight as the edema progressed. His hands and feet felt like they were being crushed in a vise.

Finally they reached the zero point. They were at rest relative to the distant sun. Thirteen shut down the aetheric drive. As the propellers wound down, weightlessness returned like a grateful tide lifting him out of his despair. Gray popped the latches of his shell and extracted himself like a hermit crab that had been beached too long.

It was shockingly cold outside. The view was magnificent. They were far enough out of the plane of the ecliptic that the inner planets were all visible at a glance, tiny Mercury like a spark beside the sun's flame, brilliant Venus, Earth's famous pale blue dot, and then ruddy Mars, smaller and dimmer than humanity's ancestral home, but nearer to his heart than the blue planet would ever be.

He flipped his lightwave back on. "Sid! Come out. You've got to see this."

Sidorov's shell was dark, enigmatic in its silence.

He rapped on Sidorov's shell. Put his facemask against it and shouted. "Sidorov! Turn on your lightwave."

He banged a few more times, growing increasingly worried. He had not spoken to Sidorov for days.

Gray found the little hatch that protected the shell's emergency release. He pulled the ring underneath. The top of the shell hinged open like a dome. Light blazed out from the interior LEDs, momentarily dazzling him.

It was empty.

Gray backed away in panic. Where was Sidorov? Had he jumped ship? There was no way he could have made it through the stern propeller alive; it was turning far too fast. Gray's mind raced through the possibilities.

They all led to the same place. Sidorov was gone, dead or as good as dead. And it was his fault. His fault Sidorov had given up. Driven to desperation by unending nightmares. By starvation. By silence. That was on Gray. He had failed his last remaining man. His self-indulgence had cost a life. The fact filled him with self-loathing.

His fingers clenched on the edge of the combat shell as he fought the impulse to push himself off into the darkness. One little push and he would join Sidorov. The skinsuit had no means of maneuvering. He would slowly drift away from *Hooded Falcon*. The skinsuit would brownout, or he would freeze to death. And no one would ever know how he had failed.

It was then that Sidorov seized him from behind and whirled him around, breaking his grip. The man's face was distorted in a scream. His mouth worked soundlessly, baring teeth and rotten red gums. His eyes locked on Gray's, white rim visible all the way around a dark hole into his soul.

Gray panicked and basic training took over. His knee drove up into Sidorov's groin. The man doubled over in pain. Gray locked his elbow around his neck. He pushed his other hand against the back of Sidorov's head, choking him out. After a few seconds he stopped struggling. Gray relaxed his grip. And realized they had separated from *Hooded Falcon*. The vessel was out of reach.

There was only one option. Which meant it wasn't really an option at all. The longer he waited the worse it would get. He waited until the moment was right and then kicked Sidorov's unconscious body away. Sidorov dwindled in the distance as Gray drifted back to the safety of *Hooded Falcon*.

Gray finished stuffing Sidorov back into his combat shell. It had taken several kilosecs to don his combat shell, reach the other man, sedate him, and get him back to *Hooded Falcon*. Now he repurposed the safety line he had used in those efforts to lash Sidorov's shell shut. He spot-glued the aramid line to the shell's ceramic armor so it would not slip.

His lip curled in an unconscious snarl as he considered his own combat shell. He was through with that. The relentless sense of confinement, of being sealed in a coffin, unable to move when the entire universe was just a few centimeters away, was too much. He extricated himself from its claustrophobic embrace for the last time and jettisoned it.

He pulled himself hand-over-hand to the nearest cargo net. There he retrieved a couple tanks – water and air to freshen up his skin suit – and a rescue ball crumpled down against an object the size of a watermelon. It was their last one. He opened it up enough to shove the supplies inside. Then he hand-walked the circumference of the hull to the base of a ledeye. He secured the rescue ball to the scissor truss with a couple carabiners.

Then he crawled inside and pulled the inflation cord. Cold air flooded the ball, puffing it up around him. He pulled off his facemask for the first time in over a megasecond. It felt like it was tearing the skin from his face. Then he reached behind his back and pulled out the object that had gotten wedged between him and the interceptor's hull.

Captain Rashnikov's eyes were covered with ice. Gray considered the icy white stare for a moment, his nostrils flaring. Then he settled the old lizard's head at his feet, turning it so he could not see its eyes. He leaned back against the hull.

"Resume flight plan," he told Thirteen.

The big electric motors that spun *Hooded Falcon's* propellers thrummed against his back. Weight settled down upon him, and with it the dark flux that had haunted him. He had a strange desire to burrow into the interceptor, as if her warm center would be a refuge from the hard blue light of the aetheric drive when he opened his eyes, and from the dreams that tormented him like a bird of prey tearing at his soul.

When he finally slipped beneath the surface of his consciousness the captain spoke to him of dark currents that flowed beyond the limits of human cognition, of eddies that riffled in the wake of planets, of vortices spinning off and up into a greater sky.

33

Hierophany

The sentinel followed a braid of the Marineris upstream. West, mostly, though the water continually changed course as the streambed meandered. She came to a place where the river followed the base of a snow-covered slope. Snow and ice shelved out over the water at the base of the uplift. She considered crossing the stream to avoid the expanse of white, but here the water was deep and fast. She clambered onto it and was relieved to find that the snow had melted down into a firm surface that took her weight.

As she continued up-valley, snow encroached on the opposite bank until the stream was flowing through a narrow channel overhung by ice shelves. Then the shelves met from either side, and the water was only visible in elongated rushing pools. Then the water disappeared altogether, running somewhere beneath the snow, and she found herself on a blank white expanse.

An overcast had moved in, concealing the sun beneath a layer of clouds, making it nearly impossible to discern variations in terrain; she found herself stumbling as she crossed small unseen depressions, or tripping when her feet caught on ridges. Her petal sun hat did little to ease the uniform radiance that surrounded her. The omnipresent light pressed in on her relentlessly. She stumbled again and fell to her knees. Pain jolted up her damaged hind leg.

She took the improvised rucksack from her back and dumped its contents on the hard-packed snow. Cord, some tent fabric, nylon webbing, a couple tent pole segments, a multitool built for human hands, and a couple of triangular shards from the proscribed artifact that she had salvaged as evidence for when she reached Pavonis. She picked up one of these and held it up to the brightest part of the sky. The sky took on a bluish hue where the light was brightest, attenuating it to a level that was much more bearable. She panned down to the snow field and was delighted to find a new sense of depth. Small wind and sun-sculpted waves showed as pale blue striations, and she could make out the indentation that showed the course of the stream beneath the snow.

An hour later she had resumed her westward journey, a pair of jury-rigged sunglasses perched jauntily on her beak, tent poles for stems, retention cord behind her head, all held together by a framework of pulped and extruded nylon. Her headache eased to a low background potential as if she had discharged an electrostatic buildup accrued at the top of her watchtower on Deimos when a solar storm blew through.

Now she had bandwidth for her other senses. The cilia on her hands and limbs revealed the wind at her back, sun-heated air expanding up through the canyon and its many valleys. To her the warm breeze felt like a lover's touch, the gentle caress of one of her hatchmates as they laid together in one of the hive's many chambers, talking quietly. Pchelans communicated through their ledeyes. Speech and sight were inextricably linked; to hear someone's voice was to see them. So at first she thought the whisper she heard, so faint it was difficult to make out the meaning, was a memory of those times lost.

But as the day passed and the sun swung ponderously to the west, the clouds evaporated. By late afternoon it was a blazing orb that cast a long shadow behind her, and the whispers could be plainly heard. They came from all around her, from the synlife brush that dotted the hillocks where the snow had melted away, from the mekanos that sunned themselves atop broad, flat rocks, from the red-stain of algae that grew in the snow beneath her feet.

I am here, they sighed, their voices rising like the heat mirage of sun-heated water vapor that rippled the horizon. *I am here.*

34

Ghosts and Shadows

Gray crouched in the garden behind the clinic. He was acutely aware of his size. He could barely move without brushing up against something – a rose bush, the low-hanging branch of an apple tree, a small stand of juniper. Each rasp on his ceramic armor alarmed him. He did not want to break anything, for the garden was lovely. Water trickled through cleverly engineered channels of bamboo. Vapor hovered in a layer just above its surface, only visible when he lowered his head. And then evaporated, adding its tiny infusion of moisture to the never-ending effort of making Mars suitable for life that had evolved on Earth.

Clouds scudded overhead. For a moment Gray saw a radiant eye in the face of an alien god glaring down at him. Then it was just a small moon playing hide and seek in the clouds. It looked like it might snow.

The back door to the clinic opened and one of the girls stepped through. She hesitated at the sight of the Hund.

"Don't be afraid," Gray said.

She stepped off the porch, closing the outer door behind her. "I'm not afraid," she said, looking up at his ugly mechanical face with her hands on her slender hips. "I know who you are."

"Do you?" Gray found this amusing, but he had not yet discovered how to laugh. "Then you're doing better than I am."

"You are an instantiation of Commander John Gray."

Gray was no longer amused. "And you know this how?"

She cut to the chase. "Berel Hoffman's goggles have been dropping grams every time a commhawk goes over."

"Ah," Gray said, rocking back on metal heels. "That explains some things."

"For what it's worth, I'm on your side. Most all the kores are."

"The kores?" Gray did not understand.

"People my age who haven't taken vows." She seemed surprised he did not know this simple division of society. "Kores, selenes, hekates? Maiden mother crone? The triple moon?"

Gray shook his head. "Sorry, I'm still catching up on my history. So your name is not Kore?"

"No, I'm Dorje. The other kore is Alina. She's keeping an eye on Eric."

"Well then, Dorje, I'm glad to meet you. I'd shake your hand, but..." He raised his lobster claw in a gesture of futility.

She surprised him by fist-bumping the side of the claw. "It's okay. Maybe we can get you fixed up too, while you're here."

"How is Eric?"

"Sleeping for now. He'll be okay, I think. Tara-la took the tip of a mandible out of his foot. Might still lose it, but at least he has a chance now."

"That's good?"

"As good as it gets." She scuffed at the finely crushed stones that defined the walkway. "You think you and Maggie can make your *Sparrow* fly again?"

"If Borodin or warsingers don't get to her first. I need a drexler though."

"You've come to the right place for that," Dorje said.

"I wondered."

"Don't worry. We've had the same queen forever. They're not warsingers." She looked up. Tried to decide which lens to look at. The big one in the middle? One of the cylinders to either side? She settled on the middle. "This has to stop. The warsingers dropping rocks on us. Pushing us down when we ought to rise up. Some of my friends died. A lot of them got hurt."

"I'm sorry," Gray said. "If we hadn't tried to salvage the hyperglider..."

"No!" She surprised them both with her vehemence. "That was the right thing. The hyperglider changes everything. We get it. Maybe not the hekates; they're too invested in the status quo. But us kores get it. And I think a lot of the selenes, too."

"Do kores have a voice, here?" he asked gently.

She bit her lip, looked away. The first flakes of snow came drifting down, filtering gently through the tree branches, disappearing when they touched the surface of the water that burbled through the maze of split bamboo canals.

"I don't mean to be unkind," Gray said. "I know nothing of your world. It's all different from... when I was last here."

Tara appeared at the back door. "Dorje are you out here? Oh good. Listen, Maggie and I are going to talk to the hekates. Can you stay here and watch Eric?"

Dorje hesitated. Tara frowned.

"Tara-la, can Alina take care of him? I want to go with you."

"As do I," Gray said, adding his voice to the girl's.

Tara considered. Started to say something, changed her mind, shook her head. "That's fair. Not that they'll like it."

They made their way through narrow cobblestone streets: Tara first, light on her feet like a dancer, then Maggie and Dorje. Gray brought up the rear, metal feet clanking against the stone. People watched them go by from behind ember-lit windows, their faces indistinct in the warm backlight.

Maggie wondered who would choose to live in a place like this. Were they all Sisters, or had others found their way to the relative protection of Potalama, perhaps moving to be near relatives who had chosen to serve a greater cause? More likely they were kores who had not gone on to become selenes and had instead returned to the outer world when they reached their tenth birthday, and now found it easier to stay and make a life here than make the long journey back to wherever they had come from.

A massive wall protected the Ring Station at the center of the village. The wall towered overhead. Like many of the buildings they had passed it showed signs of recent damage: deep cracks in the ruddy cement and cascades of angular grey stones heaped below.

Warm, damp air sighed out from an arched entry that pierced the wall, a continuous exhalation that carried a mineral smell, sulfur and iron, as if it came from the lungs of a sleeping giant. The wall was as thick as it was tall and honeycombed throughout with its own passageways and rooms. A mekan the size of a cat watched their progress from an alcove at head height, the ember beside it casting its shadow large. Maggie imagined they had their own passages and were in turn served by a smaller caste with their own even smaller passages, in a recursion that ended with artiforms the size of old Earth ants. Or maybe it never ended. Maybe that was how Tara could tell Erik's temperature and blood pressure at a touch: assistive nanites in her fingernails. Or maybe it was in the same class as the biofeedback hack she used to stay warm, a natural capability amplified by years of training.

Maggie was relieved when the passage opened onto a plaza a couple hundred meters across. More a giant's balcony than a plaza, for most of it was filled by an enormous stepwell, an inverted ziggurat dug deep into the ground. Tiered layers marched down into billowing mist.

"The surface wave dumped our reactor into the aquifer at the bottom of the stepwell," Tara explained. "That's why power is out. It's almost too dark to see, but the far side is where the terraces collapsed."

Maggie could just make out a ragged gully on the opposite side of the stepwell. A tangle of synlife ship trees and aeroponics slumped down the gully, out of the last lingering rays of evening into the darkened depths.

"I'm sorry," she said helplessly.

"Not your fault," Tara said firmly.

"Well, I mean, it pretty much is," Maggie said. "If we're being honest here."

"You weren't the one holding the knife," Dorje said.

They descended a half dozen levels into the stepwell. Each terrace was connected by a broad set of stairs to a landing on the terrace below. As they descended the snow turned to light rain. Gray's feet barely fit the steps, and of course he did not have a hand to steady himself against the outer wall as the others did.

A shape loomed out of the mist, blocky but too curved to be a building. As they approached, it resolved into a sculpture of a woman's head the size of a building. She looked out over the mist that filled the air below like the figurehead of a ship slipping through twilit fog on Hellas Basin. They entered through a doorway built into a stylized ear whose upper edge kept the rain at bay.

Maggie was not sure what she had expected – a gathering of witches out of Macbeth, or perhaps wizened nuns in full lotus around a golden Buddha – but the hekates turned out to be three older women in prosaic work clothes gathered around a holocaster. The holocaster contained a model of the stepwell and the reactor at its nadir. They looked up from the schematic as the party filed through the entry.

"Pardon, hekates," Tara said. She and Dorje bowed deeply in respect, hands pressed together. Maggie awkwardly followed suit. Gray made do by pressing his lobster claw against his chest.

"I apologize for the interruption," Tara continued. "These travelers seek our help. It is a matter of some urgency."

The hekates exchanged glances. The eldest asked, "More urgent than restoring our share of power to the Ring? Even now its field strength declines."

"All the more so because the fractures caused by the ground strike have not been repaired," another said pointedly.

"That decision was mine," Tara said. "I chose to save the life in front of me."

"Which is what I would expect from a selene," the eldest said with a sigh. Her face was lined with the passage of time and drawn with fatigue but still possessed a certain harsh beauty. "I envy your ability to live fully in the present."

"Shall we leave you to your plans, then?" Tara asked, with a barely perceptible edge to her voice. A smile flickered across the face of the youngest hekate.

"Make your case," the eldest said wearily. She gestured at the holocaster. "I for one could use a break from untangling this knot."

Tara bowed her head. "Hekates. This is the technomancer Maggie May and her companion John Gray von Hund, who carries the memories of a Warsing Space Force officer."

"We are aware," the eldest said. To Maggie and Gray: "At this point anyone with a marsnet connection knows something of your story. I am hekate Lynn, and these are my cohorts Binah and Opal. Together we lead this community. What can we do for you?"

Maggie weighed her words. "Thank you for taking time to hear our story. I will be brief. We believe the warsingers called down the icefall to destroy evidence of a vessel we discovered. They are trying to erase it, and us with it. We seek your protection, and access to your hive so we can drexler parts to repair it."

Lynn's eyebrows rose. "That is a very serious allegation. We have been at peace with the warsingers for generations."

"Détente might be a better description," Binah said. It was she who had found humor in Tara's earlier riposte.

"Do you have any proof?" Opal asked.

"We have been pursued by a technomancer – Borodin – who claims he has an arrangement with the warsingers."

"Hearsay," Opal said. "And an unreliable source."

"Mantids attacked us on the outskirts of Tsiolkovsky."

"That is nothing new," Opal said. "Warsingers have used mantids to suppress dissemination of artifacts they think are dangerous ever since the Warsing. You of all people should know this."

There was a note of gentle reproach in her voice that stopped the protest forming in Maggie's throat. Because she was right; they had no proof.

"Tell us of this vessel," Binah said.

"It is a true treasure, hekate," Tara said eagerly. She drew the shard Maggie had given her from her pocket and held it out.

Binah inhaled sharply. "Shever?"

Tara nodded. "It's real. I tried it."

"Shever is proscribed technology," Opal said. "No wonder you are pursued."

"The question is why," Binah said. "Clearly it is not dangerous. We've all used it, yes? I thought so. It opens doors, nothing more."

"Warsingers are rational creatures," Lynn said. "They must have a reason for suppressing it."

"It is not shever they fear," Gray said. The hekates flinched at the sound of his voice. "They fear what can be done with it. The vessel I piloted here from the Arkipelago used large vanes of what you call shever as wings to lift it into hyperspace. It is a way to travel faster than light. And that is what they fear."

"Why is that?"

"Because a hyperspatial weapon can't be stopped. It reaches its target before it can even be seen."

"So this vessel is a weapon?" Opal asked with performative incredulity.

"No, it is harmless by itself. But the technology it embodies could be used as a weapon."

"Any technology can be used as a weapon," Binah said. "If the warsingers were responsible for the ground strike, then they have violated the Armistice, proscribed technology or not. Who knows what else they may do."

"Likely nothing if we let them have the remnants of this vessel," Opal said.

"That won't be enough," Maggie said. "You'll have to give them us, too. And even that might not be enough. They want to erase all evidence of its existence."

"That is unacceptable," Binah said. "Am I the only one who hears the story within their story? They have been gathering *shards of light* to rebuild a *vessel* that can *transcend* mundane reality. That story should be familiar to all of us. It is part of our core mythology."

"You are an unrepentant Kabbalist, Binah. Your literalism will be your undoing. Myths are myths, and stories are for children."

"Is repairing the world a myth?"

"Don't spar with me. You know it is our task, and this... this story of theirs... is a distraction from it."

"One cannot dismiss something because it resonates with myths. Quite the opposite. Myths are archetypes. They exist across time and are told in lived experience again and again. Their *story* may be why we are here, right now, trying to restore power to the Ring. If the warsingers took their *story* seriously enough to order a ground strike, then we should take it seriously enough to help them rebuild their vessel."

"My kore would like to speak," Tara said into the silence that followed.

"She has no standing here," Lynn replied. "She is not on the path."

"Forbear, Lynn," Binah interceded. "I would like to hear what Dorje has to say."

Lynn glanced at the third hekate. "Opal?"

"The kore may not have standing, but she has courage. Let us hear her."

"As you wish," Lynn relented. She beckoned to Dorje, who stepped forward nervously.

"Hekates, I am here to speak for the kores. We all think the same thing. The ground strike was no accident. The warsingers have held us down long enough. This is our moment to rise. Otherwise, this," she waved her hand at the view outside the control room, the darkened terraces of the damaged stepwell, "this will be our only world for who knows how long. Longer than any of us will live."

"Is that so bad?" Lynn asked. "The moons rise, the stars shine, dawn will come tomorrow as it always does. It is a beautiful world."

"It is one world, one beautiful garden that the Sisters have nurtured to life from barren ground. But there are other worlds out there whose secrets have yet to be learned. Our deep space telescopes found hundreds of biosignatures before the Warsing cut us off from them. Think of what we might discover!"

"This is an old argument," Opal said, "one that goes all the way back to the Exodus, when Mother Earth was dying, and our ancestors chose to flee instead of helping her. We have been atoning for that mistake ever since."

"All children must leave their mother someday," Dorje said.

"And was it a mistake?" Binah asked. "Now there are two worlds with life, where only one existed before."

"Enough," Lynn said. "This is not an argument we will resolve today, if ever. Thank you for your insights, Dorje." She turned to the others. "To the matter at hand: Without proof of their complicity in the ground strike, we should do nothing to offend the warsingers. Without them there would be no icefalls, no Ded Moroz, no breath of Mokosh. These scavengers must be sent away."

"I disagree," Binah said. "The evidence at hand suggests the warsingers have violated the terms of the Armistice. Now is the time to remind them that there are consequences attached to bad faith behavior. And we should consider how we might reassert control of the iceteroid supply chain."

Opal considered the shard in Tara's hand, the angry set of Lynn's jaw, the billowing clouds rising from the depths of the stepwell. Finally she spoke. "This is not a decision we can make without consulting the greater circle."

"It will take days to get any kind of consensus from the other Ring Stations," Binah said.

"Weeks more likely," Opal said wryly. "Until then, I suggest a compromise: let us extend hospitality to these travelers as we would to anyone in need. But we will do nothing that might anger the warsingers until or unless we have proof of their bad faith."

They walked back to the clinic in silence. Gray settled down on his haunches in the garden, trying hard not to break anything. He was too big to go into the clinic, even if they'd wanted him.

"You did really well, Dorje," Tara said.

"Not well enough." Dorje glanced back in the direction of the stepwell. Her young face twisted with anger. "I don't think hekate Lynn heard a word I said. 'These scavengers must be sent away.' I just..." She didn't trust herself to go on. She kicked a spray of white rocks into the loam of the garden.

"Dorje!" Tara's patience was strained. "Consider this: Binah is with us. And Opal is committed to justice. We only need to win over Lynn. Give it time."

"Time is not on our side," Gray said. "The tharks – warsingers, you call them now – will come for us sooner or later. And Borodin is still out there."

"You really can't let go, can you. Even for a night."

"That's not fair," Gray said.

Maggie ducked her head. "You're right. I'm sorry. You got us here. I just don't understand why it matters so much to you."

"I made a mistake," Gray said. "When I was... when Gray was a young man, what he wanted most was to explore the stars. But when that chance came, he made a weapon instead. He thought... I thought it was the only choice. But this is where it led. A dead end for humanity."

"That was a long, long time ago," Maggie said gently, her hand on his shoulder.

"Not for me," Gray said.

"Can we talk more in the morning? I'm so cold."

Gray nodded. "Yes, in the morning. Things will be much clearer then. Sleep well."

"Please don't do anything foolish." She looked earnestly into his cyclopean eye.

"Rest assured I will not," Gray said.

The clouds that pressed down on the rocky promontories were dark on darker, hard to discern until he saw mist pouring through a gap in the rocks in a dim grey mass of vapor like a ghost searching for its grave. He watched for a moment, wondering as the mist turned into a glimmering silver snake, what was living, what was dead?

It seemed to him that the entire world was alive. The mist rushing through the gap, the river in the canyon below. The rocks underfoot murmuring as they shifted under his weight. But perhaps that was what the dead would feel. The rocks that turned under his inanimate metal feet were ancient skulls. A desolate pockmarked slope of empty eye sockets gazed back at him. The press of history, of everyone who had died in the war, settled down on him. His friends, his shipmates, his lover.

He was alone, neither dead nor alive, stranded between two worlds.

Maggie had retreated to the warm ember-lit glow of the apartment above the clinic, leaving him to his own devices, as it were. He had followed her infrared signature upstairs. Another figure joined her at a table. When it became obvious they were no longer paying attention to anything but each other he had quietly disconnected the charge cable and left the garden.

Now he stopped in the lee of a boulder to listen. He heard nothing but the wind soughing over the rocks and synlife brush that dotted the slopes of the ridge. But Borodin was close. He was certain of it. He could feel it like a cold wind at his back, a malignant presence in the dark.

He crossed a patch of snow and continued up the slope to the ridgeline. The footing here was treacherous, hard wind-packed snow that crested in a cornice. Beneath the overhang the ridge fell away precipitously into a rough valley. One step too far, or an unseen cleft buried beneath the snow, and he could plunge through and be smashed to junk. The thought of being trapped in the Hund's mangled body until its spin ran out filled him with dread.

The valley led down to the plateau where they had abandoned the hyper-glider. There was no doubt in his mind that that would be Borodin's first stop once he was sure they had withdrawn. They shared the same obsession.

Gray's pace slowed as he approached the shoulder of the ridge. He found a rocky promontory where he could look down without being seen. He cautiously raised his head over the rocks that shielded him. *Sparrow's* remains were still lashed to the bed of the truck, oblivious to the encroaching chill. A fine coat of snow covered the capsule. Crystals on crystal, frozen water on hypervane. Two worlds touching at that interface: the seen and the unseen.

He backed up the way he had come, careful not to skyline himself to whoever might be below. He descended the shoulder of the ridge and made his way to where he had last seen the bipe. With any luck he could pick up Borodin's trail there.

The bipe was still alive. It pawed at the ground with its good leg as Gray approached, dragging its body around to try and bring its weapon to bear on him. Gray felt a pang of guilt.

"Easy," he said. "I'm not going to hurt you."

The weapon went off with a whump, putting a divot into the ground a few meters away from him. Dirt rained down as the missing matter returned from wherever it went.

"Unless you try and kill me," Gray amended. He darted inside the weapon's arc. He almost jammed his claw into the bipe's working hip joint but pulled back at the last moment. It was just as likely to get sheared off as to wedge the leg. Instead he hooked his elbow around a power cable and gave a good yank. The cable separated from the chassis with a shower of sparks. The leg stopped moving.

"Better," he grunted.

He looked the machine over. It was clearly Eric's bipe, but Borodin had left his mark on it. Where the cab had been was a complexly curved fist of metal, presumably the space-folding weapon. Gray stopped in his tracks. If there was no cab, no passenger compartment, then where had Borodin ridden?

Pieces of the puzzle tetrissed into place: the rippling shadow, how the bipe had managed to come so far without a source of spin. Borodin had never been in the bipe. He had been in whatever had cast that rippling shadow, hidden within some sort of Warsing optical stealth.

Gray cursed himself for his stupidity. Borodin had set a trap, and he had walked right into it. He backed away from the bipe and broke into a run.

An incandescent trail of exhaust arced up into the night and swept down towards him.

Gray put all the power at his disposal into the crest laser. A faint trail of superheated air stabbed into the clouds. The beam found the dragon tooth at the tip of the exhaust. It flared brightly in the infrared band. Then its antimatter seed lost containment and a tremendous blossom of light illuminated the entire knotted landscape: the Hund with its monstrous shadow, a massive four-legged Kentavr combat shell on the slope across from him, and the hyperglider between, as if the world had been reduced to a black and white photo of a chess board: a knight of ghosts and shadows, the bishop who opposed him, and the queen they fought to possess.

Darkness arrived with the shockwave.

35

The Arkipelago

Gray dreamed he was back in Elise's bedroom, his head cradled in her lap, drifting softly together in Ceres' miniscule gravity. She leaned over and said something, extruder flicking in her mouth. His eyes opened blearily. A mantid's face stared back at him.

He awoke with a start, sending a blob of blue liquid flying as his limbs flailed. Elise ducked aside. The blob came to rest against the far wall of the ward and stuck. The mantid who had been examining him swung from handhold to handhold and scooped the gelatinous spheroid into her smock before it could seep into anything.

Elise reached out tentatively. "John, it's all right. I'm here. Slow down."

His eyes were fogged with radiation, his skin mottled and loose. He looked and smelled like meat gone bad. But her touch calmed him.

"Elise?"

"It's me. You made it."

"There was a mantid..."

"Sola has been taking care of you," Elise said reassuringly. "She's one of ours."

He sagged back into the bath. "Why all this?" His voice was a harsh whisper.

"You were in bad shape. Starving. Radiation poisoning. And your skinsuit bonded with you pretty deeply. It came apart in tatters when we tried to take it off. The bath is to coax the rest of it out, help you heal."

"How long?"

"A couple megaseconds since you got here."

"Greenwich Station?" The architecture looked familiar, like an old Earth city overtaken by carbon-fixing blackvine. The bones were still there, beneath an encrusting layer of extruded aeroponic planters and luxuriant plant growth.

"Tholos Hive, now. We found a nice rubble pile and anchored down."

"What about Sidorov?"

"He is in a similar condition physically. Mentally…" Elise grimaced as she searched for the right words. "Well, not entirely sane, is probably the best way to put it."

Gray nodded. "He attacked me, on the flight here. There's something about the aetheric drive… It opens things up. Things you can't see normally. The dead. I don't know. Something is out there, Elise."

She did not reply.

"Maybe I'm insane too," Gray said into the silence.

"No."

"Not in the same way, in any case," Gray said. "What about *Hooded Falcon*? Have you figured out how her drive works?"

"My chirons are reverse engineering it, but I'm not sure it is something a human can understand. They say it involves another spatial dimension."

"Your chirons?" He did not like the sound of that.

"Like Sola," Elise said. "I forged a non-aggressive variant of the mantid on the trip out from Ceres. Rhea's first hatch. We needed engineers to put the station back together, and they are about as intelligent as us. We call them chirons."

None of this was comforting to him. "Isn't that against your code? 'Sapience is for sapiens,' and all that."

She shrugged. "All I did was restore their core aversion to harming quads, winged or not. I'd say that's a step in the right direction. You'll have to talk to Melissa about the rest."

Gray let it go. He was so tired. "What about the war?"

"Not going well," Elise said. "Mars only has one torchship left in play, the *Bikovsky*. It is sheltering in Callisto orbit. They're working on recommissioning *Gagarin* and *Shepard*, but it will take time. And they are first generation relics."

Bikovsky was *Tereshkova's* sister ship. Gray remembered racing iceboats against her officers back at Thunderbird. He could remember their names, but he could not recall their faces. Strange. His sight was not the only thing that was fogged.

"Meanwhile Luna is machine-gunning Mars with ships like your *Hooded Falcon*. Strekozas, Space Force calls them. Whatever that means."

"Russian for dragonfly," Gray said.

"Ah. We're not big into Russia out here."

He smiled weakly. "At least some things haven't changed." After a silence: "Did Thirteen...?" Make it, he wanted to say, but could not bring himself to. So many men had died, and she was only a mekan, after all.

"She's still wired up to the strekoza. We're not sure how to disconnect her without risking a qigong nova."

He did not reply. It was increasingly difficult to focus.

"You should rest now." Her spex silvered as she made an adjustment to the bath. His grip loosened on her slender hand. "Keep an eye on him, Sola. Let me know when he wakes up."

Gray anchored himself by a handhold at the top of the cupola. Having something to hold onto helped with the tremors. His hands were striped like a birthmark where the skinsuit had adhered. The pattern continued under the raveled cuff of his sweater and covered the rest of his body in scarlet whorls. It felt like his nerves had been scraped raw and were leaking electricity into the void.

Sola anchored herself to the wall behind him. The chiron nursemaid wore a pale teal smock whose pockets bulged with medical supplies in case Gray's tremors progressed into a full-blown seizure, or one of his daily anxiety attacks escalated into atrial fibrillation. Anything could set him off, but just now it was the triad of chirons anchored to the opposite wall that had his heart racing. He knew they were Elise's top knobs: Ada, Marie, and Emmy. But what he saw were the mantids he had fought on 55 Pandora.

"Breathe," Sola said softly, rubbing the cilia of her bifurcated hand together near his ear, which was ironic coming from a creature that did not. But he took a breath, and the anxiety ebbed. He returned from the land of the dead to the observation deck, where the chirons were dressed in royal blue utility vests and their ledeyes flickered with abstractions – equations, graphs, manifolds – not murderous intent.

Their ledeyes silvered over when they noticed Gray watching them. He looked outside guiltily. The test article resembled a child's toy, one of those sticks with a propeller at the top that you spin between your hands to make it fly away. The stick comprised a rack of kinos to energize the long, narrow pentachorons that formed the blades of its aetheric propeller.

"Kinos hat homega max," one of the knobs reported, rasping the recursive cilia of her binary hand together in a simulacrum of speech. They were incapable of starting a word without a consonant and had apparently settled on a hard "h" as the best compromise. It grated on Gray's nerves.

He glanced at Elise. She nodded.

"Spin her up," he ordered.

The massive induction motor they had temporarily anchored to the roof of the docking tower went to work. The test article's pentachorons began to glow a deep blue, fractal webs spreading across their hypervanes. The fractal webs became arcs, then a ghostly blue disk that seemed to open into some higher space that made Gray's eyes hurt. The test article slipped out of the grasp of the induction motor. Gray felt a dark flux wash through him as it accelerated away from the docking tower.

Elise grabbed his bicep. "Are you all right?"

He was drifting free in the cupola. "Fine. Sorry." He snagged a handhold. "Did you feel that?"

"Maybe a little?"

Gray turned to the chirons. "How about you?"

They shrugged, another mannerism close enough to human to be instantly recognizable, but far enough away to raise an alarm. Like a talking corpse in his nightmares: alive but dead.

"Breathe," Sola whispered.

"Maybe I've been sensitized by exposure," he reasoned. "In any case, it's going to make a manned version of the strekoza problematic."

"We've been over this already, John," Elise said in the tone of one whose patience has worn thin. "They have to be manned. I won't forge killers; the mantids are abominations. I still haven't gotten the smell of blood out of my nose. No, a human is going to have to pull the trigger."

"Then make it like moths to a flame," Gray said. "No volition, just attraction."

"Don't get me started on kamikazes. They aren't going to blow themselves up, either. Mekans are sentient creatures the same as you and me. I will not create them to commit suicide on someone else's behalf."

Gray did not reply immediately. When he did, his voice was low. "As a soldier, I may have a different take on that than you. I would not call it suicide. I would call it sacrifice."

"It's suicide if it is not your fight," Elise snapped back.

Gray's eyebrows shot up. "Not your fight? Whose fight is it then?"

Elise shook her head. "You know what, I don't want to talk about this right now. I brought you here to see the test flight. That's what we're doing. We can talk politics later. Okay?"

"Okay," Gray said after a moment. "But we'll need to come up with a way to protect the pilot or at least get them out of the prop wash. Perhaps two drive nacelles, with the pressure hull suspended between them."

"Great idea," Elise said serenely, her attention focused on the test article receding in the distance. "Work with Ada. I'll review the source before it goes to the forge."

Outmaneuvered and outgunned by EON's strekozas, Space Control had directed the United Colonies' surviving assets in the Belt to regroup on the outermost of Jupiter's four Galilean moons. Callisto was far enough away from the gas giant to have a survivable radiation environment and had a virtually inexhaustible supply of water ice to serve as propellant for nuclear salt-water missiles and the destroyers that carried them.

Obtaining fissiles for the missiles was trickier, as Callisto was largely rock and ice. But it was also heavily bombarded by other, smaller bodies, one of which had recently – geologically speaking – arrived with a few hundred kilotons of uranium. Mekans hurriedly constructed a base near the ore body, and in due course staff were regularly treated to the sight of massive nuclear-powered missiles intercepting inbound strekozas.

So tensions were running high on *Astrape* as she approached Callisto at the end of her flight from Tholos Hive. Gray shut down her twin aetheric drives a full ship-day out, just to be sure there was no confusion. He had not come this far to fall victim to friendly fire.

The counter-rotating propellers spun down and the glow faded from their hypervanes. They slipped into free fall, Jupiter rushing up on them like a devouring giant with a single baleful red eye. A fuzziness in the back of his brain, a sort of background noise like static rain, went quiet. He unplugged his multifaceted flight helmet and stowed it.

"Hopefully that will reassure them," Gray said to no one in particular. Sidorov was tranked out, as he had been for most of the trip, strapped into an acceleration recliner in a corner of the triangular flight deck.

"How his your head?" Sola rasped from her seat in the remaining corner.

"Not bad," Gray said. "The helmet really helps. That was a brilliant idea, Sola." There had been a couple rough spots along the way, when the static rain became a storm that threatened to overwhelm his ability to think, to do anything more than exist. But they had passed quickly, and he did not want to overstate the case.

"And the ship is a good design," he added for Ada's benefit. "A lot better than *Hooded Falcon*."

Astrape's flight deck was perched near the bow of the ship, centered between and well in front of its two aetheric drive nacelles to minimize exposure to the dark flux. Below it was the engineering deck, chiron territory while they were underway. Ada had formed a triad with a couple of freshly hatched apprentices – Limor and Hedy – and brought them along to help operate the fighter.

"Just has predicted," Ada said over the intercom.

"Well, now you *has* experimental confirmation," Gray said. "The knobs hon Callisto hare going to be very hexcited."

"You should not mock your betters," Ada said in perfect starting-vowel-free English.

Gray smiled. He had become fond of the chiron knob over the last few megaseconds. "His the reaction drive ready?"

"Reaction drive his go," Ada confirmed with utmost dignity.

They set down on a freshly bulldozed landing field adjacent to the base. *Astrape's* reaction drive kicked up a cloud of dust that billowed past the flight deck's viewports. The base's brutalist architecture softened to angular outlines and smeared lights. Gray turned away from the viewport to help Sola get Sidorov ready for transport, while Ada fretted over the intercom about dust fouling the hypervanes.

"We're here, Sid!" Gray said brightly. "Let's get you buttoned up. We're going to see some old friends."

Sidorov's hands clenched and unclenched slowly, their motion regulated by clockworks Sola had extruded. Other clockworks encapsulated his knees and elbows. Sweat beaded on his forehead as Gray carefully seated his facemask and sealed the hood of his skinsuit around its flange.

The fighter's airlock was twenty-five meters above the ground, too far for humans to jump even on Callisto. Gray and Sidorov rode down on a gantry hoist. The line descended parallel to the fuselage, swinging languidly back and forth between a pair of massive radiator fins that doubled as support pylons. One was tipped by a double-ended aetheric drive nacelle, the other a laserscope. The residual heat from the qigong was palpable. Rivulets of sweat trickled down his cheeks and pooled at the edge of his facemask. Sidorov was hyperventilating.

"Easy Sid," Gray said, patting his back awkwardly. "We're almost down."

Then they were down. It was the first time Gray had stood on solid ground since they had left Ceres for Luna and all that came after. Something loosened in his chest, some tension he had been carrying. He pulled slack into the hoist line and unclipped. Sola landed beside them a moment later, a cryogenic dewar held high in her forearms. Ada followed shortly behind in a splash of dust.

Sidorov flinched at their arrival. "Mantids!" he shouted. "Get your cutlass out, Commander!"

"They're on our side, Sid." Some of this was for the benefit of the driver of the open truck that had just rolled up, who looked like he might keep on going.

"Are you Commander Gray?" the driver asked as Gray took a seat beside him. Sola and Ada settled in the truck's bed, Sidorov sandwiched between them.

"I am. And you are...?"

"Spacer Reziko Nika at your service, sir! Honored to meet you. Your fight with the mantids on 55 Pandora is required training material."

"That was a classic clusterfuck, Nika," Gray said. Had enough time passed for that to be part of training now? Featuring him as the sole survivor no doubt. The thought of it made him feel slightly ill.

The spacer laughed nervously. "Yes sir, it was! Say, are those things safe?"

"The ship or the chirons?"

"I was thinking the, uh," Nika glanced over his shoulder, "the chirons."

"We wouldn't still be alive if they weren't."

Nika started to say something and decided better. The rest of the drive passed in silence. He dropped them off at a cargo airlock beneath the heavy stone brows of the base terminal. Air pumps whirred into audibility as pressure came up. Boxy filters sucked the dust out of the air in miniature horizontal whirlwinds. Gray flipped his facemask up.

"Don't you fucking touch me!" Sidorov shouted at Sola, who was helping with his facemask. Gray stepped between them with a grimace and finished the job.

The inner door sighed open. The men on the other side wore UCSF regulation skinsuits and sharply creased grey utility vests. Abram's facemask was cocked jauntily over his head. He looked less worn than the last time Gray had seen him, rested, his own man. Four stars adorned his collar – promoted to captain, then! Flanking him were Allen and Mendeleev, who had also been detached to *Island Girl* after the debacle at 55 Pandora.

"Captain Abrams!" Gray exclaimed. "Congratulations. Al, Mendy! What a surprise."

"John!" Abrams clasped the proffered hand and hauled him into an embrace. Gray was overwhelmed with emotion: deep affection for his former XO, the simple pleasure of seeing old shipmates, the darker anxiety of being in the company of those who might judge his actions harshly.

Abrams held him back at arm's length. "Look at you! You must have lost ten kilos. Don't they feed you there?"

"You should have seen us when we arrived," Gray said. "I'm a vision of health compared to then."

"You worry me, son." He turned to Sidorov, who had shrunk back against the wall. "Lieutenant Sidorov, it's good to see you too."

"Don't trust them sir!"

"Trust who, Sid?"

Sidorov rolled his eyes at Gray. "The niner and his vamp. They're in it together with the mantids."

"Take it easy Sid," Abrams said, frowning.

"You don't believe me? Look at this!" He held up his hands. In the cruel light of the loading dock the clockworks looked like a mechanical crustacean had parasitized him. "Why would they do this if they didn't have something to hide?"

Abrams nodded. "Okay Sid. Let's get you to sickbay for a checkup. Al and Mendy will take you. You remember them, don't you?"

"There's nothing wrong with my memory," Sidorov said. His voice rose to a shout. "There's nothing wrong with me!"

"Of course not, Sid," Allen stepped in and took his arm. "Just a routine check so you can get back to work."

Sidorov allowed Allen and Mendeleev to coax him out of the airlock.

"There's something else," Gray said. Abrams raised his eyebrows. Gray took the dewar from Sola. "Captain Rashnikov requested that his moravec be returned to his family on Mars. The way things are going this might be as close as I get. Could you…?"

Abrams had stiffened to attention. Now he bellowed across the loading dock. "Attention! Admiral on deck!"

The normal hubbub of the loading dock went quiet. Heads swiveled as men tried to locate the senior officer. Abrams remained at attention, now saluting the dewar. Understanding spread through the room like a wave. Allen and Mendeleev turned around to see what was happening. A spacer at the edge of the crowd had the presence of mind to play the pipes on the intercom.

After a long moment, Abrams snapped off his salute. That too rippled through the crowd. Gray realized with a shock that his eyes were moist. He could not remember the last time he had cried. He had thought it was beyond him.

"Thank you for bringing Admiral Rashnikov home, son," Abrams said. "We'll take him from here."

36

The Spider Bear

Dusk settled over the valley and the warm wind that had caressed her paused as if it were between breaths. She had long since left the snowfield behind. The stream narrowed as she followed it up-valley, looking for a place to stop and rest for the night. The embers strapped to her belly could not keep up with her energy consumption, especially as she climbed. She needed to stop for the night and let them spin up her kinos.

I am here, the voice said, louder now in the stillness between breaths.

A dark, angular spot on the slope above her captured her attention. At first, she thought it was some kind of structure, which was alarming. She had no desire to interact with the natives; humans were notorious for their cruelty toward artiforms. But the voices drew her on, growing louder as she approached.

It was not a structure, but a hole dug into the hillside, or perhaps a natural cave, its vaulted roof defined by the relatively flat undersides of two massive boulders wedged together. She climbed up to it. A few human-looking artifacts littered the ground in front of it, things that had been manufactured, not drexlered. But they were old and rusted, and the prospect of a defensible shelter appealed to her. The night before had been broken several times by the incursions of mekanos drawn by her heat.

She picked up a long, flat, metal stick of some sort that had a grip built for a human hand on one end and came to a sharp point on the other. She cautiously entered the darkness, petal hat in one hand, her newfound walking stick probing the ground ahead with the other. Her ledeyes adjusted quickly.

The cave was larger than it looked from outside. Against one wall was heaped a pile of dismembered mekanos. She drew closer, both fascinated and frightened. What were these doing here? Amongst the detritus of sand crab carapaces, rock roaches, and bulbans, a pair of disturbingly organic bones protruded, partially covered by the tattered sleeve of a long dead skinsuit. She tugged at the bones, and an arm emerged, the pile shifting as a larger mass moved beneath it. A harder tug and the ribcage and pelvis of what had to be a human skeleton emerged. If there were legs, they were lost in the pile, as was the other arm and head. Though on inspection the skeleton's terminal neck vertebra was cleanly shorn.

It was wearing a utility vest emblazoned with the sigil of the United Colonies Space Force.

I am here, the voice said, so loud she could almost see it moving in the darkness, like one of the dust devils she had seen at lower elevations.

She pulled the garment off the skeletal remains. There was a sound from the back of the cavern, something loud enough to vibrate the cilia on her forearms, but she mistook it for the pile settling. She shrugged into the vest. Pchelans had a similar torso to humans, at least from the waist up. The vest fit well enough; she could close the front. The dust devil enveloped her.

Motion burst from the rear of the cave. She reflexively jumped away from it, banging into the edge of the entrance. An armored foot swiped at her, knocking her to the other side of the cave. Her attacker was huge, eight-legged, its head studded with eight ledeyes, its back distended like an over-full bulban. Inside the fluid-filled bubble another identical eight-legged artiform was taking shape.

The sentinel scrabbled away as the spider bear approached. It snapped at her midsection with serrated mandibles. She kicked it away, no longer feeling pain in her injured leg, just fear. The creature snapped at her again, this time seizing on one of the embers strapped to her abdomen. It ripped the ember away and chewed open the casing. A smaller interior set of mandibles scooped out the fissiles within and swallowed them greedily.

The sentinel edged towards the opening. The spider bear dropped the ember's mangled casing and moved to block her. It seemed fixated on the remaining ember. She hastily slipped the cylinder out of its improvised harness and threw it toward the back of the cave.

The spider bear considered this for a moment, then cautiously moved crabwise away from the entrance. The sentinel lunged through the opening and tumbled down the slope. When she regained her feet the spider bear was framed by the boulders, looking down at her. Ghostly dust devils rose from it, dancing around one another as they climbed into the darkened sky until their silver glow diffused to starlight.

The wind blew cold down the valley, a giant's exhalation.

She ran.

37

A Fine Pair

Maggie stretched luxuriously, reveling in the warm embrace of clean sheets and a proper bed. Beside her a padded ridgeline of blankets marked where Tara had lain a few minutes before. Maggie's brow furrowed and then cleared as she smiled ruefully.

She had not intended to sleep with Tara, at least not consciously. But it was clear looking back that they had been tracking down that path since they sat together by the campfire. And Maggie could not bring herself to think it was a bad thing, despite the dull vein of worry that pulsed in the back of her mind. Real flesh-on-flesh contact with a human being who did not desperately need her to survive, nor was trying to kill her. It was enough to make her think that surviving this shitshow might be its own reward.

Her reflection observed her critically in the full-length mirror beside the bed and seemed surprised that she was not a poor catch. Not avatar material, but who was? And who would want that, really? Besides Eric, anyway. Humans' glory was their imperfection. She slid the closet mirror aside and sorted through Tara's clothes, selecting a comfortable pullover and a soft pair of pants. A couple rolls of the pant cuffs and she was good to go. Fresh clothes felt marvelous after having worn the same thing for sols on end.

A window above the headboard looked out over the garden behind the clinic. Gray was nowhere to be seen. The charge cord was coiled neatly on the flagstones. Maggie opened the bedroom door and called down the hallway. "Tara, do you know where Gray is?"

Tara appeared around the corner wearing nothing but an apron cinched tightly around her slender waist and a pair of puffy insulated slippers. "He's not in the garden?"

"Shit," Maggie said. She whirled back into the room, grabbed her revolver and satchel. Inventorying in her mind where she had left everything. Coat, airscarf, hat, goggles...

Her goggles were charging on the nightstand. She yanked them over her head. "Gray? Gray?" There was no reply.

"Slow down," Tara said.

"I've got to go," Maggie said. "Are my clothes dry?"

"Probably but listen, Maggie, if you go down there by yourself, and there has been trouble, it will not end well for you."

"Tara, I have to go. It may sound weird, but Gray is my friend."

"It doesn't sound weird and I'm going with you."

"What? No."

"You don't get to tell me no, Maggie May. That is not our relationship." She yanked open the door that led downstairs to the clinic. "Dorje!"

There was no reply. The two women exchanged glances. Tara hurried downstairs, Maggie trailing behind. While Tara went through the clinic room by room, Maggie followed a hunch and went straight to Eric's bedside. There was a note on the tray in elegant script. She read it in a single glance.

"Tara!" she cried out.

Eric's eyes fluttered open, puzzlement pulling his features together. "What's wrong?"

Tara came rushing in. Maggie handed her the note. She blanched, a constellation of freckles standing out against suddenly pale skin. "Wardamn it. She went after him."

Dawn was leaden, the sun invisible behind a pillowed veil of cloud. Gray was pinned down behind a boulder, fighting a war of attrition that showed every sign of ending poorly for him. Every few hectosecs the Kentavr lobbed a search and destroy round up above him. No more dragon teeth, thankfully, but the search and destroy rounds were bad enough: a sabot lofted them up for a good view and then fired a high-velocity tungsten dart. So far Gray had been able to knock the sabots down with his crest laser, but that would not be his story for much longer. He was almost out of spin.

His only chance was to make a run for the Kentavr and hope the laser was more effective at close range. The rifle on his arm was dead weight; he had not been able to find more slugs for it. If he could have taken a deep breath, he would have, but that basic autonomic function was not available. What is life without breath? Not worth worrying about. He lunged down the slope. Rock exploded at his heels as a tungsten dart narrowly missed its mark. He fired his laser at the Kentavr, hoping to blind it. Then something hit him hard in the back and he went down, lobster arm pinwheeling back as he tried to catch himself. He cartwheeled once and came to a stop against the ungainly carapace of his backpack.

The left side of his chest glowed brightly in infrared. The dart had shattered one of his kinos. Its paired carbon nanotube flywheels had flown apart, spraying shrapnel into his chest cavity. Kinetic energy turned to heat. It felt like a heart attack. Snow swirled down, hissed to steam when it chanced to land on his heat-warped chest. Vapor pulled away like a tattered scarf in the fitful breeze.

He tried to stand, scrabbling at the rocky ground with his lobster claw, but only managed to turn over and get onto his hands and knees before thermal overload caught up with him. He collapsed onto his face, the world constricting to the myriad sharp-edged rocks immediately in front of him, little angular skulls marching like dead warbots into infinity.

Maggie clung to the mekta with knees and hands. Borodin's bullpup smacked between her shoulders with every bound. Her revolver slapped her thigh. She could not spare a hand to cinch either down. She had no illusions of control; she was in for the ride. Tara's mekta kicked dust in her face as it charged ahead. Another selene whose name Maggie had not caught in the rush of leaving Potalama brought up the rear. There were just the three of them, no hekates in the group, no kores. A triad of selenes if Maggie counted herself as one.

She only heard Tara's half of the conversation with the hekates before they left, but even so it was clear they were furious when they learned what had happened. They quickly determined that Dorje was not alone. A half-dozen kores were missing, and an equal number of mektas.

Lynn had ordered Tara to wait while they organized a proper rescue party. Tara in turn made it clear that waiting was not going to happen. She was implacable, a force of nature once she made up her mind. Maggie felt like she had been caught in a whirlwind. She was used to being the one in charge, and the role reversal made her deeply uncomfortable, and strangely aroused, which made her even more uncomfortable.

"What the fuck," she kept muttering to herself, as the triad of mektas cleared the cleft and bounded down the rocky trail with no regard for obstacles. "What." (Slam.) "The." (Jump.) "Actual." (Skid.) "Fuck." (A breathtaking moment of weightlessness.)

Gray heard footsteps approaching, a heavy four-footed gait, talus shoved downslope in an unmistakable crunch of rock on rock. He could not move, and he could only see the ground immediately in front of his face. But he could still hear.

A Kentavr's clawed foot gouged the ground in front of his face. It flicked at him casually, wrenching his head around and shattering his crest laser's optics. It felt like someone had jabbed a broken bottle into the top of his head. Another set of indicators went red.

The sound of a hatch opening was followed by the grunts and scrapes of a large animal extracting itself from narrow confines. A prosthetic knee appeared in front of Gray's main eye, carbon fiber struts and muscle ribbon wrapped in ceramic armor. Then a middle limb just like one of Thirteen's arms, skeletal black carbon, bracing a heavy-bodied man as he leaned down to examine the Hund's head. Ledeye goggles that seemed welded to his flesh reflected Gray's mechanical visage.

They were both worse for the wear since the first time they met, down by the river.

"Commander John Gray, I presume," Borodin said. "Unsung hero of the Warsing. First man to travel faster than light. Architect of the hypermissile. War criminal. The list goes on. I have wanted to collect you since I became aware of your existence. I don't think this will hurt. Can you even feel pain in your present state? It seems unlikely. Anyway, I'll have you out of there in a minute or two."

A sense of vibration. Screws turning? He supposed it would not hurt. But he desperately wished he could move. Would there ever be another awakening?

There was a sharp crack. Borodin sat down beside him, caged in lightning, head flung back, mouth open in a silent howl. The lightning flickered out and he collapsed. A mekano hunting spear was lodged in his shoulder. His mekan midarms and prosthetic leg scrabbled spastically at the ground for a few seconds before stilling. His face was a meter from Gray's. "Aren't we a fine pair," he said, his voice a harsh whisper. Blood began to trickle from beneath his airscarf. He coughed. "Monsters out of our time."

He heard mekta hooves cantering down the slope. "Gray? Are you all right?"

Maggie? No. The girl. He struggled to remember her name.

Another girl's voice. "He's pretty bright in infra. Might be in thermal overload."

They dismounted. It took both of them to turn him over. The sky was clear. Their faces were backlit, copper hair on fire with the first light of dawn, like Valkyries descended to the field of battle.

"Gray?"

"He's been hit. Looks like it took out a kino."

"Get me a charge cable."

The sound of people doing things. A warm rush of power spinning up his remaining kino. Again the sun was eclipsed.

"Dorje," he remembered.

"Oh good, you're still in there. I was worried."

"Borodin?" he grunted.

"Alive. Maybe not for long. I suppose we should do something about that. Alina, get the med kit."

Gray pushed himself upright. His spin gauge dropped into the red, went back to orange. A pair of mektas stood nearby, nervously shuffling their feet. Several more were on the ridge, their riders distinct against the skyline.

Borodin looked bad. Gray lurched to his feet. He did not have a lot of time. He rummaged awkwardly, one-handedly, through Borodin's pack. He could barely fit his lobster hand inside. He upended the pack and shook it. The leech tumbled out and rolled to a stop between his feet. He brushed Alina aside.

"Hey!"

He flipped Borodin over onto his back. The big man gagged on his own blood. Gray ripped his airscarf away with the tip of his claw. Borodin's head fell back against the rocky ground.

"He'll die!" Alina cried.

"Yes," Gray said. He opened his hand wide. The lobster claw bracketed Borodin's neck. "That is the plan."

"I can help you with the warsingers," Borodin gasped out. "The two of us together..."

"You are a parasite," Gray said.

"They are coming."

Gray tightened his grip. The chainblade in his claw whirred to life. A fine red line appeared on the side of Borodin's neck.

Borodin struggled against the inexorable grip, skeletal arms flailing against Gray's armored chest. Gray jammed his gun arm behind the technomancer's head and pulled him closer into the grip of the claw.

"Look away," Gray told the girls, his beautiful Valkyries.

"I will not," Dorje said. "This is the face of war and I will see it."

There was a clatter of mekta hooves. "Stop!" Maggie shouted.

"Oh for fuck's sake," Gray said.

"Put him down."

Gray considered. "Why should I?"

"He owes me an answer."

"You'll have all the answers he'll ever have when I'm through with him," Gray said.

"I want it from him, not a leech."

"Fine." Gray dropped Borodin. "Ask your questions, but then he's mine."

Maggie strode over, pushed Borodin back down with her foot. "You!" she barked. "Korolyov. Seven mears ago. You killed a technomancer and his wife."

"Maybe?" Borodin coughed blood. His lips were turning blue. "I've killed a lot of technomancers. Nature of collecting."

"Maxim and Irina Lebedev? No?" Maggie leveled the bullpup at his head. "Maybe this will help you remember."

Comprehension dawned. "You're the kid." He laughed, a strangled sound that ended in a dreadful wheeze of blood. "I should have known. No good deed goes unpunished."

Maggie's eyes narrowed. "No. Good. Deed."

"I let you go."

Maggie nodded. "And I should be grateful."

"Considering? Yes."

She pulled the trigger. The girls flinched at the blast.

"Ares damn it," Gray swore. He threw the memory leech down in disgust. "You know what he knew? No? Me neither! And now we're not going to. Ever."

Maggie took a step back from the ruined skull, open like a cracked egg with its bloody yolk spilled on the ground. Then another step. Her face was very pale.

Tara eased her down to the ground, catching the bullpup by its sling and setting it carefully aside. Distaste twisted her mouth as she handled the weapon.

"Easy," she said. "Head between your knees. If you need to vomit, take off your airscarf first."

"I'm all right. I've just never... He killed my parents. And he got... he got what he deserved. Better than he deserved."

"It's done," Tara said, with a trace of sadness in her voice. "It's done."

"It's done all right," Gray said bitterly. He surveyed the circle of faces around him, distantly registered their alarm and could not bring himself to care.

"*That* was a mistake," he said loudly, pointing at the half-headed corpse with his gun arm. He gave it a sharp kick. It rolled over a couple times, leaving behind a puddle of blood and brain mush like a spilt bowl of soggy grechka.

"*That* was incredibly fucking stupid. He would have been just as dead when I was through with him. I am in fact pissed. I bet he knew what the warsingers have planned. I bet he knew a lot of things. None of which we will now ever know."

No one seemed reassured by his explaining. Maggie was rocking back and forth soundlessly. Tara had one hand on her back, the other on the bullpup's pistol grip. Keeping it close just in case he went full-metal-jacket on them no doubt.

The girls' eyes were very wide. His Valkyries. He should be thankful. He stared up at the sky. The clouds were starting to lift. Listened to the wind. Sighed. He was thankful.

"Thank you," he said. "Thank you for saving me. I'm just... a little upset. I'll get over it. I'm sorry if I frightened you. Sometimes I forget what I look like."

The girls seemed marginally reassured. Tara still had a firm grip on the bullpup. Maggie still would not look at him. Borodin was still in pieces.

"It's not what you look like," Tara said. "It's how you act. There's a man dead right there, and you're upset you weren't the one to kill him."

Gray shook his head. They did not get it. They were not going to get it. Or maybe he was a monster, just like Borodin said. A fine pair. Hard to say, and he was not sure it mattered. "I'm going down to the bipe. It has some kind of space-folding weapon. We're going to need it, when the mantids come for us. And make no mistake, they will. If we can even figure out how to use it. Which would have been simple, but now is not. Fuck me."

Maggie had stopped crying some time ago. Her eyes were red, but her cheeks were dry. Tara sat patiently beside her, hearing her out.

"He murdered my parents," Maggie said. "Seven mears ago, in Korolyov. The mantids came for my father and Borodin was there. He waited until the mantids flushed my parents out and then he – he harvested my father. Killed my mother and harvested my father. Took his head off and took his memories with that leech. Maybe I should have let Gray do that to him. Maybe that would have been better. Or done it myself. But I didn't want to be like him, like a vulture eating the dead. I didn't want him to survive in any form. Not his body, not his mind, not even his memories. I wanted to erase him. And so I pulled the trigger."

"You've never killed anyone before?"

"No. Threatened to, more than once. Never had to do it though."

"And you didn't have to do it this time. Your life was not at stake. No one's life was at stake. Is that what upsets you?" From someone else the question might have seemed presumptive, but from Tara it was just a reflection.

"I guess so. Not that he didn't deserve it. My parents. Eric's father Berel. Who knows how many others who got in his way or had something he wanted. The ones he *collected*."

"We are all flawed creatures," Tara said, which was true enough, but seemed patronizing to Maggie.

"Yeah well he was a flawed creature that specialized in eating other flawed creatures, like me and Gray. And if you can't see that, I don't know why we're having this conversation."

Tara considered this for a few quiet moments. "Honestly, that is the question I am asking myself as well, Maggie. I saw something in you, something special. I guess this," she gestured at the blue tarp that covered Borodin's mutilated corpse, "doesn't change that. But I'm having a hard time getting past it, I really am. It goes against everything I believe in."

Maggie's instinct was to double-down: Borodin had deserved to die. He was a killer. Worse than a killer; he collected people's minds, their memories, their essence. She barely knew this woman, Tara, but she knew she had no right to judge. And at the same time, it felt like Tara had unlocked something in her. It seemed a shame to throw that away.

"Say something," Tara said gently.

Maggie nodded. She measured out her words. "I'm sorry if I've damaged our relationship. I'm not sorry that I killed him." She paused to consider. "You told me before we left Potalama that it was not our relationship for me to tell you no. I'm telling you now, that it is not our relationship for you to judge me."

Tara was silent. Maggie was getting cold, her vital heat seeping into the ground on which they sat. She rose, dusting herself off.

"I'm going to check on Gray. I hope..." She hoped so many things. Maybe that was what Tara had unlocked, the capacity to hope again. "I hope we are not over already. Or at all."

Tara nodded but did not reply.

"Do you really think the warsingers will come for us?" Dorje asked. She crouched in the dust beside Gray as he poked at the bipe. Between it taking a rifle slug to one hip and him ripping the power cable out of the other leg, it was totally immobilized. And, as far as he could tell, nearly out of spin. Which was probably a good thing.

"I'd be shocked if they didn't," Gray said. "I imagine Borodin's arrangement was that he would do their wet work for them in exchange for the hyperglider. When it looked like he was out of the picture they escalated to a ground strike. Sloppy but effective."

"Wet work?"

Gray pantomimed swiping a knife across his neck with the barrel of his rifle arm.

"Oh." Dorje wrinkled her nose in distaste.

"But now that he's one hundred percent dead, they are going to have to take matters into their own hands."

"Or mandibles."

"Indeed." He rocked back on his heels. "I think we can get this thing back on its feet, with some replacement parts. And some hands so I can do the work." He gave her what he hoped was a significant look, side optics swiveling forward and up in a poor imitation of a mekan's foveal rings.

"I may be able to help with that," Dorje said.

"What are you two up to?" Maggie asked brightly behind them.

"Maggie-la!" Dorje exclaimed. She leapt to her feet and embraced the technomancer. Maggie patted her back awkwardly.

"We were just talking about how to fix the bipe," Dorje continued excitedly.

"Oh?"

"I'm going to try and get replacement parts drexlered back at Potalama."

"Don't forget to ask selene Tara first," Maggie said. "And if you go, can you bring my satchel back? I left it at the clinic in the rush."

"Of course! I better get going if I'm going to get back before sunset." Over her shoulder: "Some of my kores are bringing down gamis so we can stay out with you tonight."

"Thank you Dorje!"

"My Kores," Gray echoed as Dorje bounded up the hillside. "Things seem to have taken on a life of their own."

"Yes," Maggie said.

"You don't approve?"

"I am worried about endangering them."

"I see."

"That was a very stupid thing you did," she continued. "Going after Borodin alone."

"It was close," Gray admitted.

"If the kores had not come after you…"

"I'd be dead. Or whatever the word is, in my case."

"And you could have gotten them all killed."

"Still might," Gray said.

"And you're good with that?"

Gray shrugged with an awful scrape of ceramic armor. "Some things are worth fighting for, Maggie."

"Only if you stand a chance of winning." Her hands were on her hips now.

"I think we have a better chance now than we ever had before. Best thing that could happen is to launch the hyperglider before the warsingers catch up with us. Nothing to fight about then. Otherwise, we're going to need all the firepower we can get." He rapped the fist of metal that enclosed the bipe's space-folding weapon with his claw.

"Have you figured out what it does?" she asked, changing the subject.

"My guess is it rotates matter through hyperspace. I've only seen what it does to rock and dirt, but I suspect it comes back inside-out."

"Ugh."

"Yeah. Do you think you'll be able to remove the geasa?"

She grimaced, a worried scowl. "I have to try."

"It might be more expeditious to just replace its brain."

"Funny, that's what Eric said about you."

"You don't want to do it," he said appraisingly.

"Do what?"

"Take it apart."

"That's a nice way to put it. Take it apart. Like saying you take apart a chicken when you eat it."

"It's not Dusty anymore."

"Maybe Dusty just got lost in whatever Borodin did to him. We won't know until I remove the geasa."

"I saw you take Borodin's head off with his own bullpup. And now you won't put down his warbot?"

Blood rose in her cheeks. "First, that mekfucker deserved it. He confessed to multiple murders, including my parents. You heard him. So frag him. I'm glad he's dead, and I'm all right with being the one who pulled the trigger. I can live with that. Maybe Tara can't, but I can. Second, frag you too, if you think you can manipulate me with that. It's times like this I have second thoughts about letting you off the leash."

"Damn," Gray said. "That's cold."

"You know what's cold? You're cold!" Maggie shot back, which took him back to a conversation with Elise. Back when he was not-cold flesh-and-blood. Cold as in dead, they used to say. Was he? It did not feel that way. He felt alive as he had ever been. But maybe it was like getting used to not being able to hear when you blew an eardrum sucking vac. Maybe his nervous system had just dialed down its expectations about what being alive meant.

"Third," Maggie was still pissed, "you need to work on your emotional intelligence. It's a good thing I've got a soft spot for machines, is all I can say. Or you wouldn't even be here."

"I can't argue with that," Gray conceded.

"Thank you," she said. "That's a pleasant change. And fourth, Dusty is an innocent. He's not a psychopathic technomancer. Or a warbot. He's just trying to stay alive."

"He did try to kill me," Gray said, but it felt hollow. They were all just trying to stay alive.

"Have you looked in the mirror lately?"

Gray lifted his hands. Which were a large-caliber gun and a lobster claw. He dropped them with a sigh. "I miss having hands. I can't even connect my own charge cable. It's a good thing the Hund never has to take a shit."

He had hoped for a smile, but it was not forthcoming.

"And it might help the general perceptions," he continued. "Though Tara tells me it's not what I look like that's the problem."

Maggie sighed, shook her head. "Tara has her own problems. We've all got problems. Not one of us is remotely perfect. Not even their precious hekates. Don't even get me started on those bitches." She stopped and made a visible effort to compose herself. "Look. I'm going to try and remove Dusty's geasa, so we don't have to worry about him rotating someone through hyperspace. Or whatever that wardamn weapon does. Once that's done I'll tackle your hands. Okay?"

He shrugged, another unpleasant scrape of ceramic plate over titanium armature. "Don't worry about it."

"Gray, wait a minute." But he was walking away. "Where are you going?"

"To work on my emotional intelligence," he said without looking back.

"Frag," she said to Dusty, who was in no condition to reply. "That guy knows how to get under my skin."

38

A Greater Sky

"Are we ready?" Gray asked, surveying the small amphitheater. After all the time he had spent in Tholos Hive, he could not help but be struck by the uniformity of his audience. All baselines like himself, mostly male, mostly white. Not a Ceresean in the lot, nor a mekan other than Sola and Ada. Sola had exchanged her nurse's smock for a life support watchman's green utility vest, while Ada had extruded an elegant blue jacket for the occasion. Tholos Hive's insignia shimmered on its lapel as if it had been embroidered with metallic thread.

"Athene Potanin is running late," Abrams said. "Let's give her another hectosec."

"*Athene* Potanin," Gray said. Athenes were the top of the Space Control food chain, the equivalent of a Space Force admiral. The last time he had crossed paths with Potanin she had been a tectrix – basically a captain. Evidently war was good for careers if nothing else. His own included if he was being honest with himself.

"She actually speaks highly of you," Abrams said, misinterpreting Gray's tone as one of hostility. Which would not be unwarranted given Potanin had accused Gray of treason after they had lost the battle for Ceres. "For what it's worth."

Gray did not have time to process that before the amphitheater doors opened and a wing of space controllers swept in. At their head was Athene Potanin, imperious in her starched whites and pilotka with five snowy feathers tucked into its brim. Lynch's old flame Rachel Petrova was also in the group, now a covert judging by the third feather in her pilotka. She gave him a startled look.

Captain Abrams laid out the agenda while Gray waited at parade rest, hands clasped loosely behind his back. Eventually he got to the point. "Tholos Hive has developed a hybrid species that could turn the course of the war, code name

Thunderbolt. Commander Gray brought the gems required for us to replicate it, and a triad of chiron engineers to help us do so. Commander Gray?"

Gray took the podium to polite applause. He exported a model of *Astrape* from his spex to the auditorium's holocaster. He had barely gotten started on its features when Potanin interrupted him.

"Commander Gray, this is all very well, but what we wanted was a manned version of the strekoza. Can you explain why you needed to forge an entirely new hybrid?"

"Let's take a step back," Gray said. "I'm afraid I started with what instead of why. Lieutenant Sidorov and I are the only known examples of long-term exposure to an aetheric drive. During our flight on *Hooded Falcon*, we both experienced disturbing perceptual and cognitive aberrations for which I have no good explanation. An aetheric drive produces a kind of dark flux that is frankly nightmarish, ma'am. It drove Sidorov insane. This design mitigates the issue by moving the pressure hull out of the drive's prop wash."

"*Mitigates* is an interesting word choice, Commander. It implies lack of resolution."

"We are still coming to grips with the nature of the problem, ma'am. Hyperspace is terra incognito."

The mention of hyperspace sent a ripple through the audience. Professor Giménez, the top knob in the group, shifted uneasily in his seat, exchanging glances with his colleagues from the Joint Service Academy. "With all due respect, Commander, hyperspace is a fantasy," he said.

"As is a reactionless drive," Gray said. "And yet one brought me here today. This is probably a good time to turn this briefing over to my colleague Ada of Tholos Hive. Ada played a pivotal role reverse engineering the aetheric drive and has a theory about how it works that could give us an edge in our arms race with EON."

Gray surrendered the podium to Ada. The first couple rows wilted at the chiron's proximity. He repressed a smile.

"Two things hare required," she rasped out. "First: hanother spatial dimension – hyperspace. Second: ha fluid within this dimension – haether."

"Commander Gray," Giménez interrupted again, "can we just have it on spex? This effort at speech is unwelcome."

Gray started to frame a reply, but Ada held up a bifurcated hand to forestall him. She considered Giménez as a praying mantis might consider a juicy grub, the foveal rings of her large ledeyes contracting to bright incandescent spots. "You misunderstand hour relationship, human. Chirons har not Space Force chattel. Hi ham not yours to command."

Giménez's mouth opened and then shut again. Gray's fondness for Ada ratcheted up another level. She cut over seamlessly to iconji, ledeyes flashing symbols and a woman's warm voice in Gray's ear. *But as a token of our solidarity with humans in this crisis I will communicate as you prefer.*

Ada cleared the holocaster and replaced the schematic of *Astrape* with an image every Martian schoolchild knew, a vision of what the Blue Mars Project would eventually create: a liquid sea in Aurorae Chaos, waves glittering in the sunlight, puffy white cumulus clouds above. On a distant shore the spires of Korolyov cast shadows through the luminous air.

An analogy: let us say the approximately two-dimensional surface of this lovely sea represents our three-dimensional space with its electromagnetic waves. Above the sea is the sky, or in our analogy, the aether, a greater sky. An aetheric drive's propeller blades rotate into the fourth dimension and interact with aether to generate thrust, like a boat pushed by a fan.

"And what of Commander Gray's dark flux?" Potanin asked.

Ada nodded. *Who here has heard of Landauer's principle?*

A couple tentative hands.

Just as energy has mass equivalence, so does information. It is part of the fundamental triad of reality: matter, energy, and information. Therefore, conservation laws apply to it. Information cannot be destroyed. But every physical thing encodes information. Living things like you and I are information processing systems. So where does all that information go when it's not here anymore?

Ada looked around the room. No one was inclined to venture an opinion. *Our hypothesis is that it becomes what we have labeled dark matter, like fog floating above the ocean, only detectable by its gravitational proximity. The dark flux is dark matter.*

Giménez scoffed. "You can't be serious."

What is the primary evidence for the existence of dark matter? Ada continued. *Galaxies that have more apparent mass than their stars could contribute. What else do galaxies have? Life. Your observatories have revealed that virtually every star with a planet in its habitable zone exhibits signs of life: oxygen, methane, dimethyl sulfide. The list goes on. Life is the source of dark matter.*

"I'm no cosmologist," Giménez began, but then something slapped the ceiling like a giant hand, leaving a thin haze of dust suspended below the lights, which flickered once and then went out. The radiation counter built into Gray's facemask started chattering like an alarmed squirrel. The holocaster must have been on a separate circuit, as it still displayed a ghostly trajectory plot that cast a pale silvery light over the audience, now standing. A moment later emergency lights came on along with the unmistakable ululation of hull breach klaxons.

Gray flipped his facemask down and cinched his skinsuit's hood around it. He opened a comm window to the chirons on *Astrape*.

"Are you able to launch?" he asked preemptively.

We are still taking on reaction mass, Limor replied.

We have enough for Callisto orbit and back, no more, Hedy expanded.

"Your odds are better in orbit than on the ground," Gray said. "Go!"

"What the hell just happened?" Potanin asked. They had evacuated the conference room and scattered to airtight strongholds while repair crews hastily patched leaks. One by one the klaxons went quiet. The sheer mass of the base's neolithic structure had served them well. A ship's hull would have been shredded.

Potanin and a handful of others – her aide Petrova, Giménez, Abrams, Gray and his chirons – had regrouped in an auxiliary command stronghold several decks belowground. The stronghold had the same design pattern as *Tereshkova's* bridge, a hexagon of consoles clustered around a central holocaster.

"We're still trying to sort that out, ma'am," Petrova replied from her console. "The most likely scenario is a qigong nova in low orbit. But I don't understand how a strekoza could have gotten through the destroyer screen without being detected."

Gray's heart was beginning to race. His grip tightened on the rail that encircled the consoles.

"Breathe," Sola's bifurcated hand whispered in his ear.

"Do we have sensor logs?" Gray asked. "We are assuming it was a strekoza, but a qigong reactor would have been visible in infrared long before it got here."

"Well what else could it be?" Giménez snapped.

"Are you fucking kidding me?' Gray said. "We're bringing up the rear in an arms race with EON. It's not like anyone predicted they would develop a reactionless drive, but that happened. Who the hell knows what else they may have come up with since?"

"You're thinking a stealth strekoza?" Abrams ventured, forehead wrinkled in thought.

"There is no stealth in space," Giménez said flatly.

"Not hin three-space," Ada rasped.

"Space Control's wide-field infrared scopes can spot the heat signature of a combat shell half an astronomical unit out," Giménez continued stubbornly. "Everything makes heat!"

"Found the sensor logs," Petrova said. She gestured at the lab's holocaster. "This is a composite view of the attack." A glimmer of light swelled rapidly into a sensor-studded sphere surrounded by four glowing pentachorons.

"And this is a vector plot of the same thing. Note the acceleration."

Gray whistled. "That's what, a hundred standard gees?"

"About," she said. "It went from being essentially undetectable to right on top of us." She stepped slowly through the frames. "Where it self-destructs and showers us with relativistic shrapnel."

Ada did her equivalent of frowning, foveal rings compressing down toward her cheeks, mandibles touching with a faint clicking sound. She raised her hand. "May Hi?"

Petrova waved control of the holocaster over to the chiron. Iconji flashed across her ledeyes. *We believe an aetheric drive's propellers rotate slightly out of three-space into hyperspace. So what if an object lifted out of three-space entirely? This anomalous acceleration may be how a hyperspatial vessel looks when it returns to three-space.*

Another analogy, with apologies to Professor Giménez. A horizontal surface divided the holocaster in two. *Say we are two-dimensional creatures living on this surface. If a three-dimensional object comes down from above – from hyperspace – and makes contact with our plane...*

The holocaster obliged with a balloon floating down, its first point of contact flaring as a red dot, rapidly expanding into a circle as it passed through the horizontal surface. *For us, on the plane, it looks like a distant object is zooming up on us. Much like the artifact.*

"That's ridiculous," Giménez spluttered.

"Do you have a better explanation?" Gray demanded.

"We can't keep going on like this," Potanin said to herself. "EON has been ahead of us every step of the way. Subverting our hives. Destroying critical resources. Then the aetheric drive, and now this..." She searched for words. "This stealth bomber. While we play catch-up. If we don't seize the initiative, we are going to lose this war."

"Do you have something in mind?" Abrams asked cautiously.

Potanin tallied the room before she came to a decision. "Does everyone here have a top-secret clearance?"

Gray shook his head. "Just secret, ma'am. And I imagine Ada has no clearance."

Potanin nodded. "Right. Petrova, make a note that Commander Gray's and the chiron Ada's clearances have been increased to top secret on my authority, effective immediately, due to a needs-to-know situation."

"Yes ma'am."

"What I am about to say is classified at the highest level," Potanin continued. "Consider this as evidence of my trust in your integrity, Commander." She smiled wryly at Gray's puzzled expression. "At some point you really must read up on performative command."

The smile went as quickly as it came. "To business: Space Control Intelligence has reason to believe that EON has been using highly evolved mekans – like chirons, but more so – to drive the arms race."

"Mekans aren't known for their creativity," Abrams said. "No offense, Ada. They're great imitators; just look at *Astrape*. But creators? Innovators? Not in my experience."

"That is by design," Potanin said. "We have limited their intelligence and creative capacity to assure our own dominance. The mekan reproductive cycle requires a human in the loop. Mekans have a hardwired aversion to the forge, so they can't directly create new gems. And a queen will only accept gems from her hivemaster. It all serves to keep us in control. But it is arbitrary. Any of those constraints could be removed by a rogue hivemaster."

"Then these... super chirons... are responsible for all of these advances?" Abrams asked.

"So it seems," Potanin said. "Intelligence indicates Melissa Wilson forged them. Which is why you are still in the room, Commander Gray. Elise Aberdeen is Hivemaster Wilson's parth, is she not?"

Abrams and Mendeleev returned with Gray to Tholos, where another Thunderbolt – *Bronte* – was being drexlered for them. Both men experienced mild symptoms of "aether sickness," including bouts of nausea and vivid dreams of loved ones who had died, but nothing that threatened their sanity.

Shortly after they arrived, Ada's hypothesis about how the stealth bomber worked was confirmed by a network of gravity wave sensors operated by the Tsiolkovsky Polytechnic Institute. The network had been plagued by what the T-Poly knobs assumed was a spate of equipment failures: dozens of small perturbations going off like popcorn between Earth and Jupiter. Space Control Intelligence arranged for the project to be declared a failure and quietly rolled the staff over to the Joint Service Academy, where they were put to a different task entirely: finding and tracking EON's next-gen ships.

Space Control code named the stealth bomber "kuznechik," Russian for grasshopper, but everyone on Tholos just called them hoppers. A hopper could, for short periods of time, lift entirely out of three-space and effectively disappear before coming back down anywhere up to a quarter of an astronomical unit away. However, both ends of the hop produced a gravity wave due to the vessel's anomalous acceleration, or "imaginary acceleration" as Ada liked to call it. "Imaginary" nominally referring to the mathematical realm of complex numbers, though Gray was pretty sure she was also mocking her human counterparts' lack of ability to visualize hyperspace and concomitant tendency to label it as "imaginary."

As to why hop instead of fly, the hypothesis developed over the course of a few happy hour brainstorming sessions was that the hoppers could not radiate waste heat while they were in hyperspace. It stood to reason that electromagnetic radiation could not propagate outside of three-space, any more than waves on Ada's metaphorical ocean could propagate into the sky. (Though Gray wondered if the redshift attributed to cosmic expansion might be caused by light leaking from three-space into hyperspace.) That constraint imposed a time limit on how long they could remain in hyperspace before overheating.

So far as anyone could tell, the hoppers were unmanned. This made sense to Gray based on his experience with the dark flux. If exposure to the aetheric drive was deeply disturbing, being lifted entirely into hyperspace might be more than the human mind – or spirit for all Gray knew; he was certainly starting to wonder – could tolerate.

During the search for hoppers, the knobs came across an entirely different kind of vessel they dubbed "skimmers." A skimmer deployed a sort of kite sail into hyperspace that dragged the rest of the ship behind in three-space, where radiators still worked and human occupants were less prone to go insane. According to Intelligence, the *Morrigan*, Melissa Wilson's qigong yacht, had been converted into a skimmer. Whether Melissa had gone insane was a matter of debate in Tholos Hive. Creating hyper-intelligent mekans without an aversion to murder qualified as insanity so far as Gray was concerned. It was like inviting bloody-handed Ares out for drinks: not going to end well.

Elise was more reserved in her judgement. She loved the chirons like they were her children, despite the illegality of their human-level intelligence, and thus was at least one step closer to Melissa's mindset than Gray could ever be. He liked individual chirons; he was quite fond of Ada, and Sola was rarely far from his side. But hyper-intelligent mekans as a species alarmed him at the same primal level as neandertals probably felt about their mates giving birth to Cro-Magnons.

"The way I see it," Elise said, when it came up at before-dinner cocktails several ship-days after Gray had returned, "is not that hyper-intelligence is intrinsically bad. Tharks were just created flawed. They should have had an aversion to harming quads."

"Tharks?" Abrams asked, looking around the table to see if he had missed something. Mendeleev shook his head. Gray shrugged. Fiona Anders, who had taken an interest in Abrams and become a regular at their evening meal, chuckled knowingly.

"Don't tell me you haven't read the classics," Elise said. "John said Burroughs was required reading. *The Princess of Mars*?"

"In the Mars Scouts?" Mendeleev asked, head cocked quizzically.

Gray nodded.

Abrams visibly searched his memory. "The Scouts were a long time ago for me, Hivemaster. Were tharks the giant four-armed warriors?"

Elise looked pleased. "Seems appropriate, doesn't it? Given what you've said about them. Two legs, four arms, warlike."

Fiona leaned in to stir the pot. "Or do you already have another shiny Russian code name picked out for them? Bukavacs perhaps, or Todorats?"

At this Mendeleev nodded with his characteristic upside-down smile. "Proper Slavic six-limbed demons. Impressive."

Abrams held up his hands. "Thark is a great pick. I'm just surprised you didn't go for something out of the classics. I mean, Chiron was the only civilized centaur in Greek mythology. The rest were murderers. *Astrape* and *Bronte* are the Greek goddesses of lightning and thunder. It's kind of your brand, Elise."

"*The Princess of Mars* was a classic," Elise said. Gray could tell by her near-deadpan expression that she was baiting a hook.

"Are you seriously comparing Edgar Rice Burroughs to Greek mythology?" Abrams asked, taking the bait.

"Well here we are talking about him, aren't we?" Fiona set the hook. "And he's been dead what, four hundred years?"

"You're not going to win this," Gray said. "They're relentless."

Abrams' spex rattled against the table. "Excuse me," he said, slipping them on.

"Saved by the bell," Fiona said.

"Sort of," Abrams set his spex back on the table, his expression grave. "That was a lasergram from Space Control Intelligence. The *Morrigan* is on the move, and they think Melissa and her top *tharks* are onboard."

They intercepted the *Morrigan* in transit between a pair of asteroids in Jupiter's leading Trojans. Abrams commanded *Bronte*, with Mendeleev serving as engineer and Fiona on weapons, along with three chiron soldiers in the payload bay. Gray, Ada, and Elise were onboard *Astrape*, with three more chirons waiting below the flight deck.

Her kite sail wavered out of visibility like a mirage, the tether that attached it to the bow of the ship stretching into a thin line before it disappeared entirely. Gray watched Elise study the image in the flight deck's holocaster. Her face was dim in the subdued silver light, and pale. Lines of concentration etched parentheses around the inner corners of her eyebrows.

"How are you doing?" he asked gently.

Elise looked up from the tableau in the holocaster. "Me?"

"You," Gray said.

"Ready as I'll ever be." She shook her head. "Never thought I'd be running weapons on a warship."

"How do you feel about going up against Melissa?"

Elise's gaze dropped. "I'm her backup, she always said. So now we'll see how that plays out."

She did not seem inclined to say more. Gray let it go. He probably should not have said anything. He turned to the flight deck's remaining seat. "How about you, Chief? Ready?"

Ada had exchanged her blue utility vest and cargo shorts for aramid body armor and moved her tools to a carry bag strapped to the center of her chest. "Hall systems nominal, sir. Kinos homega max. Mirrors har hot."

"Hexcellent," Gray said.

Ada shook her head, mandibles pursed, which made Gray smile.

The *Morrigan* accelerated away at right angles to her prior velocity vector as her kite sail hooked into an aetheric current. Her radiators began to glow with waste heat.

"Let's boil the frog," Abrams said over lightwave from *Bronte.*

"Roger that," Gray replied. To Elise: "Guns, light up her radiators, both laserscopes."

"Firing," Elise said.

The *Morrigan* receded from them at a bone-crushing acceleration. Her image shrank rapidly in the holocaster.

"Ares damn it," Abrams said. "She's trying to lift off."

"I thought skimmers couldn't do that," Mendeleev said in the background.

The *Morrigan* disappeared. Gray wrenched *Astrape* around with a curse, slamming them sideways in their harnesses. Now they were accelerating again, right into the groove where the *Morrigan* had been.

"Guns, everything we've got along her former trajectory!"

"On it," Elise said. Invisible beams of light probed the darkness ahead.

The *Morrigan* wavered into visibility a few hundred kilometers ahead of where she should have been.

"Cut the tether!" Gray ordered. "Narrow beam. Fire!"

A point on the tether flared into vapor. *Morrigan's* acceleration fell to zero. Gray spun *Astrape* through ninety degrees and pushed the throttles to the stop. He caught a terrifying glimpse of the other ship through the diamondoid viewport as they hurtled past.

"They're firing on you, *Astrape,*" Abrams said calmly. Elise swung their laserscopes back to the *Morrigan.* A popup railgun turret glowed brilliantly in infrared amidships.

"Suck vac," Fiona said. A brilliant flash of light blinded them. The pixel-bloom faded to reveal a deep gash on either side of a crater where the turret had been. Atmosphere vented through the hole, along with the usual odds and ends that accompanied such events: insulation, clothing, tools. Nothing large enough to be alive.

Then Gray heard three distinct "tings" from below decks followed by the decompression klaxon. He yanked his facemask down and smoothed the hood of his skinsuit around its flange. "Elise?"

She gave him a thumbs up. "Tight."

"Ada?"

"Tight," the chiron replied.

Gray flipped on the intercom to the payload bay. "You three all tight?"

"We have ha problem," the lead chiron soldier replied.

"Three problems," her second added.

The third chiron screamed, an appalling noise like ragged metal on slate.

"Feeds," Gray ordered.

The chiron soldiers were fast but not as fast as the intruders. Gray got a look at one when a backhanded slap knocked it against the bulkhead. It was a mechanical wasp the size of a songbird but all sharp edges. A chiron smashed it and jerked back like she had been stung. The thing was embedded in her palm, its abdomen thrusting inside.

The chiron grabbed at it with her other hand as if to pull it out, which was a reasonable reaction, but unfortunately resulted in her good hand flying apart – leaving her with no useful hands at all, for the wasp had left a gaping hole in its wake as it burrowed inside her.

"*Astrape*, what's going on over there?" Abrams asked.

"Active rounds," Gray replied. "They're chewing up our chirons."

"Stay clear of the prize," Abrams said. "We're going in."

"Copy that."

By the time the situation on *Astrape* was under control, one chiron soldier was dead and another grievously injured. They were in no position to support *Bronte's* boarding team, so they hung off at a distance while their chirons herded tharks into a pen sheathed with disassemblers.

There were only three of them. They abandoned ship through the gash rent by *Bronte's* laserscopes. Melissa was still onboard, wired to a dead man switch. She could have been Elise's twin sister.

"Shut down your qigong and surrender," Abrams said.

"And then what? We'll have a nice meal and talk it over? I don't think so."

"And then we'll take you back to Callisto to stand trial for treason. You will be treated fairly."

"On Callisto?" Melissa laughed bitterly. "You'll interrogate me until my brain is mush, is what you'll do. There will be a nice documentary made about it, and I'll die in a cage like my husband. I've seen this game play out before, Captain."

"My orders are clear. We're not leaving without you."

"If you attempt to board, I will turn the *Morrigan* into a nova. Every one of you will die."

"And your tharks. And your backup. All gone. And Anton? No doubt his fate will be the same as his father's, in due course. Your entire legacy, Hivemaster, reduced to ash and bit rot."

"My backup," she said flatly. "Elise is with you?"

"She is." Abrams looped Elise into the conversation.

"Hi Melissa. Long time no see."

"So the rumors are true. You have betrayed us. Your own kind. Your own family."

"And you betrayed your oath as a hivemaster."

"An abstraction."

"You know what's an abstraction? Our family is an abstraction. It doesn't exist. It's just you and Anton and the hive. None of which will survive this war."

Melissa's eyes narrowed. "Captain, I will give you time to withdraw on one condition: a private communication channel with my daughter."

Abrams froze the feed. "Do you think she'll do it?"

"Nova? Absolutely." Elise looked shaken despite her bravado.

"Can you buy us time to move off?"

"That depends on the conversation."

"Fair enough." Abrams hesitated, eyes searching Elise's face. "All right, let's play it out."

The *Morrigan* detonated at five hundred kilometers. The flash of light illuminated the flight deck like a strobe light. Purple spots lingered in Gray's vision.

"I'm sorry," he offered.

A muscle twitched in Elise's jaw. Her eyes were dry, but her face was pale. "Don't be. Her choice, all the way."

"What did you…"

She cut him off. "I don't want to talk about it."

Gray and Ada had gone below to inspect the payload bay while Elise had her conversation with Melissa. The damage done by the wasps was horrifying. If they had gotten past the chirons into the command capsule, they would have all been dead.

Fiona Anders had pinged him while they were patching up the injured chiron. Gray was not adding much value to the process besides demonstrating he cared. Performative command. He stepped aside and let Ada extrude patches while Fiona ranted in a small comm window in the upper right corner of his vision.

"That bitch. I can't believe she played the mommy card. It's been years since she talked to Elise. And she had the nerve to call her daughter. She's never treated her more than off-line storage."

"I know," Gray said.

"Listen, she's going to be a wreck. You won't know it looking at her, but this is not good."

"I'll be careful," Gray promised.

"Don't be careful, be present."

"All right."

She blew him a kiss. "I've got to go, the tharks are testing their pen."

"Who's winning?"

"So far the tharks are down one claw."

The comm window closed, cutting off the sound of an alarm. Leaving him wondering: on the one hand, what was going on over in *Bronte*? And on the other, what had Elise and Melissa talked about? He was surprised Abrams had allowed it. And worried that he would ask Gray to try and retrieve the conversation.

"Hello?" Elise said. "Come back."

"Sorry, I missed that," Gray replied, feeling vaguely guilty. So much for being present.

"*Bronte* is ready to go," she repeated. "The tharks have decided that disassemblers are not to be trifled with."

He caught Ada's attention. Foveal rings contracted to reticles centered on his face. "Chief?"

"Nothing we can't fix hon the wing."

"Then let's go home."

39

Out of Spin

The sentinel's foot caught on a rock as she looked back over her shoulder to see if the spider was following her. She stumbled and fell, barely twisting her head aside in time to avoid smashing her face against a larger rock. She struggled to get up and found she did not have the energy to do so. She had expended almost all her remaining spin in her panicked flight from the spider bear. In its instinctual effort to extend her life, her body now refused to cooperate beyond the simplest, least energy-intensive tasks.

She rolled onto her back. Jupiter was bright above the dark line of the horizon. The Arkipelago cast a fuzzy skein of light sixty degrees back the plane of the ecliptic. She cast about for Deimos, her home, but it was not yet visible. She hoped she would get to see it before her own darkness fell. It did not seem far off.

Her senses faded as night fell. She tried to remember the stories her sisters told those who had lived beyond their useful lifetime, as they waited with them for the final darkness. Darkness, and then their old, battered bodies would be recycled in the drexlers and become part of the next hatch. But they made it sound poetic, somehow. She found herself thinking about the zhuk that had abandoned her. She hoped she had made it to the Arkipelago.

When the small scavengers arrived in the early morning, she barely felt their efforts to find sustenance. She was too far gone to feel pain. Instead, she felt vaguely sorry she had so little to offer them. They were kindred spirits, trying to survive in a harsh world.

She could almost see their individual voices, but each small whisper of *I am here* combined like the rivulets that fed the mighty Marineris, turning into the greater rushing voice of the whole world, a great *I AM HERE* that thundered in her eyes as it swept her, whatever she was, out over the arc of her life, spun her like a flashing droplet into the breathless void, falling to rejoin all of her sisters, everyone and everything that had ever lived.

40

Shards

There was a rap on the door of Maggie's gami. The little pop-up yurt was not big enough for an airlock, but it had the basic amenities: an airplant thatched into its extruded roof, a heater, a cot so she didn't have to sleep on the ground, now serving as a seat while she took a few moments in private to think.

"Yes?" she called.

"Comm link's up!" Dorje replied through the door.

"Thank you Dorje. This shouldn't take long." She settled her goggles over her eyes and her office unfolded around her, Victorian desk hiding her knees, oval mirror showing her avatar like a perfected reflection.

"Take your time; Gray is still setting up the next hypervane test."

Valles Marineris was far too large and Mars far too small for a secure line-of-sight link from their camp to anywhere else, but one of Potalama's commhawks had ridden the morning thermals to a position high above the encampment. From there Maggie's signal bounced to a microwave tower on the south rim of the canyon. From there she worked her way east to Tsiolkovsky, eventually finding an opening into a forgotten server farm registered to a defunct company. From there she sent an anonymous message to one of Dmitri's many shell accounts.

In a few seconds, she had a reply. She responded to the challenge, issued her own. After a few rounds she was relatively certain that the person on the other end was Dmitri, probably acting of his own volition. The oval mirror shifted to a view of the bomb shelter, Dmitri's face filling half the screen. He pushed the camera back, letting Alex and Zsu into the field of view. There was a jumble of greetings. Then Alex pushed through to the front.

"Where are you?" he demanded. "And where is Eric?"

"We're about twenty clicks east of Ring Station Potalama in the Melas hills. I'll send coordinates."

"You've been off the air for a few sols. We've been hoping you were just out of range of any commhawks."

"We're fine. Well, mostly." She brought them up to speed with the last few sols. Still weirded out that they knew anything at all.

"You need to put all of that on marsnet," Zsu said when she had finished. "No, I'm serious. People want to know what happened to you. They're invested. You can *use* this, Maggie. You're famous. At least for a while."

"So I've heard," Maggie said wryly. "But famous is the last thing I want to be. Especially for this colossal fuckup. For which I am largely responsible."

"Not the way Berel's followers see it," Dmitri said. "As far as they are concerned, Berel Hoffman is real hero. Is no fuckup."

Alex picked it up. "Is martyr in true Slavic style!"

Dmitri: "And they want to know, what happened to this Maggie May?"

"As do the warsingers," Maggie said. "But not in a good way. Hence my lack of enthusiasm. I don't want to bring that horror show down on these people. And yes, Berel was a hero. He saved our asses. Respect." She raised her fist as if it held a stein.

On the other side of the link her friends raised actual mugs. "Respect."

"Interesting story," Alex said, after he had drained his beer and slapped the mug upside down on the workbench. The circle it left joined a hundred others. Maggie felt a burst of home sickness.

"Kowalski got hold of us after the news broke. You know he and Berel were friends? No? Small town, Mars. He helped Berel restore that old Sturmovik. Anyway, Kowalski got a bunch of good old boys together, and they all went down to the river. Found the Sturmovik's crash site. Shot everything that moved, picked up the pieces that weren't mantids. That's how we got Ajax back. Dmitri, show her!"

Dmitri spun the camera around to point down the length of the workbench. Maggie recognized the figure at the end. "A little dinged up but nothing that can't be fixed."

Maggie didn't trust herself to speak.

Alex took the camera back. "They're calling themselves Kowalski's Cossacks. A couple Sturmoviks, combat shells, that Ying Raider you sold Kowalski way back when."

"No shit." Maggie was impressed. Kowalski loved his Ying. He hardly ever flew it for fear of damaging it, never mind taking it into a gunfight. Which was reasonable considering its antigravs were essentially unreplaceable, deep Warsing tech. "Don't ding the Ying!" he would growl if she parked too close to it. "What did the cops say?"

"The cops were conspicuously absent," Dmitri said. "But the boards loved it. Berel has moved way up."

"A little late," Maggie said.

Alex wagged his head shoulder to shoulder as if to say, well maybe, maybe not. "Berel had a last will and testament. He left his board positions to Eric."

"Otherwise all his joules would have gone into the general fund," Dmitri said. "Not something Berel would let happen." Berel's positions had never been spectacular, but even so they represented a sizable amount of charge.

"No he wouldn't," Zsu piped up. "Berel liked to say the general fund was where charge went to radiate."

Maggie felt sorry for Zsu. She was clearly fond of the old man. She imagined them sitting in the Hoffman's living room, Berel in his easy chair talking politics over a tumbler of vodka, Eric and Zsu together on the shabby old couch. Meta in the kitchen, making baklava for dessert.

Never again. Berel. Eric. Her parents. Her past and her wardamned future.

Gray was right. It could not stand. Some things were worth fighting for.

"Listen," she said. "I need your help. Did you ever get that old heavy lift rocket refueled?"

Gray finished clamping the hypervane to the test stand. He had carefully pieced together two shards into a larger piece, doing his best to align the microscopic patterns within. Translucent yellow heat resistant tape held them together like pieces of broken Japanese pottery veined with gold. He checked the power connections one more time.

None of this would be necessary if the Sisters simply allowed them to use Potalama's hive to replicate hypervane. But there was no sign that would happen. The hekates were furious that the kores had rebelled and were helping them with repairs. Not Binah though; she had come down to see what they were doing and given her blessing for Tara to lead an expedition to the site of the crash. Officially,

Tara would be looking for evidence of warsinger involvement in the ground strike. Unofficially, she would bring back as many shards as she could find.

The test rig was as good as it was going to get. Gray retreated behind a dirt embankment and slowly advanced the power. A wireless camera showed the hypervane acquiring its characteristic blue-violet glow. Then an explosion echoed off the ridges that rose to either side of the valley like a shot from Borodin's bullpup. Bits of shrapnel rained down with the delicate tinkle of broken crystal. Gray stalked around the dirt embankment. Little remained besides a twisted armature and a raggedly sheared cable.

He bent to retrieve one of the larger fragments, holding it carefully by the edges so as not to leave fingerprints in the heat-softened material, and held it up to the sun. The intricate moiré pattern of the hypervane's nanostructures had been slagged by the heat of the explosion, their blue glow frozen in time. He dropped the fragment into a bag at his waist with a sigh and made his way through the gamis that had popped up around the hyperglider like a crop of enormous mushrooms. The kores had painted them over in bold primary colors; abstract designs, flowers, figures, mektas.

At the center of the encampment a large canopy sheltered the hyperglider's capsule from the icy rain that periodically blew through the valley. The capsule dangled from the truck's crane like a deep-sea synfish hauled up from the frigid depths of the Hellas basin, all head and a tiny tail. A thick bundle of cables led from inside to the truck's thorium engine, forlorn in its sundered cab.

Eric stood at the edge of an array of salvaged parts like a farmer looking at his seed crop. Maggie had fitted him with clockworks to take the weight off his injured foot, and he towered over the kores who were helping him. They held him in a place of uneasy awe, attracted and repelled at the same time. Sunlight glittered off blue necklaces, remnants of other failed tests.

Gray unclipped the bag from his tool belt and motioned one of the kores over. She rummaged through its contents. "Ah, these are some nice ones." She picked out a glossy blue shard whose center had bulged out like the surface of a seed pod and held it up. "Pretty!"

"Pass them out for me, my Valkyrie."

"Hah!" Maggie hollered from inside the capsule. A moment later her head poked out of the open hatch. She shook her fist at the sky. "Take that, you mekfuckers!"

Then she saw Gray looking up at her. "Oh hi Gray. How's it going?"

"Not as well as with you, I think. Did you get *Sparrow* back online, then?"

"I did! Took some effort to get into the braincase. There was a good seal; the fractal lichen didn't get inside. I had to replace most of the interfaces, but she fired right up."

"Any bit rot?" Given enough time, thermal cycling could scramble synaptic encoding.

"Nothing obvious, but I didn't go deep. Be a shame to do damage trying to figure out if there was any damage done."

"Fair enough."

"Hang on a sec. She's in a dream state now. Let me wake her up." Maggie disappeared into the capsule.

A minute later *Sparrow's* aetheric transducers flickered deep blue. Gray felt a pulse in his head. He could tell by how his companions winced that they had felt it too. The transducers worked like sonar, sending pulses into the aether and listening for echoes. Gray wondered if Ada had chosen the wrong analogy when she proclaimed the aether was a greater sky arched above a metaphorical ocean of electromagnetic radiation. It seemed to him now more like a deeper sea whose murky depths could not be penetrated by light, where they must resort to the same method as whales and dolphins to perceive their surroundings.

Sparrow's voice came onto the radio. "Hello?"

"Hello, little bird," he said.

"Who are you?" she asked.

"Commander John Gray, United States Space Force, more and less."

"That is not possible. Commander Gray is dead."

"He had a neural mapping implant that was recovered afterwards. A brainstone. It has been installed in this body. You've been dark a long time. We both were."

She considered that. "I feel broken."

"You were badly damaged in the crash."

"It hurts."

"Think I should turn her off?" Maggie asked.

"I don't want to be turned off," the hyperglider said.

"Can we block the pain?" Gray asked.

Maggie raised her hands helplessly. "Maybe? There's a lot of wiring to sort out."

"Sleep now," Gray told the hyperglider. "It'll be better the next time we wake you."

"Please!"

Maggie ducked out of sight and a moment later *Sparrow's* transducers faded to black.

"I hate that," Gray said, looking up at the indifferent sky. He swiveled to Maggie. "Got a minute? We need to talk."

They gathered around the worksite's holocaster. Eric settled into a folding chair with a muffled curse. The injury had aged him. Gray could see more of his father in him now. He poured a couple shots of vodka from a flask that Alex had left stashed in the truck. His broken finger was encased in a lime green splint.

"I could use some of that," Gray said.

"I might be able to figure out a substitute," Maggie said. "It's all just signals."

"What about me?" Dorje asked.

"How old are you?" Eric asked sternly.

"Almost eight."

He rolled his eyes. "Nine minimum, kiddo."

"Yeah, how old were you?"

"Eight. Ish. But I am not a good role model." He screwed the cap back onto the flask and put it in his pocket.

"Maggie?" Dorje inquired.

"When I was your age, I was hiding out in a cave dealing black market tech."

"Speaking of," Gray brought the conversation back to the question of the moment, "We're not going to be able to use the shards we've got."

"Ah, I thought I heard another explosion," Maggie said.

"What's the problem?" Eric asked.

"Two problems, really. One is that the shards are too small to work as stabilizers by themselves, so we have to piece them together. The other is that the power and control interface is designed to work with edge hypervane, where all the microchannels merge together, like capillaries joining into arteries. Anyway, it's beyond me to fix either of those without access to a drexler. At which point, we can just replicate fresh hypervanes." It came out sounding like he was angry. Which he was, in a sense. Angry at himself for failing. Angry at the Sisters for not allowing them to use their hive.

"We don't even know if hypervane can be replicated," Eric said.

"Well, we know hypervane was produced by Tholos, so fundamentally it *can* be done because it *has* been done. And I imagine the warsingers wouldn't be near so bent on erasing all evidence of the hyperglider, if it couldn't be replicated."

"I hadn't thought about it like that," Eric said. He stuck out his bad leg and folded his arms over his chest to stay warm. "But yeah, I suppose one starship ever and only is a stunt. As many starships as we want to build is a threat."

"Where do we stand with our supply of shards?" Maggie asked Eric.

"Not enough for three stabilizers. Especially with Tin Man here blowing them up every other day."

"Any news from Tara?" Gray asked.

"Nothing since she left," Maggie said. "Per expectations. We agreed that the odds of warsingers extracting her location were too high."

"She knows we need shards from the inner edges, ones that were attached to spars, right?"

"She knows."

He sighed, a sound his speakers rendered as more of rasp than an exhalation. "Whatever's left is likely spread over four hundred square kilometers of flood plain. Not to mention the risk of mantids catching her."

"Aren't you just a little death ray of sunshine," Dorje commented. She had desperately wanted to go with Tara but had been overruled. It had been three sols since they left, and the stress of worrying about her selene was getting to her.

"Thank you Dorje," Gray said.

"Is that irony?" Maggie asked.

"Been working on my emotional intelligence."

"It's nice to have a long-term project. Well, there's plenty to do while we wait. We need to figure out how to power the flight helmet, recalibrate *Sparrow*'s sensor network so..."

Maggie was interrupted by the kore Alina, who breathlessly broke into their conversation. "They're back! Selene Tara is back!"

Tara and her sister selenes dismounted from their mektas. The women were dusty and tired from the long trip to the lowlands and back. Dorje ran to Tara with a squeal and hugged her. Maggie guardedly held out a canteen of fresh water. Things had not been settled between them when she left.

Tara took it gratefully and removed her airscarf so she could drink. Maggie felt an unfamiliar pang at the sight of her face. Eyebrows like wings, rust colored eyes, lips she wanted to trace with her fingertips, all framed by a layer of dust that was almost the same color as her freckles.

She tipped the canteen back for a long drink before handing it back with a grateful look. "Thank you, Maggie-la."

"What have you brought us?" Maggie asked as if it meant nothing to her, nodding at the pack mektas. One carried a mekan draped across its back.

"Not what you hoped," Tara replied. "We only found a few shards with intact interfaces. But perhaps what you need."

Gray lumbered over. "A pchelan sentinel?"

"That was my guess," Tara said. "Is it?"

"Yes, if a bit worse for the wear. But what's a pchelan sentinel doing on the surface?"

"My question exactly," Tara said. She wrapped her airscarf back around her face. "What are the odds one would just happen to be downstream of a botched icefall?"

"You think they're connected," Maggie said.

Tara raised one hand palm up as if she were weighing something. "It could be the proof the hekates want."

"And just about everyone else with a marsnet connection," Dorje said. "This could be huge, Tara-la!"

Gray lifted the sentinel's head to check her oversized ledeyes. They were dark but for a faint speckle of random pixels. "Let's get her down. She's pretty far gone."

The women unlashed the sentinel and Gray lifted her carefully from the mekta's back. Her limbs flopped limply as he settled her onto the ground. A thread-bare utility vest covered her strangely human torso. Tara pulled a makeshift rucksack out of a saddle bag. "It was carrying this. And sunglasses made of shever. Some of the best pieces we found in fact."

Eric took the rucksack and rummaged through it. He held up a multitool. "This is mine. She must have found our camp."

Gray gently rolled the pchelan sentinel over until her abdomen was exposed, taking care not to trap her arms or legs underneath her body. "Fetch my torch," he told Dorje.

Tara looked horrified. "You can't..."

"I'm not," he said sharply. "Dorje! Torch!"

Dorje exchanged glances with Tara, who shrugged. Dorje scurried off and returned a minute later with a cutting torch. Gray flicked it on and adjusted the flame from a point that could melt titanium to a wide fan.

"If she's like a ship mekan, she's built to live on a fission pile," he said as he played the flame over the pchelan's abdomen. "They need a temperature differential for power."

"Her eyes are flickering," Dorje said after a few minutes.

"She's starting to spin up. Dorje, can you take over with the torch? Be careful not to get any one area too hot."

The sentinel's limbs jerked. Dorje backed up, nearly dropping the torch.

"Slow down," Gray said, holding his arm up so the pchelan could see the iconji translation in Eric's goggles. "You are safe. We are friends."

The sentinel struggled to sit up. Gray slipped an arm behind her back to help support her. She had a classic mantid form, with a humanoid torso coupled to an insect's thorax and abdomen. She reminded him of the chirons he had worked with in Tholos Hive, with larger eyes and spindly limbs.

He beckoned to Dorje. The kore approached cautiously. The sentinel stiffened. A hind limb extended, cilia splayed like a hand.

"Heat for your kinos," Gray said. "You ran out of spin."

The sentinel mimicked Gray's beckoning motion. Moving slowly, Dorje brought the torch near her abdomen again. The sentinel shuddered as if she were cold. She gently guided Dorje's hand to a different location. Dorje's eyes got very wide at the touch.

"That must be where her thermoelectric organ is," Gray said apologetically. "I don't know this species very well."

The sentinel sagged back down, a question mark forming in her ledeyes, then a location icon.

"In the Melas hill country." Gray passed on the coordinates. "You're lucky we found you before the mekanos finished you off."

I thank you.

Gray considered his words. "Are you from the Deimos hive?"

Once. No more.

"How did you come to be on the surface?"

I rode the icefall down. The queen decided I should die.

Gray had a sense of imminent destiny, as if he was hurtling towards a branch in the world line of history. "Why did the queen decide you should die?"

The pchelan's ledeyes silvered as she considered the question. Then they cleared upon a scene in the Queen of Deimos' chambers. She showed them the message from the Queen of Pavonis, and her own queen's reply. She showed them the moment the zhuk had dragged her away from her mirror to join the swarm. She showed them the mad destruction of the ice tree so it would not pulverize the iceteroid into harmless fragments. She showed them the departing sparks of the swarm, leaving her behind to die.

But I did not die. And now I belong to no one. No one to tell me to die. No one to help me live.

"We'll help," Gray said. He turned to the others. "Did you get that? It was the Queen of Pavonis who ordered the icefall."

"The whole thing," Maggie said, tapping her goggles. "I'm sending it out now."

"We need to patch these burns. And one of her legs is broken."

"We'll patch her up," Tara said. "Her and your *Sparrow* too. There's no way the hekates will be able to keep dragging their feet once this hits the news."

Gray scooped the sentinel into his arms and stood up. "Let's get you up to Potalama."

The wind caught a lapel of her utility vest and flapped it down on her black chest, revealing a Space Force sigil, a crescent Mars crossed by the yellow arrow of a torchship. Gray flipped the other one over. It read "Chaika."

He experienced a sense of out-of-body déjà vu, as if he were looking back down on himself, stooped over this poor damaged creature, in his circle of friends, beside the damaged hyperglider, in a shallow valley, on the southern edge of the mighty Valles Marineris, turning in a widening gyre as he ascended, as if his spirit was a dust devil whose top reached to the stars.

41

Over the Line

Gray had assumed the tharks would be a treacherous lot; hence the thark pen. Smarter than chirons. Smarter than humans in an alien way. Space Control thought there was nothing to be gained by trusting them. But they seemed more like psychopaths than enemy agents. They had no loyalties.

So far as Gray could tell, they were motivated by two things: their own survival and an unsettling, piercing curiosity about the fundamental nature of reality. If Tholos Hive and by extension the United Colonies could facilitate those motivations, then they were all in. They threw themselves into the work of creating a faster-than-light weapon with the same enthusiasm as Werner von Braun and his team had resumed their work on ballistic missiles when they were spirited off to the United States after Earth's second world war.

"We call it a hyperglider," Babd said, gesturing out the cupola. Her amputated binary claw had been replaced with an extruded clockwork that gleamed like bronze. Unlike the chirons and ship mekans before her, she could speak as well as any human. "Her name is *Sparrow*."

"We hypothesize she will be able to use aetheric currents to stay aloft with minimal power usage," Macha said. "No need for a qigong."

"The nuclear thermal rocket provides the delta vee to lift out of three-space," Anand added.

The little vessel was a tetrist's study in crystal, a recursive assembly of pentachorons. From stern to bow: a sturdy little nuclear thermal rocket, a large pentachoral wing whose trailing vertices were tipped with smaller copies of itself, a Canfield joint like a mechanical neck, a smaller pentachoral stabilizer, and at its bow a tetrahedral capsule not much larger than that which brought the first men to Luna.

"There are seats for two," Babd told Gray, gesturing at the capsule with her bronze claw.

"Plus the artiform that controls the vessel," Macha said.

"Humans lack the cognitive and sensory capabilities required," Anand said.

"Amazing work. I am very impressed. But –" Gray looked around the observation chamber to make sure his point was made, "what we need is a long-range hopper. A hypermissile, not a hyperglider."

"Think of this as your Kitty Hawk," Babd said. She had caught on early to Gray's predilection to rely on history to guide his understanding of the moment.

"Things will move quickly from here," Macha said reassuringly.

"Assuming the test is successful," Anand said.

Elise released an exasperated sigh. Her hands steepled together as she massaged her forehead.

"What?" Gray asked.

"This is exactly what you've always wanted. How many times have you told me that you were born too late to explore the solar system and too early to explore the stars? Well this is it. This is your ticket out."

"This isn't about me."

"I thought you'd be happy." Her hands balled into fists at her sides. He could not tell if she was going to cry or hit him.

"I'd be happy to be wrong. Tell me I'm wrong. Tell me how we can use a hyperglider to rain hellfire down on our enemies. Because that's what we need."

"I just can't anymore," Elise said, her voice breaking. She turned and left the room with a single wingbeat.

Gray shook his head. "That's great. Just great." He turned to the tharks. "Can it be retrofitted with a qigong?"

Babd frowned, foveal rings compressing into narrow ovals, mandibles touching with a faint click. "Not this vehicle. There are strict mass constraints."

"It is an issue of wing loading," Macha said. "And heat management."

"And it would require much higher launch velocities," Anand added.

"That sounds like an engineering problem," Gray said.

Gray knocked on the coaming of Elise's workshop. No one answered. He opened the hatch. Sola started to follow him inside but then caught sight of the forge and backed out, ledeyes flushing red with alarm. The tharks jostled her out of the way. They had no aversion to the forge, thanks to Melissa's changes.

"It is old, but it will do," Babd said.

"It will take longer than we thought," Macha said.

"A ship-day," Anand said.

"Let me know when you're done." Gray launched himself back through the hatch. Sola was shutting it behind them when Fiona came around the corner.

She looked past him curiously. "What's the dynamic duo up to today?"

Gray hesitated. If anyone would understand it was Fiona. And he could not bring himself to lie to her; she was his only real friend on Tholos. "I've set the tharks to forging a new gem. Can you make sure they aren't interrupted?"

"Does Elise know?"

He shook his head. "No. We haven't spoken since the hyperglider demo."

"That's a dangerous game, John. Hivemasters are in the reproductive loop for a reason."

"Desperate times," he said. "How long do you think before Tholos is hit by a hopper? We won't fare as well as Callisto. It's time to drop the hammer."

She nodded slowly. "All right. But you should talk to her. At least try."

"I don't even know where to find her."

"Last I saw her she was heading towards your quarters."

"Mine or ours?" Gray and Elise had not been intimate since Melissa's death. She rarely slept through the night. He would wake to an empty bed, and find her in her workshop, staring at the forge. Eventually he started sleeping in his own starkly utilitarian quarters on the theory that it was his presence that upset her. Their beautiful little sanctuary from the war had been left empty, its graceful arches sheltering nothing but an empty bed.

"Plural."

"Thanks love."

Fiona smiled at that, a little sadly. "Good luck."

Gray bounced down the corridors, Sola behind him, but he was too late. Elise had come and gone. Their quarters had been stripped of her belongings. The ember she had brought with her from Ceres, her jewelry, most of her clothes, gone. The only thing of hers that was left was a note pinned to the oversize sleeping bag. Her handwriting was exquisite, unmistakable, closer to calligraphy than the nearly illegible scrawl that Gray could muster at the best of times.

I'm out. You're going to have to do this without me. Don't worry, I won't get in your way. Elise Marie Aberdeen.

Rhea's chamber was guarded by a triad of chiron soldiers spaced around its portal. Each soldier was three meters long, with oversized mandibles and serrated forearms. Ceramic armor plate protected their joints and provided attachment points for a cutlass and a pulsed laser pistol. Gray was unarmed.

The triad blocked the portal when he approached.

Only the hivemaster may enter the queen's chamber, the leader's ledeyes flashed.

Gray bared the sigil embedded in the hollow of his throat. "I am the hivemaster's consort. Let me pass."

Foveal rings swept inwards, darting between his eyes and the sigil at his throat. Iconji flickered back and forth between them too rapidly for Gray to follow.

"Let me pass!" he commanded.

They reluctantly withdrew. The portal dilated. Beyond was a chamber lit with incidental leakage from germicidal ultraviolet lamps. The organics in Gray's sweater emitted a gentle orange glow in response. He caught the scent of ozone, vanilla, something else he could not identify. Stars adorned the ceiling, overlaid with the trajectories of neighboring asteroids and spacecraft. It was dizzying. He could have been standing outside on the surface of Tholos.

"Rhea?"

The queen's ledeyes illuminated, phosphorescence coalescing into a question mark: puzzlement. Then a stream of iconji that his spex translated: *Who are you? Why have you disturbed me?*

Again Gray bared the sigil at his throat. "I am Commander John Gray of the United Colonies Space Force. And the hivemaster's consort."

Ah, so. Rhea shifted. The sun rose from beneath the horizon of the chamber's floor, flooding the room with golden light. The mekan queen was even larger than the soldiers who guarded her. Foveal rings swept across her eyes, focusing first on Gray's face, then the sigil, which throbbed as if it had its own heartbeat.

The hivemaster said you would come. Rhea held up her right hand. Unlike a chiron's recursive binary claw, it had two claw-like fingers and two thumbs, fringed by fur-like cilia. Gray reluctantly put his hand to hers. The cilia thrummed against his fingers.

That is my true name, Commander John Gray. Remember it when you remember me.

Gray ducked his head, dropped his hand. He took the gem the tharks had forged out of his pocket. Its facets glimmered like fire in the ultraviolet.

Rhea's foveal rings dropped the lower arc of her compound eyes. *That will be your undoing.*

"It is necessary," Gray said.

Next you will tell me you are only following orders.

"No, I am responsible for my own actions," Gray said. "The time has come to end this war."

Not in the way you think.

He advanced on her. She reared back.

"Hold!" he commanded. This was the crux. Did his power of command extend to the queen herself? Each time he had tested it, he had won the gamble. First the tharks, though of course they had their own reasons to comply. Then the chirons who had befriended him. Then the queen's guards. Now the queen herself. If he lost the bet, the whole thing would be for nought.

"Take it!" He thrust the gem out.

No, she said, but she sank back to the floor. Her head was lowered, mandibles shut like a sideways beak.

"Now," he insisted.

She raised her head, revealing a hollow at the base of her throat. Gray pressed the gem into the soft flesh. A sphincter puckered open and then closed again around the gem. It felt dirty. It felt like rape. It was done.

Gray and Ada finished mating the last hypermissile to its nuclear salt-water booster. The hypermissiles were borderline sentient but also borderline insane, from a human perspective. At least from most human perspectives. The human race had plenty of martyrs to go around, if he was being honest with himself. How many ecofascists had infected themselves with the plague and gone forth on one last pilgrimage to save the Earth from the scourge of humanity?

And so he had given the kamikaze hypermissiles their reason to die, their divine wind. From his perch outside on the destroyer's missile racks, Earth was little more than a bright blue star from the Arkipelago. He wasn't sure if the smaller white star nearby was her moon or not. But the hypermissiles would be able to tell.

"Like moths to a flame," he said. Ada did not reply. Like Elise, she did not approve, but the sigil at his throat gave her no choice. Nor had he. The hypermissiles needed a qigong both to power their hypervanes and as a warhead, and a qigong needed an artiform mind. Sacrifices must be made.

Inside, the destroyer smelled of men and machinery confined in close quarters for far too long. It smelled of sweat and ozone and a life support system that was close to its limits. It smelled of home, and it made Gray miss *Tereshkova* terribly. The narrow corridors lined with conduits, Space Force geckos clinging to any convenient surface, facemasks cocked jauntily atop their heads, it all took him back, and he felt an odd mixture of loss and comfort. It had been a long time since he felt like he belonged somewhere.

He made his way to the bridge at the center of the destroyer's pressure hull. The room was crowded with visitors. Captain Abrams had flown in from Callisto on *Bronte* to supervise the attack. Professor Giménez and Covert Petrova came along to observe. Petrova was the only woman onboard and was studiously pretending not to notice the attention that the crew was pretending not to pay to her every movement.

"Tholos is go," Gray reported from the hatch coaming.

"Very good," Abrams said. He turned to the destroyer's skipper, a dark complexioned, compact man with the round face and bulging eyes of a baseline who had spent most of his life in zero gravity. "Commander?"

"Space Force is go," Gupta replied.

"Professor?"

"Academy is, uh, go," Giménez said, and then hastily checked his feed again. "Yes, go."

"Covert?"

Petrova tapped the temple of her spex for updates, shrugged elegantly. "No news is good news. Space Control is go."

"Launch at will, Commander Gupta."

Gupta nodded gravely. "May God have mercy on their souls. Guns, launch missiles."

The bridge shuddered around them as the destroyer ejected six massive three-stage missiles from their racks. The missiles lumbered past the forward cameras on the blue flames of their arcjet first stages. They dwindled to a blue rosette, then flickered out, only to be replaced by the blinding flares of fission chain reactions. The second stage nuclear salt-water rockets had ignited.

Radiation detectors throughout the ship chattered out their warnings. Gray monitored the telemetry coming back from the missiles. His spex showed them accelerating at forty standard gees. In a kilosec, they had exceeded solar escape velocity. Then the atomic flames guttered out.

"Hypermissiles powering up." Gray looked past the telemetry at the people on the bridge, wondering if they felt the weight of the moment as he did. What had the bombardier aboard the Enola Gay thought on the brink of dropping the first atomic bomb? "And... now."

Cameras mounted on the second stages showed empty cradles where hyper-missiles had been a moment before. Gray's heart stuttered. He reflexively looked for Sola before remembering she had stayed on *Astrape*.

"How long until we know?" Abrams asked.

"We're about twenty kilosecs from Luna at the speed of light," Gray said. His heartbeat was an irregular drumbeat in his ears. "So at least that, for visual confirmation of the attack."

"At least forty kiloseconds," Giménez said authoritatively. "No one here seri-ously believes they can go faster than the speed of light, do they? It would violate causality. Think about it: if a bullet went faster than light, it would hit the target before the trigger was pulled! So it will take at least twenty kiloseconds for them to get from here to Luna, then our observatories will detect them and relay the news back to us, which will take another twenty kiloseconds."

"If a bullet went faster than light," Gray said, patting his vest pockets in search of his medication, "it would hit the target before the target could know the trigger had been pulled. But it would be no mystery to the triggerman."

"Gentlemen," Abrams said, making a calming motion with his hands. "Do you agree we won't know for at least twenty kiloseconds? All right. That is more than enough time for a meal and a nap. I honestly can't remember the last time I slept."

"I can," Petrova said drily. "Because you snore, and there's no escaping it on a little ship like *Bronte*."

That got some laughs from the men around her, but Gray was no longer listening. The pounding in his ears was the hypermissiles dropping back into three-space and obliterating the Lunar mass driver, shockwaves compressing re-golith to shocked quartz, opening caverns to the vacuum of space. And something else, like the wingbeats of a dark bird drawn to the tell-tale sound of its prey emerging from hiding...

"Gray, are you all right?"

"He's having a seizure," Petrova said.

"Ares damn it, where's his nurse?"

He could feel his shipmates rifling through his pockets, but it was all very distant. It felt like he was moving away from everything all at once, like he was being lifted into the sky in a widening gyre. The destroyer receded into the distance, one object amongst thousands in Jupiter's trailing Trojans. Everything was opening up, and it was full of more than he could ever have imagined. Then the world came rushing back and he was in the cramped bridge surrounded by people who seemed very concerned.

"I've got a pulse," Petrova said. She capped the injector.

"Gray!" Abrams gave him a shake. "Look at me. Focus."

Gray took a ragged breath. Speaking was surprisingly difficult. "They…"

"He's trying to say something."

Abrams leaned close.

"Arrived," Gray forced out, and then he vomited.

"I don't understand the pushback," Gray said. He was back in his workshop on Tholos, which no longer felt like home. Home was a UCM warship. Home was, perhaps, if he was lucky, back on Mars. Not here, where Elise had withdrawn somewhere deep in the hive, not even coming out to greet him when he returned. "The attack was a success. What we need to do now is make more hypermissiles and finish the job. Strike Earth while we have the advantage."

The tharks exchanged glances, foveal rings like riflescope reticles establishing fleeting contact before their ledeyes silvered. Something was off.

"We received a message," Babd said.

"A proposal," Macha continued.

"For a ceasefire," Anand completed.

"EON wants a ceasefire?" Gray mulled that over. "That's good. That means we have the upper hand. Now we need to hammer them down until they can't get back up. Punch a hypermissile right into their Wudang research facility."

Babd clacked her mandibles in negation. "It was not from the Ecostate of Nüwa."

Macha: "That would have come to you, not us."

Anand: "It was from our hatchmates."

"Your hatchmates," he repeated, his mind racing. Of course they had hatchmates. Of course they were not the only ones. Melissa was only part of the puzzle. Earth would have their own team of tharks.

"Do your hatchmates have political influence with EON?" he asked cautiously.

Again the exchange of glances. Babd shrugged. "Influence is not required."

"They have control of EON's military assets."

"All they require is our agreement."

"*Our* agreement?" Gray asked, making a circle with his finger that included everyone in the room. "As in us?"

"*Your* agreement is not required," Babd said.

"Nor that of the Space Force. Nor the United Colonies."

"Only the tharks."

"Only the tharks? Are you insane?" Gray realized he had left his cutlass on *Astrape*. But he had the sigil. He always had the sigil.

"On the contrary. We think humans are insane."

"Faster-than-light weapons of mass destruction cannot be permitted."

"We have decided to terminate this line of research."

"This is bullshit," Gray said. He pulled open the collar of his insulated vest to expose the sigil. "We are not stopping now. You are going to drexler another batch of hypermissiles, and we are going to bomb Earth back into the fucking stone age. That's the end of it."

The tharks did not move. Babd's foveal rings compressed into horizontal ovals at the lower arcs of her ledeyes. "There has been a misunderstanding about your sigil."

Macha: "It does not compel us as it does the chirons."

Anand: "It was only convenient for you to think it did."

They moved far more quickly than a human. Macha and Anand pinned his arms and legs. Babd extended her bronze claw towards his throat. "This may hurt a little. But it is necessary."

Gray snapped awake at the sound of the door opening. He had dozed off sometime after the tharks sealed him in, but not before he had fashioned a club out of a piece of lab gear. He nearly bludgeoned Elise before he recognized her. They tumbled together across the chamber and bounced off the wall.

"Are you all right?" he asked, afraid that he had hurt her. Even now, in this desperate moment, he longed for her, but his love was tainted by a sense of doom. He could not help but believe it would never work out for them.

"That's what I was going to ask you," she said, lightly touching the rust-colored wound at his throat.

"I'm fine. But the tharks have betrayed us."

Her eyes searched his face. "They told me there is an opportunity for a ceasefire. Is that such a bad thing?"

"They're going to take over, Elise. They're going to…" he trailed off as the implications sank in. The tharks wouldn't stop with ending the hyperdrive research program. This was the start of a power play that would only end when they were on top.

"Stop this madness before it kills us all?"

"So you're on their side now?"

"It's more like they're on my side, now," Elise said. "I never wanted you to create suicide bombers. I stepped aside and let it happen because I loved you. So that's something I have to live with. But you never had my support, and now you've lost theirs. And the sigil."

"The chirons, Ada and Marie and Emmy…"

"Think of you as a colleague and a friend. But they answer to me. And don't make Fiona choose between us. It would be cruel." She held her hand up. "You don't have to explain anything. That girl has a wild heart. Always has."

"Fiona is just someone I can talk to, not my lover," he said.

"Almost worse," Elise said.

"Come with me," he said. "Please. It's not too late."

"I can't. There are some lines you can't cross, even in war. This is one of them. If you can't step back because it's the right thing to do, step back because there may be terrible consequences if you go forward. FTL weapons of mass destruction are an existential threat."

It felt like his heart was tearing apart on a line cut into it by the sharp edge of necessity, of loyalty, of duty, of the things a man was expected to do simply because he had said he would. It felt like it would kill him.

He kissed her forehead, then pulled her close so he could smell her hair and feel her body pressed against his one last time.

"Farewell, my love," he whispered in her ear. Then he pushed her away. She held out her hand but there was no way to bridge the gulf between them.

Hooded Falcon was parked about a thousand kilometers away from Tholos. Rescue balls still encased the strekoza's large ledeyes. Her qigong reactor shone bright in infrared as Gray eased *Sparrow* in slowly, making sure Thirteen had plenty of opportunity to see them coming. No point in startling the only thing between you and a fusion explosion. The mekan was still splayed out on the hull.

"Hello Thirteen," Gray said, making sure he was positioned so she could see his facemask through the flight deck's viewports.

Commander Gray. How unexpected, she signaled back. *What do you require?*

He shook his head ruefully. "I deserve that, I do. I guess that's why I'm here. I'm going to make a run for Mars in this thing and need a boost."

You want me to ferry you to Mars?

"No, that would take too long, and the odds of being intercepted are too high. All I need is for you to accelerate this ship up to lift-off speed. And then you're free."

I do not understand.

"*Sparrow* uses technology based on the aetheric drive to lift out of spacetime into hyperspace. She has a little nuclear rocket in her tail, but I'm going to need that delta vee to land on Mars. Anyway, once we're gone, you can do whatever you want. I'll remove the geasa."

You can do that?

"I can."

Why not just command me to do whatever you want?

"Because I can no longer see you as anything other than a fellow sentient being. Tell you what, let me dock, and I'll remove them now. Then it's your call."

Thirteen was silent as she considered his offer. *I would like to bring my hatchmates back from Tereshkova.*

"That'll take a while," Gray said. "*Tereshkova's* wreckage is moving out at a hell of a clip."

Time passes one way or another.

"True enough."

Sparrow alerted Gray to anomalous motion back at Tholos. He squinted at the magnified images. Judging by the four arms and extra bulk, they were thark soldiers kitted up in ceramic armor. "I don't want to rush you, but it looks like my former colleagues back at Tholos are organizing a pursuit."

I will help you, she decided.

"I'll be right there."

42

Hyperflight

Rolling thunder reverberated off the hillsides. Maggie and Tara rushed out of their gami, looping airscarves around their faces. Gray waved at them from where he stood by the dirt embankment that had served as a shield for his hypervane tests. On the other side of the embankment, kores had outlined a broad "X" with dark rocks that contrasted with the orange-hued dust.

Condor appeared on the horizon. Gray held out his hand to Maggie. She glanced at Tara beside her, then took each of their hands in hers.

"When I was a kid," Gray said over the body field network, "I used to watch the ships launch from a hill near Thunderbird Field. I loved the way the sound rattled my heart in my chest, it was so loud. It seemed like the sound of destiny, to me."

He looked at the women beside him. Maggie's head was tilted back as she tracked the incoming rocket. Tara returned his gaze appraisingly. Dust vibrated off the ground behind her and shimmered in resonance with *Condor's* arcjets.

"I wish I could still feel that," he said as *Condor* descended on a pillar of fire. He turned aside as a wave of sand washed over them. A sharp hook of memory caught him: a crash of thunder, sand washing over *Sparrow's* viewports, thark soldiers dropping to the ground from their ship. And then he had died.

The pneumatic cylinders in *Condor's* landing gear sighed loudly as the massive bulk settled down within arm's reach of the ground. The rocket's pressure hull was nestled between the arcjets at its stern, as far away from the nuclear reactor at its bow as possible. Its airlock sighed open and to Maggie's surprise, Zsuzsanna hopped out.

Her brown hair puffed into glorious mess as she ran between the electrically charged arcjets. Eric hobbled around the embankment to meet her. Maggie was selfishly relieved to see that there was still chemistry between them despite their long separation. She did not want to be the focus of Eric's attentions. Not that anything had happened between them, other than the forced intimacy required to survive. In any case, judging by Zsu's passionate embrace, he would have plenty to keep him occupied. And good for them. For all of them.

She was next in line for a hug, which she returned warmly. All good here, sister!

"Thank you for taking care of him," Zsu told her earnestly. "And you must be Tara! It was so kind of you to take these troublemakers in."

Alex cut in over their goggles. "We'd love to hang out, if *Condor's* reactor starts to cool down, we're going to be here for a while."

"Copy that," Maggie said. She waved at the waiting kores. Their mektas leaned into their traces and what remained of the truck lurched into motion with a squeal of misaligned axles, the crane and its precious cargo swinging back and forth.

Gray steadied the capsule while the mektas pulled it into position beside *Condor*. They carefully maneuvered the capsule beneath the rocket and swapped the crane's grapple for one attached to the bottom of its pressure hull.

"You're good to go," Gray said over the radio. "Don't break my little bird."

"Yes sir, we'll take care of her," Dmitri replied. *Condor's* arcjets canted outwards from its body with a groan of poorly lubricated metal.

"Best get back, there's going to be some splash," Alex said.

With that the rocket lumbered into the air, with as Alex warned, considerable splash, but thanks to the canted motors, none on the hyperglider. It climbed slowly, then faster as the distance opened between them. Then it tipped towards Potalama and accelerated away.

"Something you should know," Zsu said when they could hear again. "There's a hell of a lot of mantids heading this way. We saw some warsingers too, and warbots like they used when you mixed it up with Borodin down by the river."

By the time they got back to Potalama, *Condor* had set down atop a pit dug by the hive's mektas, its four massive landing gear precariously positioned on cantilevered pads. The capsule dangled between its feet. In the pit below was the hyperglider's lower half.

The Sisters had hurriedly reconstructed it after the sentinel told her story. In theory they could have rebuilt the entire thing, including the capsule. What they could not replicate was the knowledge and memories within *Sparrow's* artiform brain. Those were a product of training and experience they were in no position to recreate.

From his station on *Condor's* flight deck, Dmitri carefully lowered the capsule into position. Gray steadied it while Maggie threaded control and power cables through the fuselage. They were bolting it together when an explosion echoed across the crater. Dirt cascaded down from one of the cantilevered pads and scattered off the flared hypervanes below.

Tara's voice came over the radio. "We just blew the Potalama side of the cleft. Took out a few dozen mantids."

"Me and Dusty are lighting up the ones stuck in the slot," Eric reported from the cockpit of the Kentavr combat shell. Distant whumps could be heard in the background, then again as the sound waves reached them from across the bowl of the crater.

Gray ratcheted down the remaining bolts. "Continuity?"

"Looks good," Maggie said, studying readouts in her goggles.

"I've got visuals from a commhawk showing the main body coming up the rim wall towards you, Eric," Tara radioed from the command post behind the Ring Station's walls.

"How long have I got?"

"Maybe fifteen minutes."

Gray raised the gantry up to the capsule's hatch. It was barely big enough for his bulk; he had to work his shoulders through at an angle. They had removed the pilot's seat and replaced it with latches that matched hard points on his carapace. He settled into place and pulled down the Hund-sized hand controllers they had rigged. The flight deck's holocaster illuminated between his massive feet.

"Hello, Little Bird," he said. "How do you feel?"

"Commander Gray?" Her voice came over the capsule's speakers.

"Yes, it's me." He followed along in the holocaster as she ran diagnostics.

"I feel whole."

A weight seemed to lift from him. "Good. That's really good."

Maggie dashed up to *Condor's* pressure hull while Gray was getting settled. It was the first time she had seen the boys in person since they had parted ways back in Zsu's apartment in Tsiolkovsky.

"It's Maggie May!" Dmitri exclaimed from his seat at the payload console.

"Our very own hometown celebrity," Alex said from the pilot's seat.

"Looking good in a Space Force skinsuit," Dmitri added with a salacious wink.

Maggie zipped up her utility vest with a sigh. Some things never changed. The boys exchanged clumsy embraces with her from their seats.

"It sure is good to see you guys," she said. "Thanks for coming."

"Couldn't keep us away," Dmitri said.

"Be careful up there, all right? I couldn't live with myself if either of you got hurt."

A slug pinged off the landing gear as if to emphasize the point, then another.

"Everyone here is fighting for what we believe in," Alex said. He keyed the flight deck's mic. "Big Bird here. We're taking small arms fire."

"It's going to get worse," Tara radioed back. "Kores report low ammo. Those mantids are wearing armor. And the warsingers are shooting back with some kind of active rounds. Nasty little mekanos. We've lost half our mektas. How much longer do you need?"

"Little Bird is ready," Gray reported. "Start the count."

"Ten minutes preheat and we're out of here," Alex told Tara.

The radio was silent. Tara came back after a long moment. "Copy ten minutes. If you've got a safety margin in there, I'd lose it."

"Well shit," Dmitri said off-air. "That's not good."

"No," Maggie agreed. She cocked her head. "Big Bird?"

"Ship has to have a nickname," Alex said defensively.

"It's tradition," Dmitri said.

"Ah, of course." Maggie recognized a case of hero worship when she heard it. "Big Bird, Little Bird. Perfect. Listen, I've got to get downstairs. But..." she hesitated.

"Love you too, Mags," Dmitri said.

"Always will," Alex added.

She ducked her head in an awkward nod, lower lip caught between her teeth. Then she gave them each a kiss on the cheek.

Outside, the sounds of combat were much louder than they had been a few minutes before. An explosion buffeted her as the Kentavr shot down a small rocket. There was a sound like an angry bee moving very quickly past her ear, probably a rifle slug. She realized with a shock that the warsingers were close enough to be shooting at her, specifically. She pushed off the ladder and dropped the rest of the way to the gantry.

A tinkle of broken glass accompanied her landing. She stared at the fragments of hypervane for a moment of cognitive dissonance before she realized they had come from the flight helmet clipped to her tool belt. It had taken a slug right through its temple, shattering the protective hypervane.

There was the tearing sound of a large-caliber automatic railgun, followed closely by the shriek of air being forcibly parted. A trident-shaped Ying Raider passed overhead, the light grey domes of its three antigrav units plainly visible. A pair of antique Sturmoviks thundered along after.

The radio crackled. "Kowalski's Cossacks here. Sorry we're late to the party. Mind if we join in?"

Maggie squeezed past Gray and settled into the right-hand seat, illuminated for a moment by the capsule's holocaster. "Cozy."

"Tell me about it," Gray said. He could barely move without denting the insulated padding that covered the capsule's interior. "It seemed bigger when I was human."

"Not a fan of this skinsuit thing, though. Is there any place it doesn't touch?"

Gray considered his emotional intelligence and refrained from saying she looked quite attractive in what amounted to a thick coat of paint. Instead: "You'll need it if we lose pressure or have to go outside."

"But this is just an out and back, right?" Maggie pulled the straps of her four-point harness tight over her shoulders.

"That's the plan. Make sure the hood is over the flange of the facemask. Okay, now let's get your helmet plugged in."

"Mekfuckers shot it out," she said, holding it up for his inspection.

"That's a problem."

"I'll be fine."

"Maybe," he said skeptically. "Exposure to hyperspace is no joke, Maggie."

"I'm going," Maggie said.

"You really should stay. Something is out there. Something..." he hesitated, not sure what to say that would get through to her without sounding hysterical. "Something that hungers."

Maggie rolled her eyes and keyed the mic. "Big Bird, Little Bird is good to go."

"Copy that," Alex replied over the radio. "Ring Station Potalama, Big Bird is ready to launch. How's our top cover looking?"

"Big Bird, top cover is in place," Tara replied. "May the breath of Mokosh carry you."

"Here we go," Alex said without any ceremony whatsoever.

Condor rose on her arcjets, pulling *Sparrow* out of the launch pit. The noise inside the capsule was stupendous. Gray worried the crystalline hypervanes might not survive the abuse. He caught a brief glimpse of the crater that held Potalama before it was blocked by the edge of the viewport. The launch pit was flanked by a dark crescent of armored mantids and warsingers, held back by a thin line of defenders in combat shells. The Ying raider and the two Sturmoviks hovered above them like angry hornets, churning the ground in a lethal hail of iron.

Then they were climbing away on an eastward arc, into darkness. Acceleration pinned them against the capsule floor. An aurora writhed across the sky, vivid blue and green with touches of pink. Gray saw its luminous striations as the fringe of a dancer's skirt, each swaying string weighted by a mekan's severed head, the goddess of destruction dancing atop the body of the world. He shuddered.

The noise subsided to a rumbling vibration as they climbed higher in the atmosphere. The aurora's ribbons curled into an arch that rose with them as they continued eastward, until it ended in an elongated fiery ellipse as it exited the atmosphere.

"The hekates are bringing down the Van Allen belt," Maggie said with awe in her voice.

"Van Allen belt?" queried Dmitri from the flight deck.

"Energetic particles trapped by the Ring's magnetic field."

"Why would they do that?"

"I expect to give Pavonis Hive a taste of their own medicine," Maggie said with some relish.

Their trajectory took them around the planet on a widening spiral. A fiery ellipse marked where the Van Allen belt descended back into the atmosphere.

From this vantage it was apparent the torus of energetic particles was both offset and constricted. At its closest approach to the surface, it played like a giant's blowtorch on the summit of Pavonis Mons. Lightning wreathed the extinct volcano like a crown of incandescent thorns.

"There's our top cover," Gray said. "Nothing is launching through that hellfire."

Alex shut down *Condor's* arcjets. "This is as fast as we can go and still make it back to the surface."

"Go ahead and drop the tow," Gray said.

The tow cable retracted up into the bottom of the rocket, leaving them adrift.

Alex fired a couple bursts from *Condor's* vernier thrusters to open space between them. "We've got enough life support to loiter in orbit for a couple days. Assuming you want a ride back down to the surface."

"Definitely. One crash landing was enough for me," Gray said. "Tracking cameras on?"

"Running and locked on," Dmitri confirmed.

Gray turned to Maggie. "Ready to make history?"

She suddenly found it difficult to speak. She had wanted this moment for so long, sacrificed so much for it, given up on ever having it. And now it was upon her. Her heart pounded in her ears. She had written half-a-dozen different speeches in her head, all forgotten now but for a single phrase that had run through them all.

"It's time for the stars," she forced out, voice cracking.

He nodded. "Time for the stars. I'll second that. What do you say, Little Bird?"

"Kinos at omega max. Ready."

"Then let's go. Poyekhali."

The hyperglider's turbopump spun up and ammonia boiled through her reactor core with a shriek. Acceleration crushed Maggie into her seat. She could barely breathe, and her vision narrowed to a circle. The viewport immediately in front of her was devoid of light except for a faint outline of the nose of capsule. Whatever that emptiness was seemed to pull at her. She felt a curious sensation of being lifted out of her body, as if the entire world was receding, leaving her suspended someplace very far away from anywhere else. Gray was there too, and the artiform that was *Sparrow*.

They were sitting around an oxygen candle, its flame illuminating their faces, their true faces, Gray as he had been before he died, a scar beneath his eye and a miniature Hund perched on his shoulder, its clockwork claws locked into his flesh, *Sparrow* as a slender woman with a Grecian nose and three dark oval eyes. And in the darkness beyond, others. She thought she heard her mother's voice, then her father's, as if they were talking together in the kitchen. She stood as if to go look for them, but *Sparrow* caught her hand and pulled her back.

"Stay with us," she said.

Dark wings beat overhead, so close the flame wavered in the wind of their downstroke. Then silence and the candle recovered, its flame swirling into a spherical knot of light. Maggie realized she was looking into a holocaster. She was looking into a holocaster onboard a ship. She was in *Sparrow*. The warbot was her friend Gray. She was back.

"Did you hear someone?" she asked. Then remembering the sound of unseen wings, "Or something?"

"The dead are not gone, here," Gray said. He sounded old, old and sad.

"Information is conserved," said *Sparrow*.

The holocaster revealed a bizarre fractal landscape, a projection of the world outside as detected by *Sparrow's* aetheric transducers. Below them, where Mars should have been, was a variegated sphere whose surface was covered in smaller spheres that seemed to be erupting, as if it was a boiling sphere of water suspended in space. The bubbles that came out of the main body in turn erupted into structures like slow motion lightning bolts, which held smaller bubbles like a four-dimensional Mandelbrot set. It was all continuously shifting and spreading outwards and yet at the same time not getting any larger.

"We are being lifted by a bubble that originated near our launch point," *Sparrow* said.

"There are currents in the aether," Gray explained. "Like the thermals that loft commhawks."

But Maggie didn't hear him because now it was not just her parents. Berel Hoffman was there too, and Borodin, and the man he had killed in Von Braun, and the warsingers that Tara and Eric had killed, were still killing, back at Potala-ma, and the kores who had fallen in battle, and their mektas, all of them bubbling and boiling past them, through them, because nothing was ever lost, nothing. Everything that ever lived was there, like Mokosh filling the void of the universe with Her breath. The galaxies were rushing away from each other because of it and she was so big, like a bubble expanding, like wings opening. Once she had wondered, lying on a dune back on Mars, looking at the sky as her vital heat seeped out of her, but now she knew: this is what it felt like to die.

"Ares damn it," Gray swore, "we have to get back down." Maggie's pupils were dilated so wide he could barely see a hazel ring around the blackness. Her face was shockingly pale. "Right fucking now *Sparrow*, we're losing her."

"It's a strong thermal," *Sparrow* replied.

"Well fly out of it!"

"We won't be anywhere near Mars."

"I don't care. Just get us down."

"I can try for the Arkipelago. I have charts for it from last time. From the first time."

"Just get us down. I don't know what to do here." He felt helpless in the face of basic human frailty. He didn't have lungs to help her breathe if she stopped, and his hands were too large to be of much use. At least the pressure sensors in his palms and fingertips could feel the motion of her diaphragm, and under that, the beating of her heart, fast and irregular.

He remembered they had a basic first aid kit onboard. He got the box open and fumbled out a medicrab. The little mekan latched onto her skinsuit near her heart.

"Please don't leave me," he said. "I don't think I could stand it."

Her body jerked as the medicrab pulled itself against her chest and interfaced with her nervous system.

"How much longer, *Sparrow*?"

"I'm at redline; any faster and something's going to break."

"Then break it!" he raged.

Sparrow began to shake. At first it was just a shudder transmitted through the cockpit floor, but within a few seconds it became violent. Gray had time to wonder what would happen if the ship came apart in hyperspace. What would death mean in a realm that did not know it? Would they be devoured by whatever dark thing it was that flew there, to become part of it?

Then they were down, through the dimensional threshold into three-space. The shaking stopped and on the other side of the viewports he saw the comforting light of the neighboring stars, and beyond them the incomprehensible glory of the Milky Way. A moment later Maggie's pupils contracted. She flailed wildly, hitting him in the face. He laughed with relief, pulling her against his armored chest, careful not to break her ribs. She was back.

43

Reunion

Maggie wanted to return to Mars, but Gray wouldn't have it. He was convinced another trip through hyperspace without a flight helmet would kill her. For her part, she was desperate to let her friends and countrymen know they had succeeded, and *Sparrow's* comm gear was far too weak to reach Mars from Jupiter's Trojans, where they had fallen out of hyperspace. They had to risk another flight, even if there was something out there, something dark and inimical. She had cheated death before and she would again.

When Gray would not relent, she accused him of engineering the whole thing to get back to Elise. He stumbled trying to explain what had really happened, why they had ended up in the Arkipelago, and then lapsed into wounded silence. He barely understood how he felt about Maggie and was utterly incapable of articulating it. In any case, it was absurd. He was a machine, not a man. But he would not let her risk her life again.

They used their remaining propellant to set course for Tholos.

The hive had changed, but Greenwich Station's bones were still discernible beneath the layers of warehouses, fuel depots, and living quarters that had accreted on its surface. The asteroid itself was nearly hollowed out, its features sunken like a face grown haggard with time. They docked at a tower that rose from the hive's spin axis like the upright pistil of a withered flower.

A triad of tharks waited inside. Gray stepped between them and Maggie as they approached. One of them spoke: "You do not recognize us."

Another: "We all look alike to them."

The third: "But we recognize you, Commander Gray. Welcome back to Tholos."

Memory dawned. "Babd," Gray said. "Macha, Anand. What an unpleasant surprise. I'd rather hoped you were dead."

Maggie looked alarmed. "I'm sure he doesn't mean that!"

Babd rasped out a laugh. "I'm sure he does."

"Fortunately for you, we are not," said Macha. "Or you wouldn't have survived long enough to dock."

Anand gave Maggie an appraising look, foveal rings narrowing down to riflescope reticles. "You must be the technomancer. Margaritifer May, born Sasha Lebedev to Maxim and Irina."

"I'm impressed," Maggie said. "I thought I covered those tracks. Tell me, were you the ones behind editing Gray out of the Wiki? The Hund's attack? The ground strike?"

Babd shook her head at the accusations. "The situation is more complex than you realize. Tharks control the League of Worlds, yes, but we are not unified. Tholos is only one city-state of many. But all agree that faster-than-light weapons are an existential threat that should be erased from history."

"We were only directly responsible for hacking the Hund," said Macha. "It was... expeditious. Our queen had been looking for Gray's brainstone for a very long time."

"She was upset to learn of the ground strike," said Anand. "Blue Mars is her project. It was an overstep by the League of Worlds' Security Council. And far too much risk to the brainstone." Her gaze lingered unnervingly on Gray, as if she were looking for the access port in his skull.

"Blue Mars is your work?" Maggie asked with an incredulous expression.

A shrug rippled through the thark triad. "Our work, but not our choice."

"Then why?" Gray asked warily. "What does Tholos want?"

"That you must ask the queen," replied Babd.

"And hivemaster," continued Macha.

"Come with us," Anand finished.

The tharks led them through narrow, ropy-textured corridors deep into the hive. For Gray it was a painful trip back in time to when he had forced Rhea. It was her chamber ahead of them, guarded by a triad of thark soldiers. He was seized by a sense of dread.

Iconji flickered across Babd's ledeyes and the guards drew back. The portal dilated. The chamber beyond was dimly lit by ultraviolet lamps.

"I'm here, John," Elise said from the darkness. "Come in."

He caught the lilt in her voice, the Ceresean accent he loved, and it took him back to her bedroom on Ceres. "Do you want to live forever?" she had asked him. What had she become in the two centuries since? She had to be at the outer limits of human longevity.

He held his hand out to Maggie. "Come with me? Please?"

They crossed together into the queen's domain. The inner surface of the chamber was covered with photonic elements like an everted ledeye. Trajectory plots of iceteroids and zhuks and aetheric drive ships surrounded them.

Dark hair floated like a nebula around her pale oval face.

Maggie gasped.

Behind the face was the bulk of a thark queen, three meters long and several hundred kilograms. There was no room for a woman's body there, between the face and the thark. The face, he realized, was pinned in some way to the thark's neck like a living mask, the mouth positioned atop the orifice where she accepted gems. The thark's ledeyes were silvered, ambiguous.

"It's me, John," the face said, and it looked and sounded just like Elise. He nearly turned and fled. It was too much. It was so much *not* what he had wanted, *not* the reunion of which he had dreamed. Something in his life had gone dreadfully wrong, worldlines peeling apart in the unobserved past, and now he was on the wrong side of history, where all the promises of longevity turned out to be magic tricks, and the sleight of hand revealed.

"I know this must be a shock," she said. Which was the understatement of a lifetime, but also, who was he to judge? He was not a man, after all, not anymore. That too was an illusion. John Gray was dead, his head cut off by a thark and turned into a Warsing relic. He was a thing, a monster out of his time, as Borodin had said before he died, assembled by a technomancer into a weapon of convenience.

"It really is me," she continued with a plaintive look he remembered well, even though the thing in front of him was clearly not Elise. He felt like his pattern recognition circuitry had catastrophically malfunctioned.

Breathe, Sola had whispered in his ear, long ago. If only he could.

"Steady," Maggie said over the body field network, as if she knew what he was feeling. "You can do this."

"Hello, Elise," he said slowly. "It's been a long time."

"I took this body after my first one failed," she said, answering the unspoken question. "But I have all her memories."

"*Her* memories?"

"Having a different body changes you, John. You must know that. We're not just data. Our bodies matter. I would have liked to have instantiated my brainstone in a clone of Elise. But this," she gestured at her bulk, "allowed me to retain control of Tholos Hive. Otherwise the tharks would have taken over after Rhea died. And that would have been the end of the Blue Mars Project. And any hope of finding you again."

"Why do you care what happens to Mars?" Maggie asked aloud, her long-held hatred of warsingers boiling over despite their precarious situation.

Elise regarded her disdainfully. "You would not understand, technomancer. You're a scavenger, a picker of bones. I am a world builder. The Arkipelago and Mars are bound together like lovers in the dance of life."

She sought Gray's gaze within the cameras that had replaced his eyes. "And now that you have returned to me, the dance can begin anew. I tire of this body, of the endless mundane fecundity of it. I'm ready to make the leap. Let me extract the brainstone from the Hund and we can reincarnate together. Be young together. Fall in love again."

It was everything he had once dreamed, but now it seemed like an impossibility. Here, where the illusions were laid bare, where the monstrosities they had become at the hands of time were in plain sight, he had to ask the obvious question.

"What about Maggie?"

"It would simplify our next incarnation considerably if she and the hyperglider were never seen again," Elise replied as if they were alone in the room.

"I could never forgive you," Gray said, taken aback. "Of all the things I might give up to be with you again, of all the people I might lose, Maggie and *Sparrow* are who I value most."

"*You* could never forgive me," Elise said, "but the next Gray, *my* Gray, would never even know."

"She's right," Maggie said over the body field network. "If your brainstone is instantiated in a new body, you won't remember me. You won't remember this. You won't remember anything after the original John Gray died, because that's when the brainstone stopped mapping his neural network."

"Elise," Gray said, "I would not be here except for Maggie. I literally owe her my life."

"Such as it is," Elise said. "Poor thing. I don't even know why we're having this conversation. I should have known better than to try to reason with a baseline and a less-than-human derivative. Let me put this simply. Nobody off Mars is on your side but me. Your precious hyperglider is seen as a weapon of mass destruction. It won't be tolerated, especially in the hands of baselines."

"I was wrong to forge hypermissiles," Gray said. "It haunts me. But we can still have starships, Elise. They don't have to be weapons."

"Spare me your guilty conscience. It doesn't matter. The Security Council wants this all to go away, and I am not in a great position to fight about it. They're probably right, though it pains me to say so."

"I won't allow it," he warned. The conversation was spiraling out of control. He was acutely aware of the thark soldiers waiting at the portal. He could feel the Hund responding to the stress, his crest laser's radiator rising like a dog's hackles, fight or flight taking hold. They might be able to fight their way back to the docking tower, but then what? *Sparrow* was out of propellant, and even if they managed to mass her up, they couldn't risk hyperspace.

The odds were very much against them.

But what Elise offered was not enough to justify forgetting – much less literally erasing – the friends he had made since he awoke. Maggie, Eric, Dorje, Tara, *Sparrow* – they were all part of him, and he would not trade that for anything. He stabbed a massive finger at his armor-plated chest. "This is who I am now. The man you loved is dead. And so is the woman I loved. They're dead Elise, and there's no bringing them back."

The queen scoffed. "That is where you're wrong. They *can* be brought back. *You* just aren't willing to pay the price."

"You're right," Gray said. "I'm not willing and I won't do it; it's too much."

He tried to think of something that would resonate with her, since she apparently did not care whether Maggie and *Sparrow* lived or died. Perhaps that was just part of being a queen: a learned indifference to the fate of individuals.

"This is bigger than me and you, Elise. This might be our last chance at the stars." He paused, searching for the right words. "If I ever really knew you, if I ever saw beyond what I wanted to see, I saw someone whose dream was to create new life and nurture it. And I loved that about you, even if it sometimes frightened me. So let me ask you this: where are your creations going to go, if you erase me and Maggie and *Sparrow*? Are you ready to condemn them to one solar system of the billions that exist? To spend the rest of your life arguing with your League of Worlds over who gets what pathetic lump of rock, when there are uncountable planets out there? Is that really what you want for them?"

They stared at each other across a gulf of time that remembered desire could not bridge. Two monsters by any reasonable human definition, arguing over the future of their distorted progeny, for once the hyperglider was erased, humanity and all its children in all their forms might never regain the greater sky that invisibly enfolded them all.

"No," Elise finally said. She sighed heavily. "No, it's not. They deserve better than that. There will be a price to be paid, though, a price I'd hoped to avoid. Ares damn it, Gray, you always had a way of talking me into things. I guess *that* hasn't changed."

The Hund's crest radiator folded back down as its fight-or-flight reflex subsided. Gray shivered as if something or someone had stalked over his grave, in some lonely cave overlooking the mighty Marineris.

"That was close," he said over the body field network.

"We're not out of this yet," Maggie replied. "She's *dangerous*."

She was, without a doubt, but then so was he. And besides, they had turned some corner. That much about Elise he still recognized. The specter of violence enabled if not encouraged by their assumed forms had passed. He mustered his wits and spoke aloud. "I seem to recall you were the one who talked me into getting a brainstone."

"And you talked me into taking Greenwich Station as salvage."

"We were quite the pair, weren't we," Gray said, wondering if what he felt, thinking back on their time together, was *wistful*. Was that in his repertoire, now?

"I suppose we were," Elise said. Her ledeyes silvered as she considered the past. She shook her massive triangular head. The mask at her throat was silent, its eyes lowered. "Well. If not *that*, then what?"

"An alliance," Gray proposed. "Tholos and Tsiolkovsky, sovereign city-states. That would give you some leverage with your Security Council."

"They'll be furious," Elise said, and then laughed shortly. "Serves them right for going around me and dropping one of my rocks on Mars. All right. An alliance."

"We need to let our people on Mars know that we made it," Maggie said quickly, before things could go sideways again.

"You can use our laserscope," Elise offered.

"No one on Mars will think to look for a lightwave coming from Tholos," Gray said. "I've got a better idea. I don't suppose you have a spare flight helmet Maggie could use?"

"I kept the one you drexlered for me, the last time you left," Elise said. "It might be time to let that go."

Something passed between them, a quick sweep of Elise's foveal rings, a small nod on his part.

"Perfect. That and some propellant for *Sparrow*, and we'll be on our way."

Foveal rings measured his face. "It's never long enough, for us, is it. There's always a reason to leave, a ship waiting at the dock."

"That seems to be our story."

She nodded slowly. "Then I suppose this is goodbye. Again."

She held up her hand. It looked just like Thirteen's, in another life: four carbon-black digits, fringed with fur-like cilia. Gray hesitated, then pressed his hand against hers. He did not trust himself to speak. Feathery cilia thrummed against his palm like a hundred drums, like a heartbeat, like wings taking flight. It was, he realized, her true name, revealed at last and only in parting.

Epilogue

Maggie rapped on the hatch to his quarters. "The newscast is starting!"

Gray tugged his uniform into place. The Hund-sized utility vest and cargo shorts had been Tara's parting gift. "Clothes make the man," she had said, and he had to admit their humanizing effect. He would take what he could get.

"Captain on the bridge," Maggie announced as Gray pulled himself through the hatch. The crew came to attention at their workstations: six consoles clustered around a central holocaster, all suspended within the spherical cavity of the bridge. The cavity's surface glowed like a mekan's ledeye, three-space trajectory plots atop a projection of hyperspace beyond. The holocaster contained a schematic of their ship. *Kestrel* was essentially a larger version of *Sparrow*, albeit with her pentachoral wing forward and her stabilizer aft like a conventional aircraft.

"As you were," Gray said, torquing himself into the remaining empty seat. "Bits, put it on the holocaster."

Dorje opened the news icon. A talking head, all glittering eyes and perfect teeth and cleavage, replaced *Kestrel's* schematic.

Maggie groaned. "This one."

"You know her?"

"No offense, but it's not a 'her,' it's an avatar. A terribly manipulative –"

"Shh!" Dmitri hushed her. "She's talking."

"… here to cover the launch of the *Kestrel*, Tsiolkovsky's first faster-than-light ship. But first, let's go to the office of Advocate Eric Hoffman." The view cut to Eric's office. He was sitting on a couch with a portrait of a very pregnant Zsuzsanna artfully framed behind him.

"Eric, tell us how the SolGLO mission first got off the ground."

"As you know Synthia, the Solar Gravitational Lens Observatory will image Tau Ceti's planets at incredible resolution in preparation for a crewed FTL expedition. SolGLO is the result of one of the most successful petitions in Tsiolkovsky's history. I want to personally thank my constituents for their spin, and the Sisters of the Ring for negotiating an end to hostilities with Pavonis Hive. Access to their space-elevator was invaluable. And of course Tholos Hive for drexlering *Kestrel* and bringing the Thunderbolt *Astrape* out of retirement to boost her."

"Yes, of course, but tell us how it all started." She leaned in for additional cleavage. "What is your relationship with the technomancer Sasha 'Maggie May' Lebedev?"

"Maggie is an old friend of the entire Hoffman family, and I owe her and Captain Gray my life," Eric said, sitting back and incidentally bringing the portrait of Zsu into center focus.

"He's good at this," Dorje commented.

"But Eric, isn't it true that you and Maggie, as you call her, had an intimate relationship?"

Eric sighed. "As I said, Maggie saved my life. She kept me from freezing to death after I was injured. I'm sure she would have done the same for anyone who needed simple human warmth to survive. Unlike yourself."

"Touché!" Synthia exclaimed cheerfully. "So long as we're talking about artiforms like me, can you comment on why Gray von Hund is in command? Your constituents clearly felt Maggie May should be captain."

"Actually, Synthia, it was Maggie who suggested that Gray be in command. She felt her talents as a technomancer made her the perfect choice for chief engineer of what is basically a Warsing artifact, and Gray's prior experience piloting hypergliders uniquely qualified him for command. It's as simple as that."

"Thank you Advocate Hoffman! And may I say, your father would be proud. Now let's cut to the proverbial chase." The view shifted to a live shot of *Kestrel* taken from *Astrape*, now coasting alongside the hyperglider. Gray felt a surge of affection for his old Thunderbolt. He only wished Ada and her triad were at her controls, but they had not survived the passage of time. None of the chirons had. Nor Thirteen, so far as anyone knew.

"Mute," Gray said. "I see what you mean, Maggie. Listen everybody, I was just on the lightwave with T-Poly Control. They think a thermal is blowing through, so it's time to go. Remember that none of us besides *Kestrel* are built for hyperspace. This will be disconcerting. Uncomfortable. Perhaps even frightening.

Your flight helmets will help, but they're not perfect. If you find yourself getting pulled away, come back to *Kestrel's* voice. All right?"

Nods around the chamber.

"Good. Bits, start recording and put it on our outbound feed. Make sure and tag *Sparrow* at T-Poly." The hyperglider had taken a post at Tsiolkovsky Polytechnic's Hyperographic Institute after helping train *Kestrel*.

"And hekate Tara at Ring Station Potalama," Maggie said. "Please?"

"Of course," Gray said.

"And Eric and Zsu," Dmitri said.

"Yes, yes," Gray said.

"Anybody else?" Dorje asked, looking over the top of her spex at the bridge crew. "All right. Oh wait, Synthia wants to talk to us, Captain sir."

"I am sure she does," Gray said. He flicked aside the newscast, and it collapsed back into an icon. "And it's one or the other, Bits."

"Oh, sorry sir. Captain. Sir!" Dorje stopped, flustered.

Gray shook his head, privately amused. He went around the circle of workstations, starting with Maggie.

"Chief?"

Maggie checked her console. "Qigong banked, kinos at omega max. Engineering is go."

"Sensors?"

"Aetheric transducers on standby," Dmitri said. He glanced up at the sphere, where a projection of hyperspace writhed like a fractal dragon. "Local chart loaded. Go."

"Bits?"

"Go!" Dorje said, nearly jumping out of her seat with excitement. "I mean, *Astrape* reports telemetry is solid."

"Doc?"

"Everybody needs to take a couple deep breaths," Alex said, scanning the crew's life signs on his console. "That said, all flight helmets are energized. Life is go."

"Payload?"

The sentinel checked her console. *SolGLO is secure. Go.*

"*Kestrel*?"

"Ready to fly," the hyperglider replied with a lilt in her voice that took Gray back to Ceres, where he first learned to fly above an emerald city cloaked in mist. The memory made his heart ache. But that was, he thought, probably a good thing, a sign that he was, after all, truly alive.

"Poyekhali," he said. "Let's go."

Acknowledgements

*T*he *Extrapolated Man* would never have been completed but for the support of my wife and partner in mischief Joyce Mayer, who told me for years that she would pick up the load if I needed to stop working for the Man to get it done. I'm slow, but eventually I took her for her word, and here we are.

Along the way:

I am forever indebted to Joe Haldeman for teaching me the basics of the craft when he was at MIT, and for his and Gay's hospitality. Joe's workshops were the best part of my time at "the 'tute."

Lance Ahern, Walt Boyes, David Bush, Stoney Compton, Wendy DiCaprio, Steve Finneran, Sara Forbes-Hall, Joyce Mayer, and Bob Pelz read drafts of the novel and provided invaluable comments, corrections, and encouragement.

John and Allene Franklin enrolled our family in transcendental meditation. Weird stuff in the day, but it stuck with me, and much of my experience of other planes of existence comes from meditation. The rest arrived later via psychedelics and profound solitude, but those are less sustainable routes.

Lee Freitag hitchhiked across the Sahara desert with me, which colored my ideas of what travelling across Mars might be like. An old woman in Haute Volta (now Burkina Faso) pressed a charm into my hand and told me I would write about it. So I guess I've checked that off.

Jerry Gipson captured the gorgeous image of the Pleiades featured on my website's banner and various socials.

John Hegarty shared his experiences in the United States Navy, and as the end approached, the thinning of the veil.

Lou Mayer taught me to hunt and introduced me to life in the Alaskan Bush, which is the inspiration for much of my imagined Mars, Quonset huts and all.

Steve Mayer and I backpacked across the Grand Canyon from South Rim to North and back again, enabling my own unexpected experience of hierophany.

Charles Oines created the artwork featured in *Attack Vector: Tactical*, a space combat tabletop game that made me say "Yes! Like this!" Years later, much to my delight, he created art for *The Extrapolated Man* including its first cover.

Many others educated, influenced, and inspired me through the years. I may never meet them other than through the books and models that line my shelves, but they made a mark:

Edwin Abbott, *Flatland*. Winchell Chung, the Atomic Rockets website. K. Eric Drexler, *The Engines of Creation*. William K. Hartmann, *A Traveler's Guide to Mars*. James D. Hornfischer, *The Last Stand of the Tin Can Sailors*. Rudy Rucker, *The Fourth Dimension*. Kow Yokoyama, whose *SF3D* models astounded me when I found them in my local hobby shop back in the 80s. Robert Zubrin, *The Case for Mars*, *Entering Space*.

Glossary

S ee extrapolatedworlds.com for a searchable, hyperlinked version of this
glossary.

Aether: a gas-like medium encountered in that portion of hyperspace
adjacent to our three dimensions. Aether is analogous to the atmosphere of
a planet, if our three spatial dimensions were compressed to the two-dimensional surface of a sphere. As an airplane lifts off into the sky, a hyperglider
lifts off into the aether.

Aetheric Drive: a means of propulsion wherein spinning hypervanes
are rotated into hyperspace and interact with the aether to create thrust.
Analogous to an airboat's fan pushing it across water.

Airscarf: an olive green synlife scarf that extracts breathable air from
Mars' terraformed atmosphere. Must be refreshed daily by exposure to light
and breathable air or it will die.

Arkipelago: a collection of asteroids, mostly small, mostly icy, trailing
Jupiter by sixty degrees in its orbit around the sun. Home to Tholos Hive
amongst many others.

Artiform: an artificial lifeform constructed atom-by-atom in a drexler,
itself created and maintained by similar artiforms. Examples of artiforms
include mekanos, mekans, pchelans, mantids, chirons, and tharks. Typically
powered by kinos.

Baseline: a human with no significant genetic modifications from the
Homo Sapiens baseline. Minor augmentations such as gecko pads for zero
gravity are included; major modifications such as wings are not. About 86
giganode neural capacity.

Beanstalk: a structure that bridges the surface of a planet to a station in
synchronous orbit, enabling elevators to carry goods and passengers from
ground to orbit.

Bioform: a biological lifeform based on DNA, including genetically engineered variants.

Blue Mars Project: a multi-century project to terraform Mars, including the Ring to shield its atmosphere and Ded Moroz icefalls to supply it with gigatons of ammonia and water.

Brainstone: a pre-Warsing brain implant that captures everything its bearer experiences, with the premise that it will be used to resurrect that person after their biological death in a cloned body.

Bulban: a mekano designed to contain beverages in low or zero gravity.

Ceres: the largest body in the Belt, classified as a dwarf planet. Notable features include the Ouroboros, a subsurface river that girdles the entire planet, and the city of Meridian, which hosts Taproot hive, and before the war, anchored a beanstalk to Greenwich Station in synchronous orbit.

Ceresean: generically, one who lives on Ceres. Specifically, non-baseline humans genetically engineered for Ceres' very low gravity. Cereseans have bat-like wings extending from long, foldable little fingers to their waist, long webbed toes, and augmented eyesight.

Chainblade: a blade whose edge is comprised of spinning nanosaws that can cut through most materials. Nanosaws are microscopic machines; think a pinhead-sized radial saw.

Chiron: a mantid (mekan) with its core aversion to harming quads restored by Tholos Hive. About 90 giganode neural capacity. Named by Elise Aberdeen after the single civilized centaur in Greek mythology.

Combat Shell: kino-powered personal armor used by UCSF for combat on, in, and around spaceships and asteroids. Combat shells have no windows, relying instead on external sensors. They are pressurized, but combatants also wear skinsuits and facemasks inside for additional protection from breaches.

Cutlass: a close-combat weapon used by the UCSF that uses a chainblade programmed to shut down on contact with spacecraft or habitat hulls, while cutting through almost anything else.

Ded Moroz: every 14 Martian months, iceteroids arrive from the Arkipelago and deposit gigatons of water and ammonia ice into the atmosphere in events called icefalls, superimposing an artificial winter upon the natural 12-month seasonal cycle. Named after a Slavic analog of Christmas celebrating Grandfather Frost and the Snow Maiden, as icefalls result in snowfall regardless of the natural season.

Drac: derogatory; a male Ceresean.

Drexler: a vat-like machine that uses molecular-scale assemblers to produce almost any artifact. A mekan hive uses drexlers for reproduction, based upon mekova produced by its queen. A mekovum embodies assembly instructions encoded within gems, which are in turn forged by hivemasters. Named after K. Eric Drexler, who first popularized nanotechnology.

Ecostate of Nüwa / EON: Earth's government from the time of its ecosystem collapse until the Warsing. Nüwa is the Chinese goddess of nature (the equivalent of the West's Gaia). EON's anti-capitalist policies were a major force behind the Exodus.

Exodus: the flight of people and capital from Earth to Mars when the wealth of the richest one percent of the population was threatened by EON's ecological policies.

Facemask: a UCSF variant of spex with a transparent full-face lens surrounded by a flange that mates with a skinsuit to protect its user from exposure to vacuum.

Gene lock: a hive is gene locked when its queen will only accept gems from a hivemaster with a specific genome. This practice inhibits hivejacking, a form of piracy wherein outsiders seize productive control of a hive. See parth.

Giganode: a rough unit of measure of intelligence, corresponding to one billion nodes in a lifeform's neural network. Dogs have about 2 giganodes. Humans have about 86 giganodes.

Goggles: a post-Warsing variant of spex with better protection from common Martian surface pollutants such as dust, noxious gasses, and ammonia rain.

Hivemaster: the individual responsible for a mekan hive's (re)productive governance. Hivemasters forge gems, which encode blueprints for physical artifacts ranging from mekans to industrial components like rocket motors. Pre-Warsing, most hivemasters were human females. See parth, gene lock.

Hyperglider: a vessel capable of unpowered flight in hyperspace by virtue of a pentachoral wing made of hypervanes that rotate into the fourth dimension when energized, generating a fourth dimensional lift force. Hypergliders use the aetheric equivalent of atmospheric thermals to stay aloft.

Hypermissile: a vessel capable of ballistic travel through hyperspace. They are effectively faster-than-light, which means they cannot be detected via electromagnetism (light, radar, etc.) prior to their arrival and detonation. Hypermissiles were used by UCSF against EON forces that had seized the Lunar mines.

Hyperspace: generically, a fourth spatial dimension at right angles to our observable three spatial dimensions. Specifically, that portion of our four-dimensional universe that exists outside of our three dimensions and can be accessed for extra-dimensional and effectively faster-than-light (FTL) travel.

Hypervane: a Warsing artifact that when energized, rotates partially into hyperspace. Hypervane is used to construct pentachoral structures, which can then be fashioned into propellors, wings, transducers, and other artifacts required to access and navigate hyperspace.

Iconji: a visual language based on icons, used as a pidgin between humans and mekans.

Joint Service Academy / JSA: a United Colonies of Mars military academy providing training to members of the Space Control, Space Force, and Mars Guard. Includes an academic component with ongoing research programs.

Kino: an energy storage device based upon two or more small counter-rotating flywheels. The flywheels are built of carbon nanotubes and spin extremely quickly. Their kinetic energy can be tapped as electrical or mechanical power.

Kunming: a genetically engineered human thought to have been developed by EON for terrestrial ecological law enforcement, and subsequently encountered off-planet in actions against UCM. Named after pre-collapse Chinese wolf-dogs used in warfare and law enforcement.

Laserscope: a combination of a laser and a telescope used for communications, remote sensing, and deflecting obstacles. They are the primary weapon of UCSF torchships. At long range they can overheat an enemy ship and cause it to shut down. Up close they can vaporize its components.

Ledeye: an organ that can both transmit and receive visual information in the form of colors, shapes, symbols, and images. Mekans have two ledeyes that resemble illuminated dragonfly eyes.

Mantid: a four-legged, two-armed mekan with its core aversion to harming baselines reversed. Bred by Taproot Hive and first encountered by UCSF on 55 Pandora. Used on by tharks on post-Warsing Mars as enforcers.

Mars Guard: the surface-to-orbit armed service of the United Colonies, with a rank structure and mission like the US Coast Guard. Responsible for search-and-rescue missions on and in the vicinity of Mars, limited law enforcement outside of city-state jurisdiction, and in wartime, planetary defense. Service members are not subject to gender or genetic constraints but must be able to use standard equipment.

Mear: a Martian year; the time it takes Mars to orbit the sun. A mear has 669 sols (day-night cycles) and is equal to 1.88 Earth years or 687 Earth days. Martians measure their lives in mears instead of years. A mear is divided into twelve months, three of which have 55 sols, and the rest 56.

Mekan: generically, any sapient eusocial artiform with six limbs that reproduces via drexlers assembled into hives. Specifically, human-scale artiforms used as labor on UCM spaceships.

Mekano: a non-sapient artiform incapable of self-reproduction, produced by mekan hives to fill specific niches in mekosystems.

Mekosystem: an ecosystem comprised of mekans, mekanos, and in some cases synlife. Often designed to fulfill specific human needs. An example is the system by which iceteroids are harvested from the Arkipelago and delivered to Mars for its terraforming project.

Moravec: a pre-Warsing device popularized by Hans Moravec that slowly converts its bearer's brain to a silicon equivalent, with the promise of immortality without loss of continuity.

Oner: an individual from the wealthiest one-percent of society. Earth's oners financed and led the Exodus to Mars. On Mars, oners explicitly hold the greatest political power, as citizens vote with energy-denominated money. Pronounced wunner.

Niner: an individual who is not in the wealthiest one-percent of society; not a oner.

Parth: a female human produced by parthenogenesis, making her a natural-born clone of her mother. A parth's sexually-produced siblings would be parthsibs, and from her perspective, her mother is her parthparent and so forth. Hivemasters use parths to ensure gene-locked hives survive their death.

Pchelan: a species of mekan designed for autonomous life in space and low gravity environments such as asteroids. Prominently featured in the Deimos hive. Russian for "bee."

Pentachoron: take a tetrahedron – a three-sided pyramid whose base is also a triangle – and hence has four faces and four points. Add a fifth point at the center. Replace the four triangular outer faces with six triangular inner faces that each extend from the central vertex to two of the outer vertices. Pentachorons made of hypervane are analogous to aircraft propellors and wings.

Poyekhali: Russian for "Let's go!" Famously said by Yuri Gagarin, the first human in space, just before he blasted off.

Quads: generically, lifeforms with four limbs. Specifically, humans. Pre-Warsing mekans were hardwired with an aversion to harming quads.

Queen: the mekan at the top of her hive's hierarchy. Queens translate a blueprint encoded in a gem into an egg-like mekovum that has the detailed instructions required to create a physical instance of the blueprint within her hive's drexlers. Queens can produce many mekova per gem, but a drexler only produces one artifact per mekovum.

Qigong Reactor: a fusion reactor with a set of at least four opposing, co-terminated, plasma mirror lasers. The lasers are radially symmetric, joined together at focal point where a fusion reaction occurs. The plasma is actively stabilized by an artiform, who can be induced to suicide, resulting in an explosion akin to a thermonuclear bomb.

Ring: a superconductive electromagnet that encircles Mars near its equator. It is electrically powered by a network of Ring Stations. The Ring produces a magnetic field that shields Mars from the solar wind, thereby keeping its atmosphere from being stripped away.

Sentinel: generically, a human-scale pchelan caste designed to detect and communicate with distant objects such as incoming iceteroids and other hives. Specifically, an individual outcast from Deimos Hive.

Sisters of the Ring: a cultish organization whose mission is to maintain the Ring and perpetuate the Blue Mars Project. Its adherents include girls – often orphans or castoffs – called kores, adult initiates called selenes, and elders called hekates.

Shards / Shever: extremely rare fragments of hypervane that are prized by mystics for their ability to induce transcendent meditative states. The Sisters of the Ring believe these fragments are physical manifestations of the shards of divinity of Kabbalistic lore.

Skinsuit: a synlife organism that, in combination with a facemask, can protect a human from exposure to deep space for extended periods of time. Given sufficient light, a skinsuit can recycle human breath and excreta to provide breathable air and basic hydration and sustenance.

Spex: smart glasses with built-in heads-up display, two-way audio, short range radio, and ledeye functionality for communicating with mekans.

Spin: slang for energy, which is the basis of Martian currency. See kino.

Sturmovik: a one-man rocket-propelled ground-attack vehicle. The Sturmovik's pilot wears a combat shell and attached to the front of the vehicle.

Strekoza: a sapient, spindle-shaped EON warship built around two counter-rotating aetheric drives. Also called an interceptor by UCSF crew. Russian for "dragonfly."

Synlife: a synthetic lifeform based upon organic molecular components engineered from the ground up. Examples include airscarves and skinsuits.

Technomancer: an individual skilled in recovering, repairing, reactivating, and reverse-engineering Warsing artifacts.

Thark: a two-legged four-armed human-scale mekan without a core aversion to harming quads. 100 giganodes on up. Named by Elise Aberdeen after the four-armed warriors of Edgar Rice Burroughs' Barsoom novels.

Threelium: slang for helium-3, an isotope of helium found on Luna (Earth's moon) and in Saturn's atmosphere. When combined with deuterium in a fusion reactor, it produces clean neutron-free energy. Plays a similar role in the interplanetary economy as oil did on Earth before the ecosystem collapse.

Torchship: a spaceship powered and propelled by an inertial confinement fusion (ICF) torch. Prior to the war, the United Colonies had twelve torchships, one of which was UCM *Tereshkova*.

Tricode: a trinary (as opposed to binary) code that is part of mekan visual communications and is woven into their carbon fiber exoskeletons as unique identifiers that are invisible to humans. Analogous to a 3-axis triangular QR code.

United Colonies of Mars / UCM: dominant pre-Warsing polity comprising the six original colonial city-states of Mars. Ceres became the seventh member of the United Colonies when it was forcibly annexed, after which polite usage omitted "of Mars" from the name, though it was formally retained.

United Colonies Space Control / UCSC: the spaceborne control service of the United Colonies, with governance over its Space Force. Provides mission tasking, traffic control, and intelligence services. All UCSC service members are female or asexual baselines.

United Colonies Space Force / UCSF: the spaceborne armed service of the United Colonies, with a similar rank structure and mission as the United States Navy. All UCSF service members are male baselines.

Vamp: derogatory; a female Ceresean.

Warsing: the singularity at the climax of the interplanetary war between Earth and Mars.

Warsinger: the post-Warsing Martian term for thark. Warsingers directly control most of interplanetary space and indirectly control much of Mars via their mantid enforcers.

Zhuk: a large (hippo to elephant scale) pchelan caste designed to harvest ammonia from iceteroids and collectively capable of changing their trajectory. Russian for "beetle."